MARTYRS NEVER DIE

ENIGMA SERIES VIII

TIERNEY JAMES

MARTYRS NEVER DIE – ENIGMA SERIES BOOK VIII – Second Edition
Copyright © 2022 - 2024 - Tierney James
Cover Design by Sweet 'N Spicy Designs
All cover art copyright © 2022 - 2024 – Tierney James
All Rights Reserved

This is a work of fiction. Names, places, characters and incidents are either the product of the author's imagination or are used fictitiously, and any resemblance to any actual persons, living or dead, businesses, organizations, events or locales is entirely coincidental. All trademarks, service marks, registered trademarks, and registered service marks are the property of their respective owners and are used herein for identification purposes only. The publisher does not have any control over or assume any responsibility for author or third-party websites or their contents.

No part of this book may be reproduced or transmitted in any form or by any means, electronic or mechanical, including photocopying, recording, or by any information storage and retrieval system, without permission in writing from the author.

Publishing Coordinator – Sharon Kizziah-Holmes

Owasso, OK

ISBN - 978-1-965460-24-5 (Paperback)
ISBN - 978-1-965460-25-2 (eBook)

DEDICATION

Dedicated to all the men and women who fight from the shadows to keep us safe in a dangerous world.

ACKNOWLEDGMENTS

There are people who stand on the sidelines cheering me on each time I write another book. Their encouragement and belief in my abilities to do this amazing job of writing is one of the things that keeps me inspired. Thank you to:

My readers: Without you I would have quit a long time ago. Your reviews, discussions, and participation in my endless questions, help me get the next story completed.

Lipstick & Danger Street Team: These are the people who always stand up and shout out the news about the latest book of mystery, chaos and intrigue.

Editors: Kate Richards and Nan Sipe always teach me how to keep improving my work. They help me to see my potential and the potential of my characters with each book I write.

Paperback Press: Sharon Kizziah-Holmes never tires of holding my hand. She produces each book with the love and respect you pray for in a professional. I know she's got my back.

Sweet & Spicy Designs: Jaycee DeLorenza creates my book covers. Not only is she creative, but patient and a great listener. We have worked together so many times now that she almost knows what I want before I do.

Facebook Reader Group: This group shows up every day sharing their humor, good vibes, encouragement, pieces of their lives and support. We are a family! I love all of you.

PROLOGUE

شهيد

The dune buggy drove recklessly across the sand dunes, bouncing the two young men up and out of their seats in spite of the seat belts they wore. Their shouts of joy echoed across the drifting sands as the setting sun turned everything into rivers of wavy gold. They halted at the top of a rise and stared down toward an encampment of Bedouins who'd arrived several days earlier. The gentle wind carried the sound of flapping tent awnings. The two men exchanged how old-fashioned their families were to still follow the old ways.

"My father says I'll meet my new wife when I arrive." The driver killed the engine and stared forward. "What a waste. I want to pick my own wife. As a matter of fact, I don't want a wife. Not yet."

"Maybe she'll be pretty," his friend teased.

"Or maybe like one of my father's camels." He imitated the face of a camel followed by the way they chewed.

The friend chuckled then unfastened his seat belt and stood. "Wonder why no one is moving about? Shouldn't there be cooking fires? I was hoping my mother fixed my favorite since she knew we'd be here tonight."

The driver squinted at the camp. "Something is wrong." He turned over the engine and waited for his friend to secure himself

1

before easing toward the road that created a patchwork of shifting sand.

As they drew closer, it became obvious people and animals weren't moving, or an alert would have been sounded. Cooking fires failed to perfume the air with aromas of cooked meat from a slaughtered sheep. Their fathers knew of their arrival from the university and would celebrate with a feast. Yet, there was no hint of celebration or welcome.

Instead, the hollow sound of wind swept across the desert and brought the odor of death as they eased out of their dune buggy to stare at the carnage before them. Livestock lay bloated and cooking fires smoldered with upended pots of charred remains of what might have been a traditional Bedouin meal.

In spite of the heat, the young men stood as if frozen, afraid to speak what they imagined they might find inside the tents. The driver pointed toward a lump outside the flapping awning that freed itself from the wind. Could this have been an unexpected sandstorm?

"There? What is that?" he whispered.

Together, they walked toward the lump in the sand and halted when the stench forced them to cover their noses and mouths. The driver gagged but decided to rush forward as he covered the bottom part of his face with part of his kaffiyeh. He turned the lump over with his foot and cried out. Stumbling back to his friend, he fell into his arms.

"I recognized my father's knife in his hand." Terror caused him to choke as he spoke. "His face melted away."

The friend pushed him at arm's length. "The others must be—"

"Dead. All of them," he sobbed.

~ ~ ~ ~

Director Benjamin Clark, current head of Enigma, hung up the phone after talking to President Buck Austin. He knew being summoned to the office on a Sunday morning by the most powerful man in the world meant only one thing. Trouble. Even before he'd spoken to the president, he'd put a call in to his most trusted agent, Captain Chase Hunter, to meet him at the Sacramento office. He was waiting, as he knew he would be, when he arrived. No secretary to get in the way or make coffee. Chase held two cups. Director Clark grabbed one without asking or showing appreciation.

The soldier didn't react. This wasn't the first time matters of national security pulled him in without an explanation. The director knew he didn't have to explain to a man who'd seen too much danger and not enough common sense over the years. His heart, at times, was as cold as a research station in Antarctica on any given day. Men feared the battle-weary soldier but respected him nonetheless. The director cared deeply for the man and hated the thought someday he'd have to send him into a situation where he wouldn't return.

"How is the president, Ben?" The director enjoyed when his agent called him by his first name. When others were around, he employed a formal address.

"He's about to go cowboy on us, I think. Beat around the bush a few minutes on how the world was going to hell in a handbag, and folks have lost their moral compass."

Captain Hunter smirked. "Well, he's not entirely wrong, Ben. So, what is the burr under his saddle now?"

Unamused at the attempt to sound like John Wayne, the director sat down and pointed to a chair across from him in a silent order for the captain to do the same. "Saudi Arabia is the problem."

"What are they not admitting to now?"

"They're asking for our help. Scared out of their minds."

The obvious lack of interest and steely eyed glare reflected an abundance of unconcern and contempt. Ben was well aware how much disdain the man held for the Saudis after 911. He carried a grudge so heavy, it helped shape him into the killer and soldier he was today. A beloved grandmother died in the fall of the first tower. It was one of several losses the man experienced. Having already lost his parents serving as medical missionaries in China, he'd also suffered his little sister being murdered in college. The man didn't let anyone get too close and, certainly, not a woman.

Well, not until Tessa Scott stumbled into his life, smelling of chocolate chip cookies and batting her baby-blue eyes at him. Chase didn't think a woman with three kids and a self-centered husband could be of any use to Enigma. She was one of the innocents. But he was wrong. Although hesitant, the woman helped save the country from Libyan terrorists. For the first time Ben could remember, he heard Captain Hunter laugh. She both amused and intrigued his top agent. Day by day, she sanded off the cruel and deadly character he hid behind and gave him a reason to keep up the good fight. Everyone at Enigma knew the man was in love with the woman, in spite of him not wanting to admit it. They became unlikely friends. The upside of their partnership was both made Enigma better.

Ben continued. "A Bedouin camp was attacked a few days ago by what appears to be a chemical weapon." Ben noticed the captain blink and cock his head with interest. "Over forty people died a horrible death, as did their livestock. Two young men belonging to the group found them as they returned from college. Others were scheduled to arrive in a few days after the attack occurred. From my understanding, they were urban Bedouins who have jobs in Riyadh. They still practice the lifestyle with family several times during the year."

"Who do we have on the ground?"

"FBI landed within twenty-four hours of finding them. A sandstorm followed the discovery and compromised some of the evidence."

"Maybe it's an in-country rivalry."

"Maybe. Doubt it. The weapon was pretty sophisticated for a bunch of Bedouins. No indication it was launched. FBI thinks someone brought it into camp."

"Any identification of the dead?"

"Most had melted faces and body parts. Pieces of clothing, jewelry, and such helped with identification."

"Who do you think brought it into camp?"

"The two boys who found the families couldn't account for one of the dead. One too many. FBI thinks something went wrong. Possibly the unknown person didn't know what he had. Still too much we don't know."

"And why do we care?"

"The future leader of Saudi Arabia, Prince Muhammad, was due to arrive the following day."

Captain Hunter sighed, and his mouth twisted in disgust. "And I guess we have to babysit while he participates in the Environmental Impact Summit here next week."

"And you're going to get Tessa to be his arm candy to make sure he behaves himself."

"Absolutely not," Chase growled. "The man is a—"

"I'm well aware of his reputation. Be sure you put the fear of God in him with Zoric at your side. Tessa can take care of herself these days. Russia proved as much." Ben knew bringing up Russia may not have been the most persuasive approach. "She's coming in later. Stick around and put her mind at ease. She hasn't had much interaction with the team since the divorce." The captain remained quiet. Ben wondered if Chase would finally make his move on the woman, or did he now have bridges that needed to be burned before his confession of love? Finally, he stood and stared at Ben with laser focus.

"Future king or not, if he touches her, I'll kill him."

"I'm going to pretend you didn't say that."

Chapter 1

شهيد

Tessa examined herself in the gold-trimmed mirror. Meeting a Saudi prince for the first time gave her pains of uncertainty. And how did they expect her to keep him entertained? He had specifically requested a blonde with long, curly hair, curvy and tall. There wasn't anything to be done about the tall part, but the other two requirements she could handle with no problem.

Reluctantly, she'd allowed Agent Samantha Cordova to help her pick out a dress and shoes for the occasion. The prince apparently loved women to wear red, a deviation from the black abaya found in his country. Now, here she stood in a short dress, skintight and covered in red sequins. Although the long sleeves attempted to cover skin from the edge of her shoulders to her wrist, the collarbone and plunging neckline left little to the imagination. Jewelry remained simple; diamond earrings sent over from the prince. The six-inch heels made her clumsy, so she had practiced wearing them for several hours each of the last few days. They, too, were red.

She pulled her hair back into a messy bun, securing it with two clear chopsticks. The unruly strands refused to obey. They framed her face as she applied the red lipstick. She slipped it into a tiny handbag resembling thin cords of sparkly black licorice.

Agent Samantha Cordova walked around her for a final

inspection. "Not bad." High praise coming from her rival on everything, including breathing.

"Just how am I supposed to keep Prince Muhammed entertained? No one has said."

"I'm pretty sure he'll have his own ideas about that. Do whatever he wants until the threat has been neutralized. Understand?"

"No. I don't understand. If there has been a threat against his life, his people would have taken the lead and he'd have never come to this new Environmental Impact Mumbo Jumbo Summit, which means nothing in reality. He lives in a country with one of the largest sand deserts in the world."

"The president does have Secret Service involved but wanted us there, too. We've been taking orders from them, more or less."

"Guess I missed that meeting." Tessa gave herself another inspection in the mirror while Sam watched. "I think he's here because it's his college reunion. Wasn't he a frat rat or something?"

"Yes. Quite the party animal, I understand. Anyway, if he survives the summit without getting his head shot off, then we'll pass him off to Secret Service and they can deal with him. He's been here less than twenty-four hours and has everyone hopping and fetching for him. Think you can keep him entertained for a few hours until we make sense of this?"

"I read he likes to play games. Checkers is his favorite."

Samantha let a feline expression spread across her lips. She would have been much better at this than her. The woman was nothing short of a nymphomaniac. "I'm pretty sure his idea of playing games has something to do with jumping on his opponent."

"What?" Tessa said, putting her hand on her chest. "You can't be serious."

"Known as quite the ladies' man. I understood you were told this."

"I figured Chase was being overprotective or undermining my self-confidence. I read the prince's profile, and he sounded like more of a family man to me."

"Three wives, five children, possibly more. At least, that is what the info says. Unofficially, he has a number of mistresses in various places around the world. I'm sure there are more children. Play nice and get rid of the holier-than-thou attitude. The rest of the team will be trying to keep the threat on his life from taking place. The prince will be king in the near future, and we want him to be supportive of our government like his father and grandfather have been."

A knock at the door signaled Captain Chase Hunter was coming in. Tessa slipped into the bedroom to get her abaya and veil.

The deep voice drifted into her room, mixed with a response given by Sam. How could the woman have a sexy voice even when she was ready to go to work, and, most likely, break a few bones, and quite possibly kill a terrorist. It was irritating. She wondered if the captain was hanging on her every word as did most men. What were they talking about? There were times even she felt mesmerized by Sam. The witch must have magical powers. At least it made her feel better to think the cosmos put such gifts on certain women and Agent Samantha Cordova had managed to get all of them. Well, except a personality. She was sadly lacking in the temperament department.

With one more glance in the mirror, she admired the reflection. Under Sam's care, she resembled an exotic princess. With any luck, this would all be over in a few hours. She might turn back into a dowdy housewife with bleach stains on her best sweater around midnight, since Sam had been in charge of her transformation. Knowing her, this would be her idea of a good time. Using her powers of intimidation on an enemy, in this case her, always gave Sam a euphoric high.

Taking a deep breath, she joined the two agents in the living room. Captain Hunter turned his head toward her and did a double take. When he moved toward her, he caught his toe on the rug and stumbled then knocked a figurine over on the lamp table. The awkward movement caught him off guard, and he flashed a mischievous grin, causing Tessa to tingle from head to toe.

Everyone in Enigma knew the two of them had an on-again, off-again relationship. One minute, they were butting heads, and the next, they were trying to figure out their not-so-romantic relationship. They'd danced around being more than friends for several years, but events always interfered with it going forward. At first, it was because of Robert, the father of her children. Tessa refused to betray her husband with an affair. Chase refused to get involved with one of his agents. The list of excuses stacked up higher the longer they knew each other.

Chase crossed the room quickly and put his warm hands on her forearms. "You continue to surprise me at how beautiful you are." The awkwardness had vanished, and he was back to his charming self that drove her crazy. He glanced over at Sam who stood appraising the competition and curled her bottom lip to the side in contempt. "The prince might decide he wants to keep her."

"Be still my heart," Sam huffed.

Tessa was used to the woman's insults, taunts, and threats. This one was on the mild side. "I'm a little nervous. I've never met a prince before, and I understand this one is quite the character."

"He likes to think of himself as a ladies' man. But I've already informed him you're an agent with skills that can take him off at the knees if he gets a little too up close and personal."

Tessa gazed up into his dark-brown eyes and felt herself drowning. She wanted to touch the corner of her mouth to make sure she wasn't drooling.

"Besides," he continued, "I told him you were my girl, and I wouldn't hesitate to turn him into a eunuch if he so much insinuated a one-night stand."

"You always spoil my fun." Her face grew warm. His girl?

He unexpectedly touched her cheek then stepped away. "Don't take chances. We have agents positioned throughout the hotel, ready to act at any sign of trouble. The entire floor has been locked down."

"Sounds like all the bases are covered. My weapon is in my purse and"—she touched her thigh—"something else if needed."

Chase locked onto her gaze and didn't shy away from laying an open palm on her hip then sliding it down until he found her "something else." Her cheeks grew hot with his invasive touch. With a little bit of over-pretend confidence, she tilted her head and managed a mischievous grin with one corner of her mouth. He returned the expression, and his lips parted, as if he wanted to say more, but Sam had all she could stomach of being ignored.

"Zoric says it's time. Do you want me to step outside so you can finish feeling her up?"

"If you don't mind," he snarled off-handedly but continued to stare into her eyes. Then Tessa and Chase stepped apart quickly and moved toward the door. He let her pass in front of him, and she caught a glimpse in the mirror hanging next to the door of him checking out her backside. His warm gaze traced her body all the way up to her hair. Sam entered the hall, but Tessa paused to stare back into the mirror at Chase who narrowed those cold, dark eyes at her. Could this be the way he commenced to devour a woman? Since she was free, unattached, and given authority over her life, would he finally throw caution to the wind and capture the moment they both wanted? The thought occurred to her that the prince couldn't be as dangerous as the man standing behind her.

She felt paralyzed under his gaze when he stopped and circled her waist then bent his head as if he wanted to whisper in her ear. He pointed to her earwig, to remind her others listened. Instead of words, he kissed her under the ear and pulled her back against him.

Zoric, the Serbian Butcher, as he was known in interrogation circles, waited at the elevator with the door open. Dressed in a suit and tie, he no longer resembled the vampire she'd often compared him to. The high cheekbones, dark hair pulled into a ponytail on his neck, bloodshot eyes, and evidence of a once-broken nose often frighten those who found themselves on the end of his interrogations. His gravelly voice and a strong smell of cigarettes added a layer of caution to those meeting him for the first time. Those thin, almost-purple lips used to scare the life out of her. Now she made it her mission to make him show amusement at her spontaneous attempts at humor. He rarely did unless they found themselves alone in his art studio. She always thought how ironic it was that a man who could take great delight in torturing a would-be terrorist could paint such divine canvases.

"I will be close," he said, eyeing her with lustful appreciation. "Do not open the door unless I mention when I locked you in a cell so you know it is me."

Tessa remembered the incident well. It was the first day they'd met, and he insinuated he had carnal plans for her that may leave her battered and bleeding as well. But she survived the test, and he promised to be her protector going forward. In spite of his bloodthirsty reputation, the two had become friends. Heaven help the person who ever tried to harm her or Sam in any way.

She nodded her understanding of his instructions but paused to look lovingly at him. He had no one but Enigma to claim as family, and he protected it—them—fiercely.

"You are quite dashing tonight, Zoric."

Other than a slight uplift of his eyebrows, his dangerous scowl never changed.

He followed the three onto the elevator and remained silent. Feeling unsure of herself, Tessa wanted to engage him and the other two agents in small talk to relax. These moments made her wish she drank or took a magic pill to get her head on straight. But alcohol gave her headaches and even over-the-counter pain meds made her sleepy, so those were ruled out. All she had to rely on was her faith in God to protect her and the Enigma agents who most likely were avenging angels in another life. Either way, she had nothing to worry about. Right?

"The prince is ready for us, Captain Hunter," Sam announced as she touched her earwig and stepped out of the elevator when the doors opened. Zoric followed, and both took up positions.

Tessa slipped into the abaya and noticed the fabric had a sparkle to it. Although the face covering was clear, it, too, had sparkle. She lifted the head covering over her hair and realized it resembled more of a designer monk robe than an abaya. The prince had sent it over and requested his partner for the evening to wear it during introductions. When she was left alone with his protection, he would request its removal. Thus, the reason for the almost-inappropriate red-sequined dress.

A beefy guard stood on each side of the double doors leading to his quarters, dressed in the traditional robes of Saudi Arabian men. Tessa wondered how they could possibly guard the prince with no visible weapons. They ignored her, but she thought they took a second glance at Sam, who met their gaze with contempt and a hint of a smirk. She couldn't resist taunting them with what they'd never get to sample. For a split second, Tessa considered throwing off the abaya and doing a Lady Gaga song with all the gestures of a temptress to see if they'd notice. Fortunately, before she made a fool of herself or created an international incident, Chase touched her back and nudged her through the open doors. She wondered if this was how Christians had felt just before being led into the arena where the lions waited for their next meal.

The golden room of soft light and modern décor appeared out of place for a Saudi prince. Her steps slowed as Chase quickly moved in front of her and snapped his fingers; a sign she was now to behave as if shy and obedient rather than her usual bull in a china shop with snarky comebacks and a tendency to overreact.

How many times had the two of them butted heads over following orders? Of course, when she didn't and then had to be rescued, reprimanded, or threatened with expulsion, he unleashed Sam to take over her training.

Although many lessons had been learned, the father of her children had soured her on taking orders from a man. He wanted a dutiful wife, a person to cook, clean, and not spend too much on Christmas décor or presents like his mother had done. But, in the end, he betrayed her with lies. She didn't take being told what to do by a man lightly, not even one as handsome and overpowering as Captain Chase Hunter.

Then there was the whole mind-reading thing he practiced on her at times. He stopped and turned back to stare at her.

"Remember who this guy is, Tessa. He's the next king of Saudi Arabia. We want him alive, not dead. If he dies, we may never have another chance at real peace in the Middle East. Don't get on your high horse if he makes a move on you." Tessa felt her body stiffen at the reprimand and forced her expression to glaze over as she refused to comment. "All you have to do is say Zoric, and he will be here."

"Why can't he just stay?" She glanced at Zoric, who, with Sam, completed a final check on the suite of rooms.

"Because the prince requested it."

CHAPTER 2

شهید

The sound of male voices came from one of the suite rooms with the open door. A deep, authoritative tone gave orders resembling a drill sergeant quieting whoever else was in the room. Their footsteps grew closer as Chase took a step forward to block her view of the room and appeared to stand at attention. Zoric and Sam joined him with the same no-nonsense stance with their hands crossed in front of their bodies.

"Heads up, guys," Tessa whispered. "You remind me of a bunch of rejects from the Men in Black." She followed up with making soft pew-pew sounds that mimicked her son's favorite video game weapon. "Oops. Forgot my sunglasses." The unexpected snicker caused the three to turn stoic glares at her. "Okay. I'll behave." Humor was one of those annoying things she often used when her nerves were getting the best of her.

"This isn't a game, Tessa," Chase warned.

"Certainly feels like one, and guess who's the prize? Me. That's who."

"Shhh," Sam warned.

In spite of the three Enigma agents standing in front of her, there was still plenty of room to see five men had entered and all but one moved toward the double doors leading to the hall. The one remaining had to be the prince. Her knees knocked in anticipation. She'd never been in charge of a client before, much less a man who would soon be king. God willing, nothing would go wrong. At the mere thought of good karma, Chase turned his head and spoke out of the corner of his mouth.

"Remember, he's used to getting his way. Stand your ground."

"What?" she huffed in irritation. Why in the world would they put her in this position? Was it payback for all the times she'd screwed up, or did someone want to see if maybe she'd toughened up in the last year? News alert: probably not.

Chase stepped forward and extended his hand. "Your Royal Highness, it is good to see you again."

The deep voice now sounded calm and soothing. "Captain Hunter." The prince grasped his hand and held it with both of his. "It has been a long time. Please, introduce me to your team."

"Agent Nicholas Zoric and Agent Samantha Cordova. Two of my best."

"And who is this?" Tessa watched him fold his hands in front of his body patiently as Chase stepped aside for her to move forward.

"Agent Tessa Scott, I'd like to introduce you to His Royal Highness Prince Muhammed Omar Kadir al Saud."

Witty or coy? She decided a mix of both as she extended her hand. "It must be difficult getting a proper name tag at official events, Your Highness."

The prince pursed his lips together as if suppressing amusement and lifted her hand to his lips. He stopped and stared at her as his chin lowered but never stopped staring up through the longest dark eyelashes she'd ever seen. His mouth lingered against her hand as his light-brown eyes bored into her confidence. When he took a step back, he continued to hold her hand.

"Remove your veil," he asked firmly.

"Please remove your veil," Tessa said softly, causing Chase's frown to deepen.

"Agent Scott—" Chase warned.

The prince held up his free hand to silence Chase, smiling at Tessa. "Please remove your veil, Agent Scott."

Tessa pulled her hand free to remove the veil and let it fall down her cheek without breaking the visual connection they were establishing.

"You don't look like a federal agent." He continued to lower his head like a python ready to strike, dark brows arched.

"And yet, here I am." Tessa raised her chin in a fake show of contempt, or at least a stab at bravery. "They were all out of black suits and ties, your Royal Highness."

His lips widened, the bottom one thicker than the top, and drew her attention. When his laughter burst free, she felt as if the evening might not be so bad after all. This time when he reached to take her hand, the prince shifted his attention to Chase. "You have done well, my friend. You are dismissed." Then he bent over Tessa's hand again and kissed it before looping it through his arm and waving the team away. "Amir will show you out."

Zoric touched Tessa on the shoulder to force her to meet his narrowed gaze. "I will be close." She nodded to cover the nervousness creeping up her spine. Sam paused in front of the two and squinted those evil cat-like eyes of hers at the prince then Tessa.

"Should you need anything, Your Highness, Agent Scott knows how to reach me."

"Thank you, Agent Cordova." He raised his bearded chin at her as he pointed toward the door. "I believe Captain Hunter is waiting. He doesn't appear to be very happy, so you'd best hurry along."

Tessa wanted to throw herself at Sam's feet, hug the woman's legs, and beg not to be left alone with one of the most handsome and mysterious men she'd ever met. Instead, the years of suffering the woman's bullying left the door wide open for revenge.

"Yes, Sam, do run along," she said sweetly. "Oh, and that shade of green eye shadow looks great on you, by the way." Sam's nostrils flared. "Is it the new shade of envy you were telling me about earlier this evening?" Tessa tried to maintain an innocent tone, but her grin of retribution probably would get her a hard workout the next week. So be it.

Agent Samantha pivoted and walked calmly to Chase's side as Amir opened the door for them. Chase gave a parting nod to her and the prince's assistant followed him out. The door closed.

"Come. I will give you a tour of this place. It reminds me of a palace in the sky," he said, stepping away from her.

He folded his hands behind his back and appeared to keep distance between them. The man's clothes were simple but of fine cloth. The tunic was burnt orange, almost brown, with a stand-up collar. His keffiyeh, or head covering, typical of Saudi men, was brownish red with black checks and held in place with a circlet of rope called an agal. It had been tied back with more fabric and managed to accent his angular face outlined with a thin dark beard and mustache. Walking beside him, she guessed his height to be about five foot ten.

"I didn't know you and Captain Hunter were acquainted." Tessa followed obediently into what resembled a kitchen and game room.

"Yes. We attended West Point together." This information concerning a college reunion and being a frat rat didn't really match the impression Chase gave her. "I see by your face, this surprises you. I imagine Captain Hunter provided you the profile of me being a wild college student, attending drunken parties and doing inappropriate things."

"Sounds familiar. Yes." She ran her fingers along the frame of the pool table before walking around the spacious room.

"I did visit my cousin at Harvard a couple of times. Those guys know how to party. There wasn't a lot of downtime at West Point while in training. There are few opportunities for the admittance of foreigners to learn from the best. Fortunately, my father, being king, was able to pull a few strings." He motioned for her to follow him again. "There's more." The next room was a small library slash office. Tessa wondered what kind of books would be offered to such an important guest. Several lay open on a table with their spine facing upward. After reading the titles, she leveled an admiring gaze.

"You're reading Pride and Prejudice?"

He joined her and picked up another book. "Yes. But don't tell anyone. I have read all of Jane Austin's books. And"—he showed her the one he held—"all of Louie L'Amour's. What a cowboy. I love to read almost anything."

"Me, too." Tessa drowned in the man's soothing voice and charm.

He leaned against the mahogany desk with his arms folded across his chest like a college professor might do. She had to admit, it made him sexy as hell. They stood there discussing old and new books, which was exactly what she and Chase had always done before Russia. It had been one of the things that tied them together. Those days had disappeared over the last year.

"It is good to have a beautiful woman to talk books with me tonight. It is stressful knowing someone wants to kill me when I have so much work to do for my country."

He moved away toward another door. Tessa caught the glimmer of his terrace through a wall of glass as she entered a bedroom. With a push of a button, the wall retracted. In two steps he was standing next to her, gazing at a swimming pool.

"Isn't it a marvel such a thing can be installed on the tenth floor of a building?" Before she knew what was happening, he removed her abaya and threw it over a cushioned chair. He let no part of her be unexplored with his invasive stare. "You truly are a beautiful woman. This is my lucky night after all." He strolled over to a small device on the wall and requested jazz music. "May I have this dance, Agent Scott?" In spite of her taking several steps away from him, he closed the gap to block any chance of retreat. He reached out and stroked her cheek, but she sidestepped him when his hand slid down her throat.

"Don't get ahead of yourself, Your Highness. I'm here to protect you. Neither of us needs a distraction."

"Then you shouldn't have worn this dress or such a delicate perfume." He pulled her into his arms, and together they danced with fluid motions across the room.

Tessa found herself enjoying the man who would be king. At first, they discussed the music, then the words grew few and far between as, with each song, he managed to pull her closer until his breath was close enough to move the few strands of hair that fell across her forehead. Then they stood moving back and forth, cheek against cheek.

"Your Highness." Tessa knew she'd lost focus and pushed away. "I want you to stop trying to distract me."

"Then I must insist you call me Muhammed for the rest of the night."

"You should call me Tessa, then, and I won't be here all night. Someone will relieve me in a few hours."

The prince chuckled good-naturedly. "Whatever you say. Let's walk around the pool. The air is cool tonight." He laid his hand on his heart. "Please. I want to know more about you. I rarely get to engage in meaningful conversation with such an enchanting woman."

He spread out his palm toward the pool and moved outside. Tessa took the lead. "I'm sure your many wives and mistresses might take offense at those comments. Please. I don't think we should be out here in the open."

"More misinformation. I have one wife and one daughter. As to mistresses, none. But I have had"—he smiled wickedly—"romantic interludes. I'm a loving husband. My wife is beautiful, but it was an arranged marriage, and we have little in common. You Americans search for love like treasure hunters. It has been elusive for me."

The night breeze touched his tunic and keffiyeh and reminded Tessa of so many romantic stories of her dreams, A Thousand and One Nights being one of them.

"Tell me, Tessa, what does love mean to you?"

She felt herself blinking, a nervous habit she'd acquired years earlier that plagued her ability of being secretive. "Come back inside and I'll tell you all about love. Real love." He grasped her extended hand and pulled her closer.

"We have a connection, Tessa. Can you feel it?"

What she felt after being in the breeze and around so much water was the urge to pee. Maybe if she told him about childbirth and never having a strong bladder after three fat babies, it would cool his jets a bit. Now, that was love.

Who was she kidding? Roman Darya Petrov, a man she loved desperately, had died over a year ago, and it was time to move on, maybe with Chase or… The fact was she was lonely for the touch of a man in the middle of the night. She longed to experience a deep connection again with someone that could make you lose your common sense.

"Let's not get ahead of ourselves—Muhammed." She took his offered arm as they moved back inside. "Let me do another walk-through to make sure I know where everything is just in case. Are you good with that?"

He nodded. "I'm in no hurry. We have all night."

~ ~ ~ ~

Chase smoothed his black tie as he checked the security

measures the Secret Service put in place the day before. The top three floors had been emptied of guests. Each of those floors were a complete suite of rooms and reserved for the rich, famous, and dignitaries. Since they were provided with a private elevator, those had been locked down since Enigma took over part of the security. Except for the floor with the prince, it would be nearly impossible for anyone to enter without them knowing.

The perimeter of the building was being monitored. Chase insisted all valet parking be moved a block away, and guests were shuttled to and from the hotel by Secret Service. Every guest had been screened, checked, and double-checked. If so much as an unpaid parking ticket showed up, the guest was given accommodations at a different hotel at a big discount. So far, there had been no complaints. If there had been, a close and uncomfortable scrutiny would have followed.

The environment was being monitored for abnormal gases, wind speeds, temperature fluctuations, and noise pollution in a two-mile radius. Even the hotel's power grid had its own person keeping watch on the people who generally took care of such things.

Chase walked up to one of his people, Agent Tom Cooper, who stood so still, he resembled a mannequin. "This place is locked down so tight a flea couldn't get through."

The agent responded, "You'd think the President of the United States was here."

"A lot is riding on this. For whatever reason, someone is out to kill the prince. We don't want that happening on US soil. There would be hell to pay."

"Too quiet and easy. I don't like it," Agent Ken Montgomery said as he came to stand next to them then finally turned his gaze on Chase. "Think Tessa can handle that guy upstairs?"

"Zoric is close. She'll let him know if the prince gets out of line." Chase frowned at the agent. "Sometimes I think you're sweet on our domestic commando."

"She did save my life. It doesn't hurt to watch out for her. She tends to find trouble like a heat-seeking missile."

"That she does."

"She's such a babe in the woods," Agent Cooper said quietly out the corner of his mouth as he continued to let his eyes search the lobby. He glanced at his watch. "Midnight. Pretty quiet."

"I don't like it."

Chase didn't, either. Confidence was high with the intel concerning an attempt to assassinate the prince. By this time, a person of interest was usually in custody. He walked over to the check-in desk and asked to see a list of guests who arrived in the last ten hours.

"Do you have security video?" he asked the clerk. Chase slipped behind the desk and waited for it to be pulled up. "Wait. Back it up. There. When did they arrive?"

"Looks like around three this afternoon. Had a baby. Kept crying. The mother was beside herself, and the husband kept telling her to do something. I rushed the check-in. I felt sorry for her."

Alarm bells went off in Chase's head. "Rushed how?"

"They wanted an upgrade in their room, and with everything going on, I decided to move them so there wouldn't be any trouble. You know, like an argument about our service. It's a quiet end of the building, and several other guests canceled after we offered them other accommodations across town."

"What floor?"

"Seven. Something odd though."

"Odd? Like what?"

"They specifically asked for room 786. We don't have a room with that number. As I said, I felt sorry for them so I upgraded him."

"Was he Middle Eastern?"

"I don't think so. Mexican, maybe, and spoke Spanish to his wife."

Chase motioned for Agent Cooper and Montgomery. "Activate the protocol. I think we've been outwitted. They're here."

"How do you know?" The agent was already pulling his gun.

"They asked for a numbered room of 786. It signifies 'in the name of Allah, the ever merciful, the ever compassionate.'"

"Got it." The agent sounded the alarm by speaking into his wrist mic.

As Chase tried to contact Zoric and Sam, he entered the elevator to ride to the top floor. "Anyone on the floor besides you?"

"Nothing. There was a lot of laughing and music earlier," Zoric grumbled. "Then the prince poured on the charm. I think they went for a swim. He'd been suggesting that off and, on all evening, along with a number of other activities."

Samantha, who had been at the end of the hall, looked out toward the rear of the building, ran to the prince's suite, and banged on the door. "Zoric, something is wrong! Someone just jumped off the balcony."

"We're in trouble, Chase," Zoric shouted as he pulled out his weapon. "Repeat. Agent Scott is in trouble."

Together, they pounded on the steel door, calling for Tessa to activate the locks. Chase wasted no time in getting there. He waved the activator across the computer lock, and it snapped open.

The three rushed inside and froze. Two male bodies lay on the floor, blood covered their face and necks. The room had been trashed.

"Tessa," Chase yelled as he stepped forward with his trusted agents taking up defensive positions on either side of him.

He hurried to the kitchen/game room. Soaked from head to toe, Tessa held something sharp in each hand, covered in blood. Blonde curls had fallen across her face. The prince leaned into her body, with his arm draped around her shoulders. His once-expensive tunic was ripped and covered in blood. A gun lay on the floor on top of the small handbag she'd brought with her.

The prince and Tessa exchanged gazes before he turned his attention to Chase.

"Can I keep her?"

CHAPTER 3

شهيد

It was well into the night before everything could be sorted out enough to acknowledge mistakes had been made and no immediate threat remained. An Enigma doctor and the prince's personal physician had been called in to examine His Royal Highness and Tessa. Of the two men found on the living room floor, one was still alive who might not make it. A third man in the kitchen area also was still breathing but in bad shape.

"There's another one near the swimming pool," Tessa said, pointing a trembling finger. "Amir, the prince's assistant jumped." Her voice had been soft but steady when Chase took her aside to question.

"He jumped from the balcony. Had a paraglider suit on, I think. No body was found, and several witnesses reported seeing a person fly off the tenth floor."

She nodded and visually searched for the prince who sent her a comforting nod of approval. "Is he okay?"

Chase glanced his way and wondered what the hell had happened. Even if the prince was military trained, could he have taken down four assailants? He dared push Tessa's hair out of her eyes as the doctor finished up. The physician butterflied a cut over her eye and had given a fairly thorough exam, considering they were not at a clinic.

"Her blood pressure is a little higher than what's normal for her but well within the normal range. It should settle down now that all of you are here." He patted Tessa's shoulder and handed her a pill bottle. "You're most likely going to be sore in the morning. Looks like you'll also have bruises on various parts of your body. These are pain pills. Don't be a hero. Take them. Your body needs to heal."

"Thank you," she said but didn't take the bottle. Chase relieved the doctor of the pills and followed her line of sight. She was trying to see what was going on with the prince and his doctor. "I want to make sure he's okay."

"He looks in better shape than you."

"Who is staying with him? They might come back. I can't let that happen."

Chase resisted showing any signs of amusement. "We've got it covered. Now I'm taking you to a very comfortable room and tucking you in for the night after you get a hot shower and some clean clothes."

"Do as he says, Tessa." The prince had joined them. He nudged Chase aside and placed his hands on her forearms then leaned closer to stare into her eyes. "I will be fine. You have done enough for one night."

"I'm so sorry this happened, Prince Muhammed." Her bottom lip trembled. "If only I had…"

He slid his hands down her arms to clasp her hands then lifted them to his lips. "Would you like for me to stay with you tonight? It has all been very traumatic."

"I think we can take it from here, Your Highness." Chase bristled. "Your people are insisting to take over the rest of the night. Secret Service are also here."

The prince's expression turned dark and brooding. "My people will do as I say."

Tessa laid a gentle hand on the prince's chest. "I'll be okay. I'm sure Captain Hunter will make sure I'm taken care of."

"I have no doubt of that," he snapped as he zeroed in on the competition. "But if that is your wish, I will abide. Tomorrow is another day." He leaned in and kissed her on each cheek. "If you need anything at all, you have my cell number. I will also post a guard at your door to make sure the captain is able to handle any situation that might arise."

"Thank you, Prince Muhammed." Tessa appeared angelic in that moment. "You are too kind." As Chase tried to lead her to the doors, the prince pulled Tessa to his side and looped her arm through his.

"I am most grateful to you," he said as they stopped at the door.

"And I to you, Your Highness." They stood there gazing at each other until Chase cleared his throat.

"We should go."

Chase tucked her in bed before leaving her with protection in order to finish up with the Secret Service and leads on whoever had jumped off the roof. The prince had been moved to another suite of rooms and was heavily guarded inside as well as outside his accommodations. Chase tried to ask him a few questions, but the prince only mentioned he appreciated him sending Tessa for the most memorable evening he could ever remember. Because he refused to discuss the evening's events until the next day, he turned in and was soon sleeping like a baby.

Secret Service obtained the security video and told Chase they would study it before sharing with Enigma the following day since President Austin insisted, they be included. They filled him in on the plans for a meeting scheduled for noon the next day to review the video. They had secured a conference room in the hotel, along with a few meeting rooms. No one wanted to set up security for a second time in a new location. At least this one was safe for the time being.

Director Benjamin Clark of Enigma arrived by breakfast to quiz the Secret Service agent in charge as to what they knew so far. The Enigma team were in attendance, including Carter Johnson who had been the helicopter pilot who checked rooftops before and after the attack.

The former astronaut was an unapologetic playboy who never met a mirror he didn't like. He was the group's thrill seeker as well and enjoyed living on the edge. He and Captain Hunter had become fast friends in spite of one of them liking to give orders and the other not good at taking them.

"And where is our little Grass Valley commando?" Carter asked after taking a quick sip of coffee. "You tuck her into bed last night like a good boss?" He never shied away from making fun of the precarious relationship between the two.

Chase rolled his eyes then joined the director who had been watching. "Go to hell, Carter." That resulted in his friend chuckling along with Zoric who had already asked him the same question. "You guys should take your act to Vegas. You're hilarious." He waited for the director to address him before speaking.

"Where is she?" Carter finally asked in a low monotone.

"I left word for her we were meeting." Chase figured she'd be dragging this morning after the excitement of the night before. According to the Secret Service, the prince remained in his room and no further incidents had occurred. Since there was no pool, the only outdoor access was a patio balcony where a beefy bodyguard and one of his own agents spent the night. It may have been overkill on the protection, but there couldn't be any more slipups.

"Let's begin. We can have a face-to-face with her when this is done if there are further questions. From what I'm told, she was banged up and bloody." Agent Marco, the lead with Secret Service, walked by them and nodded to the chairs around the table. "You talk about this woman like she's a cupcake." His smirk was a little unsettling. "Pay close attention to the video and learn." He called for the rest to be seated and then spun his finger in the air toward a woman sitting at a computer. "Agent Willy Robbins will take us through the video. If you have questions afterward or need a copy, Agent Robbins can assist you with that." With his nod, the agent pulled up the video.

Samantha Cordova arched an eyebrow and elbowed Carter who sat next to her. "This should be entertaining."

"Nothing like a little blood and guts to get your motor running, Sam?" Carter asked flippantly.

"Especially if it's Tessa's." Her face brightened as she ran her tongue across her red lips. "Yummy."

"Cool it," Chase growled as he took a chair across from them. He tilted his head slightly toward the director, knowing the man had a short fuse when it came to the team's total disregard for authority and inappropriate social behavior.

Once the other Enigma team members settled in, the video paused as Agent Marco stood at the front of the screen. "Take a timeline card before you. Notice how the scene moves from room to room. Glance over it now so you'll catch when the camera makes a change. Nothing has been altered. In spite of the audio being rough, I think you'll be able to understand the gist of it." The lights dimmed as he took a seat.

~ ~ ~ ~

The Video

Prince Muhammed sighed then clapped his hands in amazement as Tessa triple jumped him at checkers. She had won for the third time. Because she allowed him to win the first two games, Tessa decided it was time to teach him a lesson. She was a bit competitive. When teaching her kids how to play games, she let them win only until they learned the game. Then she methodically crushed them until they became just as ruthless in their thinking and strategies.

"You'll thank me later," she told them then offered to make their favorite treat. They'd become quite accomplished at many things in their young years. She prayed they'd be okay, especially if anything ever happened to her during a mission with Enigma.

"Ah, Tessa. You are amazing. No one ever tries to beat me at checkers. Thank you for the challenge." The prince leaned back in his chair and laid a hand on his chest as if it would stop his laughter. Soft music played in the background of the living room. He devoured her in one long gaze head to toe. "I think if you had worn a different dress, I could have won." He stood and walked around the coffee table and extended his hand. "The bet was, if I win the most, then we take a swim."

"And if you don't, then we dance—in a respectful, friend kind of way," she said, taking his hand and standing then kicking her spike heels to the side of the coffee table.

He tilted his head with a mischievous expression. "But of course."

But plans changed. Slipping his hand slowly around her waist, he jerked her up against his chest and proceeded to dip her backward and leaned over her with an amused wolfish grin.

"Prince Muhammed, you do know I'm capable of making you

beg for mercy if the situation demands it?" she said coyly, enjoying the prince so much more than she'd thought possible.

"I am so counting on that, Agent Scott."

They exchanged more lighthearted laughter as he pulled her up into a standing position and moved her to the slow beat of the music. Even if he was a playboy, this was her first opportunity to enjoy herself in over a year.

She'd trained so hard in recent months with Samantha. Vlad the Impaler apparently was the woman's hero, considering the abuse she inflicted. Chase had been emotionally MIA, and the others had treated her like she was incapable of anything but grieving over a dead husband. A husband who'd been a drug runner, spy, and her kidnapper left her weak with grief and longing for more. Tonight was a chance to prove to them she could be a productive Enigma agent or at least an agent who could do more than provide intel on the hellholes of the world and the dangers that lurked in every corner.

The music beat picked up, but the prince continued to hold her close and slow dance. "I'm starving. Let's order from the restaurant downstairs. Or I can cook. I never get a chance to do that. Besides, it's late. They're probably closed."

"Do you really want to cook?" she teased, knowing being so close their lips nearly touched was throwing gas on a fire.

"Are we still talking about food?"

Tessa couldn't resist a deep laugh. He took her breath away. "Prince Muhammed, thank you for a lovely evening and just so you know, I'm not really hungry." She turned her head slightly and caught movement out the corner of her eye.

Then she heard the prince say, "What do you think you're doing, Amir?"

That's when things got complicated.

CHAPTER 4

شهيد

Tessa pulled free of the prince's embrace and eased in front of him, although he tried to resist. Where was her purse? Wasn't that the man the prince claimed to be his assistant? His scruffy beard and clothes that didn't quite fit, gave him a rough-around-the-edges appearance for someone serving in such a delicate position. She threw up both hands and tried to sound threatening. "Stop right there. How did you get in here?" Where were Sam and Zoric? She tapped her earwig. "Assistance needed." Nothing.

"It's just Amir," the prince sighed as he stepped around Tessa.

Amir wasn't much taller than five foot eight or nine. In spite of wearing a long white tunic and draped keffiyeh that fell to his shoulders, he stood rigid as if he expected trouble. Dark circles surrounded eyes the color of obsidian, adding a mystical vibe to his long narrow face that resembled chiseled granite. The loathing in his wide-eyed gaze that slid up and down her body chilled her to the bone.

Tessa threw her arm out to halt the prince from moving forward. "I said stop, Mr. Amir. Now you step back and hold out your arms until I can check you out." With disdain in his eyes, he raised his arms. She didn't like it. His fingers twitched, and he batted his eyelids one too many times. Watching all those Westerns with her dad told her this character was about to draw his gun.

When she stopped three feet from him and locked gazes, the prince laughed. "Honestly, Tessa. It's fine. I'm sure your people let him in."

"No. They didn't. Did they, Amir?"

One corner of his mouth turned up in a smirk as he dropped his arms then lunged at her. He spun her around, held her with his arm around her neck, and pulled her tight against his body. Reaching into his tunic, Amir pulled out a gun and pointed it at the prince.

A bewildered expression flooded the prince's face as his forehead creased in disbelief. He took a step forward, and Amir jabbed the weapon into Tessa's temple. "Amir," he snapped. "What are you doing? She is a friend. I will have your head for this. Release her immediately."

"I don't take orders from you, Your Royal High and Mighty. You will never live long enough to hurt me or anyone else in the kingdom. You are finished. My friends and I will see to that."

Four more men in black suits walked through the double doors. Tessa screamed, "Run," at the top of her lungs as she jerked her body to the side, catching Amir off guard. At the same time, she doubled her fist and slammed it backward, with as much force as she could muster, into his crotch. He released her and doubled over with a howl of pain. While he was bent over, she pivoted and clasped her hands together in a fist then pounded it into the back of his neck. On his way down to smash his face into the hard tiled floors, his gun flew up into the air.

Tessa caught the gun and glanced over her shoulder one more time. "Now, Muhammed!" In the next second, as the four imposters rushed forward, she fired the gun into the groin of one man, in case he was wearing a bulletproof vest. His scream echoed through the room as he tumbled to the floor, trying to cover the pool of blood forming on the front of his pants.

In that same split second, one man helped Amir up off the floor, when he said, "He's getting away. Kill the woman. Now."

Another man rushed her, and she fired with her eyes closed. Opening them, she saw a blood stain form on his chest as he fell. That left one more here and one with Amir.

This fourth man gritted his teeth and growled. It wasn't a stretch to figure out he planned to finish her off. Without warning, he let out a yell that terrified Tessa enough that she stumbled back against the couch. Pointing the gun at his head, she pulled the trigger, only to have it jam. With the aim of a St. Louis Cardinal pitcher, she hurled the weapon at his face, making contact. He took a couple steps backward and shook his bulbous head as if dazed.

She slipped around the couch as he approached again with outstretched arms, resembling a grizzly bear. When he reached inside his suit jacket, she assumed it was for a gun, but he withdrew a foot-long dagger with a jagged blade and an ivory hilt resembling a prop from a horror movie. It could have easily taken out a room full of zombies.

The thing to do was create a distraction he wouldn't expect. She hiked her dress up to the top of her thighs, which in itself caused him to pause. Then, with a hop onto the coffee table, she snatched the marble checkers and threw them at him, giving her time to leap onto the couch. The springs gave her enough bounce to land on the back. Before the man could react, she pulled out the chopsticks from her hair, gripped one in each hand, and lunged toward him. She jammed them into his unprotected eyes. One went in, and the other snapped in two but left a large gash in his cheek.

The howl reminded her of a wounded animal as he staggered backward, dropping the knife. Tessa grabbed it and buried it once in each of his thighs. She didn't know if she'd hit an artery until blood sprayed over her bare legs and arms. She straightened to pivot toward the voices coming from the other room. Hearing the prince's voice gave her hope he hadn't been injured by Amir and the last man who had barged into the suite. With a glance down at the man with the gouged-out eye, she doubted he could walk or see where he was going, so finishing him off could wait.

The crash of breaking glass and guttural noises came from the kitchen/game room. Lifting her spike heels from the floor, she ran into the room to find both Amir and yet another man closing in on the prince. To his credit, Prince Muhammed was fearless as he held up a pool stick and swiped it at Amir, making contact with his neck. The second man dodged the prince's jab at him but took the hit on his shoulder. The last intruder managed to catch the narrow end and tried to pull it away from the prince with no success. With one final jab, the prince released it, throwing the second man off-balance.

Without hesitation, Tessa leapt on the back of the attacker only to have him spin around and take her by the forearms. Using his grip on her, she jerked the back of his hand, knuckles out, to slam into his other arm, which would hurt like the devil. Samantha had done it to her several times in training.

As his grip released, he stepped back, but Tessa went after him and slipped a hand in his suit coat. She jammed her thumb into his upper chest. It should've felt similar to having a heart attack. He sucked in a breath and leaned forward. Tessa took advantage of the moment of confusion to snatch up the pool stick he dropped on the floor. As he lifted his face, eyes glazed with pain, Tessa slammed the wood into his nose so hard it shattered. At least he was no longer a threat.

Now her attention was completely on the prince. Amir threw one of the pool balls at the prince, who took it on the chest. Searching for a weapon, she spotted her purse and snatched it up, quickly discovering her Kyber was gone. Amir turned his attention to her now, throwing pool balls at her. Four hit her in various places, causing a burst of pain. If his aim had been better, she'd be dead of a head injury.

The last one he hurled, she caught in midair. She promised herself to thank her dad for making her play baseball with her brothers. She was one heck of a second baseman and later in high school, a pitcher.

"Looking for this?" Amir smirked as he pointed the gun at her.

The prince propelled an eight ball he'd found on the floor at Amir. The keffiyeh rope took the brunt, but the blow caused him to drop the gun, and he turned back toward his intended target. The prince secured a carving knife from a knife block set on the counter and rushed toward Amir.

Although the prince was getting the best of Amir, the traitor managed to get free without harm. When Tessa fired her weapon, he momentarily hesitated then ran for the outside. Both she and Prince Muhammed chased after him. Tessa fired again, and he fell into the pool. The prince jumped in after him but couldn't keep up.

Before Tessa could circle the pool, Amir climbed out and ran to a bench. Opening the lid, he jerked something out and slipped his arms through it. When she chased after him, she stole a glance toward the prince in the water.

Where was he? Then she saw him struggling and sinking beneath the water. Without another thought, Tessa jumped in and caught him around the neck as his eyes fluttered closed. She managed to pull him to a platforms as she rose out of the water and pulled him higher where it was dry. He wasn't breathing.

"Come on. Come on," she coaxed, performing CPR. When she rolled him to his side, he spit out water and coughed. When he tried to give a lopsided grin, Tessa pulled him up into her arms on a wave of relief. "You'll live. Are you okay?"

"Maybe you should hold on to me a minute to make sure."

Tessa choked on her relief just as the man whose nose she'd broken with a pool stick, staggered out to the pool. "I need to finish this. Wait here."

When she rose from the platform, the man pooched out his bloody lips and motioned for her to come at him. Tessa slowly approached and realized she may have gotten too close when he doubled his fist and took a swing at her head. But her training once again kicked in, and she plowed her elbow into his upper arm.

When he grabbed the arm and shrieked, she slammed the palm of her hands against his ears. A moan escaped his mouth as he bent over to meet with Tessa's knee under his chin. He spit blood and a few teeth at her then hit face-first on the pool deck.

The sound of banging on the suite doors reached her as she helped Prince Muhammed to his feet. "I think help has arrived, Prince Muhammed. You'll be safe now."

The prince surveyed the area as they moved toward the living room. "Safe? What do you call all this? Who needs them?"

Tessa picked up a knife from the floor and pulled the chopstick from the unconscious man on the floor, just in case. The front doors burst open to reveal the Enigma cavalry, staring at her as if she'd sprouted a forked tail and horns. She tried to appear nonchalant, but her face hurt. "I was just going to call you."

CHAPTER 5

شهيد

The screen froze with Tessa standing in the doorway, holding a bloody knife, and Prince Muhammed staring at her like he'd won the lottery. Chase felt every nerve in his body crash, tingle, and reboot as someone in the back of the room cleared their throat. Everyone shifted in their seat to see a woman in blue jeans and a Whitesnake T-shirt, who held a plate, staring at the screen in the front of the room.

One by one, each person rose and, all at once, they applauded, slow at first then picking up momentum. Tessa stood wide-eyed and silent as her gaze moved around the room. With her hair pulled back into a ponytail and a fresh-scrubbed face with no makeup, she looked ten years younger. She should be modeling for L.L. Bean instead of working for Enigma.

When the applause stopped, she extended the plate. "I—I brought cookies," she said softly. Her gaze scanned the room until they landed on Chase, and her face brightened innocently. His chest ached, to think she searched for him. Knowing her like he did, he realized the corner of her mouth, which raised in what had become their pleasure at seeing each other, nearly made him go into protection mode from so many eyes staring at her. This now was a common experience for him. "Ooh. Cookies," Carter said, making his way to relieve her of the plate. He winked at her.

"Good job, Agent Scott."

Samantha casually walked up to her and glared before a feline smirk toyed with her red lips. "Thanks for not making me look bad, Betty Crocker. I think I just fell in love."

Tessa raised her chin in stubbornness; Sam gave her a narrowed-eyed look. The two women were constantly at each other's throats, but he suspected it was all an act. Tessa raised her palm, and Sam gave her a high five and held onto her hand at the end. Both women glared at each other in respect.

"All the extra training on those weekend trips paid off," Tessa admitted.

Carter, with a mouth full of chocolate chip cookie, butted into their conversation. "What extra training? What weekend trips?"

Sam arched her eyebrow and frowned at him. "Don't give me that hopeful expression we were shopping, taking mud baths and wearing cucumber slices on our eyes."

Tessa put her finger to her cheek. "Well, there was that one time…"

Samantha sighed and nodded. "Oh yeah. I remember now." She landed a soft fist bump on Tessa's arm. "I never saw you for a mud wrestler."

"We won the team event," Tessa chuckled. "I wanted that trophy."

"Sorry about that. Busting that jerk's head open was well worth losing it over."

Tessa shrugged. "Yeah. You're right."

Chase couldn't suppress his amusement at what they were doing to Carter and Zoric. He laid a hand on Tessa's back. "We need to talk."

"No way," Carter insisted. "I want to hear the rest of this story."

"They're yanking your chain, Carter." Chase moaned. "You don't really think you'd ever get either one of them to work together in a mud pit, do you?"

"No. That's why my imagination is on overload. I've had dreams about this very thing."

The senior Secret Service agent joined them, lifted a cookie, and frowned at Carter then at Chase. "This conversation borders on sexual harassment, Captain Hunter. Do you allow your people to converse in this manner?" He nodded to Tessa. "Great job last night, Agent Scott." He took a bite of the cookie. "Taste's homemade." He reached for another one, but Zoric took the plate and walked away. "Anyway, as I was saying. You prevented an international disaster last night. You have a grateful president and a Saudi king who are in your debt."

She began the nervous flutter of her eyelashes, alerting Chase, it was time to move on. "It's her job, Agent Marco."

"Thank goodness someone was doing their job, Captain Hunter, because those five men nearly killed the future king of Saudi Arabia."

Director Benjamin Clark folded his arms across his chest and did a loud, "Humph." When Agent Marco's eyes locked with his, he did a hard swallow. Crossing the director of Enigma had left many a terrified agent to reconsider whether they were up for the job.

"Seems to me you Secret Service assholes dropped the ball. You passed out IDs to those morons that got in. They showed my people the official badges and password to get by my agents."

Agent Marco opened his mouth to respond, but the director held his hand up and lowered his head to give himself the image of the American eagle ready to swoop in and attack.

"No apologies necessary. Everybody makes mistakes. Maybe not as big as this one, but I'll be sure to let President Austin know next time we won't be working together. I'm hoping the fake Mexican couple with the baby can be found since they were the ones hiding Amir's men before the attack." Agent Marco tried to speak, but the director continued. "And the baby was a doll. Found it shoved under the mattress. We've already run their prints. They are Saudis who were educated in Mexico. Go figure," he smirked. "Now that we've done a big part of your job, I'll let you get to it."

"Maybe we should let them slug it out," Chase said to Tessa as he laid a hand on her back and moved her toward one of the open rooms off the conference area. She nodded and ended up following him into a dark room that lit up as soon as they crossed the threshold. The room had a stack of tables at the far end as well as chairs. He grabbed two and set them across from each other. Patting the seat of one, he took the other.

"Is this where you give me the come-to-Jesus talk?" she said quietly as she eased into the chair.

He leaned forward. "No. This is where I tell you I nearly had a heart attack watching that video. I saw you last night all bloody and bruised and I thought they had hurt you."

"They kinda did." In spite of her fixation on her hands, she was too calm and focused for his liking. "Sorry I screwed things up. I tried to reach Zoric." She glanced up, fluttered her lashes then stared back down at her hands.

"I know you did," he said, trying to control his breathing and racing heart. The temptation to touch her was too great. He reached out and cupped her face in his hand, drawing her attention to him. "Tessa," he whispered.

"So, I'm not in trouble, fired, or have to do more training with your crazy nymphomaniac of an agent? Because I don't think I could do any more of that." She laid her hand on his.

"I think I'm at a loss for words. What happened to the scared little rabbit I met a couple of years ago who was ready to nuke the house at the site of a spider?"

She pulled his hand off her face and held it tightly before meeting his gaze with a kind of sadness he'd come to know in the last year after the Tribesman died. She loved him enough to let him force her into marriage so he could protect her from the Russians. Chase had never gotten over the feeling of betrayal and heartbreak. It was his own damn fault for not telling her she meant everything to him.

"How long is this going to take? I want to go home, Chase. I'm really sore today. Is that normal?"

"After seeing that video, I'd say yes. I've got a few things to do here then I'll drive you to the Warehouse to stay until we make sure all is safe for you to go back to the apartment." The Warehouse was a place they kept in a former industrial park. From the outside, it appeared to have seen better days. The inside was another matter entirely: sleek, modern, and secluded from the prying eyes of the world.

Two of Chase's men, Marine First Sergeant Tom Cooper, and former Army Ranger Sergeant Ken Montgomery had both served with him in various capacities over the years. Both now lived at the Warehouse full-time and oversaw prisoners or so-called guests. The men often enjoyed, when it was appropriate, interrogating or scaring the hell out of uncooperative guests. Zoric, the lead interrogator, usually took care of those kind of conversations but hadn't had cause to do much of that kind of work lately. Since several of Amir's men were in the hospital, it might be a while until they transitioned to the warehouse.

"No. I want to go home. Those guys play loud music, drink beer, and watch depressing movies. If I have to watch Black Hawk Down or The Hurt Locker one more time, I'm going to come unhinged."

"Is that what happened last night? You came unhinged? Or did Prince Muhammed break my rules about interaction with you?" Her eyes widened before she shook her head. He went on. "The video indicated the two of you were having a really good time."

Her bottom lip jutted out as she released his hand. "He was a gentleman the entire time. And I did enjoy his company. Maybe if I hadn't been distracted by all his charm and appreciation, I would've done a better job."

"Don't be fooled by the charm, Tessa. He's had men put to death for crossing him. He's good at deception."

"So are you," she shot back in a quiet voice, but her hard glare wasn't lost on him.

He'd tried to stay out of the way for the last year so she could recover from losing the Tribesman. What surprised him was how it affected him. How could he have been so wrong about one man? Tessa had seen the good in Roman Darya Petrov when everyone else saw deception and a man who would double-cross you if it helped his questionable agenda.

In the last year, he'd kept a lot of things from her to make sure she could heal and get on with her life. Of course, he'd been there, at least most of the time. Making sure he was never alone with her had been difficult at first. All he wanted to do was comfort her and make sure her kids were okay with all the changes in their lives.

Their birth father had also turned out to be a less-than-stellar person, and she'd booted him to the curb in short order. That whole mess had finally been worked out. He hadn't wanted to be alone with her for any length of time because he didn't want to be a rebound love. So, he'd moved on with his life the best he could while the love of his life faded from his daily routine. He, too, needed to heal and move on. It was time to tell Tessa the truth. But not now. Not today. How long could he wait?

Chapter 6

شهيد

Two weeks had passed since the whole Prince Muhammed incident. Amir had never been found and was thought to have made it back to the Middle East. Sadly, of the men Tessa put in the hospital, one had died of complications related to his injuries. The other three were recovering in a secure location monitored by several agencies, including the Secret Service. The hospital adjoining Sacramento University of Science and Technology had a wing for such special guests. The staff specialized in trauma medicine and were in high demand when high-ranking officials required a special kind of attention.

Fearing Tessa would blame herself for the death of the man who tried to kill her and Prince Muhammed, Enigma enlisted their psychiatrist, Dr. Wu, to make frequent visits to her. The doctor had worked miracles with Tessa after Darya's death. Once again, the doctor was left in charge of Tessa's well-being and often invited her to his home where they tended to his orchid collection.

Mostly they talked gardening, but she knew every word out of his mouth was meant to relieve any stress or concerns stewing inside her head. He'd helped her on many occasions over the last few years, the first time after being kidnapped in Afghanistan. Throughout the last year, Dr. Wu had intruded on her grief and life to force her to move forward. He was annoying like that.

"Chase will have nothing to do with me now," she once told him. "He hates me."

Dr. Wu had come to her apartment with carryout from a fast-food restaurant. "He is hurting, too."

"Because he thinks I betrayed him."

"No. Because he betrayed himself when it came to his feelings for you. Maybe even misjudging Darya and the impact he had on you."

"I don't understand. Let's talk about orchids for a change."

Dr. Wu never directly mentioned it again. But all of the parables, Chinese wisdom, garden talk, and often times not speaking at all, healed her from the guilt she felt.

The other team members at Enigma didn't have much to say about the whole Prince Muhammed incident, but instead treated her like a trusted member. It was so worth whatever stupid luck she used the night she saved the prince.

Prince Muhammed demanded an audience with her, so she was whisked to his hotel two days after the attack. He acted a little surprised when she showed up in a black suit and low heels, with her hair pulled back in a messy bun on her neck. A few curls escaped to frame her face. Chase insisted on being present with Sergeant Ken Montgomery waiting outside the door of the suite.

The prince frowned a great deal at the two men but looped her arm through his and guided her to the balcony, still in full sight of Chase.

"If you ever want a job, a home, or to escape from trouble, I'm your guy." The prince took both her hands in his.

"Or my prince?" A soft chuckle escaped her mouth.

"I will never forget what you did for me. I'm forever in your debt."

"It was my honor to assist, Your Royal Highness. I see you have recovered and have attended the economic meetings. When do you return home?"

"Tomorrow. Come with me."

Tessa tilted her head. "My life is here, Prince Muhammed. It has been my pleasure to meet you."

He stepped back and bowed. "The pleasure was all mine, Agent Scott. Until we meet again."

"Yes. May your journey be safe."

When Tessa walked past Chase, he continued to stand statue still wearing his mirrored sunglasses. He continued to focus in the direction of the prince. When she glanced over her shoulder, the prince now stared at Chase. She was glad the prince wasn't allowed to carry a gun considering how dark his face had turned. Afterward, Sergeant Ken Montgomery took her home, since the prince requested Chase stay.

Two weeks later, the team was expected to invade her little apartment, eat, play cards, and swap lies about how without their specific talent, things wouldn't get done for the country to remain safe. They showed up to do this at least once a month, when Robert had the kids for a few days. Sometimes, they brought the food, and other times, she cooked. Tonight, she'd fixed a Crockpot of chili since it had rained nearly all day and left a coolness in the air.

She loved these moments. They really had become her family. Most of the time, she didn't participate in their banter but watched and listened. Laughter filled the small apartment and floated through the open doors of the terrace. It let the evening air in and gave them more room to stretch their legs.

Questions concerning why Chase didn't always come or at least stay the whole time continued to puzzle her. "Please come, Chase. I want you there tonight," she'd coaxed at the office.

His devilish grin was her undoing when he patted her cheek. "Then, I'll be there. I don't have any plans until later. You remember I'm flying out to Turkey tonight."

"Yes. That's why I want you to come. How long will you be gone?"

He shrugged. "Who knows. Maybe six weeks. Your Prince Muhammed convinced the director he needed me to watch after his niece, Soraya, since she is a big rock star. He's afraid Amir will try to get to him through her."

"Why couldn't his people do this?"

"Since she is considered trash and very worldly, the shame she brings to the family is unacceptable. However, she is his sister's kid who married a Kurd."

"Aw. Thus, the shame deepens."

"Yes. But he wants to protect her while she does a rock video shoot in Turkey."

Tessa reached to touch his arm, but he turned away and called over his shoulder he'd see her around six thirty.

Now, here they all were, playing cards and sipping the beer they'd brought, knowing she wasn't a drinker and wouldn't have any available. She gathered up the empty chili bowls and used napkins still on the table. Carter laid down his cards and yelled victory as the others threw down their hands.

"I'll help you with that, Tessa." Ken Montgomery stood and stretched.

Tessa liked the Ranger sergeant who'd once served with Chase. She'd accidentally saved his life from a Libyan terrorist on their first meeting. He worked in the shadows and remained aloof most of the time. Once in a while, he'd emerge and talk her ear off. Then there were times, like tonight, when his quick comebacks to the others entertained her.

"Great. You can slice the cake for everyone." She nodded toward the little kitchen open to the rest of the apartment. There was no way of knowing that simple act on Ken's part would force Chase to tear down the wall between them, once and for all.

Zoric elbowed his buddy and nodded toward the kitchen. "Chase, I think one of our own has a crush on Tessa."

Ken focused on Tessa like a schoolboy in love with his kindergarten teacher.

"Yeah. I've noticed. Anything I ought to know?" He shuffled the cards and waited for an answer.

"Besides you're an idiot?"

Chase squinted at the Serbian. "Meaning?"

"Meaning, you're going to let that slice of heaven slip through your fingers again if you're not careful," Carter muttered. "Considering how she protected the prince, and caught his fancy, do you think she's going to be on the market for long?"

"Oh, shut up," Samantha groaned. "I'm sick of hearing how precious she is." She leaned back in her chair and stared into the kitchen. "If you think Cupcake doesn't have...needs, then you weren't paying attention to her and Darya." She fanned herself with the hand she'd been dealt. "Ken over there"—she made a pouty expression with her lips as she arranged her cards— "is no stranger with what makes a girl happy."

"And how would you know that?" Carter frowned.

She replied with a smug chuckle. "Are you going to play or what?"

"Are we still talking about Ken?" Carter huffed irritation when she winked at him.

Tessa was passing out the cake, when Chase rose and made his way into the kitchen where Ken continued to slice more pieces. He handed him a plate and fork, but Chase set it down.

"What ya doing, Ken?"

Ken gave a bewildered glance then followed Chase's line of sight to where Tessa was being teased by the team. "Nothing you need to be concerned about, Captain. Why?"

"Seems to me you've been hovering a lot lately. Anything you want to share?"

"Nope. Not that my personal life is anyone's business but my own."

"I wasn't aware you had a personal life, Ken." Chase leaned on the counter and picked up the serving knife Ken set aside.

The sergeant squinted then tightened and released his jaw. "I'm working on getting one."

"Sorry. What are you working on?" Tessa joined them.

"Nothing," they said in unison.

"Okay, well, it's late, and apparently after cake, everyone is taking off."

"I'll help you clean up," Ken interjected as he took Chase's slice of cake and ate it himself. "Who says you can't have your cake and eat it, too?" he said with frosting falling on his lower lip.

Tessa laughed and turned away to join the others who stood to leave.

"I think I just said you couldn't," Chase growled then joined Tessa who was being teased again. It felt like he was marking his territory.

In that moment of clarity, he decided it was confession time with Tessa.

CHAPTER 7

شهيد

The street had been transformed into a movie set located in a Middle Eastern war-torn hellhole. The "actors" positioned themselves at outdoor tables, sipping tiny cups of tea, dressed in the shabby garb of the poor. A few women stood in doorways, covered to the point of being invisible; others moved through the street market, daring to wear head scarves and jackets. Occasionally attention shifted to the children who ran up and down the street, playing with sticks and a weathered soccer ball. Their small voices of gaiety and shouts of victory at capturing the ball made the hot dusty day tolerable to the onlookers.

The scene appeared peaceful until all the attention turned to a woman strolling down the street dressed in baggy khaki pants and shirt. The uniform resembled a fashion statement more than military issue. The medals fastened to her chest and the bracelets fashioned from five-inch bullets circling her wrists and waist caught the sunlight and positioned her as a person of great importance. A red-and-white keffiyeh laced with fake jewels dangled from the back of her head. Pushing it back revealed dark-brown hair streaked with a red dye the shade of a child's fingerpaint.

Activity stopped as she moved on six-inch heels the color of gold. She could have fit the profile of a model walking the runway in Paris. Even the birds stopped their chirps, as if holding their collective breath. Then their attention turned to the sky. On the horizon, a faint, horrifying sound grew louder with each second.

The side of a building exploded into rubble, sending screaming children in search of a rush of frantic mothers. An explosion near a tea shop turned dusty earth to blood red. Yet the woman continued to walk forward, unafraid. She pulled her automatic weapon, dropping her hand down by her side.

The squeak and rumble of tanks followed the explosions with men rushing forward with rifles reminiscent of those displayed in a military museum, covered with a layer of dirt and rust. The sound of live fire tapped a song of death as the woman continued to walk nonchalantly toward the danger. Her olive skin glistened with perfection, and her eyes danced with the coldness and beauty of a black swan. As her bright-red lips parted, a soldier bumped into her, knocking her to the ground.

"Cut!" a man on the sidelines yelled. Two muscled stuntmen rushed forward to help the woman up. The director hurried to her side as she dusted the pebbles and debris from her clothes.

"Soraya, are you okay? I'm so sorry." He barked at the stuntman, "Get that idiot over here to apologize to her. Now!" The director turned back to her. "You were amazing. Sexy and deadly. I love it."

"If you want to do a retake, then we'll do it in Syria. This is not how my people live. It is much worse."

"It is too dangerous, Soraya. We'll do your new song as soon as we get set up again."

"No. I refuse." Soraya stormed off toward her makeup artist and allowed the woman to touch up her eyes outlined in black. "I could have been killed, and for what? A stupid music video? My country needs me to show the truth of our pain." She threw her hands in the air. "Don't touch me, you cow. You got powder in my eye." She shooed her away with waving fingers. "Go. Now. Or I will beat you for hurting me."

"Soraya, you need to calm down." A tall man she knew with eyes the color of chocolate approached her. "You are angry because you fell walking in those ridiculous shoes. Who wears high heels on the battlefield? Oh wait. No one." His dark sunglasses hid his mood, but his voice was thick with contempt.

She enjoyed the way he spoke his mind, unafraid and straight to the point. Nothing fazed him, not spoiled directors, actors, or the sexy wiles she threw at him all day long like grenades. A grin often toyed with the edge of his generous mouth, while his almond-shaped eyes narrowed when she threw a temper tantrum or tried to get her way.

"But I look really good in these shoes. It's part of the act." She ran her manicured hand with nails polished blood red from her waist then down the side of her jutted-out hip. He switched his laser focus from the hills around them toward her sensual motion. His lips narrowed, but there was no indication he might be impressed. "Why don't you like me, Captain Hunter?" She edged closer with caution, concerned she might be pushing her luck.

"I'm here to protect you and make sure you don't become an international pawn. Whether I like you or not is irrelevant."

She ran her long fingernail down the front of his dark-green-and-khaki shirt until she touched his belt. Lifting her gaze to his, she offered a quick smile then went back to her trademark pout. "I think we could be good together."

"Although delusional, nice to know you have dreams." He grabbed her finger and bent it enough for her to wince and tried to pull away, but he held on. "Stop trying to distract me. How many times do I have to tell you, I'm not interested?"

When his grip loosened, she jerked away. "I'm paying you good money to look after me."

"Let me do my job."

"Maybe I should have been clear your job includes keeping me happy—in other ways as well."

His mouth widened in devilish amusement. "Maybe you should have." He nodded toward the director. "You're being paged. Behave, will ya? You're beginning to annoy me."

She dared lay her hand on his chest again until he arched an eyebrow and stared down at it. Carefully, as if disarming a bomb, she withdrew. "I'm going to annoy you more later tonight, Captain Hunter. Maybe I'll help you forget that little mouse you're so fond of back home."

"Doubtful," he said calmly then pivoted away from her to take his seat with the other film crew members.

"I intend to get my money's worth, Captain Hunter."

He ignored her, making her all the more determined to have him.

A young assistant, dressed in traditional Kurdish attire ran up to her with phone in hand. She had taken the position while shooting the video for free in return for being one of the extras in the music video. The allowance provided for such things went into Soraya's pocket without the slightest twinge of remorse. This part of Turkey was very poor. The girl must have been desperate for attention or starstruck. She guessed the latter. Knowing how strict the Kurdish community was, she imagined the girl would pay a price for being bold and shameless enough to associate with a Westernized rock star. She'd been that girl once. Not anymore.

"Hello?" Soraya snapped.

"Time is running out for you, Soraya," said the voice on the phone. "You are wasting time flirting with the American captain."

"That last explosion was a little close, you fool. What were you thinking?" she whispered, moving toward her trailer. Once behind its closed door, she continued, "I don't need you to tell me what to do."

"Get it done. I thought you were on board with this."

"I am," she growled. "I want more time. Captain Hunter is not so easily swayed by my charms."

"Maybe you are losing your touch," replied the male voice with amusement.

Soraya examined her appearance in a cracked mirror over the dresser. The dark eyeliner gave her a mysterious effect. She made it thicker to highlight the cunning in her eyes. "Do you remember our last night together, Amir?"

There was only heavy breathing.

"The things I did to you—over and over, until you begged me to stop." She offered a soft moan. "Then pulled me back for more for the next three days?"

"I remember, Soraya. I also remember how you did your own begging—"

"I wanted you to know, I plan to do the same wonderful things to the American captain." She expelled a breathy sigh as if in the throes of passion. "And I plan to enjoy every minute. I want you to think about that tonight while you are sitting in a burned-out building with your filthy men eating cold beans from tin cans.

Picture me in the arms of the strong American. He is so handsome."

"Shut up, Soraya."

"I rather like him, you know." She watched herself smile in the mirror and ran her finger across her lips. "He's muscular. Tall. Those eyes."

"Shut up, Soraya, or, I'll make you pay dearly the next time we meet."

"I'm counting on it." The anticipation of what he might do to her served more as an aphrodisiac than incentive to seduce Captain Hunter.

~ ~ ~ ~

Chase signed paperwork for the director's assistant concerning the security for the day. His paycheck depended on it. Although that money came from Soraya's expense account for the video, the bulk of his payment came from one of the benefactors of Enigma. This job was off the books, even though Director Benjamin Clark approved of him going. The benefactor, Enigma, and other important people suspected the rock video was a cover for something more sinister. It was vitally important the diva be protected from herself and anyone else who could take advantage of her and create an international incident.

One of the volunteers brought a tray of food for his evening meal, since he'd avoided eating with the other actors, support team, and extras. Keeping his distance increased the suspicious bubble around him that kept others leery of his movements and motives. Everyone knew he was security for Soraya and oversaw other security people who operated the tank, guns, and explosives.

The tank was a rusty piece of crap, loaned to them from a military junkyard. It wouldn't be able to spit out BBs; therefore, the biggest threat was the unreliable caterpillar tracks that ran over the rocky terrain. The very first day, during the rehearsal, the track split in two and fell off. Although the rehearsal continued without it, Soraya made it clear she wouldn't do any filming until everything was in place.

He'd taken the director aside and expressed concern about the last explosion. "I don't know where that came from, but find out.

That wasn't a fake or a prop."

The director promised to take care of it but reminded him the final decision would be Soraya's.

When consulted, she insisted on authenticity and stomped her foot, stirring up a cloud of dust, in refusal. "I need the atmosphere to perform. I can't be genuine for my fans until the scene is perfectly staged."

"We can splice that part in, Soraya. No one will ever know," the director explained.

"I'll know," came a haughty retort.

"Maybe you could do the dance segment on the tank while we wait for repairs."

"No. No. No." Then she stormed off to her trailer.

Four hours later, when she still hadn't emerged, Chase decided it was time to get involved and knocked on her trailer door. "Get the hell out there and do the rehearsal. Stop being a diva, Soraya." When she didn't answer, he entered to find her lying on her bed wearing only black-lace panties and a matching bra, neither of which covered much. A fashion magazine was open and a bowl of chocolates nearby. The place was a mess with strewn clothing, shoes, and the bling she'd wear in the video.

She rolled to her side and examined him from head to toe. "What do you want?"

"I'm your bodyguard while we're here, and you're making enemies by the minute."

"You're on my payroll." She swung her legs off the bed, accidently on purpose knocking her magazine to the floor. "Pick it up for me."

Chase grabbed a robe hanging from a hook and threw it in her face. "Get it yourself. I'm not your maid. My fee just increased. I didn't know I'd be babysitting a spoiled, half-witted rock star, or I would have refused the job."

"What if I fire you?" she said, standing up to reveal her voluptuous curves, her long hair falling across her breasts.

"Fine with me." He eyed her with contempt then took out his phone and punched in a number. "I'll notify your uncle it didn't work out. I've got better things to do anyway."

She lunged for the phone, but he held it up over his head as she pressed her body to his.

"Okay. I'll consider myself spanked, Captain Hunter."

He clicked off then pushed the temptation away. "You'll know when I spank you, Soraya, so get over yourself. You've got ten minutes to get out there and be a class act, or I'm turning in my resignation." He brought the phone down to show her he'd punched in the number of her uncle.

"You're kind of a tattletale, aren't you?" She reached out to run her hand down the edge of his vest.

"I'm kind of a lot of things." He turned and left. Ten minutes later, she was on the set, cheerfully apologizing for her earlier behavior.

The singer had avoided eye contact with him the rest of the day. He suspected it was the calm before the storm. For now, he would close his eyes and remember the last late night in Tessa's apartment when the world finally made sense. He could almost feel her touch each time he whispered her name. The scene was his safe place to hide when everything around him crashed and burned. Letting her come to him this way brought him comfort as he let the scene unfold.

CHAPTER 8

شهيد

Chase tapped lightly on the door of Tessa's apartment. The lady in the apartment down the hall peeked out at him. He lifted a hand and called to her.

"Sorry, Mrs. Wade."

"Kind of late to be visiting, isn't it?" she quipped stepping out into the hall.

Tessa opened the door and stuck her head out. "Chase?"

"Left my phone here, Mrs. Wade. Sorry if I disturbed you."

Tessa tugged him inside and locked up behind him.

"You know my neighbor now?"

"I like those older women."

"And clearly, they are smitten with you, " she teased.

Lightning flashed, followed by thunder rumbling enough to vibrate the old Victorian house now divided up into apartments. Tessa had bought hers several years ago to use when she taught night classes at the university. It wasn't much more than a thousand square feet, but she'd made every inch count. The French doors leading to the second-floor terrace on the house were open. The rain intensified, causing the empty galvanized bucket to ping rhythmically. It was long past midnight, and he was exhausted. But his unspoken desires drove him to see her before leaving the country again.

"Did I wake you?" The lights were off except for a few battery-operated candles positioned throughout the living room area. Only the night-light from the microwave helped him see her cover a yawn as she shook her head.

Since everyone enjoyed crashing at her place, it was no surprise they also enjoyed her cooking. She was the one in the group who watched the cooking channel and experimented on them. They were willing guinea pigs. In spite of the tight quarters when everyone was present, no one cared. If it was warm enough, the French doors were open to the terrace, and there was a lot of lies, jokes, and storytelling exchanged. This felt like home to him every time he visited.

Tessa, the gullible one, listened to them with wide-eyed wonder until the exaggeration grew to unbelievable proportions. Her reaction never failed to begin a tidal wave of name-calling on her behalf. Babe in the woods. Goody Two-shoes. Bible-thumper. She'd learned to take their teasing in stride and managed a sharp comeback from time to time.

The party broke up around eleven, and she'd insisted cleanup would be done in the morning, and told everyone go on home. But one glance showed the place was spotless, like always, and she probably hadn't been in bed long. The open concept of the apartment allowed him to see into the bedroom area with the large double windows. Lightning flashed and the sheer curtains lifted on the wind. The bed hadn't been turned down.

"I took a shower and thought I'd listen to the storm for a bit. With the drought, California doesn't get many of these. Makes me miss Tennessee. Next thing I knew, you were knocking at the door." She leaned back against the peninsula countertop, placing her outstretched hands on the granite. "Guess I fell asleep."

Chase didn't understand why he thought she radiated sexy in a baggy T-shirt and jogging shorts. It was obvious she didn't wear anything under it. The cardigan sweater she wore opened to her knees but did nothing to mask her curves. The night-light offered enough dappled light to enjoy her tangled curls falling out of an attempt of containment with a scrunchie.

He stepped closer and pinned her against the counter with his body then reached around to tug on the scrunchie. Her hair fell round her shoulders and into her eyes.

It surprised him she didn't object or try to escape like she'd done in the past. The temptation to touch the softness grew too great, as he ran his fingers through its thickness.

"How long has it been since you've touched my hair?" she asked, staring at him, unafraid or ashamed of her interest.

"It feels like forever." He slid his fingertips down her face then to her neck in slow motion, unsure he'd ever get another chance. The large scoop neck of her oversized T-shirt fell over one shoulder inside the cardigan as he explored in a downward direction.

Tessa reached inside his jacket and pulled him closer. "Why are you really here?"

"I wanted to see you. Alone. There are always people around when we're together."

She laid the tips of her fingers over his heart as if wanting to feel how it reacted to her touch. Flattening out her palm, she moved it around his muscled chest and applied enough pressure to quicken his pulse. His touch oscillated between her hair then bare skin.

Tilting her head, she searched his face then reached up to touch his protruding lower lip. Did she understand he was drinking her in, starved for her attention and affection? "You've avoided being alone with me ever since we got back from Russia. Why?"

"I wanted to give you time to heal. You were in mourning, and I felt responsible for your grief."

Tessa sighed and stepped into his sudden embrace. "I never blamed you that Darya saved your life. He did those kinds of things without thinking."

"I didn't want to be your rebound guy, either." He tightened his arms around her and rested his chin on top of her head.

Tessa pushed him to arm's length and shook her head. "He was the rebound guy. Never you."

"You married him."

"You pushed me so far away in Russia—I thought we would never have a chance," she snapped. "Now you're here, after all this time, to talk about it? Why now? Because you're leaving the country and won't have to face me tomorrow?"

The French doors flew back against the wall as several things crashed on the terrace. Both of them hurried to close then fasten them. A whistling sound came from the bedroom, where the white curtains lifted angrily, as if accusing them of neglect. Chase managed to get one of the windows closed as Tessa climbed onto the bed to reach the second.

"I can't get it. It must be stuck."

He eased onto the bed and reached up over her head. In seconds, the window slammed shut. He tried to move back on the bed at the same time Tessa turned. The motion put her on top of him.

His body had gone on alert with her pressed against him. Very little was left to the imagination through her thin clothing. In the electric candlelight in the apartment, she stared at him with interest. Once more, he pondered why didn't she try to escape like the few other times he'd managed to get this close. Without thinking, he took advantage of her prone position and caressed her buttocks, feeling her push her pelvis into his.

The long curly locks fell down her breasts, and he quickly moved them to kiss her. Tessa kissed him with a kind of passion he'd never known or hoped for from her. She sought his body in places she'd never touched before, knowing to let her continue would make it impossible to leave.

He rolled her over and pinned her to the bed. Her breathing was ragged and her body was his for the taking.

"Stop," he ordered then rolled off her and to the floor. "Stop," he whispered. "We need to talk."

Tessa sat up and quickly moved to the edge of the bed on her knees and stared at him in bewilderment. He tried to imagine what was going through her pretty little head. Hadn't he put the moves on her several times, knowing full well she'd bolt or throw a bucket of verbal cold water on him? Now, here she was, half naked, lonely and wanting him in her bed.

"Chase?" she whispered. "What is it? I thought…I mean, I've missed you. You've always been my best friend and…"

"I wanted to tell you I've found someone special."

Tessa swung her legs onto the floor and edged a few steps away from him. "Found, as in rescued from danger or found someone you—"

"I'm in love, Tessa. I'm going to ask her to marry me as soon as I get back from this job."

In a split second, time stood still for her. What happened? Had she misinterpreted the suggestive behavior all this time? Was it a flirting friendship they had with a mild interest in a sexual relationship?

Captain Hunter got what he wanted, when he wanted it, always successful at inviting a woman into his bed. Of all his confidences about different partners, most were one-night stands. She called them brainy bimbos if they were from the university, usually attractive and smart but smitten with his charm and rugged dark good looks.

Before Russia, they'd lunched together several times a week when she was in town; occasionally he'd come over, and she would cook dinner, keeping it low-key and platonic. The times he'd put on the romance hat was when they were on a mission. Something about being in the shadow of danger brought out both the bad boy and knight in shining armor in him. For this reason, she'd fallen helplessly in love with him, though she never dared breathe such a declaration.

There were taboos involved, along with the ethical behavior of a commanding officer on a mission. Didn't keep him from getting a little too close or her from swooning at an inappropriate time. Both were aware of the line in the sand drawn between them.

After Russia, the line was forever erased, and now they were like awkward teenagers exploring their first taste of love. Chase had found Miss Perfect while she pieced her life back together. Hadn't she told him for several years he should settle down and start a family? She wanted him to be happy. Or did she?

"I've never known you to be a loss for words." He grinned. "How often did you say I was wasting time and should settle down? Now, I'm ready."

"Does she know what you do?" Enigma had been a big no-tell secret when she was married to her first husband.

"Of course. She's incredibly understanding."

"Does she know you're going to Turkey with a rock star?" Tessa couldn't help sounding accusing and shoved her hands on her hips.

"Yes."

Tessa turned her back on him and paced. This was ridiculous.

How could he find someone else when she'd needed him all these months? "But, but—"

"You're stuttering. I know this is a surprise. But I wanted to tell you before I left—you know, in case I didn't come back—or something." He stepped toward her and pulled her closer, careful to avoid holding her as intimately as he had earlier. "I didn't want you to find out from the team."

"Are you saying all the others know this—woman?" Way to twist the knife.

"Not exactly. They suspect something is up, but I haven't said anything in a while."

"Have they met her?" Her heart pounded. Stay calm. Don't say anything stupid.

"Yes."

"And you didn't think to run this by me or let me meet her? I thought we were friends. Maybe more than friends even."

"We are. As I said. You had a lot going on."

"So, when are you going to pop the question?"

"When I get back from this job. I'll go see her dad so I can ask for her hand in marriage."

Tessa turned to storm off, but he cut off her retreat. "What about us? Our—friendship?" she blurted out.

He shrugged. "That doesn't have to change. We can still have lunch. We can watch a movie and make insulting commentary like always. Look." He grabbed her and pulled her a little closer. "No reason why we can't go out to dinner. I'll even come over and cook for you."

Tessa sucked in her breath and jumped back. "Are you serious? And what about what just almost happened between us? I guess that's okay, too?"

"Up to you. Besides, you initiated it, rubbing your hands all over my chest and then—"

"Just stop," she growled. "Do you hear yourself? Who is the woman?"

"If I told you, I imagine you'd google her or have Vernon do a profile on her. No thanks. I made Vernon remove anything about her so she couldn't be traced back to me. I don't want anything to happen to her while I'm gone, or anytime as far as that goes."

"Is..." She sighed. "Is she pretty?"

He gave a deep sigh and walked toward the kitchen to lean again against the peninsula. "She is the most beautiful woman I've ever known. I can't get her out of my head. She is the first thing I think of in the morning and the last thing at night. My life has become so much richer with her in it."

A wave of devastation washed over her. She'd lost him. There was nothing else to do but be supportive and wish him the best. Would it be wrong to hire a voodoo woman to do a little damage to the competition? Probably.

"Do you have a picture of her?"

He rolled his eyes up, as if trying to remember then pulled out his phone. "I think there are a couple on here."

Before he could scroll through the pictures, she rushed over and grabbed the device. Since it was an Enigma phone, finding a picture wouldn't be a big deal. "These are pictures of missions, Chase."

One of her after their first encounter the week they met. Another one in Washington DC, when she'd dressed up in a sparkly black cocktail dress.

"I remember this one. Didn't take long to get my beautiful dress messed up. You nearly killed me, as I remember," she mused.

"You were covered in the president's blood and holding a gun. What was I to think?" he reminded her, looking over her shoulder. "Keep scrolling."

Tessa continued through pictures she didn't know he had. Lake Tahoe where he'd rescued her from a watery grave. Standing in the back of a Land Rover in Africa as she observed elephants through binoculars. Her house all decked out for Christmas with her three rebels standing in front of the tree, clinging to her. Lunch on the university mall, and a few group shots of the team were included. There were also Russia pictures, but she decided to avoid looking at those. That would bring back dangerous memories. "These are things we did together."

"Keep scrolling."

A pattern emerged as she scrolled slower. Pictures of her in all kinds of poses, a few with him in a selfie, some of her working in the garden with her neighbors. Again, he'd taken a selfie with him in the foreground.

Then there was one of him holding a big sign.

Chase studied her as she sucked in her breath and staggered backward. He reached for her and lifted her chin. He had memorized the sign and recited it. "Tessa, I love you. I always have. There will never be such a beautiful soul in my life. Will you marry me?"

Tears pooled in the corners of her eyes at the same time he removed the phone from her hands. She instantly covered her mouth to prevent a sob from spilling out, as her shoulders shook.

"Babe, I love you so much. I'm not sure I can breathe without…"

She jumped into his arms, kissing him on his face, mouth, and neck. "Yes. Yes. I'll marry you." Then she stepped back and landed a soft fist to his hard midriff. "You broke my heart and made me fall in love with you all over again in a matter of minutes. How could you do that to me?"

"Because I wanted you to admit you loved me, too. Be jealous. Outraged." He pulled her into his arms and captured her lips and enjoyed the passion she returned. "And just so you know, I've already gone to ask your dad for your hand."

With her arms still around him, she managed to kiss his throat then beam up at him. "And what exactly did you tell my sweet country daddy?"

"The truth. All of it. Well, most of it. Your brothers were a little skeptical, but after a few days, we hit it off."

"A few days." She gasped. "You aim to impress."

"You're worth it. Your uncle Jake was a wet blanket."

"The old softy."

"Old softy? He broke my nose and nearly had me blown up with a bomb in Washington. And remember, he planned to assassinate the prime minister of Israel. The old coot scares the hell out of me." He enjoyed seeing Tessa offer a patient smile at his description. "But he did admit I was probably the only one who could keep you in line."

"That doesn't sound like Uncle Jake. I suspect it was the other way around."

"Come to think of it, you may be right."

She circled his waist with her arms and laid her head against his chest.

"Think you're up for watching my back forever?" he asked.

"Forever and a day."

"I didn't tell your mom all the dark secrets. I thought I'd let you or your dad do it at the appropriate time. I look forward to growing old with you, Tessa." He pushed her to arm's length and searched her face, now streaked with tears. "That wasn't a real proposal, of course. I want it to be special for you."

"Then stay with me tonight. Don't go to Turkey. You're gambling with fate. Please," she softly begged.

"I can make serious money on this one. Enough that I can get out of this crazy business and take us somewhere safe to raise our family." His phone chirped, drawing his attention momentarily. "Carter is waiting outside to take me to the airport. He has a few colorful comments as to why saying goodbye might be taking so long."

Tessa once more reached up to pull his face closer and stared into his dark eyes for a few seconds then took a long slow kiss, one he hoped would never end. When a car horn sounded outside, he pulled away but managed one last embrace.

"Don't be a hero, Chase. I need you."

"Martyrs never die. I'll be back before you know it."

Turned out that wasn't true. Even though some martyrs never die, they can't always come back.

CHAPTER 9

شهيد

Chase bolted out of bed and grabbed his gun. Wearing nothing but his boxers, he ran out of his tent and toward Soraya's trailer from which screams emerged. Several people had wandered out of their tents, scratching their heads and yawning to see what the commotion might be. None made a move toward the trailer however. Most of the crew was more afraid of the singer's wrath or reprimand than whatever made her scream.

The door flew open, flooding the ground with a pool of light. Soraya stood in the doorway, clinging to the frame with one hand and the other on the front of her flimsy robe.

Chase ran up the steps and edged in front of her, weapon aimed. He saw no one.

She pointed to the chair. "There!"

Curled up in a neat coil was a black viper, one of the most poisonous snakes in Turkey. He aimed and fired, splattering its body into a bloody mess then picked it up by the tail and screwed his mouth up in irritation.

"I thought I told you to leave your door shut. This is what happens. This poor guy now paid the price for your stupidity, and a farmer goes without a rat exterminator."

"Get rid of it," she whimpered. "Please."

"Now, that wasn't so hard, was it?" he quipped as he carried it outside and threw it among the weeds. He wondered if one of the onlookers had coaxed the snake inside. He waved them off. "She's fine. Go back to bed. Just a snake."

For a moment, he stared into the darkness and wondered how that particular snake made it to this area. It was usually found in farmland areas, not where tourists or a bunch of people had been working for weeks.

Soraya remained in the doorway as if frozen in place. With a disgusted sigh, Chase made his way to the top step and motioned with his gun for her to go inside.

She shook her head vehemently and fell against his chest. "No. What if there are more?"

"Then I guess the video shoots will be over, and I can go home." He smirked as he pushed her away. "I'll check the trailer. You clean up the mess from the snake."

"Me? Clean it up?" Soraya gasped. "You're kidding right?"

"Well, I'm not doing it. My knight-in-shining-armor contract doesn't cover blood splatter from a viper. Get over yourself and clean it up or leave it. I don't care what you decide."

Chase checked every nook and cranny of the trailer, finding only a total disregard for organization. "All clear, Soraya." He glared at her in spite of her pitiful expression. Was she going to burst into tears? "Clean this place up, and maybe there won't be anywhere for snakes and other critters to hide."

"You're cruel," she whimpered then stomped her bare foot on a fuzzy rug.

"Thank you," he retorted. "And you're a spoiled brat."

Tears rolled down her cheeks. "I'm sorry. You were wonderful to run out in the cold night in your underwear to save me."

He realized he wore only his boxers and a pair of flip-flops he managed to slip into on his way out of the tent. Taking a deep breath then letting it out slowly, he shook his head in disgust. "I suppose you don't have much on under that robe, either, so I'll say good night."

"Of course. I won't keep you." She sniffed. "But please let me thank you, Captain Hunter."

Before he could move, she came to him with open arms and embraced him warmly. As she did, he felt a tiny prick on his neck. He pushed her away and touched his neck.

"Sorry. Sorry. I wear too much jewelry. And my nails are—"

"Grappling hooks?" He looked at his fingers. No blood.

He felt the room spin, and he staggered toward the door, but Soraya pulled his arm around her shoulders. "Come. You should sit down. You didn't let the snake's fangs touch you, did you? Captain Hunter? Captain…"

Those were the last words he remembered.

~ ~ ~ ~

Soraya sent the pictures of Chase in her bed as instructed. The drug had been a stronger dose than she expected, and everything had to be staged. He certainly was in no shape to participate in any seduction. Getting his boxers off also proved to be a bigger job than she expected. The man was all muscle and couldn't be persuaded to help with the removal process. What a waste. At least the pictures would imply they'd made the most of what was left of the night. She wasn't sure why they were necessary. Maybe her contact got off on such things.

Rage filled Soraya knowing her contact didn't always bend to her demands. She toyed with the idea of telling Amir it was over between them. With all the profession of love he proclaimed, he continued to manipulate her to do his bidding and participate in treachery. To what end, she couldn't imagine. Didn't he also want a better life for the Kurds who suffered under the hands of dictators for centuries?

His darkness captivated her most of the time. But the plans he spoke of sounded reckless and dangerous to her people. And why the pictures? What good were they?

The captain stirred under her covers and finally sat up, dazed. The creases on his forehead hinted he was piecing things together. Then a dark look of revenge filled his face as his eyes fell on her. She felt more excited than fearful, knowing he was capable of payback. Setting her cup of espresso on the counter, she moved to the bed and sat down. Running her hand down his leg on top of the covers, she met his rage with an amused expression.

"Did your knight-in-shining-armor contract include sleeping in my bed, Captain Hunter?" She let her robe fall open, revealing her naked body. "We have all morning. The film crew won't be ready until later. Can I do anything for you? After all, you saved my life last night." She leaned in closer. "In more ways than one, I might add." Her hand slipped under the cover, only to have it grabbed by the captain who bent it back so far, she cried out. "You're hurting me."

Chase didn't release her as he kicked the covers off and over her head. He quickly wrapped his arms around her, pulling the blanket tight.

She tried to free herself, in a panic. "You're hurting me. I can't breathe."

He put his lips to her ear. "You ever pull a trick like this again and I'll put a viper in your bed myself." He jerked the cover off her head then shoved her down before crawling out of bed. "Got that?" When she merely glared at him, he grabbed her bare foot and squeezed until she fought harder to get away. "You make me sick, Soraya. I'm not interested in you, nor will I ever be. The only reason I took this lame job was for the money I'll use to start a new life with the kind of woman you can never be." He pulled on his boxers and flip-flops then headed for the door. "Behave yourself, let me do my job, and leave me the hell alone."

When he slammed the door, she grabbed up her phone to enjoy the pictures from the night before. She forwarded them to a number in Grass Valley, California, to a woman she'd heard about from her uncle. It wasn't difficult to find her number. Maybe Captain Hunter wouldn't need the money after all. It wasn't a good idea to reject her affections.

~ ~ ~ ~

The rebel commander stared at the pictures Soraya sent in the middle of the night. He felt both disgust and curiosity. Despite her claims each picture had been staged, they appeared real enough to him. Now he wanted to hurt her for being so willing to initiate such compromising positions with the American captain. The man was a brute and full of himself when he met with Prince Muhammed in California. Of course, every American he'd met had been exactly like he'd expected, self-absorbed, condescending, and a god in their own mind. Captain Hunter was the poster boy for such an image.

But one person on his team appeared different. Agent Tessa Scott. The night when he'd first laid eyes on her, he knew she would provide a much-needed break for the prince. The grind of being in charge of so much responsibility grew heavier each day. The prince enjoyed a pretty face when he went abroad. The agent resembled arm candy more than protection.

The royals always believed nothing could touch them. Maybe in Saudi Arabia this would be true, but here, the prince had to trust the Americans to protect him. Too many things could go wrong accidently on purpose in a country whose citizens didn't particularly like the Saudis. Of course, that, too, would play to the commander's advantage. One thing he hadn't counted on was the woman. She'd turned out to be a great deal more prepared than he thought.

According to his informant, the captain who guarded Soraya, was involved with Agent Scott. Maybe he could use the information to his advantage when the time came. All he wanted was a little time with the woman to add insult to injury with the prince. Flipping through the pictures again, he smirked. Maybe he'd make Soraya watch. The thought of her indignation fueled his desire to speed up the scheme.

~ ~ ~ ~

After dressing, Chase decided to contact Tessa on his computer. It would be close to midnight, but he wanted to hear her voice, see her pretty face, and know all was right with the world he craved. Would she be in Grass Valley at home or at her apartment in Sacramento? Out here for so long, he'd lost track of the days and time.

She appeared on his screen; the backdrop was her apartment. Other voices in the room told him the crew had invited themselves over again. Her wide smile warmed him as she carried the laptop to the terrace, away from the noise.

"Tessa, I need to tell you something about what happened here last night."

She listened without interruption, giving him hope she'd believe he wouldn't do anything to jeopardize their budding relationship. After he finished, he watched her push fallen curls from her face and behind her ears. Her expression had sobered, and she batted her lashes the way she often did when troubled or ready to tell a lie.

"You know I love you, Tessa."

Her lips turned up again, slightly. "I—"

"Hey, buddy." It was Carter, rushing out to get his two-cents worth in. "I cooked tonight. Warm enough to grill outside here." He pulled another person to his side, revealing Honey Lynch, an Irish assassin who occasionally worked for Enigma. She and Tessa had become unlikely partners over a year ago due to a comedy of errors. Thinking about it now almost made him laugh out loud.

Chase shook his head in unbelief and leaned back in his wooden folding chair. "Guess everyone will be going to the ER for food poisoning before long."

Honey blew him a kiss and disappeared with Carter.

Another face appeared as Sergeant Ken Montgomery put his hands on Tessa's shoulders and leaned down close to her face. "When you coming back, Captain?"

"Soon. Better enjoy your time off. I'm going to kick your butt when I get home."

Ken patted Tessa's shoulders then turned away, laughing.

"Gotta go, Tessa. The Internet is already flickering here. I just wanted to warn you—" He lost her image. Had he lost her trust, too? The woman had been through hell in the last year. Why would she ever trust another man, especially one with such a dangerous history as himself?

CHAPTER 10

شهید

The afternoon stretched into evening as the rock video shoot proceeded to unravel with Soraya insisting they finish in Syria to prove she cared about the Kurdish people and was willing to put her life on the line by doing so. By nightfall, she had finally gotten her way, everything had been packed up, and they were headed to the border.

When they reached the checkpoint, the convoy of six vehicles stopped and waited for soldiers to search the inside of the three trucks of equipment and the cars with the video folks. Soraya was identified right away and asked for autographs, which she bestowed with the grace and charm of a queen. Chase didn't like it. Too much darkness and too much distraction to keep the soldiers busy. The papers giving them permission to cross were suspect.

"Relax." The director yawned. "Soraya has these guys eating out of her hand."

Heads were bobbing, and soldiers took selfies with her, when approaching vehicles from the Syrian side stopped at the gate. No one got out.

"Get in the car, Soraya." Chase pulled his weapon, putting the soldiers on high alert. "Everyone, back in the vehicles."

But it was too late. Gunfire overpowered the screams of the wounded as dark-clad men swarmed around Chase and Soraya, who cowered against his chest as he was relieved of his weapon.

~ ~ ~ ~

Tessa completed her warm-up routine of stretches and walking around the yard full of flowers to help limber her up. The kids were at school and she'd set aside this day to relax. Her ex would pick up the kids and have them for the night. Maybe, she'd drive into Sacramento and do a little shopping, spend the night at her apartment. The junior college in Grass Valley, where she taught world geography, was between semesters.

She jogged down the circle drive and out onto the street that trailed through her neighborhood of elegant homes and manicured lawns. Tall, stately pines gave an impression of being deeper into nature than was true. The path meandered uphill and down, giving her a good workout. When she'd passed her house for the third time, she noticed a couple of other women were taking a morning jog. She sped up. The last thing on her list of things to do today was chitchat with a couple of yoga-smoothie-skinny women who, if they had kids, employed a nanny and housekeeper. Although the Ervins next door babysat hers from time to time, she couldn't imagine hiring a nanny even when things were hectic at Enigma.

The soft pad of their feet grew closer. Once more she tried to speed up, but they did as well. Then the fear factor kicked in, or maybe it was an overabundance of caution. Working with Enigma these last few years had taught her life was a cruel, evil place and, if you tried to right the wrongs of the world, someone would eventually try and stop you.

With a quick glance over her shoulder, she turned back to sprint home. Sweat poured from her body as her legs burned. There was a curve in the road, where she could steal a peek behind her. They were gone. She continued to run hard until she reached her drive, panting so hard, it required her to bend over and place her hands on her knees before she continued up the driveway. Then she heard the sound of applause coming from the steps of her wraparound porch.

The yoga-pants duo.

She took slow steps forward and watched smirks take over their mouths.

"You," Tessa growled. They weren't neighbors at all, or even unsavory characters from her past. She navigated up the steps, pushing between them and unlocking the front door with a hidden key. "Whatever you're selling, I don't want any."

The two women resembling spoiled felines followed her into the house. The shorter of the two, with bright-red hair, slipped an arm loosely around the back of Tessa's neck and pulled her in close for a hug. "I've missed you," she admitted with an Irish accent. "Aren't you glad to see me?"

"Nope." Tessa tossed the key in the wooden bowl by the front door and made her way to the kitchen for a drink of cold water. On the counter lay a box of glazed donuts. "You let yourself in my house?"

The tall one played with her black ponytail before easing up onto one of the barstools. "I brought you your comfort snack. I know it's your favorite food group."

Tessa glared at the sullen Samantha Cordova and then shifted her attention to the perky Honey Lynch. "Dare I ask why you're here?"

"Can't we drop in because we're old friends?" Honey opened cabinet doors and drawers, taking inventory before moving on to the next.

"Honey, you've been hanging out at Enigma for the last couple of months. Besides the night you dropped in unannounced to eat Carter's barbecue, I haven't seen you in over a year. That doesn't really sound like a close friend." She and Tessa had become unlikely partners over a year ago, which gave the woman the impression they were now best friends.

The Irish woman hurried up to her and embraced her so hard, Tessa thought she'd choke. "I only recently heard you split from Robert. So sorry."

"I bet. And that was almost a year ago, too."

"But since the two of you aren't together anymore, would you care very much if I, maybe, I mean if you didn't care—"

"No. Stay away from the father of my kids. I have enough to worry about right now without wondering if the first time he ticks you off, he ends up with a hole in his chest the size of a football."

Honey shrugged. "Just thought I'd ask. You see? That proves what good friends we are." She went to the refrigerator. "I'm starved."

Tessa turned her attention to Samantha, the more dangerous of the two, in her opinion. Her rare words of praise often sounded forced. It was always difficult to know what the Enigma agent was thinking, planning, or conspiring to do. Was it to take down a third world country? Make love to the prime minister of Israel to get information for the director of Enigma? And, as always, was she trying to figure out how to eliminate her so the field was wide open to make a move on Captain Chase Hunter? Although, in the last year or so, she appeared to have moved on from that lofty endeavor. Now, it was strictly personal.

"I'll make coffee," Tessa announced.

It was more of an act of taking her mind off why two dangerous women had come calling. There was no love lost between her and Samantha who'd been put in charge of her training when she joined Enigma. The woman beamed during these sessions, another rarity. Tessa had the impression it was because her sadistic nature was given full access. However, in spite of the brutal treatment she often suffered under the woman, the training had saved her life more than once. The jealousy between them had morphed into a series of angry tirades when the male Enigma agents were present.

In truth, the two of them had formed a truce of sorts and didn't want their team to know. Tessa idolized Samantha and often wondered what it felt like to have an entire room full of people freeze when you walked in. No matter where she went or what she did, men fell all over themselves for her. Women, although green with envy, and hated her, took note of her style and grace.

Tessa was probably the closest thing she had to a girlfriend, although such a description hardly fit their relationship. But even so, Tessa would have done anything for her if asked. Those few words of praise after the Prince Muhammed of Saudi Arabia incident came close to being the equivalent to an Academy Award in her book. Probably a once-in-a-lifetime achievement.

Honey Lynch on the other hand, was an Irish assassin who had been for hire to the highest bidder until a few years ago. She wasn't sure what changed in her life to give her a mild form of conscience, but it removed part of the hard edge from her. Now, she bragged she only hired on with ethical groups who wanted a better world. Tessa had explained if you go around killing people for such groups, maybe they weren't so ethical.

"I've done lots of work for Enigma, Tessa. Just ask your biggest admirer, Captain Chase Hunter," was the reply.

That ended the conversation because it was a lost cause. Honey was one of those people who either liked you or were on her list of things to take care of at some point. Fortunately, they had made a kind of rocky peace. Letting her think they were best friends had its advantages. One of those being she would certainly revenge her death, if that ever happened. Another thing was...she drew a blank then realized she couldn't think of anything. Although Samantha was harsh and unapproachable most of the time, Honey creeped her out with her psycho-antics.

After pouring three cups of coffee, Tessa leaned against the sink and let the first sip of brew trickle down her throat for the sake of a need for calm nerves to hear what these two were up to. Honey took one of the glazed donuts and scarfed it down followed by a second. It was beyond her how someone could eat like a defensive end for the Dallas Cowboys and be so skinny and petite.

Sam pinched off several bites then pushed hers away. Tessa had never seen her eat any sugar, so she waited for the woman to go into a diabetic coma. Maybe this would be a good encounter after all.

Temptation won out, and Tessa snatched a donut and ate it slowly, as if it didn't really taste all that great. Her first desire was for the two to leave so she could maybe have a second one then save the rest for lunch.

"Again. Why are you here?" Tessa found a paper napkin beside the box and wiped her mouth.

"Wondered if you've heard from Chase?"

Tessa peered into the box of donuts but resisted. "No. Why would I?"

Honey came to stand next to her after pouring herself another cup of coffee. "Everyone knows the two of you have a thing." She nudged her with her shoulder. "Right?"

"Wrong. He's my boss and, at most, we're good friends, or were."

Samantha tilted her head, played with her ponytail, and purred like a cat. "Maybe if you hadn't jumped into the Tribesman's bed, you could have been more."

Honey straightened. "Sam," she growled.

Samantha sighed and studied her nails. "Sorry, Tessa. That was inappropriate."

Tessa took a deep breath. "Yes, it was. I'd like for you to leave now." A sudden jab of pain hit her at the mention of the Tribesman. He was gone forever. The love they'd shared had been short and passionate. A rush of regret and loss overtook her.

Both women moved toward the kitchen door then turned back.

Honey transformed into the hard woman Tessa knew her to be. "While you're wallowing in your self-pity, thought you'd like to know Chase is missing."

"Missing?" Tessa felt like she'd been hooked up to an electrical socket while standing in water.

"We haven't heard from him in over a month," Sam told her. "Something is wrong. If you know anything, tell us now and get over yourself."

Tessa joined them at the door and blocked their exit. "He came by to say goodbye the night he left. Remember we were all together earlier? The first few weeks we skyped when he had Internet. The last call he was concerned about the woman he was protecting. He didn't like her. The reception was bad that day. I know she'd been pushing to leave Turkey and go into Syria to finish the video she was making."

"Did he seem concerned about anything?" Samantha was all business now.

"Yes. She'd done something he wanted me to know about, but we were disconnected. That was a month ago, the night Carter barbecued."

"What do you think he wanted you to know?"

Tessa walked into her office and pulled out a desk drawer. She retrieved some printed pictures and handed them to Sam who looked through them then passed them to Honey. They both stared straight-faced at her. She walked back into the kitchen and ate another donut while they went through the photos a second time.

"I put the pictures back in your desk," Sam said drily. "Look, Tessa, these are a trap. It has nothing to do with you."

"Clearly," she said, her mouth full of donut.

"What's going on with you two?" Honey said, shifting her weight to one hip.

"Nothing. I mean—well, we mended fences before he left and—"

"Oh stop," Sam moaned. "I don't want to know. The two of you make me sick as it is. But I will say this; he wouldn't have gotten involved with a client, especially a high-profile one connected to the royal family of Saudi Arabia."

"If he has fallen off the radar with you, then he is in trouble."

Now she wondered if he believed he might not return. What didn't she know?

"Last we heard from him, he was head of a security detail for the singer Soraya," Sam said with a serious expression on her face. "He left Turkey and disappeared. We think he's still in Syria. We know this because Soraya has dropped off the radar and some of her entourage were found murdered at the border crossing."

Her heart stopped beating for a few seconds, and the air left her lungs. "He, umm," she stuttered, "said he missed me and wanted to explain. When I got the pictures, I figured he expected them to surface and thought I deserved an explanation."

"Well, the director is concerned. No word from him in at least a month, and before that, it was hit and miss," Sam snapped.

"He's not really there to watch after Soraya, is he?"

"No. The man you let slip through your fingers? Amir? We're pretty sure he has a chemical weapon, and Soraya is involved."

Her knees wobbled at the same time Honey slipped an arm around her shoulders and pulled her body into hers.

"You know how this works. If he's in trouble, captured, or dead," Sam spoke slowly and quietly, "we can't go poking around in a foreign country to find him without a sanctioned mission. Honey and I are going to find him. We need you. Are you in or out?"

Tessa raised her chin in a rare show of strength. "When do we leave?"

CHAPTER 11

شهید

A flickering light bulb dangled from a rafter propped up by a pole. The ribs of burn marks along the middle suggested it would be better used as firewood instead of support. The uneven floor caused the chair he was tied, to wobble. The large open space smelled dusty mixed with urine and gas. A row of windows along the top of the wall, just under the low ceiling, let in enough light to aid in his ability to figure out what to do next. Even though the jagged back of the chair cut into his skin, he discovered if he leaned forward carefully, he could rub the rope up and down to weaken the bonds.

At least he could see out of his swollen eye, finally. His body hurt from the punches he'd taken over the last few days. But it could have been worse. Actually, he'd had worse treatment before this. Why hadn't they killed him when they swarmed the SUV that night on the Syrian border? They'd killed the set director and other bodyguards immediately when they tried to bribe their way out of the situation. What happened to the other drivers and support staff remained a mystery. The soldiers at the border had been forced on their knees and shot in the head.

Then there was Soraya, crying, begging for mercy for the soldiers, not for herself, which surprised him. Maybe she wasn't a spoiled diva after all. Her screams when the director and others she'd worked with were killed still haunted him. When they approached Chase, she jumped in front of him and rattled off words he couldn't understand. It wasn't Arabic, but her native Kurmanji, the language of most Kurds. A man moved out of the darkness and gave orders to the others. They stepped aside and took up protective positions around the perimeter.

The man's face couldn't be seen in so much darkness. When he continued to approach, Chase jerked Soraya behind him and her hands went to his sides, digging in her nails. Her breath was ragged and, at one point, she laid her face against his back. Reaching for his weapon would have been a death sentence. The man stopped in front of him and searched him quickly, discovering the weapon and immediately pointing it at his forehead.

"We meet again, Captain Hunter."

The man's no-nonsense voice struck a chord of remembrance. The sleek, manicured appearance was replaced by a mix of military and tribal garb. The dark hair was unkept now, and the night breeze moved it back and forth across his unflinching stare.

"Amir. I see you continue to be a bad boy. Still trying to find a woman who won't kick your ass like the one you ran into in California?"

A smile toyed with the corner of his mouth. "I escaped, didn't I?"

"Only because your camel spitters ran interference for you. Oh, and in case you're interested, I don't think they'll be coming back home." Chase made a quick scan of the area and the number of men he might need to kill to get them out of here. He dared smirk at Amir, running a contemptuous glance head to toe.

"It was their job. They knew the risk." Amir cocked his head to focus on Soraya peeking around Chase's shoulder. "Come here," he coaxed, shouldering his weapon and handing the one he took from Chase to one of his men. "Come on." He motioned for her. "I won't hurt you."

She stepped from around Chase, but he pushed her back with his arm. "Do you know who this is? Every army in the world will be searching for her soon. Let us go. Whatever you're after, it isn't here."

"Ah, but it is. I need Soraya so I can create a diversion for bigger things. And besides"—he motioned for his men to rush

Chase—"I don't take orders from you, Captain Hunter."

Chase shoved Soraya back against the SUV just as the first man got within striking distance. He dropped him with one punch, causing the second man to trip and fall into his uppercut to the chin. Grabbing his own pistol from the man who'd taken it from Amir, he killed him, but the two others benefited from his aim being off in the darkness. The wounded renegade still moved on the ground when Chase spotted the next one who rushed him. He wrestled the rifle away from his attacker with ease then jammed it into his gut and fired. Amir, thanks to the distraction, managed to stop Soraya from climbing into her vehicle, kicking and screaming in protest.

There were others, but they stood back, giving him plenty of room, Chase's visual search took in the perimeter for threats, until it fell on Amir, holding Soraya, his arm around her neck, her eyes wide with fear. Her whimper made his blood run cold, and he took a step forward. Amir lifted the gun to her temple.

"Drop the rifle and pistol, Captain Hunter. You're probably evaluating if you can shoot me before I pull the trigger." He shrugged. "Maybe. But as soon as I see you so much as flinch, I will kill her."

She squirmed, only to have Amir tighten his grip to the degree, she pulled at his arm and gagged.

"You have no idea what you're doing, Amir," Chase growled. "Let her go, and we'll be out of here."

He snorted. "Drop the weapons. Now."

Soraya managed to choke out a plea. "Chase. Please."

"Okay." He laid the guns down and Amir shoved her to the ground. Cautiously, Chase bent to help her up without taking his eyes off Amir. She struggled to stand then fell into his arms. "What do you want?"

"A world where the West shows us respect."

"And you think this is the way to do it? There's probably a drone already in the air searching for you. I put a tracer on Soraya's vehicle in case something happened to me. I'm overdue with checking in."

"You Americans think of everything." Amir smirked. "I figured as much. I am not stupid."

"That's what I keep telling people, but they won't listen," Chase said with as much sincerity as he could handle without bursting into laughter. His words did manage to turn Amir's expression into a snarl.

The man pivoted and lifted his gun in the air in a silent command. Two more of his men emerged from the shadows and grabbed Chase but not before he threw a punch, connecting his fist to an eye socket. But the second one used his rifle like a sledge hammer into Chase's gut, sending him sprawling on the ground. He became aware of several kicks to his ribs and another to his jaw before Soraya covered him with her body.

"Stop it," she screamed. "He did as you asked." Authority had returned to her voice, and the next thing he knew, he was being pulled up, only to be dragged toward the darkness. The flicker of flames drew his attention then an explosion as several of the vehicles crackled and burned. There was no way of knowing if any of the film crew survived.

In spite of the pain of being repeatedly punched, Chase managed to get away once, long enough to get a visual on Soraya. To his surprise she stood at ease, listening to Amir as he invaded her personal space. The rifle he carried had been shouldered, and he appeared to be in light conversation with the rock star. Did he lift her hand and kiss it tenderly, or had Chase imagined the familiarity between the two?

Then a final blow had rendered him unconscious. The ability to gain information from the surroundings, albeit dark, had been taken away from him. The length of time he'd traveled remained unknown, but the time he spent on the cold, dusty floor of this particular room might have been three days. His body hurt from the beatings. The cracked ribs made it difficult to breathe. Dried blood on his face and arms caused his skin to itch and peel.

But then there was Soraya, who came each day with food, water, and medicine. At first, she propped him up and spoon-fed him a kind of gruel that tasted akin to salty beef broth. She spoke softly to him and smelled like jasmine, even in this hellhole. His mouth was swollen enough he didn't want to talk but managed to convey his longing for answers to her with his blinking.

"I am fine. They have not hurt me," she whispered as she washed the blood from his face and edges of his hair that stuck to his forehead. "I have brought medicine."

She dissolved it in the cup of water then helped him sip it until it was empty. For a few hours, his body could relax without pain. Some days, she came several times, repeating the kindness. It didn't take long for him to crave her touch to chase away the pain as she whispered words of encouragement and sang softly to him. When he began to feel better, she rocked him in her arms and told him stories about the Kurdish people. Then, before she left, the healing liquid medicine would be given.

Now, here he was, able to sit in a chair, bound by pieces of rope that a child could have escaped a day ago, yet he was still trying to cut through the strands. The pain was returning, and he wondered how long it would be before they let Soraya bring him medicine. Yesterday, a man had come and held the gruel to his lips. Most of it had dribbled down his chin and onto his naked chest. There was no medicine to follow or any this morning.

At last, the ropes popped open but remained in place. At least no one would detect he was free. If he jumped to his feet when a guard entered, could he overwhelm them with his strength, or was that gone?

Cocking his head, he listened. Voices were in the distance, so he pulled his hands free then waited for the sore muscles to relax. Pain surged to his shoulders, but he knew it would pass as soon as the blood flowed normally. He took deep breaths twice, but the pain still felt like a knife being jabbed in between his ribs.

Carefully, he stood and let the stiffness work its way out of his body. Little by little, he twisted and flexed, feeling the strength flow back into his bones and muscles. He'd always been strong, and fearing it had evaporated toyed with his psyche a little, causing him to take things slower than usual.

The belief he would be okay surged through him after a few minutes, and he separated the things he knew to be fact from the mixed-up memories of the last few days. Without Soraya, he might have died or wished he had. Her care and visits had kept the spark alive to finish whatever had to be done.

Voices grew louder, closer, so he grabbed up the rope and sat down, placing his hands behind his back.

Although in pain, Chase felt the brute strength he'd relied on all these years, return. He lowered his head, as if asleep, when the man with his daily serving of gruel approached. This one spoke

Arabic, so Chase was able to understand his threats and insults. When he didn't respond, the man kicked the chair.

"Wake up, you son of a pig. I have food for you."

With the speed of a sloth, Chase opened his eyes then looked up at the man.

"Open your mouth, pig," he said, taking a step forward with the bowl in his outstretched hand.

Then he sobered and appeared to think twice about being so close. But it was too late. When he moved to step back, Chase kicked him in both knees. The man fell back, and the bowl fell to the floor and shattered. Chase grabbed up a large, jagged shard and fell onto the man. Before the man could fight, with what would be more strength than Chase possessed at the moment, he ran the glass shard across the throat of his abuser then sprang up to watch his captor gasp into death.

All he could think of now was to grab Soraya and escape to safety. American support and the Kurdish resistance couldn't be far. He searched the man who lay on the floor clutching his throat and soon stared wide-eyed. The Makarov pistol, a Soviet semiautomatic pistol was shoved in his waistband. Why they'd let him carry a loaded weapon in to feed an American Special Ops prisoner told him they really didn't grasp who they were dealing with. He found a six-inch knife; he guessed it to be homemade with black electrical tape wrapped around the hilt. It might not cut butter, but the serrated edge could still do damage if plunged deep, twisted then extracted.

He hobbled to the door, feeling the muscles in his thighs relax. Laying a hand on his rib cage, a sharp pain nearly overwhelmed him. Cracking the door open, he saw a corridor lighted, thanks to dirty windows, indicating it was still daylight. Two voices, one male the other female drew closer until he saw the figures step into the light and paused.

It was Soraya and Amir. He was dressed in Army fatigues, and she sported the latest in female military chic you might find at a stateside Nordstrom's. The red streaks in her hair appeared to be on fire as she nonchalantly leaned back against the wall. No fear in her stance, she listened to Amir speak so low, he couldn't understand.

Just as he decided to surprise the man and kill him, Soraya

pulled him into her arms and kissed him passionately, her hands seeking out parts of his body to tempt. Amir became intense in his exploration beneath her clothing as she managed to turn him so his back was to Chase. She was staring at him as he watched the display of erotic affection unfold. Her smile sent chills up his spine as he tried to make sense of the chaos unfolding before him.

Amir pulled Soraya after him, but she dug in her heels and demanded to check on the prisoner. Whatever she whispered in his ear after pressing her body against him made him relent, and she turned and walked toward where he was being held. Amir stared after her, his expression one of hunger and cruelty rather than enjoyment. She stole a teasing glance over her shoulder at him before pushing through the door to where Chase stood.

"Chase!" She sounded as if she might choke on tears. She gathered him in her arms and kissed his sweaty neck. "Oh, my sweet protector. How did you get free?" Stepping back, she examined him head to toe and made it a point to touch him in various places. The rib area made him flinch. "I've been so worried. I missed you terribly."

"Looks to me you have plenty of company, although I can't say I see the attraction." He managed to move her hands off him and collapsed back against the wall.

"Yes. I saw you watching. It's all a ruse, my love." Her lips became a pout. "I do what I have to do to survive, too." She reached for him, but he sidestepped the touch.

"I think you are enjoying this. Look at you, dressed like a princess. You come and go at will."

"In fact, by blood, I am a princess. Remember? Amir has taken very good care of me." She smiled shyly. "So what if I have showed my appreciation?" She cornered him. "I have been doing this for you. To save your neck. You could show a little more appreciation for my sacrifice." She turned her back on him and checked to see if anyone was outside the door.

"Where are we? We've moved three times."

"Near the Turkey border is all I know. I take great risks trying to listen to their arguments and gibberish. The Turks are searching for me." She fluttered her eyelashes. "I'm very popular there, in spite of being Kurdish. I have given my people something to be proud of."

"Do you think they'd still be proud if they knew you were raising your skirts for a terrorist who tried to take out your uncle? And that you were enjoying it?" His voice sounded like he'd been gargling gravel.

"How dare you be so rude to me after all I've sacrificed to keep you alive."

"Let's be honest. At any time, Amir could have had your body if he chose and passed you around for his men to enjoy. The fact your uncle is the next king of Saudi Arabia is your only advantage. He wants to flaunt it, draw him out to rescue you. Then he'll toss you to the side of the road like a headless goat. And I do mean headless."

"I don't like your insinuation. You make me out to be a whore."

"Because you are." He caught her swing at him in midair. "Whose side are you on? Tell me what is going on right now." When she didn't answer, he placed his arms around her waist and smelled her hair. "I'm sorry. I can't stand the thought of you being with Amir."

She faced him and pressed into his embrace.

"I'm grateful you've tried to come every day, or at least when you could, to encourage me, give me food and medicine." Chase stroked her hair. "Let's leave. We can't be far from help or the border. Get me a weapon." He kissed her lightly on the lips. "You don't belong here. Amir will use you up then kill what is left of your self-respect."

"I am afraid."

"How many men are here? What are their plans?"

He felt her relax as her hands trailed around his shoulders and neck. With her body pressed firmly against him, his ribs throbbed.

"Twenty. Maybe more on certain days. They come and go during the night. Some I see once or twice then no more. They plan to move farther south—to a Krak des Chevaliers."

"Why?"

"I do not know. It is an old medieval castle built by the Crusaders. Very beautiful and a World Heritage site. All I know is they plan to do something big there."

"How far are we from there?"

"Don't worry. I will take care of you." She ran her hands through his hair. "We move tomorrow. Try not to anger them.

They want to kill you but are afraid of the consequences."

"I don't plan to be here tonight. You're coming with me."

"I'm afraid. Are you sure we can do this?"

"Do you trust me?"

Soraya pulled him tighter until he winced. "Yes. When we return home, I want us to be together. What do you say?" She laid her cheek against his naked chest.

"Come back here after Amir goes to bed." He pushed her away. "That is, if you have enough stamina."

"Aww, you are jealous." She stepped back against him and kissed him passionately on the lips, but he failed to respond. "You are pouting. I love how you do that." She frowned when he pushed her away a second time. "I think there is someone else you care about more than me. Maybe a woman named Tessa?"

Chase straightened in spite of the pain. "Now who is jealous?" was all he could manage to say without panic gripping him completely.

"The night we made love"—she strolled away and sounded wistful—"back in Turkey when you came to protect me, you spoke her name in your sleep. And yes, I am jealous. I don't share things I want for myself."

One corner of his mouth turned up in a smirk. "You don't have anything to worry about. She was just another loose end I wanted to tie up." Had they made love? He had been so out of it, he couldn't remember.

Tilting her head, she let her gaze run over him seductively. "I guess we both do what we have to do to get what we want."

"And what do you want? If you say Amir, I'm going to have to hurt you," he snarled.

"I find your jealousy intoxicating." She took a deep breath. "Here is what I know. He wants to keep moving."

"Why?" He felt weak from too little food and water during his stay at Hotel Sadistic where the crazies give you a massage you'll never forget. "What's happened?"

"The attack has been planned and put in place."

"What attack?" His ribs hurt, and breathing only made him want to go to sleep. He steadied himself against the wall.

The door burst open as one of Amir's thugs ran in ahead of him and landed the butt of his rifle into Chase's gut. As he hit the floor, he watched Amir enter and pull Soraya into the crook of his arm as she laid her head against his shoulder. She stroked his chest slowly, whispering into his ear.

Chase's sideways glance up at Amir to make sure no harm would come to Soraya gave him a jolt of revulsion. Then his focus transferred to the singer. Her smile revealed how much she was enjoying all the attention. He was struggling to get on all fours when the attacker grabbed him and added a shake before shoving him back against the wall.

Amir untangled himself from Soraya's embrace and spotted the man Chase had overpowered earlier. He motioned for this new guard to remove him then came to stand in front of Chase. "You've been busy, I see. I will need a replacement for him." He nodded toward the limp body being dragged away. "She tells me you have decided to join us? I suppose that is a good thing considering you have made me a man short. Tell me why you have decided to join me." He raised his nose in the air in a show of untrust.

Soraya continued to smirk and flutter her eyelashes at him.

"Beats the hell out of being used as a punching bag every day. Besides, she can be very convincing." All she needed was a forked tail and a pair of horns to complete the look. He straightened to be sure he was a head taller than Amir. "I'm sick of constant war in the Middle East. I've learned not everything is what we are led to believe. Nothing like being up close and personal to see things clearly."

"Exactly. But why should I trust you? You've been an American soldier for a long time as well as an intelligence agent who has done your fair share of damage to our cause."

The pain in his side begged to be touched, but he resisted as he shifted his weight from one leg to the other, over and over. "Up until a few minutes ago, it would have been wise not to trust me. I was going to escape tonight. Soraya was going with me."

Amir turned a scowl toward Soraya, and she gave him an innocent shrug. He went on to finish his rant. "I'm sick of politics. I'm sick of the exaggerated news stories that tell half the story, and it's their version, not necessarily the facts. The people I've had to protect are not so different than those in charge here. All a bunch of self-absorbed power seekers. I was on my last nerve when I took the bodyguard job to protect her." He nodded toward Soraya.

"I hope the prince was paying you well," Amir quipped. "He does not always follow through on his promises. He is a very difficult man to work for and rarely appreciates the people he hires."

"Was going to take the money and disappear off grid, as they say. So, screw the good guys, you, and anyone else who gets between me and my money. From here on out, I work for me. Selling my services to the highest bidder."

"Interesting. I'm sure we could use a person with your unique skill set."

Chase chewed on his bottom lip and eyeballed the guard. "Yeah. I noticed. You have an abundance of assholes working for you."

Amir turned his head toward his guard who wore a bewildered expression since he couldn't understand English. "Perhaps you could teach them a few combat maneuvers. Maybe this will give them more confidence in our mission."

"And just what is the mission, Amir? Because all I've been seeing is, let's kill the infidels because they're Westerners. All that does is tick us off and, admit it, we're the biggest, baddest boys on the block. We also own and operate the best toys to scare the hell out of you."

"That doesn't sound like a man wanting to kick dirt in the face of Uncle Sam."

"Truth hurts. Can't change that." He shifted his weight off the hip that was killing him. "I learned a long time ago which team was going to win the game. Now I'm thinking you might have tied up the game and we're in overtime. Give me a reason to think your team can pull it off."

"I have a weapon."

"Everyone says that and, nine times out of ten, it turns out to be a peashooter. What do you have?"

"If I can get it in place, then Saudi Arabia and Israel will be pointing fingers at each other."

"You mess with Israel, and they'll make you pay. Small but mighty. I would have thought you'd know that by now. And the US is more than a little partial to the land of Jesus, or didn't you know that, either?"

"I want His Royal Highness Prince Muhammed Omar Kadir al Saud destroyed."

"Well, that is a big family to wipe out. Last I heard, there were roughly 25,000 members. Lots of angry siblings, cousins, wives, blooming jihadists, and opportunists to appease. What are you going to do? Melt them like you did with that bunch of Bedouins in the desert?"

"That was a mere practice run. If the prince had showed up like I told him to, then all of this could have been avoided."

"Royalty. Can't live with them and, apparently, can't kill them." The man really didn't have a plan, just a delusional dream. "Who do you want to run the country?"

"Allah will provide a leader, a savior to the downtrodden and forgotten."

"Where have I heard that before?" The temptation to let one corner of his mouth form a sneer was too great. "Let me guess. You?"

"If it is the will of the people, of course."

"In that case, I'm in."

CHAPTER 12

شهيد

Seeing all the young women and girls being herded into camp, with nothing in the way of supplies, took a toll on Chase. The women moved forward; their heads downturned as they held tight to their headscarves. He could only imagine the fear those young hearts held. In the ebb of twilight to dark, he could see several had bruises on their cheeks and arms. Most appeared to be between fourteen and their early twenties. The sound of crying from the younger ones tore at his soul. He knew what was coming. No woman should have to suffer such disrespect and brutality.

Amir's men lined both sides of the path as they shuffled along. Several reached out and felt them up or gave them a poke with their rifle then appeared to call them names or threaten them. They were worthless because they were female Kurds. No matter they were Muslims. Hatred swelled inside him, blocking out any reason or will to survive. This was madness. Without knowing why, he walked alongside the women, hand resting on the rifle strapped across his chest. Several of the men stepped back and watched him, no doubt knowing he had nothing to lose and would just as soon kill them as not.

The women stopped outside a building with one end crumbling from decay and bombing. The night had turned cold, and they had little in the way of protection. Several tried to huddle together. He couldn't resist staring at them then paraded up and down in front of them, memorizing their young faces. He understood why they cowered in fear of him. He hoped the coldness in his eyes gave warning to Amir's men to tread lightly.

Two days earlier, he'd caught a glimpse of his reflection in a glass door with a few cracks. Being so tall, his now-thin frame appeared wirier than muscled. The turban on his head didn't cover the long black hair falling on his ears. His Cherokee heritage hadn't prevented a sparse beard from forming, making his high cheekbones appear hollow and gaunt. He'd stared at his reflection, wondering at first who it was who looked like one of the walking dead. Had he given up?

A fighter walked up beside him and spoke in Arabic, spewing insults toward the women. He wondered if they understood any of it. He reached to touch one and, without thinking, jabbed the butt of his rifle into the man's gut, knocking him back several steps. A litany of unflattering insinuations followed as he charged back to Chase and yelled into his face. Once more, Chase shoved him away.

"Get the hell away from me. Your breath smells like the south end of a northbound camel." He'd turned back toward the women when the fighter charged him. In spite of his strength not being what it once was due to the lack of nourishment, he remained quick on his feet, sidestepping the fighter's attack so the man sprawled on the ground. "Get up," he ordered. "If I see you prowling around these women, I'll shove that rifle where the sun doesn't shine. And I'll rub a little bacon grease on it for good measure. Got it?"

The fighter reached for his rifle on the ground next to him, but Chase kicked it away and pressed his own rifle to the man's forehead, drawing a look of terror.

Amir came up alongside him and pushed the weapon away before motioning the downed fighter to get up. When he grabbed his weapon and stormed off, the leader took a deep breath. "You take pride in bullying my men, do you not?"

Chase didn't answer but pooched out his lips in irritation.

"These women will be sold. Do not get attached."

"Where's Soraya?"

"Safe. For now."

"Prove it."

Amir took out his phone and did a Facetime with her. "Soraya, how are you, my love?"

"Bored. When will you be back?" He turned the phone around for Chase to see. "Chase," she gasped. "Are you okay?"

Chase's stomach cramped. She was dressed like a million dollars while these women had nothing. They were her people—where she'd come from. Yet she turned her back on them in order to take care of her own desires. He could barely stand to look at her, but playing the game was necessary to find out where the chemical weapons were being hidden.

"Fine," he managed to growl as he turned and went back to the Kurdish captives.

Amir chuckled at whatever Soraya said before clicking off and catching up with him. "It is important for you to remember what is at stake if you decide to try and leave us, Captain Hunter." Pointing his finger up and down the row of women, he continued. "Can you handle this situation for a while? I know it is beneath you to watch women instead of fighting. But"—he shrugged then reached out and took the face of one of the women in his hand, turning it from side to side— "there should be a few perks in it for you."

"Keep your filthy men away from me and from them. They'll be worth nothing if they are pregnant, abused, or clinging to life when it's time to move them."

Amir withdrew his hand from the girl's face and stared at Chase. "Westerners have such a warped admiration for females. Why is that?"

Narrowing his eyes to slits, he gritted his teeth. "Something to do with being civilized I'm told."

Amir soured. "Maybe so, but from what I've heard of your reputation, you can be barbaric, too." He sighed. "It has been a long time since you've been with a woman, Captain Hunter."

"Is that what Soraya told you?"

He jerked his chin up and took a step closer to Chase. When he didn't flinch or step back, Amir grabbed his lapel gently. "Careful, Captain Hunter. She told me all about you and how you tried to get her into your bed by giving her pills."

Blood trickled out of the inside of his jaw where he bit to keep from telling the truth. He glanced at the women then back at Amir. "She's a fighter, that one. I guess I have plenty of things to keep me distracted now. Either way, keep your men away. I see them sneaking in at night, I'll slit their throats. I'll make sure the women are healthy and in one piece." He locked glares with Amir. "Who knows, maybe I'll teach the younger ones a few things their new husbands will expect of them."

"You do that." Amir gave one last glance at the women then stomped off toward another building. "Let me know if you need any help," he called over his shoulder.

The overwhelming urge to puke rose from deep inside him. He focused on two girls instead; the taller of the two stared at him then diverted her attention to the ground. Did she speak English? Amir wasn't aware he could speak Arabic, so they conversed in English. The way the girl watched him made him wonder if she understood the conversation. She must be terrified.

He moved to stand in front of her. "What's your name?" When she didn't answer, he grabbed her arm with as much strength as he could muster. "Name," he demanded as she winced.

"Naza," she whimpered.

"So, you do speak English," he said releasing her.

She dared lift terrified eyes to meet his. "A little. My sisters do as well." She pulled them under her arms.

Chase glanced to where Amir was talking to a few of his men. "Keep that to yourself." A bewildered expression leaped to her face. "Understand?"

The three nodded vehemently.

"Teach me Kurdish?"

Another nod.

"I'll teach you Arabic."

"I know Arabic, too. My sisters try." The oldest lowered her head shyly as if she'd said too much.

"How old are you?" Chase growled as he turned to survey the area to see if anyone was watching him.

"Nineteen." She paused. "Are you an American?"

He turned a narrowed gaze back to them and couldn't help but notice how tired and thin they were. "Let's get you inside. Too many men out here wanting to bump me off this detail."

Naza gave the other fifteen women and girls instructions to

move inside, just as gunfire peppered the camp. Screams caused more chaos as the men fired their weapons at an unseen enemy. Chase spread out his arms as if this might protect the women as he shoved and yelled for them to take cover inside. Several stumbled, but he caught them and guided them forward. Once inside, the women took cover against the wall, sliding down to a floor made with a mix of broken tiles and dirt.

"Yadi," Naza cried as she rushed toward the door. Chase caught her with one arm and lifted her off the floor like she was no more than a plucked flower. "My little sister. She's still outside. Please. Let me go for her."

"No. I'll go." Chase dropped her and pivoted toward the door.

He could see the little girl no more than six or seven, standing in the chaos, crying and rubbing her eyes. Chase lowered his weapon as he exited the building and moved toward the child in a slow, calculated motion. He felt no fear, even when bullets stirred up dust around his feet. Still, he did not rush. When he reached the child, he scooped her up with one arm and pointed his weapon out toward those attacking. He ran toward the doorway. At least, since he'd turned his back on them, a bullet would hit him, not the child. Hands pulled him through the door and relieved him of the child.

Naza and the other sister were there to help him, pushing his body downward in time to miss getting wounded. For a split second, he focused on the young woman staring back at him. Then he took in the rest, daring to watch him without fear. A new feeling surged through him; willing him to live. Hope. Now he had a purpose. He wanted to make Tessa proud of him. If he couldn't locate the bomb, maybe he could save these innocent women from a life of hell.

He moved to the door and realized he had to go do his part to continue to fit in. Stepping outside, he fired toward the gun flashes in the distance. Several of Amir's men who had decent cover fell, but he remained safe as he fired out in the open. Later, he would ponder why no harm came to him. Was it a miracle?

~ ~ ~ ~

In the hills surrounding the camp, one man held up his hand for his people to stop firing. He lifted his binoculars again to watch the man pick up a child then carry her toward the door. It was him: Captain Chase Hunter.

"Do not hit the man with the child," he ordered calmly. The random shots continued for a few more minutes, before the man took a second look. "He's back outside, so shoot the others. No harm should come to the man who saved the child."

A Kurdish fighter took the binoculars to examine the prize who demanded such safety measures. "Who is he?" he asked. "A friend?"

"Not always. But I owe him a great deal. He has been watching over someone very special to me for the last year."

"Who might that be?"

Roman Darya Petrov raised his rifle and caught the captain in the crosshairs and whispered, "My wife."

Director Benjamin Clark stood on a hillside near the military base and waited. With darkness nearly upon him, he rested a hand on his weapon then continued to stare over the valley. The man he waited for had become a twitch over his eye and a pain in his neck over the last couple of years. In spite of a lack of trust, he respected him. He had promised no one else would be with him at this meeting. Benjamin understood why. The fewer people who knew where he was, the better the chance he'd survive.

The others would arrive in a few days, and he didn't want any unnecessary problems to hinder implementing the plan. The clock was ticking on the location of the WMD. All they really knew now was it contained a chemical component like the one that leaked in the Bedouin camp in Saudi Arabia.

With terrorists, you never knew for sure who was in control. So far, they hadn't been able to pinpoint anyone willing to create a failsafe weapon for the Jihadist crowd. The ones with knowhow were either in a dark CIA site, under surveillance, or dead. There was the possibility a university research professor had slipped through the cracks, but the Israelis usually managed to get those situations under control pretty quickly. The real danger was the chance a freelancer might decide to make one from a YouTube video. This, too, had been monitored, and it didn't appear likely. Even if it were, there was enough wrong information to cause it to backfire and destroy whoever created it. Strange how that gave him comfort.

His contact was late, by forty-five minutes. The director remained patient and leaned against a tree, knowing he'd blend in a little more with the environment as the sun slipped behind a rugged hillside. There had been a dark spot across the steep crevice between his position and the area reshaped during the last earthquake. The suspicious spot disappeared ten minutes earlier, so he waited for the contact to approach.

By now, he knew Roman Darya Petrov probably had been here a couple of hours before he ever arrived. The man left nothing to chance. The man had a resolve made of steel and an uncanny ability to appear and disappear at will. If he hadn't seen him bleed with his own eyes and claw his way back from death, he would have believed the stories about him being a ghost. Without him and the work he did in Russia, a very vital piece of technology would have fallen into enemy hands. He'd owed him the medical care he provided at the conclusion of the mission when everyone else believed he'd died. As he recovered, they struck up a kind of friendship laced with caution. Darya wasn't a man who trusted easily and, in that regard, the director was cut from the same cloth.

Intel provided enough information to know the Russians, Taliban, Afghan government, and various Pentagon higher-ups would love to get their hands on him. Together, the two devised a way for him to remain dead to the world and yet an active part of the intelligence scene. The director laid everything out in black and white and let the Tribesman make his own decision as to whether Tessa should know the truth. The director preferred keeping his secret from Tessa and laid out the pros and cons of such a lie.

The woman had suffered greatly from what she believed to be the death of the wild Tribesman who had first kidnapped her in Afghanistan and brainwashed her into falling for his Robin Hood persona. But Captain Hunter went off the grid to get her back and bring her home. The two men hated each other with a passion. In Russia, the two once again met up, with Tessa becoming both the pawn and the prize. That time, Darya refused to lose and forced her into marrying him.

"I know you're here, Tribesman, so show yourself." Ben slipped his Luger from his holster and dropped his hand down by his side.

Darya moved out of the darkness from a position in front of the director, proof once more, the man was a spook.

"You are looking well, Director Clark."

The director replaced the Luger back in position then straightened. For the first time since they'd met, he extended his hand toward the once-drug dealer in friendship. The Tribesman let his attention go to the outstretched hand then up to the director's face. He unexpectedly grasped it with an iron grip.

"And you are strong as an ox again. The wilds agree with you." In the dappled light of falling darkness, the director observed in spite of being dirty, the man's clothing made him look like a native. He had been running with Syrian rebels, gathering intel for the Americans and who knew who else.

"The trappings of civilization are out of the question where I've been. Came across Captain Hunter."

The director straightened. "We've been searching for him. He disappeared about two months ago, along with the singer, Soraya." The Tribesman never blinked. The director surmised he might not be up on pop culture. He didn't strike him as a person who listened to much music. "She's a big rock star. The crown prince of Saudi Arabia requested Chase to be her bodyguard since she'd be in dangerous territory at times, filming her next rock video."

"Doesn't sound much like his kind of thing."

"It isn't. But politics and a chemical weapon played into the mix. He offered to pay him a great deal of money to get involved."

"Since when does the almighty Captain Hunter care about money?" Darya took a few seconds to survey his surroundings.

The director realized he'd stayed silent too long. "I'm guessing he has plans for the future Mrs. Hunter," he said flippantly.

Darya slowly turned his head his way with an obvious sinister expression.

"Neither of them knows you're alive so get over yourself. Tell me what you saw."

"He was marching women through a camp, southeast of here. One man I recognized from flyers circulating. I think his name is Amir. There were about twenty men with him that day. We picked a few off, but more have showed up. Chase was carrying a weapon as if he belonged, but he is not in good shape. Thinner. Favors left hip and tilts his body as if he's protecting his ribs from hurting.

Haggard would be a good word."

"And Soraya? Did you see her?"

"No. Chase got into it with one of the soldiers trying to disrespect one of the women. Looks like he is their self-appointed protector. Won't last long. Some of those men are ISIS holdovers. They would disrespect their mothers for the cause, whatever it is these days. From what I understand, Amir has promised them a place of importance when the crown prince is defeated. Israel is involved, but I'm not sure how. Could be a target for this weapon you're talking about, and Prince Muhammed takes the blame. Good way to get the US involved."

"I want you to go back and see what he has found out."

"I know you don't want to hear this, but—"

"Spit it out, man."

"He has been injured from what I hear. Badly. They control him with pain meds."

"Until he's now addicted and will do whatever it takes to get them."

Darya shrugged. "He is a strong-willed man. There are things impossible to fight. I saw it in my own people in Afghanistan. You should be prepared for the worst, Director Clark. He looked as if he were fading."

"I will give you a medical pack in case of an emergency."

Darya nodded his acceptance before speaking again. "A man has paid me to retrieve his wife and sisters. I believe them to be in that camp. I have searched for them for several weeks. When I stumbled across Amir's camp, I thought I saw them."

"When will you return?"

"Tomorrow I will go back."

"What do you need?"

"A way around the Turkish Army. They nearly caught us crossing last night. If we could hitch a ride to where the American special forces are, then we can walk the rest of the way."

"Take this." The director reached inside his vest and withdrew an envelope. "There's five thousand dollars in there. Can you secure a vehicle to get there quicker?"

Darya took the envelope and nodded a thank-you, which was all the director could expect from a man of few words.

"There's something else you should know."

Darya lowered his chin and peered back at him with suspicion.

"My team is on their way here. Tessa will be part of the group."

The Tribesman continued to glare at the director.

"She will pose as an International Red Cross representative to check on several Canadians working with Doctors Without Borders who were supposedly captured. That is her cover story anyway. No doctors missing, but there are some doctors at a refugee camp we can use as part of our story. A ransom has been requested, and she will be traveling with several others for protection. We received intel that Amir's people may be moving farther south than west toward the Lebanon border. There are a number of UNESCO sites there, so we're prepared to have some of the team represent those officials that deal with those problems in order to get inside, if that is where they're headed."

"Syria is a dangerous place, and she should not go. I will stop her," he growled, turning to leave when the director gripped his arm.

"No contact. Remember? You knew this when you agreed to work for me. Tessa has contacts and connections over here because of her work with the State Department. When Chase went MIA, all communications stopped. At first, we figured it was location and no service. A video surfaced that convinced us otherwise. There were cameras at the border crossing into Syria, and it was obvious Chase and Soraya had been taken."

"I know what I promised. She will be in danger."

"Tessa nearly grieved herself to death this last year. And whether you believe it or not, Chase felt he'd failed and misjudged you. He took revenge for your death."

"It doesn't stop me from wanting my wife or life back."

"Darya, you are a wanted man. Do you want Tessa to live like that?"

"No. She deserves better. I've had my issues with the captain, but I know he is not so different from me and will make a good life for her. I thought by now they would be together."

"So did I," the director admitted. "Beside the point now. I'll get you the supplies you need by morning. Knowing Chase, he's trying to find the weapon or the target. He has the skill to escape whenever he wants."

"Maybe that was true in the past. Not sure he is able now."

"Don't underestimate Chase. I want you to bring me news: good, bad, or indifferent. We don't have much time."

"You shouldn't underestimate me, either, or have you forgotten?" He leaned in closer and gritted his teeth. "Keep Tessa's exposure to a minimum, or Amir will be the least of your worries."

The director squinted and jammed a finger in the Tribesman's chest. "I don't like cocky. I'm the one person you can trust."

Darya slowly moved the director's finger off his chest. "Trust you? I said come alone, and yet you bring four gorillas with you." The director had left them a quarter mile down the road among the rocks and trees. "You leave a lot to be desired in the trust department."

"What did you do to them?"

"Let's just say I gave them the night off." He walked away. "Good to see you again, Director Clark. I'll check on Saint Chase Hunter for you. And you make sure Tessa stays put."

CHAPTER 13

شهيد

The transport plane was uncomfortable, loud, and oscillated from hot to cold. It was long overdue for retirement, according to Carter. But like a lot of the Sherpa planes, the agencies that like to stay in the shadows of national security found ways to refurbish them. They weren't made for comfort, only to get you or cargo to your destination. No one talked much and, when they did, it came out a shout, so privacy was out of the question. This left plenty of time for Tessa to think, probably not a good idea considering her current state of mind.

She glanced at Honey, who sat across from her and shivered when she realized the woman stared at her with one of those pit-viper gazes. It occurred to her, perhaps it may have been her first life before being reborn an assassin. A slow narrow smile spread across her lips, and she raised her chin before pooching her mouth into a kiss. Although she couldn't hear it, Tessa was pretty sure a sinister chuckle followed. All this discomfort she experienced appeared to be a walk in the park for the Irishwoman.

Tessa tried to imagine her as a little girl, but then the picture turned to her pulling the heads off her dolls and boiling them in water. She was a borderline sociopath. What conscience she possessed was weak and erratic. Many times, Tessa had wondered why the woman had decided to claim her as a best friend. Was it because she was a pushover? Or maybe it was because she'd stood up to her early on in the relationship.

Their first encounter had been when Libyan terrorists were planning an attack and she found herself snared in a web of dangerous lies and half-truths. The woman had been sent to kill her then husband, Robert, plus her children. She took a liking to them and changed her plans once Chase had read her the riot act. Apparently, they once had been not only partners but lovers. Now, here she was, buddies with the assassin, and heaven help her for being thankful for such a dangerous companion. Tessa believed on any given day, she was one misstep from being caught in her crosshairs, especially if the price was right.

The hope was as long as she could pit Honey against Samantha, then the impending hole in her forehead wouldn't materialize. There was a bit of confusion as to why the two women didn't get along, other than the fact the two were both self-absorbed and hated other women who posed a threat to men they wanted. This meant she was in double trouble when it came to Chase. Would they plot her demise if they knew he wanted to marry her? Making them bridesmaids to put their animosity on hold for her victory in landing the boss didn't feel like a plan that would work.

"Thinking about the captain?" Honey had slipped over and taken a seat next to her. She still scared the willies out of her.

"Yes. Rehashing the last day Chase contacted me. He said they were going into Syria with an escort and should be back in two days if they managed to finish filming. Soraya wanted to stop on the way back and do a performance for the Kurdish fighters there. And then nothing else."

"She's lying." Honey spoke so offhandedly, it drew Tessa to stare at her.

"What do you mean?"

"She is a trickster. My sources say she plays rough and may be playing nice with one of the Soldiers of the Divine. It's a spin-off from the ISIS group. No one knows much about them or who leads the group. But they are well funded and supplied. Speculation is the Russians, but since Soraya is involved—"

"It might be Saudi Arabia?"

"Bingo." Honey narrowed her eyes. "I understand the crown prince was quite taken with you after you saved his life."

Tessa stared ahead, preferring not to reveal her feelings concerning the prince. "Well, it all worked out in the end. Glad I could be of help. I was a flash in the pan for the prince. He has moved on to his other—interests, I'm sure."

"You don't give yourself enough credit," Honey said, adding an elbow to her side, making her flinch and try to scoot away. "Those baby blues, blonde curls, and curves are what make Samantha hate you so much."

Together, they turned their attention to Sam, who had been sleeping but like a flash of lightning, opened her eyes and glared at them.

"She knows you might replace her one of these days," Honey went on. "Once you took over Chase's affection, you became number one on her hit list."

"She has a hit list?"

"Doesn't everyone?" she said incredulously.

"Am I on yours?" Tessa dared turn her attention back to the assassin.

Next came an icy gaze. "Not anymore."

"Why is that?"

"You're probably the only genuine person I know. Well, besides my mum." She shrugged. "I like that. I feel I need to watch after you because you are too trusting. Besides, I plan to be the step mum to your children someday. I'm sure I'll need your advice from time to time."

Tessa shoved her face into Honey's so that their noses touched. "Let me be clear on something. Stay away from Robert and the kids. I will personally gut you with my garden spade if you go near them. Got it?"

Her lips protruded into a pout. "You see? This is what I like about you. One minute, you're all sweet tea and warm scones, the next, a psycho with a taste for roughness. I find that quality very endearing in someone like you."

Tessa jerked back against her seat in frustration, leveling a glance back to Samantha. The woman dragged her finger across her throat as if it were a knife then pointed to Honey, who had closed her eyes to nap. She mouthed the words, don't trust her, then raised her eyebrows in an all-knowing expression.

Great. She was actually living the saying caught between a rock and a hard place. This might turn out to be a hilarious sitcom in the future. Two Wackjobs and a Mom, or a Dateline episode with her ex-husband the prime suspect in killing her because the new wife gave the cops a hit list with her name on it. Maybe this was one more thing to test her mettle. One of these days, that new-found strength could have a nuclear meltdown.

The bump of wheels down always gave Tessa a feeling of relief. There was a time she'd not concern herself with any flight. She'd pull out a book or magazine, nibble a snack, take advantage of a complimentary drink, slip on headphones to listen to tunes, and enjoy the cloud formations outside her window.

Then she joined Enigma and discovered the horrific mess the world was in, along with the men and women who protected it. Now, the sight of an aircraft made her want to fall on her knees and pray to God he would protect the passengers and give angel wings to the flight crew. Now, when her children flew to Tennessee to spend part of the summer with her parents, she insisted on a layer of extra security. One of her parents would fly out to get them then she or Robert would go pick them up, depending on their schedules.

Waiting on the runway of Incirlik Air Base in Incirlik, Turkey, stood several high-ranking US military officials dressed in fatigues, wearing expressions that could have bent steel. A number of soldiers, who had also traveled with Enigma agents, exited the plane first. The officers stepped forward and shook hands with them and made polite comments.

Although all three women dressed in camo fatigues, Samantha and Honey carried themselves like soldiers, but Tessa still had that *what-am-I-doing-here* gait. She shut her eyes for a few seconds, enjoying the cool temperature and fresh air. The transport plane had been a mix of hot and cold, stuffy and hard-to-breathe air.

She had never been to Turkey and had dreamed of being here all her life. Of course, those dreams involved touring the Blue Mosque along with the Hagia Sophia, also called Church of the Holy Wisdom or Church of the Divine Wisdom. Knowing this important Byzantine structure in Istanbul, one of the world's great monuments, was so close made her wonder if Chase would agree to honeymoon here.

Most of Mt. Ararat had been off-limits because the Turks had fought a long guerilla war against a Kurdish separatist group called the Kurdistan Workers' Party or PKK. Hikers hadn't been allowed to climb since 2015. It had recently been reopened, and she fantasized about seeing the location of where, according to legend and scripture, Noah's Ark rested. The Internet declared it was safe enough these days, although hikers still remained vigilant against wild animals.

The sound of someone clearing their throat brought her back to the here and now. A chief master sergeant extended his hand to her. The wind touched her hair and pulled it across her forehead as she grabbed his hand and gave a weak, airsick nod. She feared if she opened her mouth, puke might hurl onto an officer's shiny shoes. He quickly introduced the general and walked them to a minibus.

The soldiers who had traveled with them carried their duffle bags across the tarmac to another waiting bus.

Waiting in a conference room at the rear of a hangar were familiar Enigma men, standing around talking, dressed in clothing resembling the hated PPK fighters. In a way, their cold indifference to their sudden appearance managed to give Tessa a sense of things would be okay now. She loved these men and rested her eyes on each one as a kind of reassurance welled up inside her.

Zoric, the Serbian known as The Vampire, leaned against a metal desk and continued to open and shut his switchblade as he watched the newcomers. From the disgruntled glare of the master sergeant escorting them inside, he and the Enigma agent had already crossed swords. Zoric wasn't a person to let orders get in the way of common sense or what he felt was a better idea. His eyes became hooded as they locked with hers. They never failed to make a chill run up her spine, knowing the macabre torture techniques he'd used to get information out of the enemy. Most of the time, he was a silent force in her life who stood in the shadows, promising to always protect her and her family. Other times, she steered clear to avoid his mood swings.

"How was your flight?" came a husky voice behind her.

Tessa turned to see a hard angular face with several days' growth of beard. Dark circles surrounded his eyes, as if he hadn't been sleeping well. With the turban-like covering on his head, his light-brown hair stuck out in odd places, softening his muscled neck. Relief washed over her, knowing he was here.

"Ken," she breathed.

One corner of his mouth lifted in a grin.

He'd been a good friend of late. She wasn't sure why he'd become a more frequent visitor in her life unless Chase had told him to keep watch when he had to be gone on a diplomatic mission of national security importance. Everyone had treated her as if she'd break into a million pieces since Darya died. But she hadn't. She'd just needed time to grieve and pull herself together, especially since she'd also booted Robert to the curb.

"A little tired and I'm afraid I'm a little carsick—I mean airsick. Same difference, I guess."

"I'll get you a soda. Maybe that will help." He squeezed her arm and moved away.

Flopping down in a folding chair, she took a deep breath. Carter and Vernon were making small talk with her two partners in crime. After a few minutes, they headed her way and straddled the chairs in front of her, folding their arms on the back of the chairs.

"You guys look rather dashing in your I'm a badass-outfit." She used her finger to point and outline their bodies. "Kind of sexy. Maybe you should go with this look when we go home. I bet the ladies would be all over you."

"Really?" Vernon, the youngest of the bunch and very inexperienced when it came to romance, was shy and tongue-tied when it came to carrying on a conversation outside his expertise of technical support. He glanced down at his outfit and smoothed the front of his long vest.

"Not me. I want the ladies to see what a hunk I am," Carter said, lifting his arms and flexing his muscles. "I don't need any props."

The ex-astronaut never failed to amaze her with his self-confidence and admiration for himself. It was often said around headquarters, he'd never seen a mirror he didn't need to check out. Besides being a brilliant engineer, there didn't seem to be anything he couldn't fly. As a pilot, his reputation was what legends were made of.

There remained speculation he and Samantha had more than a working relationship in spite of her love life with the prime minister of Israel. She knew for a fact they'd argued over this a number of times. Carter was the one person she never flirted with or made suggestive comments to concerning carnal avenues of pleasure.

Honey was walking around the room visiting with a few military personnel like she was shopping for a new coat. That Irish accent and red hair was apparently akin to catnip for these men. One or two were Turkish, and they couldn't stop trying to engage her in conversation. Tessa hoped they'd had their shots.

"Excuse me, guys. I'll be right back." Tessa went over and grabbed Honey's arm and pulled her back to where she'd been sitting. "Can you just stop?"

Honey winked at the two Turks then appeared to direct her interest toward the two Enigma men waiting. "Hello, boys," she growled in a sexy tone.

Both greeted her with a mix of admiration and amusement. Her reputation for being your next one-night stand gave her an almost-celebrity status. Tessa was sure they didn't want to tangle with her, even for a good time. Then Ken joined them and handed her a cola. He nodded to Honey but quickly refocused on her.

"Have you been briefed yet?" Ken switched to his no-nonsense tone, reminding Tessa Chase did the same thing when he meant business.

Tessa shook her head. "No. Haven't heard anything. The director was going to join us. Is he already here?"

"Yes. Came over with Tom and I. The guy says more with his hawkish scowl than he does with his mouth."

Tom Cooper was Ken's best friend, partner on missions, and all-around fixer when things turned messy. He was over six foot five and came across as a substitute for a barricade. She wasn't sure she'd ever seen him show amusement. On their first encounter, she'd nearly killed him, and he had really never gotten over the teasing and harassment he received for letting a tiny thing like Tessa land him in the hospital using nothing more than a flimsy broomstick. Many times, she'd seen him watching her. It made her wonder if he was planning revenge. Yet another person she didn't want to cross.

Ken Montgomery, on the other hand, would have stood on his head and spit nickels for her if she'd asked. She'd saved him from being killed by a Libyan terrorist, puking her guts out after the fact, watching him finish off the terrorist with his knife through the gut. That had been several years earlier.

Now look at her, going into no-man's land, searching for Captain Chase Hunter who had dragged her screaming and fighting into the dark world of Enigma. Sometimes she thought of herself as going from being a feather duster to a ragged piece of steel wool.

Ken reached down and took her forearm. "Can we talk a minute?"

"Sure. Let me go freshen up. I'll be right back."

As she moved away to the restroom, Carter's cynical words to Ken reached her ears. "What the hell you think you're doing, Ken?" She glanced back and noticed the two men appeared solemn and tense. Carter now stood with his hands on his hips. Ken turned his head toward her and lifted his chin as if to hurry her along. Zoric closed his knife and slipped it inside his vest as he slid off the table and came to stand next to Carter.

Men. They were always marking their territory. Every guy in the unit thought they should be in charge.

~ ~ ~ ~

Chase ate with Amir's men, what little there was, and hoarded his bread and the piece of fruit he'd been given, for the little girl. He'd been present when an old woman brought the women a kind of gruel and rice. No wonder they were all so thin. He carried water to them from a well in the center of what was once a village until they had had their fill then brought more to wash.

Once, he'd walked in to find a soldier taunting one of the girls. Chase set his two buckets down before marching over and grabbing him by the back of the collar and the seat of his pants. He ran him outside so fast, the other men burst into laughter, making rooster sounds. Then he threw him on the ground.

"Go back in there without my permission, and they'll be making hen noises instead of rooster," Chase growled. The man rolled over and glared up at him, but Chase kicked dirt in his face and addressed the others who had crowded in the doorway to watch. "That goes for the rest of you, too. If you want top dollar, then stay away."

Amir stood leaning against a doorframe of what had become his temporary headquarters. He picked at his teeth with a stick then spit on the ground. He motioned for them to leave Chase alone as they helped the man in the dirt to his feet.

Amir pushed off and let the others come in where stewed goat meat mixed with a few tomatoes, onions, and potatoes simmered on a fire. Chase had no idea where the goat meat came from or if it was safe to eat, but the smell was tempting. He had eaten cautiously to display a strengthening in his stamina. Better they think he was kind of a robot with untapped strength than recognize how much pain he endured.

"My men are getting tired of your attitude," Amir said, walking with him to the women's quarters.

"The feeling is mutual."

"No one is coming for you, Captain Hunter. And if they try to escape, I will kill you myself."

"And Soraya? What about her?"

"You need not concern yourself with her. She is a very pleasant distraction and of great value to me and our cause." He followed Chase into the area where the women were busy washing their faces and hair. They scrambled to cover themselves. He handed Chase a few pills. "These will help with the pain. I noticed you limping."

"No thanks."

Amir's eyelids became hooded. "You're no good to me if the pain consumes you. I need you to fight, not moan so loud you give our position away." He dropped them in Chase's shirt pocket then patted it. "Maybe you'll change your mind."

"I won't."

Amir put his hands behind his back and strolled around the girls as if he were shopping for a used car. He stopped in front of Naza and her sister who was sixteen. The little one hid her face in the older sister's skirt. He eyed Naza, head to toe, causing her to stare at the ground. "You. Come to me tonight. I think it is time we get better acquainted."

"No," Chase said, coming to stand in front of her. "I've already taken her and her sister."

Amir blinked as if surprised. "That is a surprise considering your ethical and moral Western beliefs."

"You said I could have anyone I wanted."

Amir arched an eyebrow and stepped to the side to get a better look. "So, you have broken her in for me."

"Not up for discussion. Naza is pregnant with my child." He pulled her forward and tightened her garment to reveal her bulge. "I will pay for her or do whatever is needed, but these two are now mine."

"And the little one?"

"She will age. They all do."

"Then you had better take those pills. I want you 100 percent."

Chase stared at him.

"Take them now," he ordered.

He popped them in his mouth and swallowed.

"Very good." Amir moved to the door. "Send me another girl tonight, or I'll come back for your woman."

After he left, Naza fell into his arms and sobbed. Her sisters, Rozerin and Yadi, circled his waist and hugged him tightly. Chase dropped his hand on the teen then lifted little Yadi into his arms and kissed her cheek.

"Captain Hunter, you risk everything for us. We will never be able to repay you." Naza laid her head against his chest as he patted her back.

"I have to get you out of here. It's not good for the baby." He pulled the food he'd saved from his pocket and gave it to her. "You need to eat."

She gave the overripe apple to the little one then divided the rest among the others. All refused and insisted she eat it. The juice of the apple trickled from the corner of her mouth as she chewed and grinned at Chase, patting his shoulder.

"Naza, I can get you out of camp, but you must travel in the dark for a long way to reach safety. I think we are close to where American special forces are located." He felt the pain meds take effect and stumbled. Several women rushed up to help Naza get him to the floor. "They are poisoning me, ladies."

Naza translated and several wept.

"I am afraid," Naza confessed. "If they catch us or find us, we will be separated, and who knows what will happen then. If we stay here, you protect us. I can't take a chance of losing my sisters." She pointed to the others. "All my sisters."

After two months with these women, he'd come to respect their love for one another. Even when they did chores for the men, suffered their verbal insults, and were touched inappropriately, they maintained a kind of dignity and strength. They hissed back at the men in their native tongue and held their chins high. Several had disappeared, and Chase knew they either had been sold or had died during the times he went out with a patrol. He did his best to keep them safe, but it wasn't enough.

"I will go tonight to the horrible man, Amir," Naza declared. Her friends shook their heads in protest as she patted the air for them to not fret. "Yes. Several of you have suffered enough already."

Chase tried to stand and fell back to a sitting position. "No. The baby. He's liable to hurt you to make you miscarry. You are worth more without the child." He reached up and took her hand. "I can hardly"-he licked his lips as saliva trickled out of the corner of his mouth—"move. Please, Naza. Don't. Go."

~ ~ ~ ~

Darkness fell early with no moon and heavy cloud cover. Amir planned to go out on patrol and left a skeleton crew of older men to guard the camp and make sure Chase behaved. Amir had already promised his men when they returned, they could choose from the women and girls in the American's care. They might have to fight him, so he warned them to be prepared.

He had dropped by to see how the captain was fairing and realized the pills he'd given him may end his life. Truthfully, he didn't know what they were or the dosage. His death would be inconvenient, considering he had plans for the captain. The women had gathered around him, speaking soft words. Just more proof he'd been too easy on them. The doe-like eyes of Naza met his with a challenge. Yes. He would definitely use her tonight to satisfy the emptiness he felt with Soraya away. With any luck, the captain would live long enough to see the results when he finished with her.

The captain's speech was severely slurred as he raised a finger toward him. "Stay away."

Amir huffed an amused cackle. "We will be back around

midnight. I will come for your woman then." He clapped his hands together one time. "The rest of you will also have a partner tonight. My men are tired of waiting."

~ ~ ~ ~

The young women cared for Chase, and he took comfort in their words, even the ones he couldn't understand. They were frightened, but he couldn't do anything to reassure them. When Naza ran her hand down his jaw and pushed his hair from his face, he saw Tessa before him. Her sweet, mischievous smile encouraged him to fight like hell to stay alive.

"Tessa." Not realizing it was Naza, he reached out and touched her face. "I love you. I always have."

"Captain Hunter, I am not your Tessa." Naza's fingers lingered on the side of his face. "She must be very special."

He blinked and licked his lips. "Yes. A good woman." He offered a lopsided motion with his mouth and rolled his half-closed eyes at all the ones who had gathered around him. "Just like all of you. Naza, if you can find her"—he closed his eyes— "tell her I thought of her at the end."

"Captain?" she whispered. "Captain Hunter? Wake up," she demanded. "Don't sleep. Please. We need you. You must live. Live for Tessa."

Although he could hear her voice, the weight of the drugs prevented him from responding. Life was ebbing from his body. He heard their sobs, especially those of the little one, Yadi. The image of Tessa's little girl, Heather, floated in his memories, and he longed to hold her one more time. So many regrets at not confessing his love sooner or throwing caution to the wind. Would he be here now if that had happened? In those fading moments, he saw himself holding a baby with her at his side, encouraging him and then kissing him on the cheek in pride. All the things he wanted and would never have.

Then he heard women screaming. Why wouldn't his body respond? Did the earth move, or was he shaking?

~ ~ ~ ~

A female fighter slung her rifle over her shoulder and stepped forward. She held her hands up to calm the women. Soon armed fighters swarmed inside and took up positions at the door and the few windows the room held.

"It is all right. We are here to help. Do not be afraid." She stepped closer to Naza who rose to her feet, blocking a person lying on the floor. "Is there a Naza here?"

At first, there was silence. "I am Naza. Who are you?" She cocked her head and viewed the woman with suspicion. "Are you a Kurdish fighter?"

"I am. Part of the YPJ unit. My name is Peshmerga. But, for now, I am with him," she said, stepping aside as a broad-shouldered man pushed his way through the door.

The room was bathed in darkness except for one small LED lantern in the corner. Although he dressed as a Kurd, the shape of his eyes told of a different heritage in Central Asia. He appeared out of place in Syria. Naza had never seen such eyes before. It was obvious from the thickness of his arms and legs, he was strong. He glanced at Peshmerga and raised his chin.

"Naza, we are here to take you home. Your husband has searched for you. Your family has paid us to rescue you." Peshmerga spoke in a no-nonsense tone.

Tears streamed down her face. "I thought my husband was dead." She turned to face the others. "He's alive," she sobbed. "The others?"

"We are taking all of you." The man spoke softly, but there was grit in his tone. "Where is Captain Hunter?"

The others parted to reveal the man slumped against a wall. "They have tried to kill him. Without him, we would have been sold as sex slaves. He fought every day to protect us. Now they have filled him with drugs to keep him from interfering with their plan to use us tonight." She knelt down and pushed his black hair out of his face. "You must take him, too. We owe him our lives."

The man waved her away and squatted down next to the captain. He turned his face toward his and then took his pulse. In that instant, the captain convulsed and fell completely over on the floor.

The stranger ordered Peshmerga to give him something from the folds of her clothing. It appeared to be a syringe.

"Stop. What are you doing?" Naza tried to move him away, but the female soldier stopped her.

"It is Narcan. This will save him."

The man jabbed him with the lifesaving drug then rubbed the captain's temple. In seconds, Chase gasped, and his eyes fluttered open to stare up at his former enemy, now his savior.

"Yes. It is me, Captain Hunter. You are not dead." He turned to Peshmerga. "Get them moving. Now." They didn't have time to say their goodbyes, but Naza paused long enough to thank the stranger. Then she kneeled down next to Chase and hugged his neck as he was repositioned to sitting against the wall. "I will find Tessa and tell her your words."

The stranger glared at her in anger. "Go. Now."

When they had all left the room, Chase tried to focus on his savior. "You. I thought"—he swallowed— "you were dead. Guess I'll call you Lazarus."

"It is better if others think I am, Captain Hunter. Do you have information on the impending attack?"

"No," he whispered. "But I'm close. They want to destroy both Saudi Arabia and Israel. Pit them against each other." He drank the water the man held to his lips. "Thank you," he choked. "Tessa."

"She comes for you."

"No. Too dangerous. Stop her."

"It is too late. She begins her search for you with others."

The two men grew quiet and stared at each other. "Why have you not taken her?" Darya checked Chase's bruises.

Chase broke his gaze and leaned his head back. "She needed time."

The man checked Chase's pulse. "The time has come, Captain Hunter. She can't know of this. She loves two men and believes one is dead. I want her to be happy and safe. Only you can ensure that. I have people searching for me and cannot risk endangering her future for happiness."

One of the fighters rushed in. "We see lights in the distance. They are returning. The women have been moved toward the cars." He disappeared out the door.

"The rest of us are on foot. We will distract them when they return, so the women have a chance." He edged closer. "I am sorry.

I cannot take you. I thought we'd have more time."

"That's all I want. Thank you. Naza is pregnant, so please take care of her. Go."

"I will. He stood and removed his rifle. "In order to keep you safe, I must make it appear you put up a fight."

"Help me," Chase said, reaching up.

The man pulled him up and held on to him until he could stand on his own. "I am sorry, Captain Hunter."

"I didn't ask for a character reference," he said, shaking him off. "Just do it. This might be your last chance to get the drop on me."

The man nodded then smashed the butt of his rifle into Chase's jaw, knocking him to the ground once more, then smashed it into his upper chest. He took out his knife and jabbed it into his shoulder, careful not to go deep enough to cause permanent damage or require repair. Doubling his fist, he slammed it above one eye to make sure it didn't jeopardize his vision.

"Khan, we must go," a fighter called from the door.

He squatted down to gaze at his equal and laid his hand on his own heart then onto Chase's. "I will come back for you, my friend."

One corner of Chase's mouth lifted then gave him a warning. "Better rethink that. Next time, I'm kicking your ass."

Darya narrowed his eyes as he stood. "I look forward to it." His words fell on an unconscious hero as the man known as the Tribesman escaped into the night.

~ ~ ~ ~

Whatever slammed into the bottom of his boot jarred his sore body. With the taste of dirt in his mouth, he spit without much success, until he dragged his sleeve across his mouth. A sharp pain hit his shoulder at the same time he tasted blood. One side of his face felt enlarged, and his chest hurt. Ribbons of light streamed into the room, carrying dust particles, making him cough. He rolled to his side then tried to push himself up with the arm that didn't hurt like it had been shot off. Then he remembered.

"The women," he panicked. Although he meant to scramble to his feet, he lumbered upward like a sleepy sloth. "Naza," he called, stumbling around the room as if he'd find her. "Yadi," he moaned. Pivoting, he nearly fell as his gaze landed on Amir, standing spraddle-legged, wearing a vehement snarl on his face. "Where is Naza?"

"Gone. Just like the others," he fumed. "Four of my men are dead, their throats slit. Two others were run through with a bayonet left in their chest. Considering the shape you were in when I left, I know you were unable to do it."

Chase felt his forehead pinch in bewilderment. What happened? He shook his head then realized his shirt had been ripped on the shoulder and blood oozed, leaving a dark stain down the front of his arm.

"Masked men," he mumbled, rubbing his chest. Once more, he staggered around the room searching for Naza who he remembered was gone. Part of him wanted her to be here, but he prayed she was safe. "They said…" He had to clear his mind. The image of Roman Darya Petrov leaped to his mind. "They said a family paid them to rescue the women. I tried to stop them. I didn't believe they were here to help them."

"How many of them?"

He blinked away the brain fog. "I saw four, maybe five. But others were outside. On foot, I think."

Amir took a deep breath. "Yes, we chased after them through the darkness and lost them."

Chase rubbed his head in confusion. "But they had the women and child. How is that possible?"

"Good question," he snapped. He approached Chase and jabbed a finger in the shoulder where he'd been stabbed, causing him to cry out and stagger backward. "If you hadn't taken such a beating, I would think you helped them. Were they Kurdish fighters?"

"It was dark. They wore face coverings. They barely spoke and I couldn't understand most of it. All I could hear were the women crying when I tried to stop them, not that I could do anything." He glared at Amir. "Next thing I knew was a few minutes ago." He hobbled to the wall and slid down. "I'll tell you this. If I find them, I'm going to kill every one of them in the slowest, most painful way, especially the one who did this," he said, pointing to his shoulder then his face. "And I will find him."

Amir arched both eyebrows and called for one of his men. He

gave him instructions to dress Chase's wounds and bring him food and water. "You may be of some good to me yet, Captain Hunter. You do realize the woman will probably lose the baby."

Chase snarled up at him. "Then an eye for an eye, is what I say."

"Good. Let all that hate show you how things are here. Rest now."

When Amir left, Chase felt relieved to have survived. He mumbled a prayer the women were safe, and Naza and her unborn child would remain healthy. He thought of Darya and the chance he took in the rescue. He'd protected him with the beating. When he closed his eyes, the image of Tessa swam up as it always did when he needed to feel alive. Did Darya say she was coming for him, or did he hallucinate? Would he once again take Tessa away from him?

CHAPTER 14

شهيد

How would Chase tell Tessa the list of unethical things he'd done, that he'd slept with another woman after professing his love for her? Then, there were the young girls he'd taken in to protect. Several times he'd been tempted to take advantage of their appreciation but resisted by thinking of her loving touch, frown of disappointment, and confession of her own feelings for him. It had been the one thing keeping him sane.

There had been opportunities to escape, but he chose to stay. The world going to war over regime change and supporting one of their longest allies kept him here only because he wanted a better place for Tessa's children and, hopefully, their own in the future. Each day made him doubt the last part of his dream would ever happen.

His body ached constantly. Admitting he was addicted to painkillers kept him under Amir's thumb. One thing he'd learned about addiction: he wasn't as hungry, and now his body grew thin. Forcing himself to exercise when he no longer cared became a constant battle. Then he would remember Tessa and how her touch energized him. He didn't want to return to her half the man he used to be. She deserved better.

Then there was the reminder of the Tribesman, Roman Darya Petrov, who had dared marry her only to leave her a grieving widow soon after. He had been a powerful adversary, one Chase mistrusted and hated for all the wrong reasons. At the end, a bond clicked between them, leaving Chase with more regrets than he thought possible.

The foggy memory of a man giving him a lifesaving shot, staring into his face as the young woman escaped, still haunted him. The voice still whispered in his ear. I'll come back for you. Those narrow eyes of fierce determination pierced his soul when he thought of how much he resembled the Tribesman. Did he hallucinate? It was so real. Part of him wished it were true. A lot of things remained unsaid between them. This was yet another thing he'd have to confess to Tessa and gamble she'd not run back to the outlaw or search for the truth. If he hadn't been such a stickler for ethics and doing the right thing, she would have married him a long time ago. Then she would never have met the notorious bandit who'd kidnapped and brainwashed her.

Dr. Wu, the Enigma psychiatrist, explained Tessa had experienced what is called Stockholm syndrome, a condition where you believe whatever your captor tells you. Since she'd suffered a head injury and amnesia in Afghanistan, she was a prime target for the Tribesman's advances and conflicting messages. Those days were behind them, or so he thought until he showed up to rescue the women in his care.

Whatever the reason, the man clothed in a foggy memory saved his life and said Tessa was coming to rescue him. How could that be? She was tucked in safely in her home in Grass Valley or maybe at her apartment in Sacramento. Did the pain meds he was given cause him to hallucinate? Whoever saved his life was either an angel or an aberration of the Tribesman. After all, he was dead.

"You are getting stronger." Amir handed him a cup of hot tea that tasted as if it had been boiled for the tenth time. There wasn't much tea in their camp, so it was used over and over until there was a stain in your cup. Still, it was better than nothing. When Chase didn't respond, he continued. "We move tomorrow morning. Rebels are near, thanks to the Kurds." He spit on the ground.

"Yet you don't have a problem with Soraya," Chase mused.

"She is also a Saudi. There is a difference."

"The biggest one being she stands to inherit a great deal of property and money from her family. Does it concern you at all they have disowned her for the most part? You have to be aware the crown prince finds her distasteful. The reason she has any standing at all is because her mother happens to be the prince's sister. She, too, is out of favor for marrying a Kurd." Chase sighed. "I can imagine what Thanksgiving would be like at their house." Amir gave him a bewildered gaze. "Oh. Sorry. A holiday we celebrate in the States each year. You know, to thank God for all our blessings—or something to that effect."

"You Americans love to invent new ways to waste time. Ridiculous."

Chase was scanning the horizon when he thought he saw a slight flash of light. "Yeah. There's that. Oh. And I think you're in the crosshairs of one of the rebels."

Amir's forehead furrowed. "What?"

A very loud blast hit the overturned cart Amir had been standing against a split second before. Both men scrambled on all fours around to the end as he yelled orders to the others to take cover. Several more shots were fired, but no one was hit. After twenty minutes, dust curls lifted over the horizon away from them.

"I'm guessing whoever it was wanted us to be aware they knew where we were." Chase stood and flexed his legs then his neck that hurt like the devil. Who do you think they were?"

"The Kurdish trash. They call themselves The Daughters of Kobani. A man would have hit their target." Amir rolled his shoulders and appeared shaken.

"Unless they were trying to let you know they were coming for you whenever they wanted."

"Then why not kill us now?" Amir grabbed the rifle he'd dropped during the attack.

"My guess, there were only a couple shooters. If there had been more, an all-out assault would have wiped you out. Probably went back to get the others. Now you're nervous and will make mistakes."

"Nervous? Humph! Never."

Chase sounded amused as he slung his rifle. "Wouldn't want the great Amir to be taken out by a woman, would we? I mean one nearly did that back in Sacramento. And she was a researcher."

The disgruntled expression he wore nearly made Chase

continue to taunt the man. He contained his amusement to protect himself from being a victim of Amir's fragile ego and temper. Although he now enjoyed being in his captor's good graces, there remained a very thin line he didn't want to cross. There was too much at stake now to let it slip away just to end up in the-infidel-must-die category. The most important mission now was to see whatever they planned ended up derailed and unable to turn the world upside down.

"Are you hurt?" Chase forced himself to give a once-over to the man.

"I'm touched by your concern," he growled as he moved away. "Thanks, by the way. You saved my life." Amir sounded appreciative but still scowled as if it pained him to admit this. "I want you to watch the perimeter tonight. My men need a good night's sleep." He stopped and turned around to face him. "Do a good job, and I'll give you your pills in the morning."

Panic gripped Chase for a few minutes. The pain meds were wearing off. Waiting until morning would be agonizing. Withholding them guaranteed he wouldn't bolt for safer ground or take up a position and kill his self-proclaimed pharmacist.

Chase leveled a dark look of contempt at his captor but knew to say anything would prolong getting the pain meds his body would be screaming for by morning.

"Looks like rain again," he said, dreading being soaked to the bone in a winter downpour.

Amir jerked a poncho from a nearby soldier and threw it to him. "Wouldn't want you to catch cold on top of everything else. I want to make sure you look good for the camera."

Every nerve went on alert. "Camera?"

"You'll be announcing my plans soon for your friends at the CIA or whatever your President Austin calls your intelligence agencies these days. Do you think Prince Muhammed didn't know about Enigma? That's why he requested you to protect him with the Secret Service." He waved him off. "No matter. It will soon be too late to do anything about my plans to unseat the royal family and much too dangerous to come to the aid of Israel." Thunder rumbled quietly across the sky. "I'll have one of the men bring you food. You're going to need your strength to fight."

Chase pivoted and moved toward the perimeter of the camp. He remembered all the times he spotted Tessa praying when she thought no one was watching. The first time had been at the National Cathedral in Washington DC. He'd not seen her for months; thought he never would again. Then there she was, posed like one of the angelic Madonna pictures he'd seen at some point in his life. The ache in his chest began then, and he'd dismissed it as stress or indigestion. Deep down he knew it was more: spiritual yet physiological. A gut feeling the woman with unruly curls and blue eyes was about to ruin his life, and not in a bad way. How many times had she expressed their chance meeting was divine intervention? Although he made fun of such notions, she never gave up on the idea she was there to save him. Another hilarious notion since he'd saved her butt more times than he could remember.

"You'll see, Captain Hunter. One of these days I'll be the one who saves you."

The truth was, she'd done that the day they met, and he'd been resisting ever since. Now, the one thing he wanted was Tessa to hold him and save him one more time so he could move into the next day. Tonight, in the darkness, when the pain resembled sharp knives in his side and hips, he'd remember every word, touch, smell, and breath that was Tessa. It would get him through the night, to live another day. Then he prayed. "God, if you're listening, I need help."

What he got was Roman Darya Petrov.

~ ~ ~ ~

Pacing was not Amir's style, yet he did so with nervous anticipation. Nothing had gone as planned. The chemical weapons were unstable, and he feared they would not be ready to move in time. To add to the confusion, one of the cannisters had been taken then somehow compromised, causing those Bedouins to die. It had tipped off both the Saudis and the Americans. The desert could be so uncooperative at times. Would they be able to pull it all together before the final plan was discovered? Would the multiple targets be enough to get what he wanted?

Had this all been for nothing? If it did not go as planned, he would be a dead man when the Saudis or Israelis caught up with him. Truthfully, he wasn't sure which would be worse. Both had a way of making devious men with big ideas pay for their mistakes with their soul. He feared both equally.

"What is the matter with you?" came the sleepy voice of Soraya. "Come to bed."

"Soon."

Amir glanced toward the bed draped with sheers and twinkly lights. The smell of vanilla candles burning inside Moroccan-style lanterns placed throughout the spacious bedroom irritated him. Such opulence and comfort added a layer of uneasiness, knowing his men slept on the ground most nights and ate like starving dogs without complaint to please him. If they knew the truth of his life with this woman, they might not be so loyal. The pleasures he afforded them with the captives he managed to secure from time to time went a long way to appease their appetites for the flesh. They still believed he was trying to force Soraya into supporting their cause.

The few times she'd appeared, her demeanor transformed from demanding diva to timid captive. The actress in her loved to perform, it seemed. Mostly he didn't mind since the scene always ended with him suggesting in a loud display of masculine superiority, as he dragged her back to her quarters, that it was time to show her appreciation to him.

Behind closed doors the scene flipped, and she became the dominant. Her aggressiveness pleased him to no end. She was both a demanding and creative lover. Except for her fascination with the American captain, things would be perfect between them. She often hinted during lovemaking he should try something the American had done to her. At first, he had tried to please her, and it was those moments she appeared to enjoy the most. When she asked to see the captain or for him to spend the night, he became furious. She would coo and twirl her finger through her long strands of multicolored hair, promising him it would be okay to watch if he chose.

"Maybe you'll learn a thing or two, Amir." This enraged him to the point where he slapped her so hard, she suffered a black eye. Inconsolable and resistant to further advances, she forced him to repent by sending the captain to see her. He realized too late, he'd fallen once more for her act of vulnerability and fragile nature, only to hear the lies told to the captain to gain his sympathy and comfort. But he watched nonetheless. Afterward, he'd had several of his men beat the captain for a trivial infraction. He watched and was disturbed to see he could not be broken by it.

"Amir. Please. Come to bed," she complained. "What is wrong?"

"Someone tried to kill me tonight. Captain Hunter saved my life." He watched her prop herself up on one elbow. "I wonder who knows of our plan."

"Nonsense. Unless one of your brainless soldiers have switched sides, I doubt anyone else knows a thing." A pout toyed with her lips as he approached the side of the bed. "Captain Hunter protected you. What a good boy," she cooed. "I mean, thanks be to Allah you were spared." When she chuckled, he reached over and ripped the covers off her naked body. As usual, she let him gaze as long as he wanted without moving until he removed his robes and climbed into bed with her. "Amir, I love you. Did you know that?"

He kissed her exposed flesh. "I don't care whether you do or not. You are but a means to an end."

"As are you," she said, pulling him on top of her. "As are you."

CHAPTER 15

شهید

Visiting dignitaries, businessmen, and a host of other people who tried to convince others of their importance secured the more comfortable accommodations, leaving Tessa and her two friends to stay in the barracks with the men on the Enigma team. Director Benjamin Clark passed on better arrangements, saying it was good to be back in familiar territory with his people instead of behind a desk.

Tessa had the overpowering urge to volunteer to take the plush offer but feared the consequences from Sam and Honey. She imagined having her head held in a toilet while they took turns flushing to toughen her up a bit.

With a shiver, she carried her leopard duffle bag inside and waited to be told what to do next. As she set it down next to the army green and camo bags, Zoric leveled a frown her way and shook his head before pinching the bridge of his nose in a show of impatience. He was another one she didn't want to tick off. Even though he promised to protect her a long time ago, he wasn't beyond teaching a few lessons. The evil in his bloodshot eyes now focused on her. Did the promise still hold true?

"What?" she snapped. "I like leopard. Do you have a problem with that?" She shifted her weight to one hip and folded her arms across her chest. "Just because we're in hell doesn't mean I can't look good."

Zoric gave her the once-over. "Do you want to be a target, Tessa Scott?" He always said both her names. "Asking because I think I'll stand clear of you when we head out."

"Of course not, silly." She thought pooching out her lips in a pout and tilting her head, would soften him up as it did to Chase. Big mistake.

"Stop treating me like I'm one of your children." He laid a finger, yellowed with tobacco stains, against her lips, causing her heart to almost stop. "Turn that bag wrong side out, or I'll do the same to you. Chase isn't here to keep me in check, and I've wanted to teach you a few lessons for a couple of years." His voice was a whisper as he leaned in closer to her ear. Then he moved a step away, his eyes narrowed and a slight smirk with the corners of his mouth. "Just because I swore to protect you from the evil of this world, doesn't mean you are protected from me. You jeopardize any of us here in this godforsaken place and you'll deal with my—wrath."

Tessa's hard swallow turned into a gulp. "Sorry. I'll do it right now."

His face softened as he lifted a leathery hand to her cheek, causing her to flinch, then patted it gently. "Good girl."

Tessa wanted to remind him she wasn't a girl or even a good girl anymore, thanks to Enigma, but she thought better of it. When the Serbian acted this way, everyone knew it was better to give the man plenty of space.

He grabbed her bag and carried it to a bunk then emptied the contents onto the blanket. "I'll take the top bunk," he announced matter-of-factly.

"I think Honey was going to take that one," Tessa said with a glance toward the woman.

Honey waved her off. "That's okay, Zoric. Heights scare me anyway. I'll take this one." She pointed to a lower bunk and flopped down then stretched out.

"You see?" Zoric said. "It worked out."

"I talk in my sleep," Tessa said in a hurried voice.

"So do I," he said, sitting down on her bunk and inspecting her belongings. "I've even been known to walk in my sleep naked."

Tessa felt her face take on a pinched expression of horror.

"What?"

"Of course, it rarely happens—as long as I'm not irritated or something."

A booming voice interrupted the powerplay. "Enough, Zoric," the director warned. "I think you've made your point."

He continued to walk toward a bunk away from the others. Maybe if she begged, he would take the one across from her. Knowing Zoric was above her, she felt a sense of uneasiness. After she turned the leopard print bag wrong side out and repacked the items, she did her best to level a contemptuous glare at the Serbian.

"Happy?"

He stood. "Rarely. But, in this instance, you pass inspection."

"Don't let him rattle you, Tessa," came a familiar voice. Ken plopped his duffle bag on the bunk across from hers. A wave of relief washed over her as she released a sigh. "He tries to be a badass, but he's a teddy bear."

The men locked stares.

Zoric reached over and patted her cheek once more, like a doting father. "We both know I'm no teddy bear." He refocused on Ken. "Guess we should spend a little quality time together after Chase comes home."

"Say when. I'm ready."

"Keep the attitude. It will help in the long run." Zoric smirked then strode off to another part of the barracks.

"He doesn't like me much." Ken turned away to open his duffle bag.

"Why?" Tessa asked, sitting down on his bunk and staring at the soldier who was several years her junior. "Then again, he really doesn't like anyone."

"He doesn't want me hanging around you," he admitted.

Tessa felt bewildered at such a thought. "Well, he doesn't think I have a brain in my head and does think I need constant supervision so I don't get the rest of you hurt. And he treats me as if I'm his responsibility. Which I am not," she snapped. "Since Darya died, he's hovered like a helicopter. I know he means well but sometimes…" Her voice faded as the image of Darya swam up from her heart.

He lowered his head under the bunk and gazed at her with a heavy seriousness she'd never seen before. "He doesn't want me hanging around you because he thinks I'm trying to score."

This revelation caused her to gasp in unbelief as she slapped at his arm. "Oh my gosh. You are too funny. I'll talk to him. There is no reason for him to be so rude." She pushed off his bunk and stood as he gripped her forearm.

"No. I'm a big boy. I can take care of myself." His grip eased. "We're friends. Besides, who would I get to fix me up with dates if I didn't hang around?" His teasing wink gave her a moment of peace.

"Right. I enjoy playing matchmaker, so feel free to keep hanging around."

He released his hold on her arm. "I intend to do exactly that." His smile was slow, and those light-brown eyes narrowed enough to make Tessa wonder if they were talking about the same thing.

Over the last few months, Ken had a stronger presence in her life, much like the rest of Enigma. After Darya's death and Chase's second trip to Russia to attend to unfinished business, her Enigma family treated her like a fragile baby sister. After all the hard work and experience she'd endured, they still didn't quite trust her ability to survive in a tight spot.

She'd been instrumental in saving Ken's life when they first met, and he'd been forever grateful. Over the last couple of years, they'd become friends, in part because he served under Captain Chase Hunter and he and Tom Cooper were now part of Enigma. Had she sent mixed messages of interest and failed to notice? Or was Zoric being his usual ghoulish self?

She walked over to Honey's bunk and motioned for her to scoot her legs over so she could sit down. "Why is everyone acting so weird?" Tessa quizzed as she spotted Ken cleaning his weapon.

Honey fluffed her pillow and motioned for Tessa to get her a second one off the top bunk. Propping herself up, she offered her mischievous goblin taunt. "You're such a babe in the woods, Tessa."

"What's that supposed to mean?"

"Ken Montgomery doesn't want to be your buddy, and he doesn't want you to be his matchmaker." The Irish assassin pooched out her lips in a kiss. "He's probably undressing you in his head right now, and using his gun as a distraction—if you know what I mean."

"Not everyone is a sex maniac like you and Sam." Tessa glanced over at Ken who turned and raised his chin at her before placing his weapon back in the holster. "He's a friendly guy is all."

"Men aren't friendly unless they want something. He hasn't been coming onto me in a while?"

"What?" she gasped. "You and Ken?"

"A couple of times." There was a devilish twinkle in her eye. "I think I was a little too…" She tapped her cheek as if trying to come up with the right word.

"Stop. I don't want to know. He's a good man. Be good to him. You could do so much worse. There's a really sweet side to him."

The smile didn't waver. "Hmm. I know. It was delicious, too." Tessa rolled her eyes and tried to stand but, the assassin used her legs to trap her body in a vise-like grip. "He'd make a better husband than Chase. Whatever the captain promised you is a lie, a moment of weakness. You're holding onto a mirage, Tessa. I'm telling you as your best friend."

Tessa had never said anything concerning Chase wanting to marry her. The tick from her fluttering lashes and a red heat trailing up her face, revealed her discomfort. In order to free herself from the woman's legs, she patted them gently and stroked them like she was a spoiled pet. Honey released her.

"Thanks for the tip. I'm thinking there isn't one of us at Enigma that is marriage material."

"Doesn't mean you can't let off a little steam," she said, nodding toward Ken. "How many men have bedded you, Tessa? I'm guessing two and Chase isn't one of them."

"I don't talk about my sex life."

"Because you don't have one," she teased. "We talk about your sex life all the time."

"Why can't we ever discuss anything except sex, violence, and weapons?"

"Give me a break, love. I can envision you nodding off in your Sunday School class."

"I love my class."

"I bet your favorite story is when King David had Uriah the Hittite sent to the front lines during battle because he could have his wife who was pregnant with his child. Poor slob was killed, of course."

The woman knew the story?

"Or maybe the story of Samson who was horny enough to give his secret of strength to the sexy Delilah who delivers him on a silver platter to the Philistines."

"I'm shocked you've read the Bible," Tessa offered flippantly.

"Are you kidding? It's full of tales of treachery, betrayal, war, sex, redemption, second chances, angels, demons." She sighed. "That Eve chick from the Garden of Eden will be in my crosshairs when I go to meet St. Peter."

"What makes you think he'll let you in those pearly gates after going over your hit list?"

She smiled sweetly. "If King David and Samson made it, I'm a shoo-in." She swung her legs over the side of the bed and watched a man coming through the door. "Look alive. The director is headed this way and appears to have been sucking a lemon."

When Tessa turned to see the man approach, he raised his chin then tilted his head for her to follow. He paused long enough to snarl at Honey then over at Ken. "Meeting in ten. Make sure the others are there."

"Yes, sir, right—" before Tessa could finish, he'd stormed out of the building like a rampaging bull.

CHAPTER 16

شهيد

Director Benjamin Clark stood at the metal podium like an American eagle ready to swoop in and devour his next meal. Tessa had always thought he resembled one, and although the director pretended to find her comment disrespectful, he rarely complained.

She had stumbled into a hornet's nest several years ago, landing at Enigma under suspicion of terrorism. The only thing that stopped him from handing her over to the FBI was the way his team reacted to her, especially Captain Hunter. When the captain laughed out loud at her naïve and flippant retorts to their questioning, they realized he was human after all. She'd managed to give him the slip by faking a lost contact lens, of all things. In the process, she put a Marine in the hospital, escaped her handcuffs, and managed to avoid them catching her when she left.

Perhaps it was the blatant disregard for Samantha Cordova's inflated superiority complex that won him over the most. She was both beautiful and intimidating, and the way she flirted with the captain gave Tessa the impression there might be an inappropriate relationship going on in the workplace. But it all changed the day Tessa dropped into their laps. Samantha, or Sam as everyone called her, made no bones that her idea of a good day would be to pour honey all over Tessa then dump a bucket of fire ants on her.

When Sam had been put in charge of Tessa's physical

conditioning and training, the director wondered if it had been a good decision. Although the Grass Valley housewife was more of a PTA president than a researcher for a group of shady agents, he had to admit she gave as good as she got. In spite of the constant volley of insults and threats between the two women, there had been times when he noticed respectful gazes between them, a whisper or smirk that indicated a lot of their bashing was more show than what went on between them when none of the men were watching or listening.

Although Sam was the dominant manipulator, Tessa was the sneaky friend who could easily have gotten away with murder. All she had to do was bake a batch of her chocolate chip cookies and offer them with one of her innocent smiles. He often wondered if she weren't the more dangerous of the two, mostly because no one ever expected her to lie, cheat, or break the law.

The Enigma team entered slowly and took their seats, spacing themselves out over several rows like a bunch of backrow Baptists during Sunday service. He knew full well the space between them provided opportunity to watch expressions, or lack thereof, keep people who they should trust at arm's length, and plot their own course as to what needed to be done.

Pretending to be the good girl she most certainly wasn't, Tessa sat in the front row with a pad of paper and pencil. Sam and Honey sat in the second row, one on each end, with folded arms across their chests, pretending to be bored out of their minds. Zoric sat in the back row with an open switchblade he usually dug under his fingernails. Carter sat in the middle of the third row behind Sam and Honey and did his best to engage them in conversation until Sam told him to "shut his pie hole," and Honey tilted her head seductively to blow him a kiss.

The last three, Vernon Kemp, the resident tech genius, along with Ken Montgomery, and Tom Cooper trailed in last and sat various places. Both soldiers surveyed the room as if it might hold explosives or a hidden camera. They didn't appear to have a life outside of Enigma and were loners for the most part. Having served in the military, this job probably gave them what they missed—action.

Vernon, the youngest of all the agents, enjoyed creating acts of terror on the Pentagon, FBI, and CIA for fun. He didn't jeopardize national security but resembled more of a killer whale playing with a seal before he decided to eat it. Tessa had tutored him in the ways of women and how to approach them. She appeared to be the only female that didn't make him stutter or lose his train of thought. He'd forget himself from time to time and call her Mom, much to her delight, and would pinch his cheek and invite him over for dinner.

In spite of being shy and backward when it came to dating, he was a dangerous man in front of a computer. Over the years, he'd showed promise as a field agent and earned the respect of his teammates. It always amazed the director how Vernon could ski like a bat out of hell or disarm a terrorist without batting an eye one minute then have Sam wink at him only to turn into a stuttering mess.

"Listen up," the director said, standing at ease with his hands behind his back. "As you know by now, we are here to locate possible chemical weapons and Chase. He was put in place watching Prince Muhammed's niece, the rock star, Soraya. It was all part of the plan that has gone wrong. Not unusual, of course. That's one of the reasons the president uses us."

The silence of life or death fell upon the group. Once more, the director measured their unspoken willingness to take care of this latest threat as well as rescue Captain Hunter. Although they often butted heads with him, the respect and admiration outweighed their propensity to follow their own path. They made a good team.

In his deep, slow voice, the director spoke. The podium was void of notes. He rarely used them.

"We now know there were three, possibly four chemical weapons along with materials to make other explosive devices, much like the one used in Oklahoma City in 1995. The first one was a small chemical device, destination unknown. We're still thinking it was an accident. Unfortunately, the Bedouins minding their own business paid the price. We now believe a traveler stopped and was welcomed into their camp. Whether he belonged is still unknown."

He pointed to Tessa, who added her two cents worth. "The hospitality with this group is legendary, and it is not uncommon for strangers to be welcomed into the Bedouin home. Because of the dangers and hardship of the desert, these people have fostered the approach of courtesy and respect."

"Although Bedouins also now reside in urban settings," the director went on, "Many continue to remain isolated. Encountering others is cause for celebration." He nodded to Tessa. "Thank you for the thorough report." She beamed a look of pride his way as if he'd praised her in front of the class.

"So, what went wrong? Do we know?" asked Ken Montgomery.

"Speculation is it was unstable, perhaps leaked, and detonated too soon. The FBI specialists in this area believe this to be the case. It was secured in a duffle bag, in a container so flimsy, it could have been opened by a curious child. And that we believe, given the position of the bodies, may have been the case. A small unidentified body, badly burned, to the point of unable to identify gender until an autopsy was performed, helped us reach this conclusion."

"Do we know where the weapons headed?" Honey piped in, leaning forward.

"No. What we do know is that Prince Muhammed, the future king of Saudi Arabia, had planned a visit to several Bedouin groups to garner support in advance of taking the throne. He doesn't want unrest, or dissatisfaction to cause any kind of insurrection when and if the time comes for him to be king. He's trying very hard to be a hero to the people he rules. Having said that, the prince had already canceled his trip the day before he planned to visit several camps. It's very possible this was going to be an attempt on his life."

"How do you know there's more chemical weapons?" asked Ken.

"Chatter in the usual social media outlets, a few people embedded with groups opposed to the royal family, and the usual I-hate-everyone groups popping up since the fall of ISIS. Our recent intel suggests they are planning to point the finger at Israel having a hand in this." A heavy silence fell on the room, knowing the director's brother was now the Prime Minister of Israel. "Or vice versa, dragging the United States into the game. I don't have to tell you Israel has been an ally for a long time, and we would respond without hesitation. I have been assured by the prime minister they are not involved and want to get to the bottom of this as well. They have been tracking several groups from Uzbekistan."

"Uzbekistan? Do they have an ax to grind with Saudi Arabia?" Sam chimed in.

"Tessa, could you take over now? Maybe you can explain the background and cultural nuances of this situation."

She rose and carried her clipboard to the podium then nodded to the director. "Thank you." She always thanked him for anything he asked her to do. He couldn't help but let a hint of amusement toy with one corner of his mouth while trying to level the steely eyed "don't screw up" he gave everyone on the team. Stepping back gave him more opportunity to watch the expressions of the men and women who once more volunteered to lay their lives on the line for the country.

"To answer your question, Sam, as of last year, the Uzbekistan government were in negotiations over an economic stimulus package to assist in their continued infrastructure growth," Tessa stated. "Doesn't appear to be an issue. Same for Israel. Jews that have settled there since escaping from the Nazis in World War II have found the Uzbek people to be hospitable, with no outward hatred of their culture. Even today, Jewish people speak highly of their experience."

"Where does this leave us, then?" Sam continued. "We know they were a huge asset during the early years of the Afghanistan war."

"They aren't the problem so much as the environmental situation." She pointed to Vernon who punched a few keys on his laptop. The white board in the front of the room came to life with a map of Central Asia. She used her fingers to zero in on Uzbekistan and pointed to what used to be the Aral Sea. There were two slides side by side: one with a huge body of water, the other only a slice, making it look more like a river.

"This is what the Aral Sea looked like a century ago. This is what is left. The Russians used a great deal of it for irrigation projects. There wasn't much thought put into long-lasting environmental concerns or the economic livelihood of the fishermen who had used the sea for generations. To make things worse, on several islands within the sea, the Russians used to conduct experiments on biological and chemical weapons back in the day when they ran things under the Soviet flag. Turned into a dumping ground for failures. Now that the sea is dried up to what you see here, it's become a shopping mall for terrorists."

"You can imagine the effects of communities along what used to be the sea when dust storms hit those wastelands," the director continued. "Cases of cancer, even smallpox surfaced. Those stories don't get told in the news media. However, we are confident these makeshift weapons began with the harvesting of potent elements from the careless dumping of lab rejects. There's money in terrorism."

"And when your family is sick or starving and someone wants you to harvest dangerous materials, it appears to be a means to resolve an already-dire situation," Tessa added. "No one is going to rat them out to the Russians or anyone else if they make more money in a few hours' work than they could earn any other way in a year. There is no love lost between the Uzbeks and Russians, although many Russians still live there."

"So, who are the other players? Iran maybe?" asked Ken.

"Maybe. Iran and Uzbekistan have a tenuous relationship. In spite of both countries being Islamic, Uzbekistan isn't as fundamentalist. Women have more rights and opportunities as reflected in the Gender Equality Act passed several years ago. Don't get me wrong, it is nothing like the West, but, compared to Iran and Afghanistan, it's paradise."

"Thank you, Tessa." The director pointed for her to take a seat.

As she settled in her seat, he spotted Ken watching her with admiration. He hoped that wasn't going to be a problem. The man was bullheaded, not so different from the captain who controlled him on a short leash. When she sat down, Ken shifted his attention to the director with a narrowed gaze. It was as if he knew he might be taken to the woodshed for admiring the backside of the "hands-off" princess of Enigma. The director also knew Ken well enough that it really wouldn't make any difference.

The director's cell phone buzzed, and he pulled it from his shirt pocket. Pulling it free, he glanced at the number. Before answering it, he waved off the others. "Let's take five. Coffee in the back."

As the team rose from their seats, the director held the phone to his ear. "The hell you say!"

CHAPTER 17

شهید

Roman Darya Petrov was known by several names, the Tribesman in Afghanistan, and here it was Khan. He stood in the deep darkness of a Syrian night that wasn't so different than in the high mountains of Afghanistan, except it wasn't as bone-penetratingly cold.

He looked skyward to see what looked like a bouncing moon and a few scattered stars through the clouds. Next, he refocused on Amir's camp where several men stood guard at each end. He nodded toward his soldiers who immediately left on stealthy feet.

Unlike Amir's men, who stood relaxed and smoking, Captain Hunter positioned himself in the middle of camp and behind an overturned vegetable cart the size of a small car. His body had remained statue still for the last hour. The other four shuffled their feet and chatted, their voices traveling on the night breezes to dangerous ears.

When he had left the captain before, he'd wondered if death would take him from the drugs. Perhaps the shot saved him. Why he cared confused him more than he wanted to admit. The respect he now held for the captain mingled with the jealousy he also carried, knowing they shared a love for a woman who neither deserved or might ever fully possess.

Captain Hunter had saved his life in Russia and stayed beside him while he lay dying. Darya had willingly given both him and Tessa permission to find a life together as he took what they thought was his last breath. A few scientists and Director Benjamin Clark of Enigma knew the truth. It had been touch and go for weeks, but he fought hard. The last year had been a miracle only to realize he was a hunted man and marked for death.

He spotted the fall of Amir's men and his own people stepping in to replace those positions, donning their outer garb in case anyone came to check on them. Then a pistol pressed into the back of his skull.

"So, you are alive," Captain Hunter said, stepping back to let Darya turn to face him.

"I underestimated your ability to spot us." Darya didn't raise his voice or his hands to strike a defensive pose.

"I smelled a skunk."

"I didn't think Syria had skunks."

"They don't. That's how I knew it was you." Chase lowered his weapon to his side then grinned. He glanced to where his men had taken up positions. "You know I'll be blamed for this. Are they dead?"

"Depends if they struggled. Does it matter?"

"You see a cockroach, step on it is what I've always said. However, I don't think Amir will be happy I'm still alive if his future martyrs are being picked off one by one."

"I see your point. You could come with us." Darya took a position next to Chase, paying close attention to the camp. "Or we could finish all of them off here and now."

"One thing I've learned is Amir is not in charge. I don't know who is, but that numbskull couldn't find his way out of a paper bag. He's a bully and gives orders as if he's a badass, but deep down, he's another cockroach doing another man's and, very possibly, a woman's bidding."

"Woman?"

"I think it is Soraya. She has the connections from all over the world, including inside Saudi Arabia. Her uncle is the next king, and taking him out at the appropriate time—well, fill in the blanks from there. Amir was his right-hand man for a time and now is playing house with the prince's niece. He thinks he's what the country needs, but I'm sure Soraya has her own agenda." He paused and shook his head in disgust. "What they did to those young women…"

"I know you tried to save them all. The rest are back home or soon will be."

Chase nodded as if satisfied and relieved. "Thank you. And Naza. Did she…"

"She is strong. I took her to a doctor to make sure the baby was well." Darya heard the weathered soldier exhale as if he'd been holding his breath for too long. "She says she will name it after you." He elbowed Chase. "I think the child won't be the last one to carry your name in the future. Those women told us what you did for them and how you suffered for it."

"Let's change the subject. As long as they're okay I'm good. But I swear, in the end, I'm going to kill those pigs who touched them."

"Tessa." The name was always on the tip of his tongue. Speaking it to the captain pained him.

"What about her?" Chase's voice took on a bland tone, as if he didn't care.

"She is here. Enigma is using her as a pawn. I don't like it." Darya turned his focus away from the camp and stared at the man who he once hated but now respected. "She will pose as a representative of the Red Cross to try and see Soraya. Word is she's being held against her will and others are also being held."

"Soraya is up to her eyeballs in this and hardly a captive. As to the others in the film crew, I'm the only one who survived, to my knowledge. If there are others, I don't know where they are. They think I'm helping them now and plan for me to publicly make a statement to renounce the infidels of the world along with the great Satan, the United States."

"Do you know where they are keeping the weapon?"

"We are moving tomorrow and Amir is beyond giddy. Soraya mentioned a medieval castle in western Syria. I suspect it will be there. How they intend to deliver it to the intended target is still a mystery. I'm hoping to persuade Soraya to trust me on the information."

Darya lowered his gaze to the ground. "How is Tessa doing now that she thinks I'm dead?"

"It's been a tough year, Darya. She grieved for you and, if the truth be told, still loves you. Although I know she loves me, too, there is no way she'll desert you a second time. And I won't keep your secret from her. Her happiness is what is important. I promise you, if I survive this, I will protect and love her, but I won't lie. If she wants to be with you, then I will extend the same protection and honor to you. I'm ashamed I didn't see you for the man you were when we first met."

Darya smirked remembering how they had fought. "Well, what fun would that have been. I needed to be put in my place and I enjoyed you trying."

"I kicked your ass, and you know it," Chase reminded him.

"We have always seen things differently. But I must insist you keep my secret a little longer for the safety of this mission." He paused as he straightened his body. "I am a marked man. I've become a ghost to those who hunt me. Tessa will be safe if I am thought to be dead. And I trust her with no one except you. I know she loved you first, Captain Hunter, and the reason she isn't with you now is because of your ethical sense of honor. Those obstacles have been removed."

"Except she is still legally married to you."

"That can be fixed. Your director promised he would take care of it. He has the papers. Please keep my secret for now. Who knows if either of us will survive the evil of this world? Wear this," he said, handing him a tiny button. "It will let us know where you are headed. My people will follow. Vernon's skills created this. Attach it on the inside of your clothing. When it is activated, the director assured me they will know."

Darya watched the captain slip the tracer inside his T-shirt. "Happy? Now get the hell out of here before Amir returns."

"I have eyes on him, and he is occupied for the night with the devil you call Soraya while his men stand guard and amuse themselves." Darya took a fighting stance and, before Chase could lift his gun, the Tribesman kicked it from his hand then landed punch to his rib cage before dropping him with a spinning back kick to the jaw. He tumbled onto the ground like a deflated blow-up clown. "You let your guard down, Captain Hunter." He let his satisfaction show in his amused voice.

Chase wiped the blood from the corner of his mouth then moaned as he grabbed his side. "Damn it, Darya. My ribs were just starting to heal." He gasped for breath several times, followed by a moan as he struggled to rise.

Extending his hand to the captain, he realized the vise-like grip was stronger than expected. Chase jerked him off-balance so that he fell forward. He braced his fall, only to feel long legs wrap around him like a boa constrictor. Before he could react, Chase knocked his arms out so his head bowed to come within inches of his face. In the split second of surprise, Darya felt his body rolled to his own back with the soldier now on top of him and a serrated blade held to his throat. The blade nicked his skin, and he wondered in that moment if the American officer had indeed switched sides. The anger and darkness in his face, now inches from his own, gave him warning the man was sick, both mentally and physically.

The two men stared at each other, measuring the possibilities and outcomes of their actions. Neither exhibited fear of the other.

"I'm kind of glad you didn't die, Darya," Chase said, rolling off and pushing slowly to his feet.

Darya stared up at him as he touched the trickle of blood on his throat. "I'm kind of sorry I didn't let you try and finish me off when you were so close." When Chase offered his hand, it was waved off. Darya sprang up and evaluated his equal. "Now I'm going to have to hurt you."

"I know. Just wanted you to know I can still best you on my worst day. Whatever you're going to do, can you make sure I'm not lying out in the rain?" Lightning flashed across the sky like spiderwebs. "Wouldn't want to get pneumonia on top of everything else."

One of Darya's men approached and tossed him a rifle. "You are in no position to make demands." The follower reached over and relieved Chase of the weapon now in his holster. "It is hard for me to say this, Captain Hunter, but it is good to see you."

"I know what you mean. Please don't say, 'This is going to hurt me more than it is you.'"

"I won't." Retribution filled him as he pondered his options. There had been a lot of bad blood between them. In a burst of speed, the Tribesman landed a blow with the butt of his rifle into Chase's gut then to the side of his head as he fell forward, unconscious. He caught him with one arm around his back then lowered him to the ground. He turned to two men who now walked up. "Drag him from the camp then torch this place." Thunder rumbled as lightning made flashes behind scattered clouds. "I want Amir to know I'm coming."

CHAPTER 18

شهيد

The director entered a Quonset hut at a brisk clip with the aide assigned to him. At one point he stopped abruptly, causing the corporal to crash into his back. He turned in slow motion to level a gaze that would have changed the course of the Mississippi River.

"I'll wait outside, sir," the corporal said. "Your protection detail is already waiting."

Benjamin nodded then continued the penetrating glare at the young soldier who backed away. Before the director reached the door, one of his detail pushed it open and stood at attention, focusing straight ahead. The director was well aware of the rumors to stare into the eyes of The Eagle, was to find yourself on the end of a mixed bag of being sent to the front line of some third world hellhole, KP duty, sparring with whatever special forces happened to need to blow off a little steam, or spending the winter counting brown bears on the Aleutian Islands.

The director was a retired United States Army general and still responded in kind when one of the men saluted him. He would always be military to his core and didn't make apologies for it. Enigma had flourished under his leadership. It had been a smooth transition from giving orders to troops to the misfit geniuses he now commanded.

"Sir," one of the protection detail dared speak as he approached.

He handed him a tablet with information displayed. "The people you see are Kurds. Just arrived from Syria. They were brought here by our people on the border. Because they are Kurds, it wasn't disclosed to the Turks they were here."

He took the tablet and glanced over the facts then handed it back to the lieutenant. "Thank you."

"Would you like for me to—"

"No. I can take it from here," he interrupted and let the soldier pivot away.

He saw them sitting stiffly in metal chairs as if they were prepared to make a run for it. The only one who stood was a woman of slight build dressed in mismatched camo fatigues with a long black vest overlay. Her head covering had slipped back off her dark hair and fell to her neck. Unlike the women sitting in the chairs, she held her head high and met his gaze with contempt and self-confidence. When Ben opened his mouth to speak, she stepped forward and stretched out her hand.

"I am Peshmerga."

Ben was surprised at the grip of the woman. "Benjamin Clark. How can I help you?"

"It is I who have come to help you, Director. But that can wait." She nodded to three young females who stole glances their way. She motioned for them to stand and come forward. "They are three we rescued from the man you know as Amir."

One of them was a little girl. The second one was a teenager, and the one who stood tallest appeared to be pregnant. He wondered if she'd been raped during her captivity. Rage surged through him at the inhumane treatment of women in part of the Middle East, and especially with terrorists' groups such as ISIS and Amir's ragtag group of idiots.

"Ladies." He didn't want to frighten them by stepping toward them. "Welcome. I understand you have been in the Amir camp. I'm glad you are now safe. We will make you comfortable until your family arrives to take you home. I'm told they now reside in this country."

Naza offered a shy smile. "I did not know this until Peshmerga found us. They tried to escape Syria many times. We were separated and taken to Amir. My husband helped pay for our return. Do you know when they will arrive?"

"I'm sorry. No. The Turkish government is very cautious of the Kurdish people and want to make sure you are not a threat and that your family isn't involved in any mischief."

"I understand."

"I will do my best to speed things up, if possible. However, I need a little information from you."

Peshmerga took a step forward. "Excuse me, but Naza requests one of your agents be present."

Ben pulled his shoulders back and tilted his head. "And who would that be?"

"Tessa," Naza whispered. "I want to talk to Tessa. My words are for her."

With a snap of his fingers toward the lieutenant and lifting his chin toward the door, the request was set in motion.

"Thank you." Naza extended her arms, and the other two girls hurried to be folded in them. "These are my sisters, Yadi and Rozerin. They speak a little English, thanks to your Captain Hunter."

"You know Captain Hunter?" Hearing the man's name was enough to get his heart pounding. "You've seen him?"

"They are very tired, Director." Peshmerga stroked the cheek of the youngest. "I will tell you everything you should know after this Tessa comes," she said in a haughty tone. "So, please be patient."

The director resented her request. She reminded him of one of the rebel soldiers, maybe one of the Daughters of Kobani. Those women were tough and didn't take orders from a man who demanded everyone snap to attention with not much more than an arched eyebrow.

"Of course." He pointed to a small card table set with bottles of water, cheese, crackers, and a few pieces of fruit. "Please help yourselves. I'm sure you must be hungry."

The little one bolted forward but Naza held her back. "We will wait for Tessa."

Ben nodded and pulled Peshmerga aside so they could talk quietly. "Who are you really?"

"We have a mutual friend from Afghanistan. Some call him a ghost."

They were standing off from the others and spoke in muffled voices but continued to steal glances toward the door, then the three, who once more took their seats.

"The Afghan that goes by Khan? How is it that you know him?"

"He fought with a few of us, and I decided to help him when asked. We knew these butchers were taking people and children for their perverted pleasures and to make money. Naza's husband found us several months ago after they had been taken. We had nearly given up hope of finding them. Captain Hunter was in the last camp we checked. I believe you already know this."

"Is he still alive?"

"I believe so. Amir does not trust him and will kill him once his usefulness is over. The woman, Soraya, we now believe, is behind the plan to use these chemical weapons to encourage the Americans to get sucked into another war they cannot win."

"Any idea where they are keeping the WMD?"

"I have not seen our mutual friend for several weeks but received a message last night that Amir's camp burned to the ground. This will force them to keep moving. Rumors are they have a place ready called Krak des Chevaliers, a castle in Western Syria."

"I've heard of it. A series of tunnels beneath an ancient city that have been used to hold prisoners."

"Correct. Amir knows little of how vast this network is or of its reach. But keeping prisoners there is easy because of the prisons built into the wall of tunnels. It is a dangerous place, even if you know what you are doing or where you are. It is not impossible however to navigate through these tunnels if you have someone to guide you."

The door creaked open with the same soldier who'd held the door for him earlier, standing at attention. Tessa moved inside, wearing sunglasses. He was taken aback once more, seeing her dressed in fatigues, hair pulled back in a bun on her neck, and a confident stride in her step as she moved toward him. Where was the young housewife who was scared of her shadow and thought spiders should be labeled a weapon of mass destruction?

The once apple-pie-and-all-things-innocent woman had disappeared in Tessa Scott. She had toughened up both physically and mentally. Enigma had thrown her to the wolves of the world, and she'd survived. The cost had nearly destroyed her several times: ruined her marriage to the father of her children, stranded her in Afghanistan with the Taliban hot on her trail, introduced her to the corruption of people she had always trusted, and served her up on a silver platter to a man known as the Tribesman in order to get information and support. She'd married him and loved him for a short time, only to lose him, too. There had been many other things she suffered for the love of country. Maybe she did it for a man named Captain Chase Hunter. Everyone at Enigma knew there was a cat and mouse game going on between the two.

"Director Clark? You sent for me?" Tessa had taken to standing at attention when she addressed him if strangers or soldiers were in the room. Other times, when they were alone, she treated him like a beloved member of her family. She'd called him an "ole sweetie" once. He'd fumed over her choice of words. She'd promised never do it again.

"This is Ms. Peshmerga. Sorry I don't know your last name," Ben added in an unapologetic tone.

"Peshmerga is enough."

Ben didn't appreciate her sudden rigid posture as she focused on his agent. "This is Agent Tessa Scott."

Peshmerga's expression changed from unreadable to contempt when she examined Tessa from head to toe. Although his agent wasn't rude, her nostrils flared, and she clenched her jaw several times. Neither woman extended a hand of welcome.

Women. It was probably a good thing they didn't rule the world. Otherwise, they'd move all the men underground and use them only for breeding purposes.

Tessa cut her gaze back to him as if waiting for further instructions. "Sir?"

"Yes. I have someone who wishes to speak to you. Follow me."

The young women eased to a standing position and held hands once they approached. They whispered to each other but stared at Tessa in expectation as Ben introduced each one.

"You are Tessa?" It was Naza.

"Yes. The director says you wanted to see me?"

The three spoke to each other in their native tongue for a few sentences then apologized. "Sorry. We are so excited to meet you," Naza gushed with excitement.

"Me? But why?"

"Captain Hunter sends you a message." The Kurdish girl

sobered.

Ben stepped up next to Tessa when she became a bit unsteady on her feet. Naza laid a hand on her baby bulge. "My unborn child will be Chase. I wanted you to know this when I tell you the rest."

CHAPTER 19

شهید

The mist of leftover rain was cold, and his body throbbed from being punched. The memory of Darya smashing the butt of his rifle into his gut caused him to pull up his shirt to find yet more bruises. With a touch to his aching head, he discovered dried blood. Then the pain in his hip and ribs returned with a vengeance, and he vomited on the ground in a mud puddle. He retched a second time when he watched several dead men being dragged to an open ditch and slung inside.

"Ahh. You're alive. I was afraid I'd have to bury you with the others." Amir resembled a caged tiger that paced back and forth. He stared out across the field then behind him where the camp smoldered. "I will tell you, Captain Hunter, this is very disturbing. How is it you are alive and my men are dead?" He stopped his pacing long enough to glare at him as he propped one hand against a burned-out truck bed. "What do you have to say about all this?" He glanced over his shoulder at the curls of smoke and spotty fires that sent clusters of sparks up when a piece of wood shifted.

"Karma is a bitch?" he said flippantly. When Amir appeared puzzled, Chase took another approach. "Your fan club got out of control." Chase shook his head in disgust. "I think the leader said he was being a ghost."

Amir jerked his chin up as he squinted. "The Ghost of Kobani.

Yes. I've heard of him. He's a coward who sneaks around like a woman."

"I see he left a calling card," he said, pointing to the side of the truck out of Amir's line of sight. "Let me see if my Arabic is still any good. 'Death to the pig Amir. I'm coming for you.'" Chase shrugged. "Or something like that."

Amir appeared to reread the words several times before hustling back around the truck where he could quickly take a position of safety. Chase managed a quiet snicker, but his ribs hurt, and he needed pain meds to get him steady. No use in ticking off his pharmacist. He would hold out as long as possible before he had to ask—or beg, which would be the case since Amir was in a mood.

He shoved his hand in his pocket and found two pills. Even though he didn't know exactly how it might affect him, he knew the pocket was empty the night before. Darya left him this comfort to manage the pain. The sky opened up, dumping a hard rain. Popping the pills in his mouth then tilting his head back, he let the rain wash them down his throat. He followed Amir to a military vehicle that had seen better days. But it was dry, and he was wet.

"We'll leave soon. I hope you can wait until we reach our next destination to get dry clothes. How long have you worn those?" Amir sniffed in disgust then laid on the horn over and over until the rest of the men loaded up in the remaining vehicles. "Get out. You stink."

Chase climbed out like a misplaced sloth from a rainforest canopy. The truck had a canvas cover over the back and was already loaded with impatient men. Two extended a hand and pulled him up to a seat on the end, completely exposed to the rain. He gathered his collar up and prayed he'd live long enough to see Tessa one more time. His body was weak and failing. How much fight was left in him was hard to measure.

Along the way, he fell asleep or unconscious, he wasn't sure which. The soothing voice of a woman stirred him awake. He found himself dry, warm, and lying in a soft bed covered in slick sheets that smelled of honeysuckle. Candlelight flickered, causing shadows to dance along the walls.

"Ahh. My sweet Chase lives." Kisses dotted his forehead, and a cool hand stroked his naked shoulders. "I am here, my love. I have missed you."

His vision focused on the dark-haired beauty bending over him. "Soraya."

~ ~ ~ ~

Tessa stared at Naza's belly then up at her young face. For the first time in a long time, she felt old. The rumors of Chase's romantic and sexual exploits had come home to her since the day they'd met. The two of them often made light of how exaggerated they were—well most of them.

"Tess, most of what you hear isn't true," he'd assured her. "There have been very few romantic involvements. I don't have time for such nonsense. Three dates, and they're ready for me to meet the parents. No thanks. When that happens, I bail."

"I want you to be happy," she'd insisted. "Settle down. Have a couple of kids."

He would moan then kiss her on the temple as he stole one of her fries. "Get rid of that husband, and I'm yours. And you come with three kids to boot. You're the whole package. I'll even meet your parents. Robert's a waste of oxygen, and you know it."

This led her to defend the father of her children out of a sense of obligation. Eventually, it got harder to do because they drifted apart, thanks to Enigma. Or was it because of Chase? They did a lot of pretending at first. Lunches on the university mall, sitting next to each other in meetings, which led to being partners during research or missions. Next came the accidental touching that lingered longer than necessary.

During the growing familiarity came Roman Darya Petrov, half Afghan-half Russian, who stepped in and took what Chase thought would eventually be his whenever he decided the time was right. The Tribesman, as everyone called him, was a thorn in Enigma's side, but she didn't care. She went to great lengths to defend and believe in him.

The Enigma psychiatrist, Dr. Wu, explained she suffered from Stockholm syndrome: the feeling of trust or affection experienced in cases of kidnapping or hostage-taking by a victim toward a captor. She never believed the explanation applied to her. However, the man did a number on how she perceived things, both good and bad.

Then Darya died, leaving her to pick up the pieces of a shattered life. Chase had been there for her when he wasn't saving the world. The kids loved when he dropped by or played ball with them. Through it all, even when she was with Darya, her love for the American hero never faded. He had become an impossible dream a long time before Darya. As long as he didn't get involved with another woman for more than a few dates, Tessa was content to believe he might discover how much he loved her.

Staring at Naza, the dream felt as if it had shattered again.

Tessa swallowed hard, her eyelashes fluttering nervously. "Oh? You're carrying Chase's baby?"

The girls giggled as Naza covered her reddening face. "No. No. I was pregnant by my husband when Amir caught us. The captain protected us, protected me by telling Amir it was his baby so no one would touch me. He claimed my sisters, too, so they would be safe. None of the girls suffered with him watching over us." She looked warmly at Tessa and took her hands in hers. "He is a good man."

Tessa exhaled and fought back tears of relief by nodding then raising a stubborn chin. "I know. How did you escape? Why isn't he with you? Is he all right?"

"No," Naza whispered then released Tessa's hands. "He is very sick. Those horrible men beat him when he fought for us. But he always win. He bring us food—for the baby, he says." She laid her hand on her stomach. "They give him drugs."

"Drugs?" Tessa's stomach lurched. "What kind of drugs?"

"For pain. Now he must have them. Sometimes he did not think right."

"I don't understand."

"He talk to me like I was you. He would smile and asked me if I remembered things you did together. I always listen, but I did not understand."

"Who rescued you, Naza?"

"I did," Peshmerga snapped. "There were several of us, a few men who wanted to help and a few others like me. Captain Hunter was in bad shape. He was near death, in no shape to travel, and we couldn't take a chance on missing our opportunity to rescue so many women. We planned to return for him, but..."

"You left him to die!" Tessa stormed.

Director Clark stepped forward and grasped her arm. "Peshmerga, let's speak privately away from these ladies. They look tired and I'm sure they are hungry." He continued to grip Tessa's elbow, a sure sign he was sending her a signal. "Could you help them and maybe show them where they can clean up and take care of any personal needs?"

"Yes, sir."

The director's brow had furrowed. This usually meant he was smoldering or worried; in this case, it would likely be concern for Chase. Her own heart was beating so fast, she thought she would hyperventilate.

Tessa led the young women to the restrooms and assisted the youngest. It felt good to have a little one to help. Leaving her children for the sake of national security was getting old. At least they were with their father and had no idea what she did for a living. Neither did Robert.

She had to demonstrate how to use the liquid soap dispenser. They washed their hands over and over, laughing and exclaiming about the softness and water mixture. Finally, Tessa had enough. "Naza, what really happened when you were rescued?"

Naza slowly dried her hands on a rough paper towel.

"Peshmerga didn't tell me the whole story, did she?" Tessa asked.

"No. There was a man who led the rescue. He was dressed like others I'd seen in the terrorist groups, but he was not the same."

"What do you mean?"

"He was not from here. His eyes different. Like the people from the East. Captain Hunter knew him."

"Was he a terrorist? Maybe ISIS?"

"No. But the captain was confused. Say he should be dead. If he not come, the captain would have died. This man gave him a shot and saved his life. I know Amir must have been very angry we escaped. He is very jealous of the captain. Another woman keeps asking for him. Amir doesn't like it. Threatens to kill him all the time, but he show no fear. But I could tell this man who rescued us gave the captain much concern. He promised to return for him."

"You said the captain had a message for me."

"He wanted you to know he loves you. All the time, he talk about you. You are the one who kept him alive." She stepped closer and whispered, "Peshmerga angry when the man who rescued us asked about you."

"Me? How does he know me?"

Naza shrugged. "He spoke of you by name. Peshmerga fought with him afterward. I think she might be his woman, but the man ignored her temper. She did not want to bring us here, said there was too much to be done."

"Then what happened?"

"He say she would help me find Tessa or he find person who could follow orders. We hid for several days with the Daughters of Kobani fighters. The leader went back several times to check on him. But he always came back without him. I don't know what happened then. I'm sorry."

A chill crashed over her body. How would anyone here know her? That could be problematic. Who else was working this mission? But the worst of it was Chase might be dead.

CHAPTER 20

شهيد

The candlelight flickered when the door opened, followed by sounds of soft footsteps moving around the room with pungent, nutty aromas. The earthy scent of cumin reminded him he should eat to stay strong. The outline of a woman wearing a hijab or headscarf. He knew it covered long dark hair streaked with red dye. The dappled light made the dark-blue fabric sparkle along her neck and shoulders. Her tight camo-styled shirt and pants left nothing to the imagination. Soraya loved making an entrance.

Letting his body stretch to release tight muscles caused pain, but he'd experienced worse when he first arrived. He'd eased himself down on the bumper to escape the confines of the crowded truck. It was an accomplishment to not have fallen flat on his face. Several men pointed toward a building where points of light showed in small circles within the structure. It took everything he had to put one foot in front of the other as he followed the others inside.

In another life, the structure must have been a place of government or residence of a high-ranking official. The scars of war had left holes in the walls, crumbling plaster, and the debris abandoned by people who wanted to escape. Once upon a time, it must have been grand, and he wished he could read the history of such a place.

Amir stopped and called out. Then Soraya materialized out of nowhere, fuming in her usual diva tone. Her voice, that most of the time irritated Chase, stopped. Part of him was relieved she was safe, and at the same time, wanted to kill her for playing house with Amir. As hard as he fought it, fog then blackness overwhelmed his consciousness. She called his name, and he reached for her as she rushed toward him. But his body had had enough, and he collapsed.

How long ago had that been? He vaguely remembered waking up in Soraya's care and then slipped back into unconsciousness. Even in his dark state, pain lurked for a while. Now he felt nothing. Once more, he'd been drugged.

Pushing up on one elbow, he waited for the room to stop spinning long enough to swing his naked legs to the floor. At least he wore clean boxers, and a ragged T-shirt. His body was clean, with all traces of dirt and blood from his wounds gone. Touching his temple, he winced at the tenderness.

A fleeting thought swam up that he would even the score with Darya next time they met. The man took too much pleasure in both saving him and dishing out more pain. Darya could have killed him at any time to clear the playing field for Tessa. Although he'd agreed to keep the Tribesman's secret from her, that didn't set right with him. If she found out, their relationship would be doomed. When this was over, he wanted to know why he'd been kept out of the loop regarding Darya's resurrection. There was no doubt in his mind, Director Benjamin Clark was behind the deception. But why?

Chase didn't realize he'd been staring at the floor, puzzling over the pieces that didn't fit together in his life, until Soraya's shiny combat boots, probably purchased at a high-end store in the States, appeared in front of him. The camo fatigues had a sheen to them, free of wrinkles. As his inspection trailed slowly up her legs, her fingers pushed through his hair gently.

"Ahh. There you are. I was so worried about you, my love." Her hands slid down the side of his face and lifted it to gaze up into her own. She lowered her lips close enough Chase could smell a hint of jasmine. After landing a kiss on his forehead, she pulled his face into her breasts and sighed. "We must be very careful. Amir is a jealous man, and especially of you, since he knows I favor you."

Chase pulled back, feeling suffocated from the smell of her.

"Where am I?"

"Krak des Chevaliers, which means Castle of the Knights." She tugged him to his feet. "Fitting, don't you think?"

"How so?" His legs felt stronger than he expected. Although he was shaky at first, he attempted to walk around the room.

She followed slowly, watching him carefully, as if he might not be up to the task. "Well, you are kind of a knight in shining armor, like the famed crusaders in Syria and Palestine. At one time, it was occupied by the Kurds, which makes me very proud. When you're stronger, I'll give you a tour. It is one of the most notable and surviving examples of medieval military architecture."

"And where exactly is this place you're so proud of?"

"What does it matter?" She shrugged. "You aren't going anywhere. Amir says you're one of us now, so you'll have plenty of time to acquaint yourself with our base of operations."

"I'm guessing you're also one of Amir's lap dogs now? Guess I put too much confidence in your judgement."

A sigh escaped her dark-red lips. "Enough talk of Amir. At times, I find him a bore and very lazy when it comes to making love." She slipped her arm around his waist and adored him with her penetrating gaze. "Unlike you. Even beaten and pumped full of drugs, you know what I want, Captain Hunter. I simply will never let anyone else have you."

"Good thing I'm available," he growled, more from a sudden pain in his hip than her words. "Surely you don't expect me to share with Amir?"

"I like the sound of that," she cooed. "I want to watch when you hurt him."

"You're one sick bitch, you know that?"

"Unlike Tessa?"

Chase frowned down at her and pulled away. A new kind of pain clutched his chest, realizing the woman he loved was in more danger than he imagined. The next time he saw Darya, he would insist he get her out of harm's way before these maniacs got ahold of her. Only Darya had the power to protect her now.

~ ~ ~ ~

The director had the three Kurdish women escorted to guest

quarters to wait for their family. Several of his security detail made sure they were comfortable then stood guard afterward. The Turks didn't trust the Kurds because of their terrorist activities against the government of Turkey. The sooner they left for their new homes, the better. The director had arranged a transport for the entire family to the Netherlands, where they would be met by an organization who handled these sorts of displaced families from war-torn parts of the Middle East. She wasn't sure where they would go next.

Tessa wanted to tag along to make sure they wanted for nothing, but the director ordered her back to the conference room to wait for his briefing. Peshmerga stood patiently beside him, glaring at her with contempt. She ignored the silent snub and returned to her friends.

"What's going on?" Carter stepped forward first with Zoric on his heels.

The others formed a semicircle, different degrees of concern on their faces. Tessa knew they weren't going to like what she told them. They were a lot of things, most either borderline sociopaths, poster children for obstruction of justice, or addicted to breaking the law and getting high without getting caught. It was all fun and games to some degree. But when it came to Captain Hunter, their loyalty and ability to follow commands was beyond reproach. In spite of disagreements, they regarded his word as gospel. They trusted and respected him more than anyone. He'd led them through fire many times, and they'd survived because of his leadership.

With a sigh, she shared what she knew, and, at one point, Honey stepped up and stood beside her as a show of what she imagined, as invisible support. Then Sam stepped forward to touch her arm lightly and take her place on the other side. Determined not to break down and cry, she felt safe in the moment, knowing they were her friends. Their strength became hers. Maybe if the men weren't present, they would shed their badass persona and hug her. That was exactly what she wanted, but the two women would see her as weak. Tessa looked from one to the other, and accepted this small token of sisterhood.

The silence was deafening. Would NORAD sound similar if they went to DEFCON1 for nuclear war. She loved this family of misfits and brainiacs, daredevils and career soldiers. They were preparing for their own kind of war to bring Chase back. Their solemn faces gave her reassurance and determination.

Her self-control was about to be tested when Peshmerga walked into the conference room.

~ ~ ~ ~

Amir couldn't hear what they were saying, but it was obvious Soraya loved playing the dutiful nurse to the American captain. The smell of food cooking on the stove wafted into the corridor where he stood. He'd given her the last of the meat to make a stew. Vegetables had been purchased in the village surrounding the castle, but it wasn't much. The food he and his men had been eating the last few weeks was not fit for the heroes they'd become in a few days. The best selections and portions always went to Soraya. She insisted on being kept in the manner to which she'd become accustomed.

"Do you want me to appear emaciated when I go before the cameras and call our brothers and sisters to rise up? They will think I've been starved into submission."

He had agreed that wasn't the wisest move, yet he wanted to find a way to make her submit. No matter how he tried to intimidate the woman, she managed to tangle him up in her wiles and make him beg for more. Watching her stroke the captain's head and shoulders drove him mad with jealousy. Was she planning to escape and take the American with her? Or was this a plan to embarrass her uncle, Prince Muhammed? Enough was enough.

Pulling out his automatic weapon, he stormed into the room and pulled the trigger.

CHAPTER 21

شهید

Peshmerga wandered into the conference area and motioned Tessa to follow her. The woman was attractive in her loose, mismatched clothing. The headscarf draped carelessly around her dark hair and exposed neck. The angular face and round eyes reminded Tessa of the pictures of kittens she used to save in her school notebooks. Below the narrow nose, her dainty mouth gave her a girlish appearance. Tessa guessed her to be in her late twenties. However, this kind of life aged a person at a rapid speed. Although the Kurdish woman came across earlier as hard and obstinate, Tessa understood war, deception, and death could initiate a no-nonsense personality and appear unapproachable.

"Peshmerga. Is something wrong? Are Naza and her sisters okay?"

"Yes. They have been reunited with their family. Her husband was very appreciative."

"Where will they go?"

"Your director has provided a way for them to go somewhere in the US. I believe he called it Nashville? Said there was a place called Little Kurdistan there."

"My parents live outside Nashville. And yes, you are correct. Most of the Kurds there immigrated from Iraq and Iran, I believe."

"That will be good. They will first stop in Europe where a group is standing by to make final preparations, thanks to Director Clark. I believe Naza's father lived in Iraq before escaping to Turkey then Syria. He will be of great help to your military and to the director after they settle in their new home."

"Thank you for telling me." Tessa took a step back, thinking the conversation had concluded until the woman grabbed her by the wrist.

"What did Naza tell you about the rescue?"

Tessa glared down at the woman's grip then pried her fingers off and jerked her arm back. "Careful, Peshmerga," Tessa warned. "She said you were assisted by a man who was friends with Captain Hunter. Care to explain that to me?"

With a hooded glare, Peshmerga lowered her chin like a bull ready to charge. "He is a rebel leader for my people and a friend to the women soldiers I lead. I didn't mention it earlier because the captured women were traumatized enough. Naza and Captain Hunter had a"—she arched her eyebrow— "special relationship, it seems. He protected her and the sisters and, in return they, as well as, the others, I'm guessing, showed their appreciation to him."

"I think you're trying to see if I'll be upset at your suggestion Captain Hunter had a physical relationship with those women."

"Are you?"

"No. I think you are upset because the man called the Ghost of Kobani, who saved the captain's life, has an interest in me." Tessa pulled her shoulders back and pooched out her lips in impatience. "More of an interest in me than in you, according to Naza. Who is this ghost, and how does he know me?"

"I'm not sure. Maybe through his friendship with the captain. That's all I know. He refuses to discuss it." The others in the room stood at a distance but continued to steal curious glances their way. "The Ghost and Captain Hunter carry secrets I know nothing about."

"Does the Ghost have a name?"

"Khan is all I know."

"Khan?" Tessa felt herself getting irritated. Was this a joke? "That is used in northern Afghanistan among tribal communities. Is he an Afghan?"

"You ask a lot of questions? Maybe you do know him."

"All the Afghans I knew of any consequence are in prison or

dead."

"I heard the captain refer to him as Lazarus. Does this mean anything to you?"

A chill ran from her toes and moved like a wave up her body until she shivered to shake it off. "Why do I get the impression you're trying to unnerve me?"

"I want no harm to come to him. He has done my people a great service. He sent me here with Naza. I want to know why these men think you are important."

"Maybe, if you had rescued the captain, he could have answered your questions."

"It was impossible. Besides"—she lowered her voice—"Khan returned to follow the movements of Amir. I am here to assist in the mission. I can help."

The sound of scraping chair legs against concrete floors drew Tessa's attention when the door opened for the director. The narrowed glare he offered in her direction meant the conversation with Peshmerga had been terminated.

Tessa took a chair in the second row next to Vernon, since she always felt a certain amount of calm with him. There would be no challenges to her abilities, and he certainly wouldn't say things with double meanings. He was too shy to make her uncomfortable since he thought of himself as one of her family.

When Peshmerga sat at the end of the first row, she turned to stare at Tessa until Honey kicked the back of her chair.

"Eyes front," she ordered.

Peshmerga turned in her chair and snarled at the Irish assassin then faced the director. Honey crossed her arms across her chest and stretched out her legs before winking at Tessa.

"She scares me," Vernon whispered.

"Try sleeping with her."

When the young tech genius shot her a bewildered glance, Tessa held up her hand.

"No. It's not what you think."

He blinked several times. "And I wasn't saying you should sleep with her." She patted his forearm. "Please never do that." At his nervous gulp, she covered the amusement toying with the corners of her mouth.

"Let's begin." As usual, the director's voice held the warmth of a cold rain. He had a knack for making a chill creep up her spine. The others never appeared to be as affected by his hard gaze and direct words. At their first meeting, several years earlier, Tessa had learned the director wasn't a man to take lightly. However, there had been times, when they were alone, he was calmer, and gave the impression he held affection for her welfare. If the other team members were present, then she was treated accordingly.

"Thank you, Peshmerga, for bringing word of Captain Hunter."

She nodded to the director.

He went on. "Although the captain has suffered under Amir's control, he has been given medication to alleviate the pain. There is a good chance he has become addicted to painkillers as a result of his injuries. With his help, and that of Peshmerga's people, a number of Kurdish women were rescued and returned to their families." Once more, he nodded to the Kurdish woman sitting stiffly in the metal chair. "Thank you." He sighed. "Although he has been a captive, Amir believes the captain has betrayed his country to join the efforts of his group to wreak havoc on the free world. We fully expect for Amir to be the one to put the WMD in place and perhaps activate it. It is likely he plans to use the captain to assist him or be the one responsible for the chaos and devastation that follows."

"How do we find him?" asked Zoric who had been the captain's friend longer than any of the other team members.

"Here is what we know. With the help of Peshmerga, and a number of rebels, they have been able to track Amir and his people who are moving to the southwest. Our boys put a drone in the air and spotted movement of what we believe to be his convoy four days ago."

"They're headed for Israel," Sam breathed. Tessa couldn't determine if she was concerned because of the world-wide consequences or because her on-again, off-again, lover was the Israeli leader.

"Actually, Krak des Chevaliers is a medieval fortress, approximately 40 kilometers west of the city of Homs, close to the border of Lebanon. Although it is old and suffers from the effects of time, it remains an impressive example of Crusader architecture. Amir could hole up there for a long time without fear of attacks from a number of enemies."

"The SEALS or Delta Force could be in and out with a few strategic explosives, and his goose would be cooked," Ken Montgomery offered. "Hell. I could do it."

"It's a World Heritage Site and UNESCO would cause more trouble than it's worth, considering they would throw up roadblocks to prevent us from doing anything. I'm sure Amir is aware of this and taking the fortress will ensure his plans won't be interrupted. Fortunately, we've convinced them it is in their best interest to send us the schematics of several fortresses in a hundred-mile area. The only one that fits the needs of Amir is Krak des Chevaliers. Vernon will download the layout of the castle to your devices. He'll also include your scripts and cover."

"And the singer, Soraya?" Tessa interrupted. "Do we know what happened to her?"

The door squeaked open in the rear of the room, causing everyone to turn. A man dressed in an olive-green flight suit stepped inside. He removed his dark sunglasses and stared around the room as if he owned it. A thin dark beard outlined his narrow face and the blue beret gave his tan-colored skin an added softness to his high cheekbones.

"Soraya is playing a dangerous game," he said in a nonchalant tone. "Unlike your Captain Hunter, she is not patriotic to anything except herself. My sources say she is a willing participant to Amir's plans. By using her notoriety as an international star, Amir is convinced the world will be watching."

As he stepped forward, Tessa eased out of her chair and watched him slip into the row of seats behind her. He leaned over and took her hand.

"Agent Scott. We meet again."

He lifted her hand to his lips and kissed it, before sandwiching it between his other hand. "It is good to see you, Prince Muhammed." It never occurred to her the Crown Prince of Saudi Arabia had just ignored the most important person in the room, Director Benjamin Clark.

CHAPTER 22

شهید

They all had their assignments, and the situation was about to get real. Carter would head to Israel to meet with the powers that be about the possibility of sending in air support when the escape plans were activated and the WMDs neutralized. Hopefully they would make it out alive. He hung back to walk with Sam. It took a great deal of willpower to act nonchalant and cavalier around her on any normal day. Knowing she was going to a hellhole in search of his best friend and a chemical weapon caused him an unusual amount of dread and anticipation.

Over the last couple of years, a growing attraction had sprung up between them. Maybe it was from being partners on numerous missions. Or had the brief sexual encounters meant more than just blowing off steam in a stressful situation? Until Tessa came along, he'd always figured she and Chase would end up together, but he showed little interest, claiming he didn't think it ethical to get involved with one of his team. Along the way, Carter imagined Sam as more than an Enigma partner.

Now he was headed off to Israel to negotiate with a man who had a relationship with Sam. He continued to be one man she'd spent the most time with over the last couple of years. Not only was he the prime minister but the half-brother of Director Benjamin Clark. The director frowned on the relationship but not enough to end it. Sam's ability to gather vital information because of their romantic involvement seemed like a reasonable trade-off. Men melted at the first sight of her and became willing to share information for just a little more time with her. The woman was a she-devil and used every trick in the book to get what Enigma requested. It was all a game to her; one she knew how to win.

Several incidents had changed the trajectory of the relationship between Carter and Sam. The first was when they pretended to be husband and wife in Botswana to complete a mission. Next came the whole discovery of American scientists missing in Russia. He rekindled a relationship with a tempting female astronaut he once worked with on the International Space Station. There were a few moments when he could have sworn Sam was jealous, making him see for the first time what a relationship with her might mean.

"You're awfully quiet," Sam said offhandedly after they picked up his duffle bag at the Quonset hut. They approached a Jeep where a driver waited for him. He continued to take long strides, keeping his attention focused on the plane he'd be taking to Israel. "What did you think about Chase?"

He managed a shrug. She hurried to step in front of him, causing him to collide into her chest. Refusing to step back, he stared into her catlike eyes that reflected both fire and ice. "Talk to me."

"Do you have any endearing words you want me to deliver to your lover in Jerusalem? Figured that's why you're following me around like an obedient puppy." Another poor choice of words. Sam didn't follow anyone in a submissive style. "If so, be quick about it."

"Oh yeah. Almost forgot. Tell him the diamond earrings were lovely," she cooed.

Carter squinted and tensed up. How could he compete with such gifts? "Anything else?"

"Also, tell him to expect a return box with, thanks, but no thanks." Sam sobered as she reached up to touch the blonde hair around his ears then let her fingers trail down his jaw. "It was a bribe to get me back. He isn't what I want. I thought you knew that."

"Everything is one big game to you, isn't it?"

"Yes. Except for one thing. You. I don't want to—"

Carter dropped his duffle bag and jerked her into his arms, kissing her mouth with the pent-up passion he'd been carrying around far too long. Her arms circled his neck and encouraged him to continue. The sound of the Jeep horn broke them apart, but their lips still touched.

"I'm afraid for you this time, Sam. This could go wrong in so many ways, and I'd never see you again."

"Then you better make sure you rescue us when the time comes." They fell into an embrace that felt new. "I don't know how to do this, Carter."

He stroked her back and kissed the side of her head. "Just give me a chance. We'll figure it out."

"Okay." She placed a quick kiss on his lips. "Carter, the prime minister will be difficult. Promise him whatever you have to in order to get his support. Do you understand?"

"I'm tired of this kind of life, Sam. The deals, lies, and sacrifices…"

"Last time. When this is over, can we go away for a while? I'm tired."

"We all are. Hell of a job we chose. Keep your head down, and don't let Tessa shoot you in the butt." He grinned.

"I'll play nice if I have to."

One more short kiss then he ran to the Jeep, more energized than a few minutes earlier.

For the first time since he took this job, his future might be taking a turn for the better.

~ ~ ~ ~

Gilad Levi was a formidable man, both in stature and power. His influence as a leader and former soldier resonated around the world. The intense scrutiny he gave to the most minute of details was legendary when it came to the battlefield or politics. Political leaders found themselves treading lightly when it came to decisions made for and against Israel. World War II bestowed a certain amount of guilt on European countries for what they ignored concerning the Jews. The prime minister was not shy about wielding that weapon if it got him what he wanted.

The difference between him and Director Benjamin Clark was

the director was an American citizen and the prime minister was not. They shared the same father but didn't share a mother. Although adopted by his stepmother, he'd spent half the year in the US and the other half in Israel with his father. The boys grew up with a love for both nations and knew someday, each would play a role in protecting the other. Maybe the time was now.

Carter Johnson ran all these things through his mind as he waited several hours to have an audience with the prime minister. Both General Ginsburg and Dov Kemper, head of Mossad, had met him at the airfield earlier in the afternoon, sour-faced. Pleasantries were exchanged, with the two Israelis taking turns at asking the former astronaut about his work with NASA and was it true Area 51 had an alien ship.

"All true," he said mischievously. "Seen it myself. The alien didn't die though. In exchange for his help, he now runs new project development at an unnamed aeronautics company. But you didn't hear that from me," he whispered then pretended to look over his shoulder as if checking to see if anyone was listening.

"Very funny. You Americans are never serious about anything," the general quipped.

"Yeah, well, that's what happens when you're the biggest badass on the planet, I guess." Carter slipped an arm around the general's shoulder, much to his disgust. "Lucky we're on the same side, I reckon. Sure do like you boys," he drawled in his Texas accent. He fist-bumped Dov on his sleeve. "Now, what do you say you take me to your boss and let me chew the fat with him a bit."

The general removed Carter's hand from his shoulder as Dov dusted his jacket from his touch. "The prime minister is very busy. He'll try to fit you in."

Carter squinted at each of the high-powered men then slapped his hands together. "Excellent. No worries. You might want to tell him it is a matter of life and death."

"Life-and-death matters are an everyday occurrence in this part of the world. I doubt that will get you in any faster."

"You might tell him I have a message from Dr. Samantha Cordova when he decides to make a little time for me. Oh, and be sure he knows it's me, will ya?"

Both Israelis exchanged concerned glances but didn't address the matter further. Carter continued to whistle the song "Yellow

Rose of Texas" then put several pieces of gum in his mouth and proceeded to try and blow bubbles, only to have them pop. He knew his cavalier attitude was getting on their nerves, especially when he asked about landmarks they passed.

"Home of the three great religions of the world," he commented. "Judaism, Christianity, Islam. Never been here before."

The important Israelis sat on each side of him as two beefy-looking characters chauffeured them through the city. Their obvious inattention to all the world heritage sites they flew by, as if withholding any thought of enjoyment, forced him to be cynical, edged with obnoxious ignorance.

"Always wanted to see the Church of the Nativity. Think we could do that?"

Dov turned a cold expression his way. "That is not in Jerusalem. You are thinking of Bethlehem."

Carter started humming "Oh Little Town of Bethlehem" before blurting out, "If I'm not mistaken, a Muslim family holds the keys to the church."

"It is tradition."

"Tradition." He couldn't resist a big grin and cleared his throat to belt out another song when Dov gave him a warning.

"If you plan to sing 'Tradition' from Fiddler on the Roof, I will shoot you, then bury your body at the Alamo with your ancestors who couldn't leave well enough alone. Now, be a good washed-up astronaut and shut the hell up."

Carter shrugged. "Ouch. You don't know what you're missing."

"I expect I do," Dov mumbled.

In spite of the car flying through traffic like a bat out of hell, Carter pretended to take in the sights by stretching his neck one way then the other. The two men ignored him, staring straight ahead as if he were not there. To add to their irritation, he pulled out several travel brochures from inside his flight jacket and thumbed through them, turning them this way and that as he extended his hands enough to invade their personal space. Once both men leveled a dangerous glare at him. He spotted the recording device in the car.

"Oh. Sorry. I'm just so interested in your great country." He made an effort to fold the brochures, but they wouldn't fit back inside his jacket, and dropped them, only to fumble on the floorboard to pick them up again.

The driver slammed on the brakes, throwing him into the back of the hard leather seat, head-first. He was completely off the seat when the general grabbed him by the collar and jerked him to a sitting position.

Carter shook his head and, in his best Elvis Presley imitation, he said, "Thank you. Thank you very much." To his surprise, he caught a slight smirk from the driver in the rearview mirror.

They slowly moved through an underground parking area until they reached concrete doors, which were opened by more-serious-than-a-heart-attack-looking men in black suits. As Dov and General Ginsburg scooted out the door, Carter tapped the driver on the shoulder.

"Thanks for the ride, buddy. Might ease up on the sudden stops. You're a lawsuit waiting to happen." The driver raised his chin and responded in Hebrew, giving Carter the impression, he'd been told to F-off. "You, too," he said, adding his middle finger as a parting gesture.

Once outside the car, Carter made it a point to stretch while he took in the surrounding area. His scoping things out in a nonchalant way probably wasn't lost on these guys. They wrote the book on being observant and never missing the slightest hint of trouble. Probably why their nation had survived surrounded by countries who hated them.

The concrete door opened with yet another set of guards wearing Men in Black attire, one of whom announced the prime minister would be going to dinner soon. He had made room in his schedule for Carter who'd once worked with a brilliant Israeli astronaut at NASA in the glory days of the space shuttle. In order to prepare the man for flight, Carter helped him improve his English. Turned out, they learned from each other. His Hebrew was more than a little rusty, but it felt like it was all coming back now.

After a short elevator ride followed by a number of security checks, Carter followed his escorts down several halls. Not only did they need retinal scans and body X-rays but also a breathalyzer for each person in the group. Once he passed with the appropriate bells and whistles, he found himself in an office decked in a mix of contemporary and traditional furnishings. He recognized the man sitting at the desk. They first met in DC when he accompanied the prime minister as his assistant.

Carter stuck out his hand. "Daniel. Good to see you."

The secretary shook the hand warmly. "It has been a long time. It will be a few more minutes. I believe my boss is talking to his counterpart in Russia. You know how they are—always want something for nothing. I understand you are on their hit list."

"Heard the same thing about your boss. But what do I know?" Carter slapped Daniel on the back good-naturedly. "Ahh, well, bullies are always making threats. Anything happens to me, and the world will know what they did to all those scientists they kidnapped. He'll be a good boy. Not worried at all."

It was common knowledge that Carter and President Austin, both from Texas, were big buddies. Sharing intel, sitting in front of a cozy fire at Camp David after a dinner with the family, probably wasn't out of the question. From the way Daniel's eyebrow arched and his smile faded, Carter imagined the man made a few mental notes to pass the slipup on to the appropriate people.

Daniel shot a narrowed look to Dov and the general as if to question whether they knew anything about a threat on the prime minister. Carter wanted to tell them he was just messing with them, but the inner circle of the prime minister rarely had a sense of humor. He had to get it out of his system before he came face-to-face with Gilad Levi. The guy could be intimidating as hell, and he wanted to be on his game.

A tiny light on Daniel's desk changed from red to green, and he stepped toward the inner-office door. "I'll check to see how the prime minister is doing with his schedule. It shouldn't be much longer, Carter."

He gave him a thumbs-up and flopped down in one of the more cushioned chairs. Dov and the general remained standing. Spreading his arms out then behind his head, Carter pretended to admire the room's elegant style instead of searching for security cameras. He could almost feel the probes measuring his body for a funeral suit. "Take a load off, boys. Not like I'm going to hightail it out of here."

"You Americans have such a way with words," General Ginsburg snarled.

"Ain't it the truth," he responded, taking the gum out of his mouth. "Where can I put this? Don't want to appear uncouth in front of your boss." Dov swiped a tissue off Daniel's desk and held it out for Carter. After placing it carefully on Dov's hand, the director of Mossad folded it and put it in his pocket. This in turn made Carter chuckle. "Lots of spit in that piece of gum to add to your DNA profile on me. Need anything else?"

"Perhaps you would be up for the new games we've created for uncooperative prisoners. I think you would find them very interesting, and it would indeed assist in our research. Always in the market for a kidney, too."

Daniel opened the door and motioned for Carter.

He quickly stood and smoothed his clothes. "Maybe another time. Looks like I'm up. Thanks for picking me up at the airport." He extended his hand, and Dov gripped it, only to feel Carter tighten his hold. "Next time you're in DC, let me know, and I'll be sure to stay home."

This time, Dov gave him a thin smile fit for a black mamba. "If I'm ever in DC again, I doubt very much you'll know about it."

Carter wanted to make a retort about never being able to find a cockroach when they hide all the time, but Daniel cleared his throat as warning it was time to move along.

As soon as he passed through the doorway, he spotted the prime minister standing at the bulletproof windows. It reminded him of his brother who often did the same thing at Enigma. The director once said it cleared his head and helped him see a way forward. If anyone needed to see their way forward in a dangerous world, it was the prime minister of Israel. Carter pulled his shoulders back and tried not to imagine him with Sam. The age difference alone confused him as to why she found him to her liking.

"Carter Johnson." The prime minister pivoted and stepped around his massive desk, stretching out his hand.

"Sir." Carter hurried to grasp the show of friendship. "Thank you for seeing me. I understand I'm holding you up from a dinner. I apologize."

One corner of the prime minister's mouth turned up as he moved to a wingback chair in front of his desk, motioning for him to do the same. "Saved me from a boring evening with a bunch of climatologists wanting Israel to do more." He threw his hand up.

"Or was it less? Hard to say." A heavy sigh followed. "So, what is going on that Enigma has sent one of their fair-haired boys?"

Somehow when he said the description, it sounded like a slur. Carter decided to take the high road and not let the man get to him.

"It's my understanding President Austin has informed you of the possible chemical weapons attack. At first, we thought it might be intended for the US, but recent events suggest it will be in the Middle East."

"Yes, your government has been very forthcoming about the threat. It is much appreciated. We are taking precautions, of course and understand Saudi Arabia may also be in jeopardy." He displayed a devious smirk. "Wouldn't Iran just love that, having both their enemies destroy each other and they couldn't be blamed. Needless to say, even if the intended target was us, the US would get involved, since we are allies."

"Hopefully we can find the WMDs before that happens."

The smirk continued. "Your track record for finding them is less than stellar if I remember correctly. If the full force of the United States military couldn't find them in Iraq, then what makes my brother, or the president, for that matter, think Enigma can find it?"

"Well, our Grass Valley commando usually says we have divine intervention."

"Ah. Tessa Scott. Yes, I forgot about that little bumbling housewife."

"Not so bumbling anymore. Dr. Samantha Cordova saw to that." Carter enjoyed watching the smirk fade off the prime minister's face. "Our little 'bumbling housewife,' as you call her, managed to save Crown Prince Muhammed's life, all by herself."

"Very surprising, considering her skill set. Of course, I always thought the prince a big baby compared to his father. Probably didn't take much to push him out of the way and let gravity take its course. I'll say one thing, the woman had an abundance of luck."

Carter opened his mouth to speak, but the prime minister held up his hand to stop him. "I forgot—divine intervention. I never figured you for a religious man, Carter."

"There's something else you probably didn't figure on."

"What's that?"

"Samantha is in Syria by now looking for Captain Hunter. She is leading the team, impersonating envoys of UNESCO. With any luck, our Grass Valley commando will have plenty of divine intervention to sprinkle on my—partner."

CHAPTER 23

شهيد

When Soraya screamed, Chase tackled her. Adrenaline pumped through his veins, enabling him to get his wits about him. Amir suddenly appeared when the curtain jerked back, waving a loaded gun. His gut told his body to react before his brain registered what was happening.

"Get up," Amir shouted angrily.

The shots had peppered the upper wall, indicating he never intended to kill them, only put the fear of Allah into them. Mission accomplished. Chase managed to pull himself up onto the edge of the bed then reached down for Soraya. She clamped onto his hand as if her life depended on it. Catching her breath, she pulled herself to a standing position and glared at the crazy lover she'd created. Although painful, Chase forced himself to stand. Taking the sudden spill on the floor had done nothing to make his hip and ribs feel better.

"Put that thing away, you crazy idiot. You could have killed me." Soraya fumed.

Chase noted he hadn't been included in the being-killed part of the scenario. The next thing he knew, Soraya was running into Amir's outstretched arms. Thankfully, she pushed the outstretched hand with the gun pointing at him, down to his side before nuzzling his neck.

"No need to be jealous, my love. Just trying to get the captain ready for his intended job." She backed away and cast Amir a smug expression. She might be suffering from a kind of psychological condition—a mixture of being a pathological liar and a heavy dose of narcissism. "Do you really want to kill me?"

Amir's eyes became so hooded, Chase wondered if he were high. "You make me crazy, Soraya," he admitted.

She stroked his face then added a quick kiss to his lips. "I've made something special for you. Eat with us. Let's clear the air. I want my two favorite people to be friends." Leading Amir to a chair at the makeshift table, she gently pushed him down. She motioned for Chase and leveled a haughty look of disgust and mouthed the words, "I'm sorry."

For a split second, he felt empathy for the clueless Amir, knowing he was being played. From the way the man was breathing and exploring Soraya's body with his appreciative stares, it didn't take a rocket scientist to surmise three was definitely going to be a crowd. He had no desire to watch what appeared to be unfolding. "You know, why don't I give you kids time to catch up? I could use some fresh air and to stretch these muscles." Could they discern his tone of sarcasm, or was it too much to hope for?

"Good idea," Amir said, laying his gun on the table before gazing up at Soraya as his hands circled her body and pulled her forward.

The woman certainly didn't need Chase to rescue her. Chances were good she'd orchestrated the whole thing to measure each man's worth. He was betting the poor slob would suffer her wrath before the night was out, and she would demand a gift for letting him near her. The one thing Chase cared about at this point was whether she believed in his interest in her well-being. Maybe he did on some level. For whatever reason, she'd kept him alive when Amir, at first, had wanted him dead.

He grabbed his jacket from the chair next to the door and exited as Soraya complimented and expounded on the strength and virility of the other crazy person in the room. Moving down the corridor lit with candles dripping wax so that it resembled waterfalls, he became aware of the grand fortress where he now hid. Although cracks and missing pieces of stone scarred the path he explored, it was free of debris. Arched windows looked out over a vast landscape under a sunset streaked with purple and pink.

His increasingly muddled thoughts shifted to Tessa and wondered what she'd say about the sky. The pain in his chest came not from his ribs this time but his heart, knowing she probably would never forgive him for betraying her love by being in the clutches of such a despicable woman as Soraya. If she was to be believed, he'd taken advantage of her several times, although those memories were shrouded in whispers, dim light, and drugs given as a reward for something he couldn't remember. One thing for sure, Darya needed to reveal himself to Tessa and take her home.

Thinking of her in the Tribesman's arms again gave him a familiar pain, but deep down, he knew how much the man loved her and would do whatever it took to keep her safe. Promises be damned. If he had to lose her because of this doomed mission, then he took solace knowing Darya would make sure Tessa returned to her family.

But for now, he wanted to pretend she stood next to him overlooking history created by the Crusaders and a myriad of other people who occupied this once-great land. He could smell her hair and sense her feathery touch when she wanted to show him a discovery. The laughter escaping her dainty mouth and the way she batted her eyes when she tried to tell a lie gave him pleasure, although it hadn't always been true. As he often did since being separated from her, he remembered drowning in her blue eyes the first day they met and how she'd outsmarted him at every turn. Even then, he couldn't get enough of the gullible and naïve Grass Valley housewife.

It took him too long to realize the emotions and confusion he felt when she was present was not a new illness. The process of falling in love often caused him to believe he was developing a heart condition. For the first and only time, he'd become consumed with her safety, or that's what he'd told himself to justify being near her. His ethical conduct as an officer kept him from being a home-wrecker, although on more occasions than he cared to admit, he plotted her husband Robert's demise.

The fact that he spent more time with her than the father of her children did gave him a false sense that it was enough. He'd played it cool to the point where she tried to fix him up with her friends, got him to tell her about his latest conquest, and listened to why he wasn't married yet. He pretended to flirt with her every chance he got with no success.

That is until they were in Africa pretending to be husband and wife. She frustrated him to the point where he lost control and embraced her long and hard, kissing her with more passion than he thought possible. They both came close to death. Afterward, they had danced a dance of avoidance, afraid of what might be happening to a friendship turned upside down. Tessa would never hurt or leave her husband. She was committed to saving their struggling marriage. That meant they had to slow things down and be more nonchalant about their budding relationship.

Then Russia happened, and the Tribesman, Roman Darya Petrov, stole her, never giving a second thought to whether anyone else might get hurt. All Darya wanted was Tessa, and he would do anything to make it happen, even if it meant betraying his country, destroying what Tessa believed to be true, and convincing her only he could give her the love she craved. Now, here Chase was in Syria, breathing the same air as the woman he longed for in his life, knowing Darya desired the same thing. This time, he would surrender to the Tribesman. No way he would come out of this a whole man, probably not even alive. Darya would be the ultimate winner.

~ ~ ~ ~

Dinner had been cold by the time the team made their way to the mess hall. No one made small talk. Tomorrow would be the beginning of the end for what Tessa suspected was another opportunity to outwit the witless. The more she came into contact with the evildoers of the world, the more she realized there was a high degree of stupidity in those who wanted to control with terrorism.

While pushing her food around with a disposable fork, she glanced up to watch Peshmerga devour her food with gusto. A part of her grasped the idea the woman might be hungrier than she'd ever been in her entire life. The group Peshmerga led, Daughters of Kobani, were known around the world for their fighting skills, ability to outwit, out shoot, and demolish the enemy. She'd seen them featured on popular news shows over the last few years.

What they didn't cover was how often they went hungry, got wounded without much in the way of medical help, were cold, and had no place to sleep but on dirty floors and missed their families.

"Want my dessert?" Tessa pushed her pudding to her.

She nodded as she dipped her spoon in and ate.

The others had said their good nights and wandered off, leaving her with the Kurdish fighter. Pouring herself a cup of coffee, she took one sip and realized it was cold. When Peshmerga chuckled, Tessa sent her a bewildered frown.

"I'm sorry. The people I fight with would love coffee even when cold. You are very lucky, Agent Scott, to have so many comforts. I know little of this kind of life."

"I know. I'm sorry for the way I treated you earlier. I'm worried about Captain Hunter. He means a lot to me. You took a great risk coming here considering the way the Turks have treated you and your people over the years. I appreciate the information and how you took care of Naza and her sisters."

"Of course." She finished the pudding and sighed with satisfaction. "I have never had this before. I like it very much. I wish I could share such a thing with my sisters on the battlefield."

"I'll see what I can do when this is over. Come on. I'll walk you to our quarters. It isn't much, but the sheets are clean, and you can take a hot shower."

They exited the mess hall into a chilly wind of evening. The moon was unusually bright. Although Tessa pulled the collar of her jacket up closer to her face, Peshmerga walked casually, unaffected by the temperature difference. It was a little embarrassing when she tripped over her own feet and felt the grip of the Kurdish woman's hand on her arm to steady her.

"Thanks." Tessa stopped and gazed up at the sky. "I guess I should stop pretending everything is going to be okay."

"What do you mean? We will do our best to find the weapon."

"I was thinking about Captain Hunter and how he would take my arm when I stared up instead of where I'm going. Those moments turned into special moments for me. The touch of his hand. His nearness. The careful attention to my well-being." She sighed. "Now I wonder if he thinks of me when he sees a sunset or the moon."

"He means a lot to you."

"Yes."

"My friend talked to the captain about you."

"How does your friend know me?"

Peshmerga took a few seconds to answer, but continued to walk. "He would not say and I was told to never speak of it again. Maybe they served together in Afghanistan."

"Maybe." Tessa figured this man known as the Ghost and Khan among his men sounded like every other man she'd met in Afghanistan. In her opinion, a goat had more value than a woman. Captain Hunter knew a lot of people in the country and was welcomed to many villages.

"Were you there?" Peshmerga asked.

"Yes. As I said earlier, everyone I knew of any consequence is in prison or dead."

"When the Kurds lose a fighter we say, martyrs never die."

Tessa nodded. "Captain Hunter told me that when he was getting ready to come here. What does it mean?"

"It is our job to honor the fallen because of their bravery and service. By thinking of them, honoring them, even beyond death, their memory never dies. Martyrs never die."

"This I understand." Tessa opened the door to her quarters. "Thank you, Peshmerga." As the woman stepped through the doorway, Tessa touched her arm. "I have someone I'll never forget, too. He martyred himself for my team and our country. He'll always be in my heart for what he did."

Peshmerga raised her chin and leveled a hard stare then nodded as she disappeared into her quarters.

Tessa turned to stare up at the moon once more.

CHAPTER 24

شهید

Prime Minister Levi picked up his intercom phone and told Daniel, his secretary, to make arrangements for his next meeting to be delayed another hour. He never wavered from his penetrating gaze toward Carter Johnson while speaking.

Part of Carter found it amusing and wanted desperately to crack a joke about the powerful leader not being able to control the comings and goings of a woman who toyed with his affections. The sane part of him knew better than to tick off the man who had spies, assassins, and Mossad in every nook and cranny of the world.

Except for a slight flaring of Levi's nostrils and his eyes changing to a darker shade of gray, there was no abrupt response or angry outburst. The man was too smart to let emotions show on an impending national threat, so it stood to reason he wouldn't come unglued discovering his love affair with Samantha might be in jeopardy because she had slipped into Syria. He probably was wondering whose head he needed to remove for failing to notify him of this bit of information.

"Guess she didn't mention it," Carter said, leaning back in his chair.

Levi let a devious show of amusement toy with one corner of his mouth. "We don't talk much when we're together. Other things come up, if you know what I mean."

Carter felt like a bucket of ice water had smacked him in the face. He had to fight the rising jealousy and disrespect of a world leader, to remember what was at stake. "Really? From what I hear, she's been a great asset to your brother."

The condemnation for him showed in his eyes. "That street runs both ways."

This time it was Carter's turn to grin. "You keep telling yourself that, sir."

"Why are you here? I'm sure it's not to discuss your continued frustration with me getting more attention than you with your Samantha infatuation. It is what it is. Let's move on, shall we?"

"I will be requesting support in a few days. I'm thinking since Iran has been behaving themselves the last few months, you won't need your F-35I stealth fighter jets on standby to scare the crap out of them. I, on the other hand, could use a little backup."

"Backup. And would you be flying one of my planes into Syria?"

"No. I'll be flying one of the Black Hawk helicopters the US sold you like the good allies we are. I have to pick up my friends."

"You sell them to everyone."

"We both know that yours are specially designed. And from what I understand, you've been begging for one of the new Black Hawks that nobody knows about—well, except you. Sam did let that slip—accidently on purpose, I might add." Carter forced himself to sound diplomatic instead of confrontational. He wasn't sure he pulled it off.

"Beg. I never beg."

"Not what I heard," Carter retorted. "Speaking geopolitically, of course. What were you talking about?"

"You are a dangerous man, Carter Johnson. I don't like dangerous people in my country." He took a deep breath of impatience. "And why should I do this? You should have come prepared to do your own dirty work. Surely your special forces in Syria have equipment to help you. Or perhaps your friends in Turkey where my brother and your team of misfits are waiting." His lips thinned into a straight line. "Surprised? Of course, I know my brother is there and his—people. I also know Captain Hunter is missing. I even have information for you on him."

Carter couldn't stop his look of surprise.

"Oh, sorry. Should I have led with that?"

"Maybe. Let's get this over with. We're prepared to give you one of our latest Sikorsky UH-60 Black Hawks with all the new bells and whistles for your help."

"Let's say three Black Hawks and three more in the next year."

"Let's say two and, if you haven't been vaporized in the next year, we'll discuss it further."

"The contracts for increasing our fighter squadrons with the new F-15EX have been bogged down in negotiations."

"I'm shocked. Unacceptable. Fixable ASAP. Anything else?"

"Stay away from Samantha."

~ ~ ~ ~

Chase wandered around the fortress, taking mental notes of open spaces, cover for a firefight, where Amir's men gathered, and how they spent their time. Location of the guards. Smells. Sounds. Anything that felt normal now could change in a subtle way, changing his ability to survive in a split second. If Darya was correct, Enigma was looking for him. He had to locate the weapon and destroy it before anyone could use it to start a war.

Darkness came too quickly here. The castle was eerie with sounds echoing softly and reminding him of ghosts. The flickering candlelight and fiery torches on columns along the stone walls slowed his steps to take in the beauty of the vaulted passageway.

"I see you're feeling good enough to explore, Captain Hunter," came a familiar voice.

Chase turned to see Amir, arm in arm with Soraya, who had changed clothes once more and gave the impression of a Middle Eastern princess with the world at her feet. Her dark hair had ribbons and pearls woven into a few braided strands that fell down her breasts. "It's an incredible castle."

"Soraya is very fond of telling the history of this place to anyone who will listen. Unfortunately, I have no interest in anything the Knights Templar had anything to do with."

"Templars. I've read a great deal about them."

Soraya tilted her head at him with interest. "Then let me show you the highlights."

One of Amir's men entered the corridor and quickly whispered in his ear. He nodded as the fighter scurried away. "I have to attend to other matters. I'll catch up with you on the tour as soon as I can." He lifted Soraya's hand to his lips. "Be sure to show the captain our special place for uninvited guests."

She gave him a tight-lipped smile, staring after him until he disappeared then turned to Chase, letting loose an exasperated sigh. Slipping her arm through his, she moved forward, making sure her hip touched him.

"Problem in paradise?" he asked.

"Aren't you the least bit jealous?"

Chase knew he had to tread lightly. He chose to shoot her an angry glare before he spun her around and kissed her viciously on the mouth then neck. When she surrendered to his touch, he shoved her aside. "Why would I be? I can have you whenever I want."

"He would kill you for what you just did." But she tilted her head and made her red lips pooch like a spoiled child. "Would you fight for me?"

"Would that please you?"

"Yes," she whispered seductively. "But only if you win, my love."

The woman was seriously mental. This was a dangerous game he played, and no good would come of it. "Are you going to show me around or not? I feel like crap and won't last much longer if you plan to continue this charade of being a sex slave to a terrorist."

"I belong to you and no one else. Together, we can accomplish my dream."

They walked apart now through the vaulted mural passageway and stopped outside a large area with a barrel-vaulted ceiling. "This is the chapel. It was built for Emir of Aleppo in 1031 CE before given to the Nights Hospitaller in 1144 CE. They, of course, chose to extensively rebuild it, along with the area we are coming into now called the Hall of Knights."

"How is it you know so much about this place?" It was an incredible fortress and a masterful piece of architecture.

She fanned her hand out toward a staircase that spiraled downward into darkness then she pointed at a flaming torch. He removed it from the iron sconce. They carefully navigated down the stairs as she continued to speak in a tour-guide tone.

"It might surprise you my college education included the study of medieval architecture with a concentration on Middle Eastern structures."

"Beauty, talent, and brains," he commented nonchalantly.

"Yes. Well, my brains didn't pay the bills so I went in a different direction. Doesn't mean I have forgotten my first love. History has always fascinated me. Syria is covered in it. As many as twenty-five world heritage sites have been damaged or destroyed during years of war here. Even this castle has sustained damage. An air raid hit one of the fortress's towers. There is footage showing a huge blast as a tower of this magnificent Crusader castle appears to take a direct hit. You can see large clouds of smoke followed by falling debris in the air. Makes me sick. After seeing the video, I decided I could make a difference with my fortune from my music career."

The smell of mildew assaulted his nose as the torchlight split the darkness. Something scurried across his foot at the same time she jumped sideways into him. He switched hands with the torch and grasped her arm to steady her.

"Take care down here," she warned. "The floor is uneven, and rats can be a nuisance, along with an occasional viper that keeps the population down. But, of course, they are very poisonous, so the local population has managed to kill most of them. Now they are mostly found along the coast of the Mediterranean."

"What is this place?"

"The dungeon, now. Notice the temperature difference? I'm uncertain of this, but I'm guessing at one time, it was a good place to store food."

"And now?" Chase let himself adjust to the dimness as he moved the torch around to brighten different areas.

"See this?" Soraya stepped toward a spot on the floor pooled with light from above. She pointed toward a hole in the ceiling the size of a base drum. "There are several throughout this area. The great hall above us is flooded with light during the day. These openings make this area easier to see. Acts like ceiling lights."

Chase came upon jail enclosures. The bars were thick and corroded with grime. Stone benches lined the walls of the ten-by-ten area. He imagined cockroaches and vermin feces might dot the floor, although it appeared swept. No trash or debris that might be used as weapons or tools. The smell of dampness grew heavy here, and the sound of dripping echoed from an unknown source.

"I take it this is the guest accommodations?" he asked drily.

"Yes. But it gets better. Come." She towed him after her as they approached a railing made of stone posts. The same iron as the jail cells went between each post, except for an entrance. "See here?"

Chase stopped short, blocked by her outstretched arm from falling into a cavernous hole. Darkness swallowed up any light shined upon it. He picked up a rock the size of his hand and tossed it into the abyss. Ten seconds later, it splashed down. Swinging the torch light around and forward revealed a bridge less than three feet wide stretching across the blackness. Except for ropes strung across the crevice, there were no railings here.

"And the other side?" he asked.

"Several more cells. These do not have walls, only a ledge. Between each ledge is a distance of one meter."

"Three feet," he mumbled.

"Yes. The floor is slick from rainwater seeping down the stone walls at certain times of the year. The ledge is one meter wide as well. I think they were used as a kind of plank to cross to each one. There are two on each side of the bridge there." She pointed back and forth. "One must jump from the bridge to the ledge. No easy task if you are wrestling with a prisoner who doesn't want to be restrained."

"Then, how did they manage?"

"Beat them first, I'm guessing. Robbed them of the will to resist. Starvation." She shrugged. "It was not uncommon to use such treatment for the worst of the worst, I think. As you can imagine, it could easily break a man's—or woman's spirit."

He cut his attention to her and saw the reflection of excitement in her eyes. "I'm guessing you have plans for this?"

She pivoted quickly and slipped onto the bridge before Chase tugged her back with his free arm. The gasp that escaped her mouth showed fear at the almost-fatal fall. "Let's leave. I'm frightened," she said, laying her head against his chest. "Take me back to my room."

He pulled her after him toward the stairs. The experience had left him drained and his pain meds were wearing off. The place felt as if it were a forewarning of death. Was it his own approaching death?

Soraya moved slowly up the steps when a box caught his attention. It rested in the corner near the stairs with faded numbers written down the side. He couldn't completely make it out since the light was barely enough to enable them to walk, and a tarp had fallen partially over the edge. He'd try and return to check it out later. Maybe this was the chemical weapon he'd been searching for.

CHAPTER 25

شهيد

Prince Muhammed clicked off his phone and watched Tessa escort the Kurdish woman to her quarters, steps away from her own. The American team had returned earlier, with loud joking and music, but soon most of the lights inside were extinguished. His quarters were simple, not at all like he was used to. Since the Turks didn't know who he was, he thought it best he fly under the radar. Since there were several bodyguards in attendance, posing as other military personnel, it made sense to share the same facilities.

It didn't matter. At times, pretending to be of no importance appealed to him. It gave him an idea of how the common man felt every day. His family knew nothing about such things. People. Real people. Those were the ones who suffered, laughed, felt joy and sadness, carved out a life for themselves without the help of untold wealth and influence. Many times, he wondered if he'd be able to survive in such a world. Other times, he was grateful he didn't have to. When he took the throne, he wanted to make a difference for his people, less fearful, less dependent on the monarchy. Of course, other things would not change.

He watched the American woman who had saved his life and acted with a great degree of bravery. The memory of her in the red dress and sheer black burka still gave him pleasure. She was smart, clever, and unafraid to beat him in the games he enjoyed. Most of the time, the women sent to him fell for his suave attention and ended up in his bed. Not so with Agent Tessa Scott. The sound of her joy was genuine and refreshing. Her unassuming personality loosened his tongue and he'd found himself sharing his plans for the future. She listened intently, like it mattered to her.

The man in charge of her, Captain Hunter, went to great lengths to ensure the prince and Tessa spent zero time alone together after the attempt on his life. Someone was always in the room listening. Were they protecting him or her? This was where being a prince usually paid off, but the captain apparently didn't get the memo. It should be up to Tessa if she wished to spend time with him. They had a connection.

"You shouldn't be walking out here alone, even if it is on a military base," he said, strolling up to Tessa. He dropped his cigarette and rubbed it out with his boot. She caught her breath, pivoting toward him, a pleasant smile crossing her lips.

She bowed her head slightly in respect but never took her eyes off him. "Prince Muhammed. You are the one who is taking chances being out here alone. Where is your detail?"

"I'm sure they are peering out the windows and sneaking around to make sure you don't pose a threat. They are aware of what you are capable of, my dear. Your reputation precedes you."

"I see you bounced back nicely. I'm glad there were no lasting effects."

"And how would you know that? What if I told you I often suffer from déjà vu at the oddest times?"

"I'm so sorry, Your Highness." Sincerity filled her voice.

"You should be, since you are the cause."

She laid her hand on her heart. "I'm sorry, sir. I warned Captain Hunter I wasn't the best fit to protect you. I regret my job has caused you pain."

His laughter burst forth unexpectedly. "No. No. You misunderstand. I'm grateful for your excellent job at protecting me. I enjoy your presence a little too much. I think of you often at times when I should be focused on matters of state."

"Prince Muhammed, your reputation for being a charmer does not do you justice. I should have known you were teasing. But thank you."

"I didn't expect to see you on this mission."

"My part is the face of peace and goodwill. Apparently, I don't have a threatening vibe like some of your friends."

"Oh, if they only knew."

She expelled a light chuckle.

"And what is your real job?" he asked.

"I am here to check on a few doctors taken for ransom and convey concern for their health. We will do our best to have them released. I'm also supposed to be checking on Captain Hunter and your niece, Soraya, since they have been in captivity. The director will pose as a UNESCO representative, along with several others."

"I see. This is a very dangerous game, Tessa. Have you ever been in this part of the world before?"

She shrugged. "No. But I have been in Afghanistan."

"Ah. Well, that is also a dangerous place." He locked his fingers in front of him. "My niece is, at times, difficult to understand."

"How so?"

"She is a woman without a country, culture, and family. She has no idea of her place in this world. Being surrounded by the glitz and glamour of a musical career has left her shallow, overindulged, while sacrificing the beliefs of her people."

"The Kurdish people?"

"I suppose." He took a step closer. "Her mother, my sister, grew up in a royal household, instructed in following the ways of the Prophet. She eloped with a Kurdish man, a soldier from a family of farmers. I tried to keep in touch, but it became more difficult when her husband joined the rebels in Syria. He became nothing more than a terrorist."

"And what of Soraya? Did you reach out to her?"

"When she was younger, her mother asked if I would take her. I did, and I accepted her, but she never did us, rebellious, wild, and a bully. My father, the king, found out I'd been hiding her and demanded I send her away. I had no choice but to return her to her mother. I never spoke to either Soraya or my sister again."

"And yet you have financed this operation to rescue her."

He took a step closer, drawn by her fresh scent and the outline of her mouth in the moonlight. "She is still family, and I once loved her mother very much. She was much older than me and would sing to me when I was but a small child. I guess Soraya inherited her voice. I've listened to her music often. Do you sing,

Tessa?"

"I've been known to croak a tune out in the church choir."

"Maybe you'll sing for me one day." Another step closer, but this time she shied away. "I have thought of you often. I hope you have remembered me fondly as well."

She lowered her gaze then lifted it to meet his with determination absent a second earlier. "Yes, Your Highness. You are a difficult man to forget. I am honored to have met you." She glanced toward the door of her quarters. "But it has been a long day. Perhaps we can talk again over breakfast. I'm very tired."

As she turned to take her leave, the prince cut off her exit. "My quarters are quite comfortable. I would very much enjoy your company for a while longer." He reached out and slid his hand down her forearm then took hold of hers.

"Your Highness, I am unavailable. There is someone else in my life right now."

The prince had opened his mouth to insist when the door of her quarters flew open and Ken Montgomery stepped out.

"Tessa, we've been waiting to go over a few things for tomorrow." He turned his attention to the prince, who dropped her hand, deciding this might be one of those stand-down moments. The soldier, although speaking to Tessa, remained focused on him. "Coming, Agent Scott?"

She inclined her head in a nod. "Yes. Good night, Your Highness. I'll see you tomorrow." She disappeared inside leaving the soldier who continued his confrontational glare at him.

"And here I thought it might be Captain Hunter who had won Agent Scott's heart," the prince said.

"That's the thing with Agent Scott. She has a way of making men get a lot of crazy ideas. Know what I mean?"

The prince didn't appreciate being chastised and warned. "Good night."

When the prince reached his quarters, he turned to see the soldier standing against the door to the Enigma team's quarters, with his arms crossed across his chest. These people who worked with Captain Hunter needed to be reminded of their place when dealing with a prince.

~ ~ ~ ~

Ken didn't trust the man, well aware of his playboy image. Tessa turned out to be a real handful with those terrorists, but the woman was clueless when it came to men and what they were capable of. There had been rumors of her and Chase since day one. His own hidden admiration for her turned into something more along the way. Maybe it was because she'd saved his life or because she was so innocent. But would Chase get out of his way? He had his doubts, so he appointed himself watchdog until he could have it out with his captain.

Peshmerga emerged from her quarters and slipped across the grounds to where the prince stayed. She tapped lightly at the door. One of his men opened it, flooding light on her body. In seconds, the prince appeared and took each of her hands, then kissed her on each cheek, before slipping an arm around her shoulders. He straightened when she disappeared inside with the prince.

"What the hell?"

CHAPTER 26

شهيد

The road was dusty and not exactly pothole free. Tessa ripped a hole in the seat from digging her fingers into the upholstery. Their Turkish driver must have been a competitor at Daytona in a former life. Director Clark reached out and braced his hand against the dash a few times but remained quiet.

Honey and Sam sat on each side of her, so, other than the seat, there was nothing to grab onto as they bounced along. Their stoic persona reminded her of a military ad she'd seen as a child; be all you can be. Dressed in camo fatigues, she might appear to be a badass. Maybe if she could smear slick dark goo under her eyes and around her chin and chant "hoo-rah," she'd feel braver. The other women had been to hell and back so many times, this new mission must feel like a walk in the park.

When the truck swerved around a corner with a steep drop-off and hit a bump at the same time, Tessa let out a yelp. Each hand grabbed the thigh of the woman on either side of her and squeezed. What in the world was she thinking to come here?

Sam clamped her hand on hers and applied so much pressure, Tessa winced but fought back a cry of pain. Her nemesis arched an eyebrow before lifting her hand then tossing it away as if it were a piece of trash.

Clearing her throat, Tessa nodded. "Sorry." Then she realized her right hand still clenched Honey's thigh. It flexed beneath her fingertips, as the assassin patted the back of her hand. She hesitated to sneak a glance but lowered her head and did anyway. Honey continued to stare out the window and, when Tessa tried to remove her hand, she tightened her grip.

My best friends are a psycho assassin and a nymphomaniac who probably have been planning meetings on how to turn me into their kind of crazy. This was not the first time the thought ran through her head. She'd survived these last few years by acting dumb, innocent, or smarter than them—none of those actually applied to her. To make up for faking it, she'd taken to being the class clown, with one-liners or making fun of them. That alone was a dangerous attempt at fitting in, but somehow it had kept her alive under their training and friendship.

Tessa jerked her hand free then elbowed Honey to move over. In slow motion, the assassin turned her head and stared deep into her eyes, in the zone. No threats or words of advice this time. Although they were two of the scariest people she knew, it was comforting to know Honey and Sam would have her back. At least, she hoped they would and not have a gun jammed into her spine.

The other trucks followed, the rest of the team probably also in the zone, calm, fearless, and prepared. Why had she continued with this kind of life? What about her family? What would happen to them if she were to die or become so injured, she couldn't care for them?

She didn't choose Enigma. It chose her a long time ago. When she was a kid, she fantasized about doing this kind of thing. Maybe her living with Robert had been jeopardized by her own dissatisfaction with her everyday existence. Captain Hunter burst into her world, uninvited and dangerous, and she fell for him hook, line, and sinker. Enigma offered her adventure and she grabbed it. But it was time to end it. Chase loved her and also wanted to start over. They both deserved it. And, in the end, that was why she came this time. It was her turn to save him.

Tessa leaned forward to speak to the director. "How much longer until we cross into Syria?"

"As soon as we can get past this." He nodded at the line of traffic in front of them, vehicles and people walking into and from Syria.

"Is this normal?" Sam asked, also leaning forward to get a better look.

The Turkish driver wiped at the inside of his windshield, removing a layer of grime. "It is a frequent place of crossing for Syrians trying to reach the refugee camp in nearby Reyhanli. Vehicles with Turkish registrations entering Syria can be held up for days."

"Can't the government do something?" Tessa asked.

The driver shrugged. "The crossing is a major route for smuggling, particularly oil and gas, and during the Syrian Civil War, there has been a dramatic rise in weapons smuggling." He turned to glance at Tessa. "From time to time, the rebels from the Free Syrian Army have seized the border and defaced images of the Syrian president. Other times, foreigners raised the Jihadist flag of al-Qaeda at the border post, leading to a confrontation with the Free Syrian Army. Although things have quieted in the last six months, in the past, car bombs have exploded here."

"What are all these trucks carrying?" Tessa wondered.

"I understand it is humanitarian supplies," Director Clark interjected.

"Yes. That is right," the driver agreed. "This enables Turkey to be in charge of the crossing. We can check to make sure no contraband gets through. It is a very bad place. No place for women like you three. It is good you bring protection."

Both her companions cocked their head at the suggestion. She could have sworn their necks popped into a cyborg-ready mode toward a defensive stance on the matter. Good thing the director was there to protect the driver.

When they were five vehicles back from the crossing, a lot of hand-waving, horn honking, and angry voices generated confusion.

"I will go see what the problem is." The driver opened his door. "We have International Red Cross plates. I'll take the UNESCO packet, too. I need cash to get across."

The director refused to hand over the important papers or the money. The driver shrugged and turned off the ignition. "You go see what's going on then we can talk about the papers and cash," the director growled.

"I don't like it," Sam said through clenched teeth.

Honey pulled her serrated blade from the sheath attached to her belt and twisted it in her palm. The director, sour-faced, glanced back at Sam then Honey.

"Ladies?" he mumbled then stared out the windshield before navigating his body to the driver's side. He restarted the truck.

"Ready," Sam said, pulling out her Khyber and slipping it between her and Tessa's hips.

He used the walkie-talkie to call the truck behind them. "Better send Ken up here to be my second."

"On it," came a reply. In seconds, Ken was opening the door and taking his place in the car. He nodded to both Sam and Honey and ignored her.

"Whoa. Whoa. Whoa. What is going on?" Tessa said as she landed a nervous pat to the back of the front seat.

"I believe we're going to be detained. Our driver slipped away and down that ravine. When we move forward, let me do the talking." He glanced at Ken, who was dressed like a local. "How's your Turkish?" The battle-worn soldier gave him a thumbs-up as he turned his attention toward the checkpoint. The director spoke again in the walkie-talkie. "Look alive, people."

~ ~ ~ ~

Chase was certain staying in Soraya's rooms, now that he was awake and lucid, meant a beating, or possible death sentence from Amir whose masculinity seemed to be hanging by a thread. Thankfully, the decision was made for him when Amir returned unexpectedly with one of his faithful followers in tow.

"He will take you to where my men bunk."

"I prefer my own space. If you want me to help you, then treat me like a valued asset. I can just as easily make this go sideways for you."

"I sincerely doubt that, Captain Hunter."

He was standing two feet from Amir and, in a flash, disarmed him and tightened his arm around the man's neck then held the gun up to his temple. Both Soraya and the soldier gasped. The captain chuckled and released him then patted him on the back and returned the gun.

"I'm not the enemy, Amir. I support you. After all, when you take over Saudi Arabia, I expect to be compensated as a loyal follower should be."

Amir rubbed his neck before pulling back his shoulders. "You play a dangerous game, Captain Hunter. I should kill you."

"Then do it. I'm sick of your threats. Either let me help you or end it. Here. Now."

Amir took two steps away from the captain and pulled Soraya under his extended arm. "All right. We'll see how tomorrow goes."

"Tomorrow?"

"Yes. We're going hunting. If all goes well, I'll have a nice surprise for you."

CHAPTER 27

شهيد

The vehicles rolled forward. A few were waved on impatiently, and others endured a search followed by a lot of yelling and waving of weapons. Tessa saw money being slipped into the palms of the soldiers at the checkpoint. But maybe they were something else. Their uniforms didn't resemble the Turkish soldiers she'd seen mingling with the American military personnel. These men were rougher, less polished. Then it was their turn.

The soldiers swarmed both vehicles. Tessa guessed the emblem of the Red Cross was recognizable as a soft target. They had UN license plates since they were also representing UNESCO. A burly man with close-set eyes and a bulbous nose leaned in to inspect the passengers.

The guard jabbered as he pointed to the women who quickly covered the lower parts of their faces to show respect.

"He wants to see your faces," Ken translated and handed over their passports, "to make sure you are who you say you are."

Ken spoke carefully to the guard then turned to them, so they quickly dropped their coverings. "Be cool and don't make eye contact."

The man handed back their passports and smirked after staring longer than was respectful. He yelled at another man in the guard shack and pointed to the women. Ken burst into a tirade, waving his hands and growling what must have been insults. The guards narrowed their glares and spoke to the director. Surprisingly, he responded in his usual calm but threatening voice. One more command from the guard, and the gate arm lifted, and they were allowed to pass through.

"What did you say to them, Ken?" Tessa asked.

He shrugged and turned back to stare out the windshield, but Samantha filled in the answer for him. "He told them they were disrespectful when we were trying to follow the ways of their people. I think he may have insulted their parentage as well."

Without turning around to address them, Ken spoke drily. "I quoted the Quran, more or less. 'Men shall take full care of women with the bounties Allah has bestowed on them. And the righteous women are the truly devout ones, who guard the intimacy which Allah has ordained to be guarded. Surely, Allah is indeed the Most High, the Greatest.' At least, that's what I meant to say. Left a few words out, but they were taken aback and probably didn't want to appear foolish in front of foreign women when I took up for you." He glanced at Tessa and grinned. "I told him you were married women, and I was your protector."

"So, he doesn't know you couldn't fight your way out of a paper bag," Honey said coolly. "Or make them beg for mercy, I guess."

He turned around further to level a hard gaze at the Irish assassin. "I sort of remember you doing that very thing not so long ago."

"Whoa!" Tessa said, shaking her head. "I don't want that picture in my head. Just stop." Everyone but Ken burst into laughter. He pushed his bottom lip out, amused then winked at her.

"I think she took notes, Tessa, if you're interested," he added.

"Oh my gosh. No thanks."

~ ~ ~ ~

Except for the wind gusting around the outside of the castle, the silence hung heavy. Most of the men slept as if they didn't have a care in the world. Chase wondered if they knew there was a chemical weapon that could melt their faces off. Accidents happen when you are clueless and exhausted.

Wandering around the structure, now that most everyone was asleep, was simple enough. Amir had provided him with a separate room off the main hall. Privacy was at a minimum, though, with the barrel archway open for others to keep watch on him. But the ragtag bunch of so-called soldiers could do nothing without Amir drawing them a picture of what needed to happen. Lately most of the men had included him in their moments of humor and downtime. Since the Quran forbid gambling, they invented other games with cards that didn't involve money. Chase taught them a few he'd learned as a kid. A good deal of joking at the fun managed to keep his attitude from spiraling down a dark hole.

Grabbing a torch from the wall near the stairs he'd used earlier, he recognized he should create an escape plan soon. He wasn't sure he could defuse the weapon without killing himself in the process. Once it was located, he might be able to get to the few special forces still in Syria to let them call in an airstrike. The thought of losing such a magnificent piece of architecture labeled a World Heritage Site nearly made him sick. However, a war or death of countless innocent people was more unacceptable and a greater risk for world peace.

Once at the bottom of the stairs, he stood still to adjust to the deep darkness. The flickering flame lessened his anxiety. His pain earlier gave him a warped sense of time and space, but now, after being allotted his pills, a calm had allowed him to focus on the problem at hand. Where had he seen the suspicious box?

He caught movement on the perimeter of his circle of light. He hadn't been allowed a weapon to defend himself. Whatever it was, the movement had stopped, but he sensed it was man rather than beast. Had Amir slipped away from Soraya's bed to join his men and found him gone? Or maybe one of them was put on guard duty.

"Whoever you are," he said in Arabic, "come out. I have no weapons."

The shape of a man formed on the edge of darkness then stepped into the light.

~ ~ ~ ~

By the time the trucks rolled into the refugee camp, thirty

kilometers from the checkpoint, Tessa's nerves were on edge. No one spoke. They just watched out the windows for trouble, checked their phone GPS, and stared into oblivion as if they were plotting against the world. Why couldn't she do that? During these times, instead of anticipation of things to come, she went into self-doubt and reflection. Events of her life turned into rapid flashbacks. Mistakes. Roads less traveled. Children hugging her. Christmas presents made from scrapbook supplies by their little hands. The adventure of a lifetime, thanks to Roman Darya Petrov. The warm, passionate kisses of Captain Chase Hunter and him sweeping in to save her too many times to count.

Her deep breath then long release caused Ken to turn his attention to her again. He observed her with concern then looked away. Tessa figured he was worried she'd get in the way or trip over her own feet during this mission. She didn't want anyone getting hurt because of her inability to respond with the appropriate rhetoric. Hopefully there wouldn't be a firefight, but her training had increased her accuracy and confidence. Could she pull the trigger and take an enemy combatant down in the blink of an eye? She thought of Chase. Yes. Her fingers twitched. She'd pull the trigger.

Such an idea would soon be tested.

CHAPTER 28

شهید

This would have been one of those times Chase drew his weapon and leveled it at the unknown who dared sneak up on him. It appeared such a choice had been removed for everyone's safety. Otherwise, he'd have shot his way out of this mess weeks ago. If only Soraya had chosen to leave with him, things might be different now, but by then, her true colors had begun to emerge.

The man stepped farther into the light with his hands extended to reveal he carried no weapon. Chase relaxed.

"Darya." An unexpected release of air in his chest helped him realize he was glad to see his once-former enemy. "Never thought I'd be so glad to see you."

The Tribesman's eyebrow arched in surprise as he moved closer. "Never thought you'd be so warm and fuzzy."

Chase chuckled softly. "Probably the drugs. I'm sure I'll get over it." He tilted his head, a bit confused. "Why are you here? Better yet, how did you get in here without anyone seeing you? You really are a ghost."

He glanced back over his shoulder. "There's a tunnel leading into here. Probably put in place by Crusaders. But it is a good way to make a fast exit."

"Got a feeling it will be in use soon. Amir let me know we were going hunting tomorrow. Said I'd be surprised."

"Enigma is in Syria now. My contacts along the way are watching but we are far and few between. They are in a refugee camp handing out food, clothing, and medical supplies. Tessa should be in her element there, being the do-gooder, she is. Probably go home with another child in tow."

"Tessa is with them? I thought you were going to stop her from doing that," he said hotly.

"I sent Peshmerga with the women we rescued to fill in Director Clark on our situation and yours, of course. She was to encourage him to leave her behind. I don't believe he listened."

"Or maybe Peshmerga told her you were alive, and she decided to come see for herself."

"Peshmerga knows nothing of me and Tessa. I plan to keep it that way. I'd bet your director decided Tessa would be an asset and couldn't jeopardize the mission, or he didn't like me telling him what to do."

"If you had gone in person, he would have listened, and you could reveal yourself to Tessa. She would have done anything you asked," Chase growled.

Darya sobered then nodded. "Perhaps. Why are you so eager to hand her off to me? You've spent the last couple of years trying to erase me from her life."

"Because I love her. I'm damaged goods now. Who knows what is going on inside my body with this constant pain? I'm addicted to pain meds or whatever it is they're giving me. I've not exactly been a Boy Scout when it comes to being faithful, either. Her happiness and those kids of hers mean everything to me."

"You did what you had to do. Besides, I thought you believed I was too evil when it came to being with her."

"I guess neither of us is good enough. But we both love her. She deserves better."

"The woman has a taste for roughness. It probably isn't going to get better than us." He admitted. He had a point though. "If I don't find this bomb, we're going to have bigger problems than drawing straws for her. If I die, here in this hellhole, promise me you'll take care of her and leave this kind of life."

Darya's solemn face spoke volumes as he extended his hand in friendship. "Same to you."

Chase grasped his hand and was reminded again how strong the man was, especially since his own strength had been tested these past weeks. "If she ever finds out we made this pact, she'll have neither of us."

"We'd better get busy. Then I'll show you the way out of here in case you need to leave in a hurry."

~ ~ ~ ~

Tessa felt the air grow colder by the minute. Lightning spiderwebbed across the sky, and the low rumble of thunder promised rain in this parched land. The sound of tent flaps clapping in the breeze fanned the smell of cooking fires throughout the camp. Many of the people had rushed to be in line for the supplies they desperately needed to feed their families. Most were Kurds who had escaped their homes from the advancement of governments troops or ISIS. Being so close to the Turkish border, they had protection from UN groups.

Entering Turkey was a waiting game because the government didn't want more trouble entering to support the PKK. The Kurds wanted their own section of Turkey to call Kurdistan. As it was now, the Kurds had to agree that the refugees would consider Turkey their home and melt into society. The PKK were considered terrorists in political circles. Tessa figured the British thought the same thing about the colonists in 1776 America. The threat of rebellion continued to run in Americans' DNA.

Tessa had tagged along with Peshmerga to greet elders and mothers with concerns about their children. They wanted to hear about life in America, as their children stood by with weak cries and bellies swelling from hunger. After going to the medical clinic and seeing the sick children and the mothers who held and rocked them, she escaped to get some fresh air. There was no stopping her tears of helplessness at seeing the children.

"What's wrong?" a masculine voice asked.

Looking up, she found Ken and his best friend Tom Cooper scoping out the surrounding area with their weapons ready like they were patrolling the streets of Kabul.

"You have been gone a long time. Your ghoul sent us after you," Tom piped in.

They were talking about Zoric. The director already forbade

him walking around since he had the dark aura of a ghoul, vampire, or creepy unearthly creature. Since he was Serbian and had a less-than-stellar reputation, there was always a possibility he might be recognized.

"Are you okay?" asked Ken.

Tessa pulled her shoulders back then dragged her sleeve across her face. "The children," she whimpered. "I've never seen anything like that before."

"Where is Peshmerga?" he continued.

She managed a shrug and pointed inside.

He tilted his head in that direction, and Sergeant Cooper slipped inside. "Let's go. I want to talk to you."

"But Peshmerga—"

"Tom will escort her back."

"But it might not be appropriate for them to be alone."

"Fine. But when we get back, we have to talk."

"What is this about?"

His jaw tightened and released, making his mouth tight and drawn. His cinnamon-colored eyes narrowed, and he never stopped searching the area. Although he wore native garb over parts of his fatigues, there was no doubt of his toned body.

"Have I done something wrong?" she asked. "You've given me the cold shoulder ever since last night when you saw me with the prince."

He swung his weapon to his side. "Yes. Damn it. You…"

Peshmerga opened the door, exiting with one of the visiting doctors. They spoke pleasantly for a moment before the doctor slipped back inside to attend to those with more comfort than solutions.

"Let's go. You shouldn't have been out here in the dark," Ken snapped.

"These are my people. There is nothing to worry about, Lieutenant." Peshmerga bristled. "I am able to take care of myself. I have been doing it since I was a girl."

"I bet you have," he retorted. "At what cost?"

"What are you accusing me of, Lieutenant?"

"Peshmerga, please, it's his job to protect us," Tessa soothed. "Let's just go back. We're all exhausted. Hot food and a good night's sleep will go a long way."

The other woman stomped toward the entrance gates. "Hot food?" she fumed. "And these people? What about them? There was barely enough food for each family to share one meal tonight."

"More is coming," Tessa promised. "You know that. Two days. Three at the most. Maybe twenty trucks full of food and medical supplies. Today was an act of goodwill to get us where we need to go."

"Don't you mean information? You don't care about these people," she snapped as the gate opened for them.

"Yes. Information." Ken circled around to cut her off. "I'm not walking into an ambush. It's my job to keep your ass out of trouble. After we're done, I don't give a rip what you do or where you go. So, yeah, I don't care about them nearly as much as I do my team."

"Ken, that's enough," Tessa warned, laying her hand on his chest.

Peshmerga pushed past them and toward the tent where hot food was being served. The first drop of rain hit so hard on the ground, a puff ball of dust floated up before repeating over and over until the entire ground grew wet.

"Let's go," he ordered.

Tessa followed him to where Director Clark stood in a tent doorway, the flaps resisting the wind that twisted hair out of her bun. He stepped aside and let them pass. Inside, in the glow of an LED lantern, were a cot and a table topped by a layer of dust and a bottle of Jack Daniels.

"What is this about, Ben?" She didn't realize she'd called him by name until he frowned at her. "I mean Director Clark."

Ken poured himself a shot of the whiskey into a paper cup, gulped it down then gritted his teeth.

"And what was that back there, Ken?" Tessa fumed. "You were rude to Peshmerga."

"And you need to be better at who you pal around with."

"What's that supposed to mean?" she growled. "If you're talking about Prince Muhammed last night—"

"Enough," the director said. "Prince Muhammed is a necessary part of this mission. He is a player; however, he feels like we rushed you away before he had time to—" He cleared his throat. "To get to know you better. You impressed him, and he has requested your services in his security detail for an indefinite amount of time."

"He's harmless. I can handle him," she said firmly.

"You really are clueless, Tessa," Ken said, exasperated. "If he wants you, then he'll make that happen. Please tell me I don't have to spell that out for you."

"Be that as it may," the director continued, "Ken will keep a close eye on you—"

"What? No. I'm not a baby. Why can't you treat me like everyone else?"

"Because you aren't like the rest of us," the director said calmly. "At least not yet, in spite of showing—improvements of late. Ken and Sergeant Cooper will be watching you, Sam, and Honey. This is a man's world over here, whether you like it or not." He held up his hand to stop her protest. "There is more. Ken?"

"Last night when you went inside, I waited for the prince to go back to his quarters."

"And?"

"In a few minutes, Peshmerga slipped away from where you left her and went to the prince's quarters. He kissed her on the cheek before they embraced. She was inside a couple of hours. I waited until one of his guards took her back to her quarters then left. When I came in to talk to you—you were already asleep."

Tessa was going to be sick. It felt hard to breathe in this confined space. This was exactly why her teammates didn't trust her 100 percent. Her bad decisions and a tendency to be gullible were not endearing personality traits when working with traitors and terrorists.

"So, what are we going to do about it?" Director Clark asked.

Tessa swallowed hard, never thinking she'd ever say this in a million years. "Let Zoric have a crack at her."

CHAPTER 29

شهيد

Tessa walked into her tent, where Sam and Honey played cards at a small table. Each had a bottle of water and took an occasional sip. Staying hydrated in this land and any mission helped with clarity of mind and body. She'd better chug a gallon or so of purified water to make it happen.

"What's up with the boss?" Honey said, laying her cards down.

Sam frowned before standing up. "I don't know how you cheat, but I know you do," Sam said flippantly. She turned her attention to Tessa. "You're as pale as a ghost. What's up?"

Tessa shared every bit of conversation she'd had with Peshmerga, including the part where she'd apologized for being rude. The savory tidbit concerning how the woman met secretly with Prince Muhammed appeared to cause the two women to glance at each other. Once more, she wished they would just once, look at her as if she had a mental understanding of the situation and a plan to initiate.

"How could I have been so wrong?" Tessa said, flopping down on her cot. "I figured she was tough as nails and had been treated unfairly her whole life because she was a Kurd."

"Probably true. Doesn't mean she gets a pass to hide information." Sam came over and sat down next to her on the cot. "As to the prince, Ken is right. You should be careful around him.

I don't know if he is infatuated with you because you saved his life or what. You showed him up. No doubt about that. Insulted his masculinity maybe and wants to show you what a man he is."

"I find that hard to believe."

"And this is why the men come sniffing around our little Grass Valley commando," Honey whined. "Grow up, Tessa. The men we deal with aren't like the people you've known all your life. You've got to shake a wee bit of that unicorn sparkle off you, if you plan to have a life in Enigma."

"Thanks, Honey. Like I didn't already know that," Tessa quipped. "I can't help it if I see the good in people."

"Yes. Even that ghoul, Zoric, who would slit your throat if you took a carrot stick off his plate." Honey shivered. She'd never pretended to like the man, probably because they were alike.

"That's not helping." Tessa placed her face in her hands and shook her head in disgust. "I told Ken to take her to him for interrogation."

Both women snickered at her.

"There's hope for you yet," Sam said, slapping her on the leg. "I'm wondering who this Khan is that Peshmerga talked about. Sounds as if he might be an Afghan. Why is he here when his country is in turmoil?"

"Apparently fighting for justice and the Syrian people. Helps the Daughters of Kobani with weapons, intel, a safe place, whatever they need. I think she has a serious thing for him considering he led her to believe we've met. She didn't seem to like that much."

"Ring any bells?" Honey said, coming to stand in front of her cot. She crossed her arms. "A jealous woman with a gun is more than a little dangerous. Besides Darya, did you have any interactions with any other Afghans?"

"Only Darya's family and village. They rarely left there. There was Massoud, who vowed to kill me. But I doubt he survived the bombing. Even if he had, his injuries would have been severe and left him incapable of carrying out any threats. He certainly wouldn't be able to leave Afghanistan without being tracked. I'm thinking the Taliban probably found a replacement for him as soon as they heard about the bombing."

"Now you're talking like an agent," Sam mused. "Chase had

both friend and foe in that hellhole. Maybe that is why he was taken."

Tessa rubbed her face vigorously with both hands to keep the tears away. "I just want him home. Safe."

"A little horny, are we?" Honey cooed.

"Shut up, Honey. I'm sick of your smutty mouth all the time and your threats. Not everyone has to sleep around to fall—"

"You've never slept with him, have you?" Honey sounded accusing.

"Lots of times."

Sam sighed. "She's right. However, they've never had sex, if you can believe it."

"No wonder the two of you are so sexually frustrated."

"I'm not sexually frustrated," Tessa growled. "Why is everything about sex with you two?"

"I bet you've never even had a three-way," Sam said, leaning back on her hands behind her.

Tessa felt confused. "A three-way? Why on earth would I want a three-way light bulb, and what does that have to do with anything?"

The two women burst into laughter. If not shocked at hearing Sam laugh for the second time in one evening, she might have been offended at their continued prodding.

Honey leaned over and took Tessa's chin in her hand and squeezed. "You're so adorable. A three-way is a ménage. You know, two on one sexual experience."

Tessa's face flamed as she slapped the woman's hand away. "Oh. I know that. Duh." She pushed herself off the cot and found herself chest to chest with Honey, who smiled like the wolf about to eat Little Red Riding Hood. "Move," she demanded, although her heart felt like it was about to jump out of her chest. Honey's good humor faded as her eyes squinted. Prepare to die kept playing in her head.

A knock at the door then in walked Ken Montgomery, all military macho and serious. "Heard loud voices. What's going on?"

Sam pointed to Tessa. "Just tutoring Tessa on what a ménage is. She's never participated in one. So, we were thinking—"

"Count me in," he interjected.

Tessa opened her mouth to object but fell mute.

"How can I help?" He tilted his head and appeared innocent of the torment. "I'm at your service. Anything to make the world a safer place."

Honey stepped aside and let Tessa move into open floor space as she waved them off. "Ha. Ha. Ha. Once more, I'm the butt of your jokes when I'm trying to be serious."

"I was being serious," Sam said, wide-eyed with fake innocence.

"Me, too," Ken said in a matter-of-fact voice. "How should we do this?" He removed his vest and turban hat. "Any rules I should know ahead of time? Safe words? Things like that?"

"Stop it," Tessa moaned. Finally, she chuckled and shook her finger at Ken. "You should be ashamed of yourself playing their little mind games."

"Oh." He put the vest back on. "So embarrassed," he lied. This caused Sam to sober, although the lines around her mouth indicated she remained amused, but Honey kept staring at him as if he was a piece of steak. "Probably just as well. The boss wants all of us in his tent ASAP. I'll walk you over."

"What now?" Tessa wondered if Zoric had hurt Peshmerga during her interrogation.

Ken sobered and took a deep breath. "Peshmerga has disappeared."

~ ~ ~ ~

Chase pulled back a tarp he'd seen earlier. A crate of missiles with various markings on them and the signature green band told him all he needed to know. Mustard gas.

Darya squatted down to get a better look. "Wonder how they plan to launch these."

"Knowing them, they'll lay these puppies on the ground and have target practice until they leak or explode. Even if we manage to call in an air strike to set them on fire, there is no guarantee the bombs would have any effect at all this far below ground. We'd just manage to destroy this UNESCO site and have the world hating us for yet another incident they believe was carried out by war mongers."

"There's got to be more." He counted them. "Eight won't have the impact they're wanting if Saudi Arabia and Israel are to get involved."

"Let's keep looking."

Once the area was thoroughly searched, Darya remembered several places in the tunnel and suggested they look there. Chase gave him the flaming torch and followed him through a hidden door. The area was at least twelve feet wide and walls constructed of stone. The floor was a mixture of flat stones and perfectly formed brick that may have been added later in the castle's life. They were a bit uneven from previous earthquakes, settling, and age, so navigating the awkward steps that were wide and spaced a meter apart caused Chase to lose his focus. A wave of dizziness swam up to overtake him, until he had to lean against one of the walls.

"Sorry. I'm a bit wasted."

Darya stopped and waited for him to revive. When he didn't, the Tribesman told him to stay put. "I'll be right back. The area ahead is where I thought might be used as a storage area."

"Go ahead. I just need a minute."

Darya handed him a small flashlight. "Use this if you need light. Can't see your hand in front of your face down here."

Watching him disappear down the tunnel gave Chase a sense of abandonment. Fear bit at his sense of location when something scurried across his feet. He clicked on the flashlight in time to see a rat moving inside an opening in the wall. This part didn't match up with the rest. It was loose and made of different stones. Moving two caused several others to fall. The opening was big enough for him to shine his light.

The movement of a torchlight caught in his peripheral vision as Darya made his way back to his side. "What's this?" he asked.

Chase leveled his light through the opening for the Tribesman to get a better look. He stood there for a few seconds as if trying to make sense of what he saw then withdrew to stare at the captain. "I think we struck pay dirt."

~ ~ ~ ~

The following morning, Chase felt a hard jab against the bottom of his foot. Startled, he rose up on his elbows to see Amir standing to the side of him, and one of his soldiers holding a rifle at the foot of his bed. He realized it had been used to wake him. Once upon a time, it would have been easy to snatch it away from the soldier and slam it against his face for waking him. Today, it was a memory of his past ability. If he survived this, his goal would be to get back in shape and teach these idiots a lesson to never disturb a sleeping bear.

When he was a boy growing up, his mother, a full-blooded Cherokee, had called him Yona, meaning bear in her native tongue. His father had been a big man, of Nordic heritage, and Chase inherited his physique from him. His maternal grandfather had taught him the ways of the black bear roaming the Smokey Mountains. He longed to get back to being Yona once more. But now was not the time or place.

"Tell your social misfit if he ever touches me again, I'll ram that rifle down his throat."

Amir hmphed. "Tell him yourself. You speak Arabic. I think by the fear on his face, he knows this may have been a mistake." He waved the man off with instructions to get the others ready to leave. "Pull yourself together, Captain Hunter. We are going to do a little hunting today. More of my men arrive tonight from all over the Middle East to join me in this glorious time of transformation and regime change."

"What the hell does that even mean?" Chase stood and dressed. "Who are these men you're talking about?"

"I always have the impression your questions are actually a kind of soft interrogation. Why do you think that is?"

"Oh, I don't know. Maybe because you're a narcistic sociopath with trust issues."

Amir chuckled good-naturedly. "Big words again. In this day and age, these traits would come in handy when ruling a country, especially one as big as Saudi Arabia."

"So, what's the plan? You think you're just going to march into Riyadh then the king and Prince Muhammed will hand you the keys to the palace? The prince is not a forgiving person and very much wanted to deal with you himself if you were ever caught."

"Well, he hasn't managed to do that, now has he?"

"No. But I wouldn't underestimate him."

"Whose side are you on anyway?" Amir sounded confused.

"The side that keeps me alive and gives me what I want."

"And what is that?"

"Money. Lots of it. I have plans of my own. Doesn't appear the cash I was promised from Soraya's production company or her uncle is going to come through. I'll kind of like being on the winning side for a change, too, if you think you can pull it off."

A slow smile spread across Amir's face. "I think we'll make a good team.

"Give me my meds."

"Of course. Right after you make a little video for me to send to your news outlets back home."

A hard knot formed in Chase's gut. Professing his anger and outrage against the country he loved more than life itself would kill him. He'd never be able to run away from such disgrace. If people found out he did it under duress and in captivity, there would be many who thought he should have resisted the brutal intimidation. Maybe he would die, and Darya could tell Tessa the truth. She always saw him as a hero, and she would be the one he wanted to know the truth.

CHAPTER 30

شهيد

Chase was escorted before a camera by a couple of guys who dressed more or less in Western-style clothing. There was fancy lighting and a black backdrop with the flag showing a large sword dripping with blood hung on the stone masonry. He picked up on the lack of notable details to pinpoint where they might be located. Maybe they weren't as stupid as he first thought. He wondered how this would play out in the news.

American Special Forces soldier turns his back on America.

American soldier decides to take revenge on the country he served.

Who is the man who betrays his country?

Has one of our own been brainwashed to turn his back on America?

The lead-ins kept hitting him to the point where he thought he would lose his mind. He had to hope there would be someone left to tell the truth. What if his team saw the video? Would their confidence be jeopardized, or would they see it for what it was: propaganda. What if Tessa's kids saw this? The thought of their disappointment in him was too much to bear. He wanted to be their dad, to be there through the good and bad, play catch, coach their baseball teams, go on vacations, and watch them grow up. Everything was at risk. The love of his life might never forgive him.

"Stand over here, Captain Hunter," one of the videographers instructed.

He moved to where they pointed and spotted a large piece of cork wrapped partially with butcher paper propped against an equipment case. The Arabic lettering was crude, but what he was able to read made him sick to his stomach. One of Amir's men picked up the cork board and held it in front of him. "Can you read this?" he asked.

"Yes. Can you?" he snapped. From the way the man glowered at him, he assumed the answer was no. "Ah, too bad. I don't believe what it says about your mother anyway."

Amir tapped his chin as a frown deepened the lines round his mouth. "You have a death wish, Captain Hunter. Let's have a rehearsal first, then we'll begin the filming. Ready?"

"Let's get this over with."

~ ~ ~ ~

The Enigma team searched for Peshmerga, but she was gone, disappeared into the night in spite of the storm, or maybe because of it. The sky opened up, and a downpour ensued for nearly ten minutes followed by a slow, steady rain for the next few hours. Rivers of sludge, mud, and human debris made searching in the camp impossible. People were tucked inside their tents, trying to keep warm and in no mood to answer questions with crying babies and hungry bellies. Hunting the unfamiliar landscape surrounding the facilities ended up being a hopeless endeavor.

"What if she's hurt or was taken?" Tessa offered as they entered the director's tent after an exhaustive search.

"Your unicorn sparkle is showing again," Honey moaned.

"Up yours," she retorted. "I'm sick of your and Sam's constant torment."

Everyone appeared to freeze in place and stared at the aggressive comeback to a woman who was known for having the last word in any confrontation. Honey squinted as a smirk thinned her lips. She raised her chin at Tessa, and a wave of relief washed over her.

When no retribution happened, the team appeared to take a sigh of relief, except the director.

"I don't have time for female drama, so whatever is going on between you three, get it under control or I will."

"Yes, sir," Sam said stiffly, cutting a sharp gaze to Tessa then Honey. "Won't happen again."

"Tessa, you'd better stop acting like a rookie and get your shit together. Understand?" The director snarled.

She blinked, startled he spoke so harshly to her, when most of the time he acted like a loving father. "Of course, Director Clark. I'm just a little—"

"I don't want excuses. Either you're a team player or you're not. I'll send your ass back to Incirlik Air Base if you can't pull your weight and use that big brain of yours. Got it?"

"Yes, sir."

The obvious silence would have been deafening if not for the rumble of thunder outside. She dared sneak a look at the others, and they were either staring straight ahead or at their feet. They hadn't heard the director speak to her in this manner. To say she was embarrassed would be putting it mildly.

"Peshmerga can take care of herself," the director continued. "She has friends here. If she wanted help, all she had to do was ask. Chances are good she took off to meet contacts and will be back by morning."

"Do you trust her?" Ken asked.

"No. But she is the only way we have right now to contact the man called Khan. I'm hoping we'll have a better idea if Captain Hunter has found the WMD soon. According to Peshmerga, he is in pretty bad shape. It is imperative we get him out ASAP, even if he hasn't located the weapon. It may have been moved or be already in place."

"And Prince Muhammed?"

"He has his own agenda I won't share at this time. I believe, for now, we can trust him."

Vernon, Enigma's tech wizard, had been playing around with his equipment during the entire search. He had managed to secure his equipment in hidden compartments before the border inspection. Now, he stared at several screens like they held a map to the location of the Holy Grail.

"Director, radar shows a lot of movement south of Damascus. I estimate maybe several hundred troops."

"Keep me posted, Vernon. Thanks. Anything on Peshmerga?"

"The tracker I put in her backpack activated several minutes ago. Signal is in and out. Probably improve when the weather clears. Not one of my best toys. Anyway, she's currently five miles from here."

"Alone?"

"So far. Looks like she's stopped. She took cover. Maybe waiting out the storm. Can't tell if it's a structure or possibly a cave. As I said. Not so reliable in this weather." He then addressed Tessa. "I think she's okay, Mrs. Scott." Vernon couldn't give himself permission to call her by her first name. He was the youngest of the crew and the only one who treated her with respect.

Tessa mouthed "thank you."

The director let his gaze go back and forth between Vernon and Tessa, with a little contempt. "The rest of you get some sleep. We leave at dawn whether Peshmerga is back or not. Hopefully, we'll have more information to what Amir is up to and where by then. Our intel believes he's at Krak des Chevaliers."

"Our UNESCO cover should help get us that far," Zoric said as he made his way to the door. "I'll study the layout again tonight."

"I'm watching the place. The movement of those troops, or whatever they are, might be headed there." Vernon turned back to his computer toys.

"Night. Now beat it," the director said, throwing up a dismissive hand. Everyone stepped toward the exit. "Except you, Tessa."

The team gave her sympathetic nods and disappeared. She wondered if he indeed would send her away. Although this place frightened her, the thought of leaving without knowing Chase was safe and getting the medical help he needed was torture.

The director turned his back and checked on Vernon's progress before pivoting toward her.

"Sir, I am so sorry I let Honey get to me. I'm just—"

He held up his hand for her to stop. "I want to caution you about ticking off the wrong people."

"Honey or Sam? Seems to me I'm screwed no matter what I

do."

"I meant Prince Muhammed and Peshmerga. Both are from different cultures than us, and what you think you know or understand could be something else entirely."

Tessa nodded in agreement. "I'll be careful. I was blindsided by Peshmerga. Why would she cozy up to the prince?"

"Zoric planned to find out. Truthfully, I think the woman is too dedicated to the cause to throw in with anyone from Saudi Arabia, especially the prince. I'll admit it does puzzle me. But that is beside the point. It is Prince Muhammed causing me concern. He is fond of you because you saved his life. He approached the Secret Service about hiring you. Even though you don't work for them, they refused the offer."

"Thank you, sir," she said more formally than she ever had before. In the past, she'd played coy, along with the I'm-so-innocent card to get under his skin. She didn't think it would work here. "Is that all?"

"No." He folded his arms across his chest and leveled a narrowed look on her. "One more thing. Chase isn't doing so well. He's injured and has been given enough drugs to kill a horse a couple of times. Thanks to the man named Khan who saved his life, he continues to search for the WMDs even though he could have left. He's also protecting Soraya. However, it appears she is up to her neck in this. Are you and Chase in a relationship I should know about?"

Tessa blinked nervously and wanted to tell him it wasn't any of his business, but instead she told the truth. "Yes, we're in a relationship, but there isn't anything you need to know—except…"

"Except what?" he said slowly.

"This may very well be my last mission. I have a family to think about, and the world keeps getting more dangerous every day. I believe Chase may want that, too, or at least to be removed from the line of fire. I want my life to be normal again."

"You should have thought about that before you agreed to join Enigma."

"I really wasn't given a choice, sir."

A devious, thin smile touched his lips then disappeared.

"There's always a choice."

"Jail or Enigma. Now, let me think," she quipped.

"Well, I didn't say choices were always ideal." He dropped his hands to his waist. "I'll admit, I didn't think you'd have the guts to stick it out. But your transformation has been remarkable."

"Thank you. May I go?"

"As to Honey and Sam…"

Tessa went on alert.

"Be careful. Both are a little…" He tapped his head and rolled his eyes.

"Yes, sir. I know."

Once outside, she took a deep breath, relieved to be out of the director's crosshairs. Everyone at Enigma had their way of intimidation, but Director Benjamin Clark was the king. All he had to do was lower his chin and look down his narrow nose at you to make you stutter or scramble to get answers. Usually, she wasn't a victim of that treatment, but tonight she could feel it.

A match lit and highlighted Ken's face as she stepped toward her quarters. He took a drag from his cigarette and exhaled. "Have you been taken to the woodshed?" Once more, she picked up on the no-nonsense tone in his voice.

"More or less. Shouldn't you get some sleep?"

"Wanted to make sure you made it back to your charming roommates."

"With any luck, there won't be any booby traps. I wasn't gone long."

"Don't let them get to you." He dropped his cigarette in the mud. "I think they enjoy embarrassing you."

"I wasn't aware you and Honey were involved." It wasn't any of her business, but curiosity killed the cat.

"We've hooked up a few times but definitely are not involved. She is pretending to like you, so watch your back."

"Why would she do that?"

"Probably because she knows I'd kick her to the curb if I thought I could be your number one."

She stepped back.

"Don't worry. I know we're friends. Good friends. You and Chase have been going at this cat and mouse game so long, you don't even know how to stop. I'm just saying, I think you're all right. I'm proud of you. Proud to be your friend."

"So, you were just teasing about the three-way," Tessa said,

giving him a soft fist bump to the arm.
"No. I was pretty much all in for that."

CHAPTER 31

شهيد

Prince Muhammed stared across the open terrain and calculated his next move. The anticipation gave him an itch he couldn't scratch. Knowing he was close to the time when he could correct a lot of mistakes from the past gave him the ability to see his future clearly. His father had favored his oldest son to take the throne upon his death, but that all changed when Muhammed's brother was killed in an midair collision over the Nefud Al-Kebir, a large sand dune desert in the northern part of the Arabian Peninsula. There had been rumors of foul play, but no evidence proved the theory.

The older prince had been known in some circles as cold and distant, whereas Prince Muhammed made it a point to mingle among the people and show compassion. He practiced Islam openly, donated to causes, and appeared to be a devoted husband—most of the time. Internationally, he developed a playboy reputation. However, his military career showed a more focused and motivated prince, one who had plans for his country. Although he enjoyed the lavish life his position afforded him, he also had a taste for roughness and danger. Once his brother died, he was no longer allowed to be a test pilot for the sake of the throne and a grieving father. That didn't mean he was denied access to the latest military toys that took a great deal of practice and intelligence to master, which he did.

His good looks got his picture on the cover of several European magazines and caused quite a stir among the royal family. This failed to inflate an already overconfident ego but managed to open doors for him. The world saw him as the future king and did what was necessary to secure a position in his good graces in order to keep the oil flowing their way.

Now, here he stood, bodyguards at bay, with the dry winds of change touching the hem of his robe and twisting the red-checkered keffiyeh headscarf on his head. Although the Turkish government had now been informed of his presence, the prince knew they would be suspicious of him working with the Americans.

Saudi Arabia's relationship with Turkey had always fluctuated between cooperation and distrust. Once asked about their on-again, off-again relationship on a TV program in France, he responded merely that it was complicated. In spite of being economic partners, the political agenda led Saudi Arabia to campaign against Turkey being a part of the United Nations Security Council for several years. It was a touchy subject between them.

On a personal level, he resented that his sister had lived here, married to a PKK member, and they did nothing to help her get back home to her family. Although his father and mother had turned their backs on her, he had not. She had been his friend, playmate, and protector growing up. Once Soraya, his niece, had become an international celebrity, Turkey decided to claim her as a citizen and let her be their ambassador of sorts for their international tourism. The woman was an embarrassment to his royal family.

Now, here he was, a victim of their treachery. After all he'd done for his sister behind his father's back, his niece's part in this possible attack on Saudi Arabia with a chemical weapon was unforgiveable. To involve Israel into it and ignite an unnecessary war, dragging the world into chaos, was beyond anything he could imagine. This would destroy them. He'd promised his father he would take care of Soraya himself.

Then there was Peshmerga, a typical Kurd through and through, brave, hardheaded, and willing to feed him the information he wanted to keep his finger on the pulse of what was happening.

What to do about her afterward would be decided later. For now, her curiosity toward him and his importance played in his favor. So far, she had been a willing participant. If at any point that changed, her disposal would be simple enough. His inner circle could see to those matters. Getting involved in a scandal wasn't an option. He didn't tolerate messy or loose ends.

His thoughts drifted to Agent Tessa Scott and their first encounter. To say she was lovely was an understatement, but it was her wholesome, American-apple-pie persona that charmed him. He found her aura of innocence and sincerity refreshing in spite of her being able to take down the men who tried to kill him. Most American women he'd met were players. Whether they were politicians, business CEOs, celebrities, or escorts, they all wanted something from him because he was a wealthy member of a royal family. He took advantage of their weaknesses and greed.

Tessa was cut from a different mold. Not once did she flirt or take advantage of his generosity. She requested only his friendship. There was no pressure between them. Perhaps he shouldn't have been so forward a few nights earlier, when they'd finally found themselves alone. She'd transformed from a goddess dressed in red at their first meeting to army fatigues and no makeup. It made him feel young and vulnerable again to enjoy a woman merely because she was pleasant to be around. The sound of her voice and laughter helped him forget who he was and the weight of responsibility on his shoulders. Maybe that was why the director of Enigma had chosen her for him.

Captain Hunter appeared to take a special interest in Tessa as well. Was he her boss or something more? After investigating the offshoot of the president's National Security Agency offices, along with Homeland, he realized Enigma was a watchdog with sharp teeth, unlike the Secret Service, FBI, and CIA.

"I would very much like to offer your agent a position with my people who protect me." He had taken the captain aside after Amir had invaded his quarters. "If I know Amir, he'll not stop until he kills me."

"I'm sorry, Prince Muhammed. Agent Scott is not in the protection business. She's more of an analyst."

"A very well-trained analyst it seems."

"Lucky for you."

Later, the prince found out the two of them were very close outside of work and had worked as a team on several missions. Now, here she was, part of the rescue effort to find Captain Hunter. Thanks to Peshmerga, he'd known all along where he was. Perhaps it could be used as a sort of enticement to get to know Tessa on a more—personal level. It wasn't so much he wanted a romantic experience with her, but he did want her undivided attention, similar to the night she saved him. What if it had been the other way around? Maybe he should try and create such a scenario.

Seeing Tessa with Peshmerga concerned him the Kurd might reveal their relationship. She reassured him their secret would remain hidden. He had reprimanded her for sneaking over earlier than advised, but apparently no one noticed. He'd watched the two women and compared them during dinner. He'd been seated with high-ranking officers who made small talk and performed their diplomatic duty flawlessly. But he hardly listened. Several times, he'd made visual contact with Peshmerga, warning her to be careful.

Now he would move forward with his plans. Being a prince had its advantages.

CHAPTER 32

شهيد

Chase knew Darya needed time to remove the chemical weapons in the dungeon area. He wanted to make sure his men had protection in case there was a leak. The tricky part was replicating the boxes and cannisters with decoys. The Tribesman assured him there would be no problem getting them out. If they could be taken to another location a few miles away, then the coordinates could be called in and the fly boys do their thing. Hopefully they would incinerate the menace before they could be launched into Israel or Saudi Arabia. Keeping Amir and his men from going down and checking on them might be tricky. Thus far, there had been zero activity toward checking on them.

The video of him pronouncing his loyalty to Amir and regime change in Saudi Arabia made him sick to his stomach. He read the script of lies on how the US had given money under the table to keep the royal family in business in the name of oil. The US was the cause of human rights violations and the oppression of the common man. The fabricated lies sent chills up his spine. Would the people of Saudi Arabia rise up against the royal family?

There was no mention of chemical weapons. To admit they had them would put both countries on high alert. Amir wanted the weapons to cause chaos, misinformation, and mistrust so he could more easily slip in the back door of Saudi Arabia and unseat the king. His knowledge of the coming and goings of the family, security systems, and various palaces gave him a definite edge.

"Thank you, Captain Hunter. That wasn't so hard, was it?" Amir said calmly as they walked outside to where a line of supply trucks waited. Several had men packed inside and others appeared to be empty. "Now if you'll come with me, we'll head out to meet your friends."

"My friends?"

"Yes. The ones looking for you. I suspect they are also searching for the WMDs I have stored away for safekeeping."

"What are you talking about?"

Amir arched an eyebrow and opened the door of the truck. "You ride in the back with my men." He reached in his pocket, pulled out two pills, and shoved them into Chase's hand. "These should help you. The road ahead is pocked with holes from shelling over the years. Wouldn't want you to be uncomfortable."

"I want a weapon," Chase growled.

"Very well," Amir said with a sigh.

He motioned for a ragtag follower dressed in black from head to toe. The only defining feature Chase could describe were small beady eyes set too close together and a limp. After being handed an AR-15, this new terrorist hurried to the other side of the truck and pulled himself into the driver's seat.

"Let's hope there isn't a cause to use it," Amir quipped. "I would hate for one of your friends to get hurt."

Chase remained quiet to keep from saying he would prefer to mow everyone down now, but there were too many others in the area anxious to return the favor. And if he failed in killing Amir, then Tessa would be the victim of his wrath, along with the others who depended on him.

As the trucks moved out, Chase noticed few people of the village enter the castle with baskets of food for their return. Their gaunt faces gave him the impression they didn't have it to spare. They were all men, and the question arose to where the women might be. Hidden most likely against any interest these men might take in them.

~ ~ ~ ~

The refugee camp was awake and stirring as the Enigma team loaded up to move to their next task posing as a UNESCO team and inspect Krak des Chevaliers as permitted by the Syrian government. It was a sign of goodwill, and they would be checking several more sights along the way. They were warned of the dangers and given permission to bring a protection detail.

"Director, a signal was sent out from Krak des Chevaliers with a video attached. I captured it." Vernon's forehead creased.

"Let's see it," he said as they rode side by side in the back seat of the truck rolling down the road. It was Chase. "Good heavens, what have they done to him," he growled.

"They left a way in so I can destroy the original through their operations. Child's play. They don't know what they're doing."

"Copies?"

"No way to tell, but I'm guessing they are sure of their ability to keep it safe on their equipment and didn't bother in case they wanted to send it again. Most of these guys couldn't find their way through a simple puzzle and only know the basics. I'll keep an eye on it. But this one is dead in the water. No one will see Chase like this."

The director nodded and could never remember feeling so desperate. Chase had been like a son to him, and to see him a shadow of the man he was two months ago caused a wave of murderous rage to swell inside him. The thing he had to hold on to was knowing Chase Hunter was a man above all others. He loved his country and was the ultimate officer and a gentleman right up to the point where his life or the lives of his team were threatened.

"Thank you, Vernon." He laid a hand on the young man's shoulder, causing Vernon to stiffen with a startled expression on his face. "We depend on you, son."

Except for a few puddles pooled in hollowed-out stones, most of the rain had been sucked into the dry earth and left little hint at the downpour the night before. The air was cooler, cleaner but when the sun emerged from behind the clouds, the temperature spiked enough to make the team uncomfortable.

Zoric, Ken, and Tom Cooper kept their weapons readied as the others stretched their legs and nibbled on MREs provided at the air base. Sam and Honey alternated with the men so they could take a break, but Tessa pored over maps, intel, and the video of Chase.

Everyone took their turn to view the video.

"They're going to pay for that," Ken promised.

"I managed to upload a virus to their system, so not much chance it went anywhere. He looks bad though. Never seen him so thin," Vernon said, shaking his head. "Makes me sick."

Tessa covered her concern with a hard gaze at the surrounding environment, as if she might be trying to manage this pain.

"Tessa—" the director whispered to her.

"I'm fine. He'll be fine. We just need to get him out of there and bring him home." She pivoted and moved to lean against the truck.

"Let's load up, people," the director ordered.

Pulling back onto the road, they had gone no more than a half mile when part of the road collapsed with an explosive blast. Tessa was one of the team that slammed against the door as the truck crashed into a boulder protruding over the edge of a steep cliff. She was pinned inside as the mud, from the night before, caused the truck to slide toward the edge.

CHAPTER 33

شهيد

The truck stopped after the back tire popped and the wheel became wedged between two large rocks. Sam managed to push the passenger side door open with her foot, and a person on the outside held it for her as she slid out. As she did, she reached a hand back inside for Tessa, who grabbed it like a lifeline. Scooting across the seat made the truck unsteady, especially as Ken and the director also exited. Honey, Zoric, Tom, and Vernon were in the second truck and she didn't know their status until her feet were on the ground.

She was momentarily distracted by the groan of the truck as gravity pulled it downward off onto a ledge and it rolled into the deep ravine.

"What happened?" She pivoted around to check on her teammates.

With backs to her, the others had their hands raised, facing roughly twenty men with rifles aimed at them. Several ran, yelling, around the team, waving with one hand on the rifle, the other in the air. Ken stood rigid next to her, chin lowered, along with his AR-15, his finger on the trigger.

"Ken, please. Don't do anything stupid," she pleaded quietly.

He locked gazes with her and blinked slowly before turning his attention back to what appeared to be bandits.

"Ken," she said again. "Please."

The director stepped in front of him and raised his hands to distract Ken whose eyes were narrowed and his forehead creased in anger. It was enough time for the bandits to swarm in and grab Ken's gun and shove her aside causing her to stagger. The only thing that kept her from falling was Ken reaching for her. He then moved to help Sam who had already been shoved to the ground. Grabbing his hand, he yanked her to her feet. Tessa spotted Honey's uplifted hands, but her fingers twitched, and her expression had turned sinister. The woman was already plotting who would die first.

Several trucks pulled up, and more men jumped out of the back as the passenger side door opened and Amir emerged. The driver now joined him along with another man Tessa didn't recognize until he locked gazes with her with a solemn, dead expression. Her heart lurched when she realized she was seeing Chase for the first time since they said goodbye a couple of months ago. Thinner, a dark stubble of a beard, shaggy hair, and hollow cheekbones turned his Cherokee good looks to evil. She'd loved how his face lit up when she walked into a room over the years. There were times it was his mischief kicking in, but other times, when they were alone, his eyes showed a deeper, more personal connection. The way he appraised her now frightened her. The total lack of respect he showed to the team was unsettling.

Amir followed his line of sight to Tessa. A slow smile spread across his thin lips as he pushed through the others to approach her. Chase followed, surveying the area around him for danger.

"Ah, Agent Scott. We meet again." Amir sounded almost welcoming. When she didn't respond, he glanced from Chase to her. "Surprise. We have a new recruit." He then moved to stand in front of Director Clark and extended his hand. "Director Benjamin Clark, I am pleased to finally meet you. I've been an admirer of yours." When the director refused to shake hands, Amir glowered and pivoted toward Chase, slipping an arm around his shoulders. "I think you know my friend. He's decided to join us these next few days. So much to do." He glanced over his shoulder then back at the director before cocking his head at Tessa. Ken postured his muscled body in front of her as if to intervene. Before he could get closer to Amir, one of his soldiers rammed a rifle butt in his gut, bending him over, only to get another one to the side of the head, sending him sprawling on the ground.

Tessa gasped and reached for him, but the same man shoved her into Sam who caught her with both arms.

"Easy," she whispered as she tightened her grip.

Tessa didn't fight the hold and felt a kind of security with Sam's breath on the side of her face and the pounding of her heart against her back. Sadness filled her when Chase appeared unaffected by the mayhem. There had been a time when he would have taken out anyone who dared get this close to her, much less threatened or touched her. His attention shifted to Ken trying to get to his feet. How could the man she loved be so disengaged?

Amir came to stand in front of her. "We meet again, Agent Scott. I see you brought reinforcements this time."

Sam tightened her hold as if to warn her not to react.

"I'm assuming you are searching for Soraya to check on her welfare?" When she didn't reply, he yelled at her. "Answer me!"

"Yes. H-her fans are worried about her as is her country," she stuttered.

"Which country would that be? Turkey? Saudi Arabia? Syria? US? All apparently claim her now that she is an international sensation." His eyebrow arched, and his nose flared. "I assure you she is fine. Very fine." A few of his men elbowed each other at the insinuation. "But perhaps you'd prefer to see for yourself?"

"We would indeed." Director Clark's voice remained deep and strong as Ken took his place next to him. "This would also be a good time to turn her over to us. It would be a sign of good faith on your part."

"I'm sure it would, but I'm not too concerned about any of that. Besides, I have big plans and I'm going to want something for returning Soraya to you."

"We can discuss it like civilized men."

"I'm sure we could—if I were in the mood for compromise. But I am not." Amir raised his rifle and shot the director in the chest, spinning him around and face down in the mud.

Between the curses of the director's team, screams of protest from Sam and Honey, and sobs of Tessa who tried desperately to pull away from Sam to run to the father figure she'd come to love, orders were being given to the men to take the prisoners to the trucks. Amir aimed his weapon at the tires of the Enigma truck and let loose enough firepower to also do damage to the fuel tank. It exploded into flames as he passed Tessa then reached back and grabbed her by the arm to drag her after him.

Chase lifted his gaze from the body in the mud to her. There was no pain or remorse expressed on his face or revenge in those dark eyes. Where was the man she loved? Had he died as well?

~ ~ ~ ~

The last few days in Israel, Carter had spent time discussing rescue operations with the military. They were on standby, but prime minister Levi had left things up in the air as to whether or not he would participate. Even though Carter taunted the prime minister about Sam's possible new love interest, or maybe because of it, Levi remained stoic and informed him, "Israel will do what is best for Israel. If you get yourself in yet another debacle, don't expect Israel to bail your people out."

"I'm sure the president will be very understanding at your attitude," Carter said, knowing Levi would always put his country first. On the flip side, he thought he could leverage his help with getting more military technology while promising to prevent other countries from receiving the same advantage.

Carter's phone hummed. He saw it was an unknown number and opened it to see Director Clark being shot. The truck was shot up and the other team members were herded into other vehicles. A quick picture of Amir in the background, Tessa sobbing, and Ken getting up off the ground finished out the video. He could have sworn his heart stopped for a few seconds before he turned to the stare at the prime minister.

"What is it?" he said coldly.

"It's your brother, sir. I think Amir just killed him."

CHAPTER 34

شهيد

Amir lifted his chin toward the director's body. "Throw him over the side. I don't want trash on the road. Can you do that, Captain Hunter?"

"The truck in the ravine might have equipment we can use. Not very deep. I'll take a look." Chase shouldered his weapon.

"Good idea. Take Kareem with you. We'll leave the small truck for you to use. I want you there when I question whoever these people really are." Amir stole a last glance at the director lying in the mud then snarled at Chase. "I should have made you shoot him."

"Anything else?" he growled.

Amir tossed him the keys to the truck. "Hurry it up." His impatience was showing as he strode off toward one of the troop trucks.

Chase watched them pull away, the prisoners in the last truck. Tessa sat on the seat nearest to the open flap, wiping away tears. Zoric sat next to her, Ken with the other two women across from them. The others he couldn't make out. No doubt, there were a few radical jihadists in the mix. Hopefully, they would behave themselves.

Turning toward the director, he watched as Kareen poked him with his rifle. In two long strides, he approached the man and snatched the rifle away from him. In Arabic, he scolded him. "Have a little respect, you stupid fool."

"Who do you think you are? You are nothing but a spoiled American trying to hang onto the coattails of Amir, the next ruler of Saudi Arabia," he snarled.

"You're right. Sorry," he said drily.

Kareen raised his chin and puffed out his chest as if he'd won the war of words. "I'm going to go down to the truck. Take care of the trash," he ordered.

"I don't take orders from you," Chase said coldly, causing the man to stiffen and take a step back. "You know the woman you touched and shoved?"

"More trash."

Chase, in a split-second decision, grabbed Kareem around the neck and twisted with all the strength he could manage, until he heard a pop. He let his body slip down far enough so he could lift him up in his arms. He carried him to the edge of the road and dropped him over.

Next, he squatted down by Director Clark, rolled him over onto his back, and wiped the mud from his face. "They're gone," he said matter-of-factly.

Director Clark opened his eyes and blinked several times. "Took you long enough."

He offered a lopsided grin. "Payback is a bitch. Kept thinking about all those times you gave me hell during my training." He rose then extended his hand to pull the man to his feet. "Glad you had on the vest."

"Felt like I was hit with a sledgehammer." He ran his hands over his chest. "Where's the misfit who poked me?"

"Got a headache."

"And?"

"I let him go."

"You have a warped sense of humor, Chase. I think Zoric has rubbed off on you. How are you? I mean really?"

"Well,"—he surveyed the area around them— "I hurt like hell, most of the time. They give me drugs for the pain. No idea what they are. Good stuff though. Pretty sure I'm addicted. Not sure if there is any coming back from this."

"We'll get you good medical help, Chase. You can trust me on that."

"Trust you?" His temper rose. "Darya is alive, and you never thought to mention that?"

"No one expected him to live. I thought it best."

"Tessa should have been told."

"I wasn't made aware until after we had the funeral. I couldn't put her through that again. There was little hope he would survive. I made sure he had the best medical attention available. It was a miracle he pulled through. Then intelligence discovered Russia was searching for him along with the Taliban and anyone else he screwed over in his shady deals. One by one, his enemies believed him to be dead, thanks to a web of lies and half-truths. He's still a marked man and has had to reinvent himself."

"I guess you gave him a new identity and a way to do your bidding if he kept quiet. Who would believe Enigma's ability to raise Lazarus from the dead? He is good at being a ghost."

"Besides you," the director said, "I don't know anyone else who can blend in or disappear like Darya. He gathers intel and support as if he were a magnet. It's only a matter of time before an enemy finds out. There was no way he wanted Tessa to be caught in the crosshairs."

Chase took a few steps away and sighed with irritation. "Neither do I, but she has to know the truth. It's not our decision." He ran his hand through his hair. "Dammit, Ben, I asked her to marry me before I left for this protection job with Soraya. We were finally going to make a life together."

"I never dissolved the marriage between them. For all practical purposes, they are still married. He wanted her kept in the dark but didn't want to deal with divorcing her. I wondered if he didn't plan on contacting her."

"I know." He stared up at the sky. "I promised I wouldn't tell her until this mess was cleared up, but I will tell her if he doesn't. No more secrets, lies, and sleight of hand. There is enough of that at Enigma as it is."

"She may stay with him."

"It's her decision. Not yours. And not mine. Darya saved my life several times, and I'm here because of his help. He could have let me die several weeks ago but chose to be honorable, even though we've been at each other's throats for what seems like forever. If I don't make it through this, he'll make sure Tessa and you guys get home. Right now, that's all I can ask for."

"You trust him," the director said flatly.

"I do. Maybe more than any other man I've ever known. Maybe more than you." He strode to the edge of the road and stared down. "Anything in the truck I should go get?"

Director Clark continued to rub his chest. "Yes. Might come in handy, too."

~ ~ ~ ~

A two-hour drive turned into four, trying to avoid government troops and hiding from the Kurdish resistance groups not far behind. Amir separated the team to ensure they couldn't make any plans to escape or overtake his men. After being Prince Muhammed's assistant for so long, he was well aware an organization called Enigma existed and had the full support of the president of the United States.

After seeing what just one of their agents could do when he tried to kill the crown prince, he had no doubt as a collective group, they would do their best to unhinge his best-laid plans. After all, Captain Hunter had a reputation for being a ruthless killer to anyone who tried to terrorize his country or his team.

Now that the captain had seen Tessa Scott again, he realized there was no romantic interest at all. Most likely a loyalty matter since he'd barely reacted to her being pushed around. She didn't resemble the glamorous woman he'd seen back in California. She was dressed in camouflage, like the other two women. However, military fatigues couldn't hide the softness in Tessa's body. No matter how hard she'd fought to protect the prince, she wasn't military. Maybe he could cause her to fight again with the right incentive. Would it be the tall, olive-skinned woman who held her back or the captain?

He had moved Honey inside his truck and cocked his head to get a better look at the redhead. She wasn't very big; all angles and grit, he thought. The mouth was too wide and the eyes too big for such a delicate face. When she turned her head to stare back at him, a kind of unhinged expression caused a shiver to run up his spine. This one wasn't afraid of him and might throw caution to the wind if she tried to escape.

"What are you doing with this bunch?" he asked.

"Looking for a cause to believe in," she answered calmly.

"And what would you do if you found one?"

"Hmm. Lots of really bad things." She leaned toward him so fast, he pulled back. She smiled and let her gaze search his face then rest on his mouth. Her hands had been bound, but she rested them on his thigh. "Maybe you'd like to find out." She pushed herself back against the seat. "I needed a job and the market for my"—again the coy expression— "kind of expertise has been a little slow. I'm like a shark."

"How so?"

"When I smell blood in the water, I get really excited." She ran her tongue on the outside of her lips then sobered.

"And if I offered you a job?"

"Depends on the target and the pay."

"The target would be Tessa Scott, and the pay would be your freedom."

"Sign me up," she mused.

"There's one catch."

She tilted her head with interest.

"You do it slow, and I want to watch."

CHAPTER 35

شهید

Soraya walked along the top of the outside wall, stopping occasionally to peer through the rectangular openings in hopes of seeing the approaching vehicles. Spending a whole day here without one thing to occupy her was drudgery. Maybe she should offer to give a concert for all the volunteers to the cause. Then she thought better of it; there would be those who frowned upon her type of singing. Amir would make them listen. She wanted to woo all of them so they loved and desired her.

The one person who remained unaffected by her charms was Captain Chase Hunter. This both irritated and excited her senses. Everything about him forced her to admit she wanted him for herself—forever. He didn't allow her to walk all over him and couldn't be tricked or manipulated into doing her bidding like Amir.

Chase's body, still strong, in spite of the drugs, was her doing. She made sure he had enough food, water, and comfort to override abuse from Amir and his men. Although only a few times, she'd offered her bed when Amir was occupied elsewhere, Chase had to be pretty stoned to accommodate her. Once she'd let Amir watch, hoping he could learn a few things. If he hadn't been so high, he probably would have killed her afterward. The trouble with Amir was that he wasn't the captain. And the trouble with the captain was he tended to talk in his sleep about someone named Tessa.

An old woman who'd come from the village to cook for them approached her to announce the men were returning. She checked once more to see dust rising in the distance. With a nod, she extended her hand for the woman to guide her down the narrow steps then rushed to freshen up before they arrived. She ordered the woman to bring her water to bathe.

She changed into a long red dress with yellow trim. With no one around during the day to admire and fuss over her, Soraya was more than a little ready to be adored, and pampered. She missed the American captain any time he was away, but especially today when they were bringing captives from UNESCO, or was it the Red Cross, to check on her safety and good health.

Perhaps she shouldn't have primped so much, she thought as she stared into the mirror. She blew herself a kiss then ran her fingers down her long dark hair streaked with bright-red tints. Slipping a few bracelets on delicate wrists and shiny earrings that dangled down her neck, she caught the woman who had waited on her throughout the day staring at her.

"You are very beautiful," the woman said, lowering her voice.

"Yes. I know," she said, admiring her reflection. "Please announce I am on my way to meet our guests. Have Amir stand at the far end to the colonnade so he can observe me as I enter."

"Yes." She bowed, covered her face, and hustled out.

"Peasant," she said softly and sighed. "The poor are so boring." She fastened a sheer face covering to loop around her ears and double-checked to make sure it was thin enough so everyone could see her face. After a long hard day, it was important Captain Hunter knew what was waiting for him. Now, how was she going to get Amir out of the way?

~ ~ ~ ~

Amir strolled into the castle with the others following. A few of his men were guarding the prisoners, since he had insisted there be no signs of restraints. His vehicles roared through the village with lots of onlookers pointing and clapping as if he was an invading army rescuing them from the current oppressive regime. Of course, he was well aware the village displayed this welcome whoever came these days.

It was advantageous to be hospitable and accommodating to whoever the invaders happen to be. He paid them well to be his eyes and ears and assist with the day-to-day needs of his men and Soraya. The annoyance of her demands and temperament often weighed heavily on him, but then she would… He couldn't think about that right now.

~ ~ ~ ~

Darya watched from afar, as the Enigma team trailed into the Krak des Chevaliers castle. He watched Tessa vomit after going only a few steps. It must have sprayed on one of the soldiers because she received a hard shove and would have fallen if not for Ken Montgomery catching her. Then he was jabbed with the butt of the rifle for his efforts. The Tribesman sighted the bully through his binoculars and memorized his face to deal with later. He watched Tessa pull back her shoulders and drag her sleeve across her mouth. Most likely she was carsick, which wasn't uncommon for her. Seeing her for the first time in over a year nearly overwhelmed him.

All this time, he'd stayed hidden. It took several months of hard work to get back to his old self. Only pure determination, thinking he might be able to be with his wife again, made him press on. After he'd overcome so many obstacles, he soon realized reconnecting with her would put her in jeopardy. There was a good chance she had been watched, although Director Clark assured him her safety was a top priority. Approaching her meant more complications. He'd made a pact with the devil, the devil being Director Benjamin Clark, in order to keep her safe. Then he'd stumbled across Captain Chase Hunter, nearly dead and begging him to take care of her. With a great deal of reservation, he'd come to respect the captain and made him promise to keep his secret. Being an honorable man, he promised, but only until this latest crisis was solved. He wanted Tessa to know everything, even if it meant losing her to him.

The captain would do anything for her, and this he understood. However this played out, he longed to touch her one more time. To feel the warmth of her body and the silkiness of her hair twist between his fingers that would remind him of happier days when they first married. She was more than he could have imagined and, even now, staring at her from afar, he felt her heartbeat against his chest and heard the whisper of her words in his ear.

Lowering the binoculars, he wondered where Chase might be. He didn't want Tessa going into that situation without him present. Why was Director Clark absent? What had gone wrong? He decided to backtrack to see what the trouble might be. There were people on the inside he could contact to make sure he kept apprised of the team's security and treatment.

He stole one more glimpse through the binoculars when she suddenly turned around and stared right at him. Her forehead creased, and those blue eyes he loved searched for something. Was it him? Could she feel his presence? More than anything, he wanted to think so.

~ ~ ~ ~

"What is it?" Sam said, coming alongside Tessa. "Still have motion sickness? You're pale as a ghost."

"I don't know. Nothing, I guess. I felt a chill come over me like we were being watched." She put her hand on her heart and glanced toward Amir who had stopped to talk to a few locals who'd wandered up. "Sam, I'm really scared. Chase never even acknowledged us."

"The scary part is he didn't acknowledge you. That bothers me even more."

~ ~ ~ ~

Chase shifted gears as they navigated their way toward Krak des Chevaliers. They figured the castle was no more than an hour out. Amir called him on the radio only once, in case someone was listening in, to let him know they had arrived and to be aware of several tricky places to avoid. One of those places was manned by Kurdish forces, who had already set up roadblocks. The resistance surrounded Chase's vehicle before Amir could notify him in time.

He stared at a Kurdish soldier who looked a mere nineteen, maybe younger, and thought how tragic such a senseless war had to be fought by children. Amir had signed off before finding out where he was, not that he would have shared that information, since the director was with him. Both men stood outside the truck being patted down while others searched their truck. They were rough men but came to no harm after they found the bullets still lodged in the director's vest.

"I speak a little Kurdish," Chase mumbled to the director. "I'll see what they want."

"What they want is freedom, Captain Hunter," came a familiar voice.

Both men cautiously turned to see Roman Darya Petrov parting the group of soldiers with another familiar face, a woman, walking beside him.

"Don't we all," Chase said, extending his hand, which Darya gripped firmly.

Director Clark shook his hand as well but kept his focus on the woman. "Peshmerga. Nice of you to show up. We were concerned."

"Humph. I bet. You want to lecture me."

"No. I wanted to interrogate you for holding out on me."

Darya glanced her way, and she waved him off. "It is nothing you don't already know."

"It appears you were left for dead, Director Clark," Darya said as two men brought a box from inside the truck. "What do we have here?" he asked as they opened it, causing him to whistle then level a questioning gaze toward Chase.

"I'm going to need that back," Chase growled.

"Do you plan to take it from me yourself?" he asked as one corner of his mouth quirked and his eyes narrowed to slits.

CHAPTER 36

شهيد

The Enigma team was still reeling from the death of Benjamin Clark. What would become of Enigma without him? He was the steady hand that guided them, ran interference with other Homeland officials wanting to disband them permanently. Each of them had crossed swords with the man at one time or another. He'd pulled them from the fire whether instigated by a self-absorbed congressman or a political official. The director had been a man to be reckoned with. Beyond those everyday occurrences, he became the father figure, the wise sage, the sheriff with the shining tin star who they counted on, respected, and loved. He was their rock.

Now, it felt like the world had crumbled beneath their feet. Tessa remembered the devastation she experienced the first time she'd seen a movie where Superman died or Batman was destroyed. But both returned miraculously to fight another day. In her heart of hearts, she knew in real life, this wasn't going to happen. Her heart ached. By the expressions on the teams' faces and the way their shoulders sagged, the dire situation they were in without him weighed heavily on them as well.

She needed to grieve. Scream in protest. Sob a really ugly cry like a baby. Hit something. Eat a quart of ice cream covered in whipped cream and caramel sauce. First, she lost Darya. Now, the director. From the looks of him, Chase wasn't far behind.

The image of her children flashed in her brain. What was she doing here in hell? If by the grace of God, she made it back home, she was done with this crazy life. Heaven was waiting for her in Grass Valley. In that moment, she decided, if she did make it home in one piece, then no matter what the father of her children said, she was moving back to Tennessee to be near family. This wasn't living. It was barely surviving these last few years. A broken heart could take only so much.

~ ~ ~ ~

By the time Chase arrived at the Krak des Chevalier, the sun hovered over the horizon, partially blocked by darkening clouds. When he exited the truck, he hailed several men he'd seen from the village to carry in a few things he'd rescued from the truck in the ravine where they'd attacked the Enigma Team.

A movement in a window where he'd watched the sunset caught his attention. Tessa stood there staring down at him. He couldn't tell anything from her expression but guessed from experience she was crushed by the death of Benjamin Clark. He wanted to go to her and hold her tight, making the world go away and pretending life would soon be better, but he continued to wonder if this was possible.

Neither broke their visual connection until one of Amir's men came to retrieve him. He strode off, feeling more determined than ever to kick the drug habit in order to fulfill the promises he made Tessa, the only woman he'd ever loved. His body already ached from withholding his meds for most of the day. But as each thread of pain intensified, it reminded him what he wanted to live for.

~ ~ ~ ~

Soraya stared down at Captain Hunter and felt rejected when he didn't return as much as a wave when she blew him a kiss. Whatever he focused on had nothing to do with her. Then she saw the American woman in the window. They had not yet been introduced, but she'd watched them being paraded into the castle when Amir returned. All she knew was they were a mix of Red

Cross and UNESCO representatives sent to check on her, along with preservation of the castle.

She took inventory of the four men and guessed they were the muscle of the group. The three women were a great deal more interesting. One annoyed her immediately with her tall toned body and olive skin, cat-like eyes, and other perfect features. The men couldn't keep from staring at her as she leveled a dangerous glare at them. The second woman, much shorter, wiry, but still attractive with her red hair and pale skin, appeared curious, surveying her surroundings. There was something off about her, but she couldn't put her finger on it. These two women, given their circumstances, were more focused than afraid, appraising the entire scene before them.

Then there was the blonde who resembled a pathetic, scared rabbit. Her eyes were puffy, and her skin appeared blotchy, as if she'd been crying. Her baggy camo fatigues did nothing for her figure. Soraya guessed her to be the negotiator for her release and the least experienced of the party. Nobody special. A wimp. A person she could easily fool and manipulate at will. So why was Chase staring at her like a lost puppy? Who was she really?

~ ~ ~ ~

Carter Johnson watched as Gilad Levi slowly sat in his chair and absorbed the news his brother had been killed in Syria. Was it possible, the man would lose self-control and order an air strike, undoing the plans Benjamin Clark had put in place? If there was one thing he knew of the prime minister, his vengeance was legendary. You threaten Israel, there would be consequences. You murder one of her citizens, and you and your village would pay the price. But the man had never faced a situation when a person he loved was taken from him. Benjamin meant the world to him. Although they shared the same father, their mothers were different. Benjamin's mother had raised him from the time he turned two.

"Sir, Ben is an old warhorse, and you know it. He may have been shot, but we have no way of knowing if he survived. It's possible," Carter continued carefully. "Vernon apparently had to cut the feed. Let me work with your people to find out what happened."

Gilad cut his eyes to him like two laser beams. He nodded calmly as if he'd been asked a simple question concerning the weather report. "If I need your help, Agent Johnson, I'll let you know. I appreciate your offer and will take it under advisement."

"You're stubborn as your brother. Don't jeopardize his life because you dislike me or feel –"

The prime minister appeared to snap out of his shock and rose to his feet in complete control. "I don't feel threatened by you, if that was your thought. As to liking you, I find your obnoxious, self-inflated importance repugnant and childish, along with your propensity to check yourself out every time you pass a mirror. If you are concerned about actions I may or may not take because of my brother, you can rest assured as prime minister of Israel, I have the whole country to consider, not just myself. Now, leave. I have a lot to do."

Carter raised his chin and chewed the inside of his lip. Sometimes you had to know when to walk away. This was one of those times. He moved toward the door and stopped in front of an ornate, antique mirror, ran his hand through his hair, and winked at himself. Then he turned to make sure Gilad Levi still watched him. "You know where to find me."

~ ~ ~ ~

The recovered items from the crashed truck were piled in the corner of the room. Chase knew they rested over the area Chase had explored and found the WMDs with Darya. Stone barricades around the holes in the floor ensured no one would fall through the openings, but still allowed a large amount of bright light to tunnel straight to the area beneath them. At night, the lighted torches and lanterns also provided streams of dappled light. When a person's vision adjusted to the dimness, it would have been enough to move about carefully.

Searching the room resulted in no clues as to where the prisoners had been taken. Amir would want to parade them before the men arriving later. It appeared the large numbers of volunteers for change had fallen short of what was expected. Maybe there wasn't as much support as he claimed.

The possibility of these poor slobs giving a rip who ruled Saudi

Arabia was slim to none. Most likely, Amir had promised a grand prize to the current Syrian government in order to secure help. He would need their support if Israel and the United States rattled sabers. Iran and Russia would throw support to Syria, since there was no love lost between them and the royal family.

"Aw. You're back," Amir's voice echoed across the open space. "I understand Kareen did not return with you. Why is that?"

"He poked the wrong bear one too many times," he said sarcastically.

Quiet fell across the men standing around eating and drinking.

"Yet you came back anyway," Amir replied. "I find that remarkable."

"I thought we were in this together. Was I wrong?"

Amir revealed a smug expression and swung his arm out toward the men staring at the two. "Do you see, my friends, how loyal this former American captain is to me? Even he knows what the winning side looks like." There was a loud rumble of agreement and bobbing of heads. He walked over and embraced Chase then thumped him on the back. "Welcome back."

"Where are the prisoners?" Chase accepted a plate of food from an old man from the village.

"I will take you to them," he said with enthusiasm. "The expression on their faces when you showed up to stop them gave me great pleasure." He slapped his hands together in excitement and continued to beam pride. "Oh, and the fear on that Scott woman's face was very gratifying." Sobering, his gaze turned hard as he motioned for Chase to follow him. "She set my plans back. Now I have to take care of the prince myself."

"I thought you already tried that once." He sounded flippant, but the man didn't appear to notice.

"The man is a coward. Letting a woman defend him. He doesn't deserve to be king of such a great country."

"Where are we going, Amir?" he asked, impatient with the grandstanding.

"We're here." He stopped and tapped the duffle bag Chase carried. "What is this?"

"Show you in a few minutes. I think your prisoners will have a rather negative reaction. I want to witness it with you."

CHAPTER 37

شهيد

Chase followed Amir into a smaller room with a barrel ceiling. It felt cold and smelled of dust. Several LED lanterns were placed around the room on tables and in indentions in the stone walls that once held candles. The soft light gave the room a calm ambience, tricking one into believing everything would be okay. It wasn't going to be okay ever again for him.

When Amir stepped aside so that the Enigma Team could see Chase, they all stood, as if waiting for him to lead them out of this mess. If only they had stayed home, he wouldn't need to worry about their actions or frame of mind. Each of them were killers when it was required of them and could improvise at the drop of a hat.

Fortunately, Tessa had come a long way toward being like them, except for the take-no-prisoners mentality. She second-guessed too much; maybe they were traumatized as a child and required a little kindness. Those possibilities were beside the point in his world. Now she was part of it, too. The woman had complicated his life since the day they'd met. Along the way, he'd decided he couldn't live without the rapid heartbeat he experienced when she entered a room or the tingling sensation that came over him when she lied to him. Now, here she was in the most dangerous situation she could possibly have chosen, all because of him.

"Good. Everyone is here," Amir said, motioning for Chase to come stand beside him. "Soraya is running late as usual. She does love making an entrance." He elbowed Chase in amusement, causing him to bite his lip to hide the pain.

"I hope everyone has eaten and been refreshed for your stay." No one spoke. "I'll take that as a yes. It is my understanding you are here to check on Soraya since, apparently, someone has taken a fancy to her." He glanced at Chase. "She is kind of big deal in the West. In my country, not so much. But soon she will be."

"I will be what?" Soraya appeared to float into the room.

"Be a star in the entire world."

"I'm already a star of the entire world. You just aren't aware of it."

He took her hand and kissed it. "Of course. How could I forget." He gazed around at the team as if inspecting a line of troops. "Would you like for me to introduce you?"

"Yes, please," she cooed.

"Come." He pulled her after him and pointed to Vernon. "Introduce yourself for the lady."

One by one, they moved from person to person. Normally, when people met Zoric, their first impression and comment gravitated toward him being a vampire. Not this time. Soraya met his harsh gaze and spoke kindly to him. The Serbian gave her one of his yellowish smiles. The woman could have no idea what must be going through his brain. If she did, she wouldn't be trying to impress him.

His two soldiers, Ken Montgomery and Tom Cooper, were polite, but he could tell from their stance they didn't trust her. Soraya barely acknowledged Honey and Sam, except to give a snide head-to-toe once-over. But when Amir stopped at Tessa, he made it a point to give a little background.

"And this is Agent Tessa Scott."

Soraya turned around and glared at Chase then narrowed her eyes in anger.

"She was quite protective of your uncle the night we parted ways."

"She kicked your ass," Ken said, raising his chin toward Amir.

Soraya turned back to focus on Tessa. "Really? You don't look much like a person who could fight."

Tessa's nostrils flared as she shifted her attention to Amir. "I'm not usually. I was just as...surprised as Amir that I overwhelmed his men and put him on the run." She tilted her head and her bottom lip protruded. "The most action I'd ever seen before was trying to keep from burning chocolate chip cookies I made for the Christmas bazaar. I hope you weren't terribly hurt. I mean, besides your pride."

In that split second, Chase thought he'd have to kill the man if he mistreated Tessa, but Soraya burst into laughter and pulled her out of Amir's reach. She patted his arm and linked hers through Tessa's. "So now you work for the Red Cross?"

"That's right. Mostly I work for the US State Department, and I'm one of their representatives for a variety of committees, especially when called upon to intercede on important issues or political prisoners. It's more of an all-encompassing title. Just knowing the US is behind one of our visits carries a lot of weight."

"So, you were asked to check on my welfare?"

"Yes. The Red Cross wanted to check on Doctors Without Borders, several refugee camps and you, of course. My friends"—she pointed toward Sam and Honey—"are UNESCO representatives and had this trip to check on Krak des Chevalier set up for months. I was lucky enough to tag along."

"Interesting," Soraya said, glancing coyly at Chase. "Let me assure you that I have been well treated and never abused in any way. Besides, Captain Hunter made sure I was safe—and satisfied."

This time, both women turned their attention to him. Even from where he stood, Chase could see the hurt in Tessa's eyes. Fortunately, Amir had had enough of Soraya's drama.

"I asked for ransom. Yet it hasn't come." His temper showed in his reddening face.

Chase tossed the backpack on the floor hard enough to slide it to his feet. "Lucky you didn't shoot the truck in the ravine. It held your money." He stared at Soraya. "Guess your uncle, Prince Muhammed, thinks more of his niece than expected. There's over a million dollars in there."

"I told you to ask for more," Soraya cooed. "It's getting late, and I'm tired. All these strangers in the castle frighten me. Can

Chase escort me back to my room?"

"Take her then come right back," Amir ordered.

"I don't want to be alone," she fumed.

"Stay or go. I no longer care now that I have my money. You will be sent back if you continue to complain," he yelled. "I'm sure your uncle has a great many lessons he'd like to teach you."

With a huff, she stormed past Chase, snatching his hand to pull him after her.

Once out in the corridor, he shook her off and refused to let her touch him. The sound of music from the grand hall drifted throughout the castle and sounded a lot merrier than he felt. Soraya continued to stomp and blabber, in Kurdish, he guessed, since he understood only a few words. Every ten steps or so, she'd stop, pace, throw up her hands in frustration then progress toward her room.

Entering her bedroom, he smelled incense. Her attendant had lit enough candles that it felt like he'd fallen into an Indiana Jones movie. The bed had layers of thin covers trimmed in brocade and fringe. She'd demanded purple and red silk because the fabric warmed the skin on such cold nights.

"Make love to me, Chase," she said, wrapping her arms around him. Speaking between kisses on his face and neck seemed to calm her down.

"I've got to get back. You heard him."

"Don't you love me?" she pouted, stepping back enough to stare at him seductively.

"No. I don't. And you don't love me. What we have could never be labeled anything but convenience. You know what I do love? My head, which would be rolling across the floor in a second if Amir caught us." He pushed her aside and watched flames of anger redden her face, and half expected laser beams to shoot out her eyes any second.

"I hate you," she stormed.

"Ditto. Now you're talking." He casually walked out, her ranting and cursing at the top of her lungs following him.

Mumbling to himself, he admitted, "I'd rather run with a pair of scissors in a dark room full of crocodiles than spend one more minute with her."

Amir was exiting the room that contained the Enigma team,

holding the backpack against his chest as if it were a newborn baby. He approached Chase then leaned against the stone wall, dropped the bag, and lit a cigarette. "Did she calm down?"

"She will, since she doesn't have an audience."

CHAPTER 38

شهید

Benjamin Clark rubbed his sore chest gently as Darya and his men moved into the tunnels located under the partially bombed-out church that led to the underground section that held the weapons. Except for Darya, each man had donned hazmat clothing. The director hoped the suits were in better shape than they looked, but they'd know soon enough if they dropped like flies. When he'd reached for a suit, Darya held up a hand to stop.

"This is not a job for you, Director. I want you here in case things don't work out. Someone will need to get the team out. I showed you the way, so now you must wait. The weapons have not been compromised, but if we are caught, then you'll have to finish this and get help. Call in air strikes to burn this place down. That's the only way to destroy the weapons."

"We don't have planes in the area that can do what you're asking."

"Israel does. So does Saudi Arabia. We are going to move them to another location farther away from here. This way the air strike will not affect the castle."

"Well, if it isn't possible to do that, then the world will say we destroyed a World Heritage structure. They won't remember the lives saved or how we prevented world war."

"Can you reach Carter on the equipment Peshmerga provided?

She is willing to reach out to Prince Muhammed and get them ready. Trust her."

"I will do my best." Darya had turned to leave when the director took hold of his arm and turned him around.

"Godspeed, Darya. The world is depending on you."

Darya stared down at the director's grasp then up into his eyes. "And I on you, if I'm caught." He stepped away and glanced down the dark tunnel. "Be ready."

~ ~ ~ ~

When Amir finished his cigarette, he crushed the butt in the stone floor. Chase had the urge to catch him by the scruff of the neck and force him down to pick it up. What kind of man disrespected Middle East history and culture? Such apathy spoke volumes of the man.

The time grew near when he could take revenge on the man who had made his life a living hell. Killing him was too easy. Turning him over to the Saudis might be a fitting end. There was no doubt Prince Muhammed would design a form of retribution to satisfy both of them. Although she was banished from the royal family, he wasn't sure what he'd do with Soraya, considering she was the prince's niece. But, for now, he wanted to focus on the problem at hand, his team and the WMDs.

"What are you thinking about, Captain Hunter?"

"That my team is lying to you."

"Yes. I figured as much." He picked up the bag of money and pooched his lips out in indecision. "You could have run with the money. Why didn't you?"

"I told you. I'm fed up. There's more to life than saving the world. Now is the time for me to make a new life for myself. You have a vision, and I want a piece of it. A million dollars is nothing to what is out there."

"Think you can find out what is really going on with your team?"

"They trust me. Probably haven't seen your video you posted."

"And the woman, Tessa Scott?"

"What about her?"

"I want her." His face hardened. "I saw how she looked at you."

Chase rolled his eyes in disgust as his forehead creased. If Amir knew the depth of his involvement with Tessa, she would suffer Amir's attention. "Hero worship on her part. Comes with leadership. I'm sure you know all about that. Look at the way Soraya begs for your attention."

"Soraya needs a little lesson in sharing. Maybe if she knows I'm still attracted to other women, she'll behave herself."

"Good luck with that." Chase would have to do something to convince the man Tessa didn't interest him. "Want me to see what they're up to? As you say, they once trusted me. Maybe they still do. We'll see."

"Let's go."

The team went on alert as they walked in. Amir waved his guard off to move near the door. "I'm going to separate you now. The women will remain in here, and the men—we are making arrangements for you," Amir said with a degree of wickedness. "I'll be right outside should you need me," he said, glancing at Chase as he left.

The team appeared to be frozen as they stared at him. Were they waiting for an explanation or guidance? Tessa's lips became pouty, the way they did before a good cry, and she took a step forward. Ken reached out and pulled her back. Good man, he thought. Don't be too trusting. Protect the helpless, although he wasn't so sure Tessa was so helpless anymore.

Tom Cooper, the big Marine, moved with Zoric to stand next to Sam and Honey. Another good man who didn't say much but was an absolute brick wall if anyone tried to go through him. Vernon stepped forward.

"Boss, are you okay?"

Vernon was the youngest but no less dangerous, even if it was mostly with a computer. When Chase pointed for him to take a step back, he obeyed. The kid had seen his share of action, but Chase still worried he'd get hurt trying to live up to everyone else's reputation.

"Chase," Tessa whispered desperately. It broke his heart to see her confused and hurt. What must she be thinking? "Tell me you're okay."

He shifted his attention from Tessa to Ken. "I want you to make it appear Tessa is your—"

"Got it," he snapped.

"The director?" Sam asked in her usual harsh tone. "How could you stand by like it meant nothing to you?"

"And the money? Where did that come from? We don't negotiate with terrorists by paying ransom," Zoric interjected. "We gave our money to the doctors at the refugee camp."

To tell them too much would jeopardize the mission. If they were tortured into telling the plan and how it was being implemented, it would be a death sentence for all of them.

"Give me intel to share with Amir. It'll go easier on you. I'll see to it."

"Screw you. We're not telling you a thing." Honey spit on his shoes.

He stared down at his boots then at Honey. "I wish you hadn't done that." When he pulled back his hand to slap her, Zoric stepped in front of her, but she pushed him aside and jumped on Chase so fast, he stumbled backward, holding her tight against him, as she bit his ear. He twirled her around to shove her up against the wall and applied pressure on her throat. Leaning into her ear, he whispered only to have her break his hold on her neck and knee him in the groin.

Amir and the soldier rushed in and shoved Honey to the floor. Zoric scrambled to help her up and pull her back with the others. As Chase rubbed his privates and stood, he leveled a dangerous glare at Honey.

"You'll pay for that," he fumed. "I should have taken care of you in Belfast years ago."

He then watched with even more pain as Ken forced Tessa into his arms. Burying her head in his chest, he tightened his hold on her then kissed the top of her head. "Leave us alone," he ordered Chase.

Although Ken did exactly as he instructed, seeing Tessa in the arms of yet another man did nothing for his morale. Ken had carried a crush for Tessa nearly as long as he had, but in the last year, he'd showed more than a little interest. Tessa was one of the people you liked immediately and felt comfortable around. She was a safe place in the chaotic world they chose to live. Sometimes she played the part of a funny little sister, and other times, a mix of beauty and brains.

Several soldiers filled the room and ran at the Enigma men. When they reached Ken, they punched him in the gut, causing Tessa to scream. He managed to stand up long enough for her to circle his neck and plead on his behalf. This, too, disturbed Chase as Ken reached out and laid a gentle hand on her cheek. To his surprise, Ken's tone reassured her. She nodded and clung to him until he was jerked away, along with Vernon. Ken managed to slip out of their hold and landed a fist to Chase's jaw, staggering him backward. He reciprocated the punch, but Ken was ready for him and landed a second one to his chin.

Zoric and Tom mumbled a few words to Sam and Honey, but they were more focused on Chase than any words of encouragement.

"I'm going to take care of this. Are you coming?" Amir said as he walked through the door.

"Yeah. In a minute."

Once he was out of earshot, Chase turned to the women. "Are you okay?" he asked in a gruff voice.

"Go to hell." Honey had a way of making her voice sound like a pit bull.

Then he locked gazes with Tessa. She took a step forward, wearing a look of hopelessness. She mouthed the words, "I love you."

It was too much. He pivoted and rushed out without saying what he had planned.

CHAPTER 39

شهيد

Rubbing her arm vigorously didn't rid her of the cold seeping into her body, especially her heart. The man she loved for so long had vanished, leaving a beast in his place. Those few hours before he left for his latest job, she'd never known such happiness. Finally, they had come together, admitting their love and making plans for the future. This had consumed her thoughts from the moment he left. When she'd mouthed "I love you," he hadn't so much as flinched. But his hard, cold frown of contempt was obvious. The strength and safety in those arms that had protected her faded to a distant memory. Yet, he'd asked Ken to imply they were together. Why?

"Why are you so glum?" Sam quipped. "Besides being a little thin, Chase looks pretty good. That Soraya is a piece of work."

"Chase was cruel to Honey. Doesn't that bother you just a little? What he did to her was inexcusable." She pointed to the red marks on Honey's neck. "And Ken? I thought they were going to kill each other the way they went at it."

Honey waved her off. "No problem, love. It was all an act. He whispered in my ear that help was coming."

"What?" she gasped. "Sam, do you believe him?"

"Sam? Why ask her?" Honey fumed. "I'm the one he was talking to. When he said he should've taken care of me in Belfast years ago, that was a message."

"What message?"

"When we worked together in Belfast, the IRA got in a twist about me working with an American agent. They roughed me up a bit. He said he'd never let anything happen to me again if he could stop it. He was telling me he had a plan is all. I don't know what it is, but if Chase says he'll do it, then he will. Stop looking like you lost your best friend," she moaned.

"It kind of feels like I did," she said softly.

Honey threw up her hands in frustration. "Hello. No. You didn't. I'm right here, sweetness."

Tessa finally hugged the crazy Irish assassin then reached an arm out for Sam who stepped inside the group hug with a little hesitation.

"If either of you tell anyone what just happened, I'll put a cobra in your bed. Got it?" Sam said, shoving them away. "I don't do group hugs."

"Kind of makes me wish I hadn't promised Amir I'd off you," she sniffed and wiped at an invisible tear.

When Tessa put her hands to her throat in horror, Sam huffed in frustration. "Pay her no attention. She was just getting on Amir's good side. She does that shit all the time."

Honey patted Tessa on top of the head like an adoring parent.

Tessa backed up to the wobbly table in the room and eased up on top but kept a suspicious eye on her Irish friend. "How could Chase not respond to the director's death? Shouldn't he have reassured us or something?"

"He may be all touchy-feely with you, but he expects the rest of us to suck it up and move on."

"Seems a little harsh. I loved Director Clark."

"You love everybody," Sam said as she searched the room for a weapon. "And that isn't a compliment. I'm thinking when Amir is through with you, you'll stop looking at the world through rose-tinted glasses."

"Amir? Think he'll take revenge on me?"

"After you whipped his ass and all those clowns he was with—aw, yeah. If he had taken down the prince that night, his timeline for all this would have been a great deal shorter. He needed him out of the way. Whatever you think of the royal family, Prince

Muhammed can get things done. He'll make a good king. He is admired by much of the population. It's the outliers, the ones still living the ISIS dream, who are causing the problems."

"Wonder what the director would want us to do next?" Tessa sighed.

"When this is over, I'm definitely going to drag you up and down a gravel road to get that unicorn sparkle off. It's beginning to annoy me." Honey joined Sam in looking for a weapon.

Tessa bit back the words, *up yours*, thinking it might be a little confrontational since Honey was hyped up and ready for a fight. "Why not use the hot wax dripping down the sides of the candles. You know, wrist snap it so it sprays on their face then jab it in their eyes," Tessa said matter-of-factly. She shrugged. "Probably won't last long, but those iron stands are probably heavy. Bet while their digging at their eyes or crying for help, you can smack them in the mouth and kick them in their balls."

Both agents turned and stared at her then at each other.

Tessa eased off the table and pushed her hair away from his face. "How's that for sparkle?"

~ ~ ~ ~

Down in the tunnels, the dimness this time of night made navigating the twist and turns tricky if you didn't know where you were going. All the weapons had been moved, but the other surprise Chase found was next to be moved. Five of Darya's devoted men had removed their protective suits the last time out. Now, they followed him to a second chamber where the prize of a lifetime waited.

"What do you think?" Darya Khan asked the men who had worked so hard for the Kurdish people and for Syria. Their faces filled with amazement as he opened two chests of ancient gold coins. "These are worth more than you can ever imagine. This will help your people start over, wherever you wish to go. Educate your children, make doctors, teachers, farm the land, and bring back the ways of the old ones so you can live as free men."

"You must come with us, Khan. You have given us the will to keep fighting. You are one of us, too."

"No. I plan to return to my home, far away from here. I am

trusting you to do right by your people and to those who tried to help you."

"We will, Khan. Thank you."

"Let's get this to a safe place. We may not have much time. Soon fire will rain down, and we may have to still fight to escape."

Two men lifted each chest of gold coins. They took them to another part of the city and secured them in the basement of a small church where they were locked in a vault. An Eastern Orthodox priest kept the key around his neck. When the coast was clear, he led them back to the abandoned cathedral where the director and Peshmerga worked to get the radio transmitter to work.

"Any luck?" Darya asked.

"We'll see now," he said, attaching the microphone. "This thing is a dinosaur. Good news is it isn't complicated."

"I'll leave you to it. I'm going to see how it's going with Chase. If I can rescue Vernon, maybe he can help here."

"Good idea." The director nodded.

Darya secured a flashlight to return to the tunnel that exited the crumbling church they were in. He moved carefully as if a ghost, the reputation he'd earned and relied on. Maybe he could find out about Tessa. Hopefully, Chase had managed to keep her safe from these monsters.

He returned to the enclave he'd discovered earlier by pressing a hidden lever. He checked the contents, his men had stored, to assist the team when the time came to escape. He felt maybe they'd be able to escape without anyone getting hurt. Snatching up a pair of night goggles he'd left here earlier, he decided to grab several more for later, along with a couple bulletproof vests. Carefully, he closed the door then moved toward the area where the prison cells were located. He hid the goggles and vests when he heard the sound of voices.

The dungeon section of the castle came into focus as Amir's henchmen wrestled Captain Hunter's men down the steps. The two men who had served with the captain managed to free themselves and do some damage to their captors. Being outnumbered, they ended up getting a beating in spite of the Serbian and Vernon trying to intercede. They, too, received a beating, but it was short-lived as the iron doors were opened and the men were shoved inside. The echo of the iron slamming shut, then the rattle of a lock to prove they had no escape, didn't keep the Enigma men from yelling obscenities at them.

He watched Amir stroll down the stairs with Chase following. Since Darya was dressed completely in black, and his mask covered his face, he didn't worry he'd be spotted. The soldiers left as Amir and Chase approached.

"Tomorrow will be the beginning of the end for you," Amir fumed. "You should not have interrupted my plans. Our chemical weapons are over by the steps and down that tunnel. They will be driven to two locations."

"And how do you think you're going to manage getting them there?" It was Ken.

"We managed to steal several Red Cross trucks months ago. The word is out to let them pass. They carry medical supplies for refugee camps in great need. We have equipment that will send the WMDs to predetermined destinations." His mouth made a lopsided grin. "And I will have your woman with me to watch, so she knows her feeble attempts to protect Prince Muhammed were in vain."

Ken took the bars with a firm grip and then reached through to grab Amir's military-style jacket, only to have Chase place his hand on Ken's face and shove him back.

"You'll pay for that," Ken snarled.

Amir patted Chase on the back. "I doubt my friend will be around for you to collect on such a threat. You'll be left here to starve and waste away. The rats will be well fed for a long time."

CHAPTER 40

شهيد

Darkness was enough cover for Darya to watch in silence. Observing Chase in this role disturbed him. For a moment, he believed the man had turned, but then he spotted a kind of signal he gave with his index finger behind his back. The prisoners quieted for a few seconds then yelled obscenities at him. Chase rushed to the bars and yelled words he didn't understand. The others moved to the rear of the cell and spoke quietly to each other.

Emerging from the darkness, he stepped into the entrance tunnel. A torch was lit here. He stood like a statue, feet apart, arms out from his side, and his mask covered the lower part of his face. Several minutes passed before they spotted him.

"Are you our guard, you miserable piece of crap?" Ken still fumed over Chase's treatment. Darya knew of their partnership while serving. He must feel a deep sense of betrayal. The act was very convincing.

Darya stepped closer and shook his head then held a finger up to his lips. Even though his voice had changed to rough and gravelly, from the time he was brought back from the dead by the lifesaving treatment he received, he wasn't ready to take a chance on them recognizing him. In the dappled light dancing across the tar-colored walls, he stepped closer then pointed to the tunnel and ran his fingers across his other palm to indicate escape.

"A way out?" Zoric asked.

Darya nodded and stared hard at Zoric who returned the gaze with more curiosity than fear. This man knew him from Afghanistan and might possibly recognize him. Vernon pushed forward then grasped the bars and stared at him. From the first time they met, Vernon accepted him without question or judgement. They became friends of a sort. Now to see him with a swollen eye and bruised cheek made his blood boil. He was so young to be a part of this madness. The Tribesman knew, just like the rest of Enigma, and in spite of his age, Vernon was gutsy and fearless. In the near future, he would be a force to be reckoned with.

Vernon's lips parted to speak his excitement at recognizing him, but Darya shook his head slightly and held his finger to his covered mouth to keep his secret. A slight nod of acknowledgment and, for an instant, Darya thought he saw a tear pool in the corner of his eye.

"Can you get us out of here?" Vernon asked.

Darya nodded and pointed to the stairs.

"It leads to the grand hall and the rooms." It was Zoric. "Our female agents are up there. I don't have a good feeling about it. I'm not sure if we can count on Captain Hunter to assist them if they get into trouble." Darya shifted his attention from the steps back to Zoric. "Whose side is the captain on?"

Darya pointed to the prisoners followed by the okay sign and a thumbs-up. From underneath his cloak, he pulled out a tube of ointment and pointed to their cuts and bruises. A knapsack was slung around his shoulder, holding several bottles of water and stale bread. He passed it out and watched them guzzle the water before returning the bottles to him. With his fingers, he motioned for them to eat then turned and disappeared back into the tunnels.

But he didn't go far.

~ ~ ~ ~

Soraya waited until Amir was asleep in her bed before going in search of Chase. He wasn't in his room or the great hall where most of the men lay sleeping. She slipped quietly down another corridor and saw him standing outside the door of the room where the three American women were being kept.

His appearance had changed again. He stood taller, stronger, and more confident. Had the woman, Tessa, caused this to happen? A surge of jealousy filled her. The woman was a plain, uninteresting rag. How could he favor such a creature over her? What made her different? He knocked on the door, and it cracked open. The woman Tessa peeked out then swung it open and fell into his arms. He lifted her off the floor and buried his face in her hair before carrying her inside. The redheaded woman took a glance outside before shutting the door.

That would never do. Captain Hunter belonged to her, not a mousey agent with more brains than beauty. She turned and stormed back to her room. Lying awake the rest of the night, various plots took form as to how to correct this terrible mistake on the captain's part. Glancing over at Amir, she realized perhaps she should have treated him better. Instead, she put her own physical needs first and turned to the captain whenever it suited her. Maybe he was having his pick of the women and enjoying himself before Soraya killed them. Sharing was not in her DNA.

~ ~ ~ ~

As he set Tessa's feet on the floor, she continued to hold onto him and lay her face against his jacket. "Ladies. I see by the mischief in your faces, you have things under control."

"I'm not so sure I like you right now." Sam crossed her arms and glared menacingly at him.

"I'm not sure I like me, either," he snapped. "Guess from here on out, I'm an acquired taste." Honey pretended to gag and puke in a nearby bucket. "Point taken, Honey. I hope I didn't hurt you earlier."

"I was thinking the same thing about you."

"Always have to get the last word."

"Keeps me alive, I think, love." She walked around him, inspecting his tall form from head to toe. "Besides, I knew it was an act. I caught your little walk-down-memory-lane reference. I'm not sure this counts as saving me. Seems to me, I need to save you from the Botox queen you've been sleeping with."

The last statement caused Tessa to retreat and stand next to

Sam, who remained in I'm-going-to-kill-you mode. "Director Clark." Sam spoke his name flatly, like he was an item on a grocery list.

"Wasn't supposed to happen."

"You didn't so much as blink when he was shot," Tessa groaned.

"It wasn't like I could do anything to stop it. I was too focused on the rest of you not getting your heads blown off. All I can say now is, I'm sorry, and I'll do my best to get you out of here."

"And the WMDs?" Honey quizzed. "Were you able to find them?"

"Down below. They'll be moving them out tomorrow night or the next day. Or at least that's what I've been told. I've taken care of that, too."

"How?" Sam had taken on the determination of a killer. He'd seen it many times before when she was angry or in the zone on one of their missions. She was the strongest woman he'd ever known, and one of the most resourceful. The bravery she showed under fire often made him wonder if she was a robot. Men both loved and feared her. One of the reasons he'd put her in charge of Tessa's training was because she was the best. The fact the two never got along was important because she would show no mercy. Chase knew he would have gone easy on her with the first bruise or complaint and taken her to dinner to apologize.

"Cool your jets, Sam. I know what I'm doing. You're going to have to trust me."

"No."

"That's a direct order, Agent Cordova."

"Not until I know you are able to tell me what's going on. You're favoring your left side. You're injured. Eyes are dilated, so I'm guessing you've been pumped with drugs long enough that now you need more and more each day. You've lost about twenty-five pounds, probably a lot of muscle mass, too, and there's a tremble in your right hand. Your gun hand."

"I trust you," Tessa said softly.

Sam pulled her back when she took a step toward him. "You'd trust Satan's spawn if he told you he'd changed his ways. Stay put. And that really is an order, Tessa. I'm in charge here."

The woman won out, and Tessa didn't approach Chase.

"It's okay, Tessa. Listen to her. She'll keep you alive if I can't. Rely on your training." He tilted his head toward Honey. "I'm counting on you."

"Since when?"

"Since forever." He turned toward the door and motioned for Tessa. "I need a minute with her, Sam."

Sam nodded in compliance as Tessa timidly stepped forward, and he grabbed her hand and pulled her after him. "Thanks, Sam."

Honey propped the door open as they stepped outside into the corridor. They'd listen in case Tessa needed a rescue. The trio had become unlikely friends. Chase pulled Tessa in front of him and placed his hands on each side of her face. The questions in her blue eyes made his chest hurt, similar to when they first met. Back then, he thought something was wrong with him, only to learn much later, he was falling in love with the biggest pain in the neck he'd ever met.

"I've done things, Tessa. Things you'll never forgive me for. But I want you to know how much I love you, have always loved you. My life without you is empty. If I don't make it back…"

"No. Don't say that." Her arms circled his waist but was pushed back so he could stare into the depths of her eyes.

"I am saying that. Please don't turn your back on love if you ever get another chance."

"Chase, what are you talking about? You're it. No one else. Ever."

"There will always be someone else." He leaned down and kissed her gently on the lips for a second then walked backward. "And whatever happens tomorrow, I love you."

"Chase, I don't understand. Don't walk away. Please."

"Get some rest. I have to go."

Walking away from her was the hardest thing he'd ever had to do. She clearly wanted him. How long had he waited for such a time or a declaration of love from her lips? Now he had to leave to save her. Darya would pick up the pieces. He was good at that. Most likely, Chase wouldn't survive the next twenty-four hours anyway. Knowing she'd be loved and cared for would have to be enough.

CHAPTER 41

شهيد

The morning sun broke through the horizon full of storm clouds black with the threat of danger. Overcast skies became burdened with rain and teased the morning with an occasional quick shower that barely settled the dust. It wasn't the time of year for heavy rain. It was barely enough to sustain the once-fertile fields the farmers had worked. Mother Nature apparently had taken on a new partner called global warming, and together, they decided it was time for a few surprises. This would be one of those days.

The castle stirred with life. Workers from the village showed up to cook at dawn. Others did household chores that involved cleaning up after too much celebration or the lack of decorum and respect of property. The people in the surrounding village called al-Husn took pride in Krak de Chevalier. Chase assumed they jumped at the chance to work because of the fear these men would do permanent damage to the structure. Although the money they were paid, what they earned didn't compare to the tourist trade that had all but dried up. This would have to do and allowed them to keep watch on their World Heritage site.

A young man, no more than fifteen, tapped at the door of the room where the Enigma women spent the night. He brought tea and a basket of hard-crusted bread and honey. They insisted he take part of it for himself, considering his cheeks were hollow and his arms the size of a much younger child. But he refused and spoke in broken English, telling them it would be rude.

"I would love to have a cappuccino at this little café near the Eiffel Tower that has the best pastries." Honey blew across the cup of steaming tea. "It's one of my favorite places."

"Sounds wonderful," Tessa said, letting the warmth of the chipped cup seep through her fingers. She dropped her bread back in the basket. "Not hungry."

"Eat up," Sam said, chowing down on her portion. "You need the energy. Going to be a long day—or maybe not, but you need the calories either way." She reached in and snatched it up then tossed it to her.

Tessa wanted to say no thanks, until Sam pulled off a bite and chewed slowly and glared at her with one eyebrow arched. She decided there was enough confrontation in this castle, and making Sam erupt into one of her glorious acts of violence wasn't anything she wanted to experience this morning.

Before the boy left, he'd built up the fire in the small fireplace, brightening the room and chasing away the chill. They'd extinguished the candles the night before since the fireplace provided enough light. Soon, they would light them again in case Tessa's plan as a last resort had to be put into action.

They had talked into the night. At first, their conversation concerned Chase, the other agents, and how to fight if push came to shove. Then, slowly, they shifted to their pasts, their missteps and regrets. Tessa had been riveted by their stories. When it was her turn, she talked softly and after a while realized both women had fallen asleep.

Thanks to God, her life had been safe and boring. Her two friends had lived lives of intense adventure, danger, and sexual prowess. Several times, she'd stopped them and asked, "Are you making that up? Is that even physically possible?"

As she lay there, listening to them breathe deeply, stretched out like powerful lionesses, she realized how much they meant to her, especially through the bad times. Their friendship, and she used that word loosely, was dear to her heart in spite of having nothing in common, except for Enigma.

The sounds of life outside their quarters echoed softly in the corridor. Dropped pans, masculine voices she imagined drinking their first cup of hot tea the color of crude oil, the shuffle of feet, and other creaks and groans that came with being a medieval structure. The white stones, tarnished with grime from age and environment, cooled the room, making the fireplace a good place to stand to get the stiffness out of her joints.

Honey dared open the door and stick her head out. "Well. Well. Well. No guard this morning. Maybe we could take a stroll. Surely this place has jacks." When Tessa gave her a bewildered expression, she huffed. "Toilet. That's what we call it. You Yanks say restroom, which would be social suicide if you asked for that in Ireland."

Tessa saluted her. "Good to know. But we have one right here. I—"

Sam smacked her on the arm. "Honey means we're going to find a way out. Someone stops us, we'll say our toilet," she said rolling her eyes, "is stopped up."

"Oh. Right."

The three eased into the corridor and saw a couple of old women carrying bundles of what appeared to be thin blankets. It wasn't difficult to make them understand what they wanted and be escorted to the proper facilities. When they exited, the old women had disappeared, and two scrawny soldiers stood patiently smoking cigarettes. Their rifles were propped against the wall, and Tessa's friends were plotting on how to relieve them of such a prize.

"Why don't you bat those baby blues at those maladjusted gentlemen and get them to follow us back to our rooms?" Honey elbowed her.

"I most certainly will not. How do I know you'll protect me?"

Sam sighed. "She's right. This is my chance to be rid of her sickening smell of chocolate-chip-cookie lotion and her annoying perky smile. 'Oh, look how cute I am.'" Sam mimicked her in a very unflattering tone. "Do you know how many times I've fantasized about creative ways to off her?" She spoke to Honey now in a calm, unnerving voice as both women watched the two men.

"I know what you mean. I use to feel the same way, but she kind of grows on you."

"So do warts," Sam reminded her.

"True." She cocked her head and gave Tessa one of her pyschodeceiver smirks that always made her blood run cold. "Strut your stuff, and show some of the unicorn glitter you're always dropping."

Tessa bristled. "Or what?" she stormed.

Honey reached out and grabbed the front of her shirt and jerked her against her chest. "Or I'll take you back to the room and pour hot candle wax down your throat."

The two men straightened, stomping out their smokes. Grinning, they resembled teenage boys who had been admitted to a mud wrestling event with naked women as competitors. It was too much.

Tessa jammed the palm of her hand under the Irish assassin's chin and managed to throw her off guard. "I'm sick of you. You're one crazy bitch, Honey Lynch. Stay away from me. If you touch me again, I'll—"

Before she could finish, Honey let out a growl that would have had a serial killer in a ski mask backtracking. But she stood her ground, as Sam decided to get in the fray. She caught hold of each of their collars then gave them a shake. Neither woman could match her strength, and her height had her towering over them.

The two men stepped forward to stop the commotion and made the mistake of putting their hands on Sam to pull her off the other two. Then it became kind of a blur as she pivoted around and landed a fist against one man's mouth, sending him staggering against the stone wall. Honey landed a punch to the other one's throat so that his eyes bulged. Before he could act, Sam landed a side kick to his gut. As he bent over, Tessa locked her fingers into a fist and brought it down on the back of the man's neck so he fell at her feet. The other one recovered enough to reach for his rifle, but Honey got to it first and jammed the butt with more force than Tessa thought possible, into the man's forehead. He dropped unconscious to the floor.

Honey took a deep breath as she handed the second rifle to Sam. "That was so gratifying."

"You planned this?" Tessa fumed. "Without letting me in on it."

"Oh, for heaven's sake." Sam moaned as she reached down and caught the arm of one of the men and dragged him toward their quarters. "If we had told you, you'd be stuttering and batting those baby blues like you had an incurable disease."

Tessa helped Honey with the other man, each taking a leg and following Sam's lead and dragging the body back to their room. As they entered, they found a length of cord to bind their feet and hands before shoving them under their beds. Tessa fashioned gags from the pieces of greasy cloth used as napkins in their breakfast basket.

With that accomplished, the women checked out the newly acquired weapons.

"So, when you called me a 'bitch,' you were kidding, right?" Honey's forehead furrowed as if she were confused.

"Absolutely. Just kidding." Tessa gulped, pushed her hair from her face, and nodded a little too much.

"I thought so," Honey said simply and went back to checking her rifle.

She shifted her focus to Sam who had raised an eyebrow and smirked at her, knowing she just lied to an assassin. "Bitch? Tessa, we may have to wash your mouth out with soap if you keep up such language. Whatever has gotten into you?" She sighted the rifle then lowered it. "I may have to tell your good reverend about your potty mouth."

"Ha. Like you know Reverend Paxton."

"You mean Harley?"

He'd told the youth group he was called Harley in college when he belonged to a motorcycle club.

"You know what they say. Once you've had a holy man, you never go back," she said offhandedly.

Tessa covered her ears. "I'm going to pretend I didn't hear that."

"She's right you know," Honey said matter-of-factly.

Both women now stared at Tessa, waiting for a negative reaction, so she surprised them. "Maybe he could be a part of our ménage when we get home."

They burst out laughing as Honey put a tight arm around Tessa's neck and pulled her in to her side then kissed her on the cheek before she squirmed away. "You got a little sass about you, Tessa Scott."

"Well, thanks to you two, my unicorn sparkle is turning into sand and ashes."

"What are friends for?" Sam asked, slinging the rifle strap to her shoulder.

"So, we're friends now? For real?" Tessa hoped.

"Don't be ridiculous," Sam said, breezing past her, but stopped long enough to pat her on the cheek.

"Just checking. I knew that," Tessa stuttered.

CHAPTER 42

شهيد

Chase rolled off his cot at the sound of a lot of chatter outside his room. There appeared to be excitement over two men leaving their post and failing to return. They were called a number of unflattering names and various threats were leveled for when they decided to show up. He guessed Sam had taken things into her capable hands and now was armed. Those jerks wouldn't be found for a while. There was an element of comfort knowing she and Honey were with Tessa. A fleeting thought of how Tessa had handled Amir and his men to protect Prince Muhammed also gave him a little more confidence she would help buy them time.

He was able to get a mug of hot tea once he joined the men in the grand hall. The heat of the cup seeped through his fingers, and the rich smell of the brew gave a momentary hope that the caffeine would delay taking pain meds. But the thought had washed away with the last drop of tea. A slight throbbing in his legs spread to his side where he'd been beaten a number of times. Then the headache roared to life. He felt cold and hot at the same time. Within minutes, he'd swear something was crawling on his arms and neck.

"Where's Amir?" he asked, grabbing the arm of one of his men.

"With Soraya, I think."

Chase hurried their way, bypassing the room Tessa occupied. The thought of her seeing him less than 100 percent and weak was not anything he wanted to risk. If he could head this off, he hoped he'd be able to do the job that needed to be done. He tapped on the door.

"Morning, Captain Hunter," Amir said, yawning. "You are a little late for your pain management."

"Let's call it what it is. I need my drugs. Now. There's a lot to be done in the next twenty-four hours. I want this to go right."

"As do I." Amir glanced over his shoulder at Soraya who lay on her stomach, covered with the silk sheets she'd demanded. "Soraya, we have company. Keep yourself covered."

She rolled over on her back then sat up, letting the sheet fall to the top of her breast. She held it loosely and offered an impish gaze. As she yawned and dropped the sheet, Chase turned away to avoid looking at her. The woman loved to be the center of attention.

"Here." Amir handed Chase extra pills. "Space them out. I'll trust you'll not abuse these. I have only a few left. These have to last two days. I want you to have them in case we get separated."

"Sure." He popped one into his mouth and shoved the other two in his vest pocket.

This was more of a threat than a promise. It was yet another way to control him.

Amir walked over to the bed and handed Soraya an elaborate embroidered robe the color of the same red streaked through her long, tangled tresses. Without all the makeup, she wasn't much to look at, he decided. She stood taking Amir's hand, who tied the belt around her waist. He kissed her then pointed to the door. "Let's talk outside while Soraya gets dressed."

Chase dared glance back at her. She pooched out her lips in a kiss then blew it to him across her palm. He hated her. Hated what she'd help him become and hated the things he'd done to survive. Maybe he could still get her back safe and sound to civilization to collect his payment. Then again, the idea he'd live long enough to spend it became a rather far-fetched dream at this point. But maybe Tessa could use the money and build the new life she wanted. So, he winked at Soraya, to keep up the illusion he was interested in appeasing her self-addiction.

"We will load the weapons later today. Storms are rolling in, and I don't want anything to go wrong in transport. And there's too big a chance some clumsy idiot might drop one, causing a leak."

"You've never told me where they are?"

Amir took a deep breath and let it out slowly. "Down below in a room off the main holding area."

"The place where the cells and cavern were?" Chase hoped Darya had completed his job of removal.

"Yes. The trucks are worthless and often break down. They have been equipped to keep them steady."

"How will the weapons be deployed?"

"The Iranians provided what we needed along the Lebanon and Jordanian borders. They have assured us the weaponry is in place and can easily launch our WMDs into Jerusalem and Riyadh. Do not worry."

"What worries me is if one malfunctions and misses its target, drops into Amman, Jordon, or maybe Cyprus. Iranians aren't known for their failsafe weapons."

"They have reassured me many times that these are the latest and best they have."

"And what are you paying them for this new technology?"

Amir shrugged. "They are more than willing to help us destroy two of their enemies."

"Sounds like to me you're testing equipment they don't even know works. If it fails and gets traced back to them, they'll say they were stolen and untested. They had no way of knowing they were gone because they were still under development. Why would you trust the Iranians? They've got nothing to lose here."

He twisted his mouth into a frown and rubbed his chin as if considering Chase's words. "It is the will of Allah that I am successful. It will be fine."

"Oh, now I feel better."

"You worry too much, my friend. We are doing them a favor. They won't screw with us."

"They screw with everyone, Amir. I hope you're right."

"I have things to do. Check to see if the trucks have arrived and that they are in good working order."

"What about the prisoners? They need to eat."

"Why? They will soon be dead."

Chase slowed his heartbeat, a trick he'd learned a long time ago from a medicine man, to keep from getting drunk on adrenaline.

"Very well. Take someone with you."

"Still don't trust me?"

Amir frowned and walked away.

As Chase turned to leave, Soraya reached out the door and grabbed his hand. She tugged hard enough; he had no choice but to enter her quarters. She'd made herself up but still wore the robe over what felt like her naked body.

"I wanted to come to you last night after Amir fell asleep. I put a little something in his tea." She rubbed her hands up and down his chest. "But you were not there."

"Couldn't sleep. Took a walk."

Soraya gazed up into his eyes then kissed him passionately, only to have him gently push her away. "You need to stop this," he said. "Amir is getting crazier by the minute. He won't like it."

"I don't care about Amir. I want you. Tell me you feel the same way."

"Get dressed, Soraya. I'm busy," Chase said, walking out the door. As it closed behind him, he heard a crash against it as a result of one of her tantrums.

~ ~ ~ ~

Darya moved among the local people, head down, feet shuffling so no one would pay much attention to him. He'd borrowed clothing from a family he'd been helping and walked with them, using a cane. When he spotted Chase giving orders to the truck driver who had just arrived, he limped over and held out his hand as if begging. Without warning, Chase knocked him down, then caught him by his vest and dragged him kicking to the side of the road. Jerking the cane from his hand, he pretended to smash it into his shoulder but actually struck a rock. Darya cried out nonetheless.

Struggling to his feet, Darya watched Chase move in front of him to block sight of him.

"I think you took too much enjoyment in doing that," the Tribesman growled.

"I honestly did," he admitted. "Guess my aim was off with the cane."

"Must be the drugs." He took back the cane and hoped the insult got through to him.

Chase narrowed his expression for effect. "They're planning to load these trucks later today."

"Already moved the WMDs. We replaced them with similar cannisters. Contents stink, but unless you drink it or breathe it for long periods of time, it's harmless. Wanted to make sure they thought they still had the real ones. Repacked them in the original crates, too."

Darya listened as he informed him of the Iranian launchers and the locations. He said he had already rescued Vernon the night before with the help of several of his men.

"The rest of your team were as thrilled as a pit of black mambas." Darya took a moment to search the area around them.

"Didn't recognize you?" Chase quizzed.

"Kept my face covered, but Vernon knew before I got him back to the director and Peshmerga. He's a good kid."

"How badly was he hurt yesterday?"

"Nothing he couldn't handle. He went to work right away. The guy is a magician with technology. I'll be sure to pass this new information along to the appropriate people. I think I can mark the truck so the fly boys can find it. Their sensors will pick it up," Darya said.

"I have to go." Chase paused and stared hard at the Tribesman. "I'm counting on you."

"Same here. Remember your promise, Captain Hunter."

"Remember yours."

He turned and strolled off, yelling orders at several of Amir's men.

CHAPTER 43

شهيد

Dodging several of Amir's patrols led Darya on a secondary way back to the bombed-out church which appeared to be sealed off from the world. Debris surrounded the skeleton of a church, and what once was the entrance now remained blocked by tons of concrete and burned timbers. But there was an opening between it and what might have been a school. It, too, resembled a hopeless cause, but the opening was revealed after moving a few crates of the rotting carcass of a couple of rats to make going any farther disgusting even to a terrorist. Slipping inside occurred after Darya was convinced no one had followed.

"Darya, I was getting worried," Vernon said, reaching out to shake the Tribesman's hand. "Were you able to see Chase?"

He nodded and went to stand in front of an old computer Vernon had been working on. "I see the solar batteries have you connected."

Director Clark joined them. "The satellite connection helped, too. Getting ready to call Carter now."

"Before you do, there is more information you should pass along." After sharing the last bit of news from Chase, Darya covered his face again and backed away into the shadows. "I need to remain anonymous."

"Of course. Vernon and I will handle this part. Any news on the women?"

"Only that they are alive. Soraya, too, if Prince Muhammed wants to know." Peshmerga entered and came to stand beside Darya. He glanced at her and nodded a greeting but did not speak.

The connection took too long, and Vernon tried several times before he connected with Carter in Jerusalem. At first, the screen appeared snowy, but it cleared up soon enough.

"Well, hell's bells, if it ain't my little buddy. What happened to your face? Are you not playing nice with the terrorist?"

"I tried to tell those jokes you always get a laugh with, but this is what happened to me. Guess I don't have the same delivery as you."

"Gotta learn to read your audience, kid. And it's all about timing."

"Gotcha. On the other hand, someone here wants to talk to you."

Director Clark sat down next to Vernon and stared into the screen. A sudden intake of breath then a slow grin greeted him. "Never thought I'd see the day when you were at a loss for words."

"Sir, you can't imagine how glad I am to see you. We received a message you were dead."

"Most of the team thinks I am. Fortunately, Chase worked a little magic and got me out. Well, magic and a bulletproof vest. Although, I'm sure when Tessa realizes I'm alive, I'll have to listen to all her divine intervention stuff."

"Whatever. I'm glad you're okay. And the others?"

"Don't know much except what Chase has smuggled to us. The men are behind bars, and the women are kept in another part of the castle."

"How is it Vernon is with you?"

The director avoided mentioning Darya. Instead, he said Vernon managed to escape and let that be enough. Carter didn't push the matter. He went on to tell him the information Chase had discovered.

"I'm waiting for the prime minister and his security people," Carter told him. "Your brother has been one scary dude since we heard you were dead. I was afraid he'd do something stupid."

"Not possible. Israel is always first. But I'm sure within days, Amir would have met with capture or an untimely death. In the end, he would have begged for it."

"Kind of sorry I'm going to miss that," Carter admitted. He stood up, phone in hand. "Here they are. Dov Kemper, head of Mossad is not going to be happy I have a phone in here."

"I can imagine."

"How did you get a phone in here?" fumed Gilad Levi. He turned and gave a nuclear glare to his two-security people, blaming them without saying a word.

"Calm down, Gilad. We have our ways, too," the director said sternly.

His brother grabbed the phone out of Carter's hands and stared into the director's stubborn face. A deep breath was released from deep in his chest, as if he'd been holding it for a while. "I should have known you were too stubborn to die."

"So I've been told."

"And the others?"

The director figured his concern was for Sam. "Alive. The men have been neutralized by being placed in a kind of dungeon. The women are being held in a separate section of the castle, and my sources say they are well."

Gilad nodded then shifted his attention to the matter at hand. "What do you have for me, little brother?"

After catching Gilad up to speed, the director encouraged him to put in a call to Prince Muhammed for both military and geopolitical support.

"Tell him what you know and who has the money he sent for Soraya's release and her involvement with this plot. As I said earlier, the weapons have been replaced, and the fakes will be moved later today. It is imperative both of you form a united front. Get your stories straight. There isn't time to bring in security and state department representatives to pile up the BS for days. It's happening. The two of you can do this yourselves."

"I'll also call the president of Turkey to be sure he's on board, since the prince is already there at the military base." Gilad took a deep breath like a tired old man.

The director wasn't surprised his brother knew where the prince waited. "I should have guessed you knew exactly where he was."

"Always. I'm glad you're alive. When this is over..." Gilad paused.

"I'll do my best. In the meantime, go easy on my agent. He's one of my best."

"Has he been a crybaby while I was out of the room?" the prime minister mused as he once again shifted his attention to the Enigma agent.

"No. But I know you, Gilad. Give him what he asks for please." The director spoke sternly.

"For Israel."

"Yes. For Israel. Peace depends on it."

Gilad nodded, clicked off then handed Carter his phone. "Thank you."

"You promised to give me whatever I want." Carter wanted to push him a bit since he now knew Sam was okay.

Gilad didn't take the bait but motioned for his men to escort Carter into the lobby where he would wait for two hours before being called back inside to discuss the plan.

~ ~ ~ ~

"Let's get out of here," Sam said, checking her weapons while Honey slipped a knife into the sheath she'd taken off one of Amir's men. "Think if I give you a gun you won't shoot yourself?" she said, handing Tessa a small caliber handgun.

Tessa snatched the gun away from Sam, checked it then slipped it under her robe into a pocket. "Positive. But I might accidently-on-purpose shoot you." They locked confrontational glares until Sam pushed out her lips and raised her chin.

"If that's the case, you'd better do it right the first time."

Tessa pulled her shoulders back and tried to match the intimidating tone. "Noted."

"I love all this touchy-feely back-and-forth between you two." Honey laid her hand on her heart and puckered up and sniffed as if she might cry.

"Shut up," they said in unison.

The smile on Honey's face faded, and the crazed expression of a psycho returned. She lowered her head like a bull ready to charge.

Together, they stepped out into the corridor to search for the rest of the team.

But Soraya watched from afar.

CHAPTER 44

شهيد

Not surprising Amir had set up a technology room where he could keep his finger on the pulse of what was going on with his circle of misfit freedom fighters, and the world. Chase didn't believe he had the knowhow or the wherewithal to complete the big picture and oust Saudi Arabia's royal family. Although working for the prince had primarily involved secretarial duties for Prince Muhammed, such a job also meant he had to wear many hats. He doubted the job included social media and other technology resources. Of course, he would have had a minimal working knowledge of computers. Soraya, on the other hand, was addicted to social media, and you could barely turn on various outlets without her picture or comments showing up.

That's where he found her after he returned inside the castle. Amir was outside giving last-minute orders and asked him to check on the weather radar. What he didn't realize until he saw Soraya leaning over to stare at the monitor was, they had access to plenty of indoor and outdoor security cameras.

"I see you found clothes to wear," Chase said, walking up behind her. She moved to block his view and slipped her arms around his waist. "Only you could make a military-style outfit a fashion statement. He pushed her hair off her chest and admired her with appreciation. No doubt she was a beautiful woman.

"Have you come to apologize for ignoring me this morning? I was very hurt."

He ran his hand down her cheek. "I know how you like for me to play hard to get."

"Forgiven." She kissed him lightly on the lips.

"Good. Now tell me what has caught your interest. Surely it wasn't the weather radar."

"It appears your friends have entered the grand hall. I suspect they are going to go down to the lower level if they make it across the open space without anyone seeing them. Given most everyone is outside, I think maybe I'll take care of this myself."

"Care if I tag along?"

"I insist," she said calmly and moved away from him then tilted her head to follow.

~ ~ ~ ~

Tessa found herself standing in the middle of the corridor after her two friends gave her a shove. Nothing like having your so-called partners decide you should be bait. Other than a few workers from the village, everyone else milled around outside. Without warning, several men rose up out of the staircase, carrying what appeared to be long wooden boxes. Once they were at the head of the stairs, the process was repeated by yet more men.

Since she'd managed to cover herself with a sheet from their room, pulling it partially over her face kept her identity hidden. She turned her back on them and pretended to be busy as she meandered closer and closer. They disappeared out of the castle onto what must have once been a drawbridge, fortified now for safety. Trucks lined up on the other side. A lot of activity, excited voices, and hand motions urged the men carrying the boxes as if they should hurry.

Her peripheral vision caught sight of Sam and Honey moving along the outside wall, protected by the open corridor, arches, and barrel ceiling. Compared to the open grand hall, the area was bathed in shadows. They were slowly coming around to where she watched the removal of what she guessed were the chemical weapons. Panic washed over her, especially when one of the men stumbled when he reached the top of the steps. He'd spotted her and realized she wasn't one of the workers when her head covering slipped onto her neck, revealing her blonde hair. The other man yelled at him, out of fear, she guessed, and she was forgotten. But it was enough of a distraction her partners were able to watch the last of the men exit the lower level.

The three women headed down the stairs carefully, pulling their weapons to readied positions. When they reached the bottom, three men appeared into the well of light on the floor. The bright light flooding the upstairs had filled the stone wells in the grand hall. There was enough light to see, but outside the circle was nothing but shadows.

"What are you doing down here?" one man shouted at them, waving a fist.

Tessa realized he didn't recognize them because of being partially covered. She followed Sam's lead and bowed her head and hunched her shoulders in a submission stance. When they stood their ground with downturned heads as the men approached, she experienced an adrenalin surge in her veins.

One of the men dared put his hands on Sam's shoulder. Before he could say a word, she grabbed his hand and twisted his arm tight enough, Tessa heard it snap. He screamed out in pain as he fell to his knees then caught her elbow in his mouth, spewing blood and teeth out on the second and third guy who stood stunned for a moment.

Both charged at Honey and Tessa who sidestepped them and shoved their heads into the stone wall. Dazed, they staggered back several steps only to receive a kick of their boot in their crotch. This collapsed them on the floor. The first man rallied long enough to use his good hand to pull a weapon. He lifted it toward Sam, but Honey shot him in the head, then turned and finished off the other two. Sam nodded her thanks to the Irish assassin and pointed to the dark side of the room.

As they dragged the men out of sight, a familiar sound reached their ears. They followed the voices and found their friends locked in a small cell.

All three men rose from the floor and grabbed the bars and expressed relief they were okay. Ken was the first to speak. "You are a sight for sore eyes. From the gunshots, I guess you took care of our most recent jailers."

"Where's Vernon?" Tessa asked in alarm.

"Not sure. A guy came and took him last night. Had a couple of tough characters with him." Ken nodded toward the tunnel opening that was nearly invisible if you didn't know it was there. "The one in charge didn't speak, but one of the others said not to worry. They meant him no harm. There was a lot of activity after that."

"What kind of activity?" Tessa inquired as Sam went to investigate the area he indicated.

"They were in and out all night. Something important was back there." It was Zoric. "Considering what they hauled out of here, I'd say it was the weapons."

"Can you get us out?" asked Tom Cooper. Tessa always felt a little surprised when he spoke, since he was the definition of the strong silent type. It was twice the shock when he addressed her, since they had never been on good terms. She'd put him in the hospital with a concussion the first day they met, and his ego had never fully recovered.

She pulled on the large lock as if it would magically open. Maybe if she hadn't made so much noise attempting the impossible, she would have realized they had company.

"Looking for this?" Later, Tessa would remember this new voice resembled scratching fingernails on a blackboard. Soraya held up a large skeleton type key and twirled it around a manicured finger. Chase stood next to her with five armed soldiers dressed in black, head to toe. She leveled an innocent expression. "I'd drop your weapons if I were you. Or not. I don't really care."

Chase pointed to Sam and Honey who had lifted their weapons, too. "Put them down on the floor now." A few seconds of a staring contest ensued, with Tessa aware of who would win. Although his loyalty remained a little foggy, and he lacked the physical intimidation he once had, Chase remained a force to be reckoned with.

Her friends stood on each side of her. Honey's jaw flexed as she raised her weapon. Tessa threw her body into the woman and grabbed the rifle. The captain stepped forward and snatched it away from Tessa then reached for Sam's weapon. He stood nearly toe to toe with Tessa and leveled a menacing observation. A chill ran up her spine before he returned to Soraya's side.

Soraya offered a snarky reaction. "You know, for being Red

Cross workers and UNESCO representatives, you have caused a great deal of chaos. Somehow, I believe you're not the peace-loving agents you pretend to be."

"Not true," Honey said through gritted teeth. "Before this is over, I plan to show you my specialty—piece by piece."

"Amusing," Soraya retorted. She moved to the cell and laid the back of her soft hand across her nose as if protecting herself from the stench. "Don't mean to dash your hopes of escape, but…" She laughed, "Oh yes, I do. You're going to die here."

Tessa expected a flood of uncomplimentary descriptions to ricochet off the grimy walls, but the Enigma men remained in a state of deadly calm. To Tessa, this was more frightening since she knew the pain and mayhem each could inflict.

Soraya turned around and sniffed at the women. She touched each woman's apparel lightly before coming around to face them. She appraised the three then paced in front of them. Soraya's designer clothes resembled a military uniform. It was all for show when the cameras were rolling, right down to her high-heeled boots and flawless makeup. The sheer veil she wore across her face didn't leave any doubt about that. The generous red lips puckered and released often, as if flirting with the soldiers around her. In a traditional Kurdish home, she'd have been beaten for her brazen behavior. Tessa guessed being a big music star and garnishing lots of attention helped and enough money to excuse her behavior.

She moved to face Tessa. "You disgust me."

Tessa wanted to give a witty comeback to cast doubt on her heritage but refrained from throwing gas on an already-blazing fire.

"You pass yourself off as a peacemaker, an envoy for the US State Department. But I know who you really are." She pointed back to Sam and Honey. "In truth, you work for the CIA or one of many national intelligence agencies in your country. You should die for butting into our business."

"I see you feel pretty confident standing in front of us with your henchmen pointing those guns at us." Sam remained matter-of-fact.

"Yes, actually it's quite comforting." Soraya glanced over her shoulder at the men who held weapons ready then looked back at Chase. "And Captain Hunter has given me so much comfort these last few weeks." She pooched out her lips to send him a kiss.

Tessa couldn't stop the fear from boiling over inside her until she retched on the floor in front of Soraya. It was mostly liquid because she had hardly eaten in twenty-four hours. Although the fluid barely splashed on her fancy shoes, Soraya stared down at the mess as if a dump truck full of garbage landed at her feet. She had swung back to strike when Chase caught her fist in midair.

"Thanks, Captain Hunter," Tessa said, wiping the liquid from her mouth, then reared back her fist and landed it as hard as she could against Soraya's upper cheek. Soraya sprawled across the floor in an undignified heap. In spite of now having a huge X on her life, the satisfied grins spreading across Sam and Honey's face made her decide it was well worth the risk.

CHAPTER 45

شهید

With Chase's help, Soraya struggled to her feet and managed to gather her wits about her then stomped forward, only to be jerked back into his arms.

"Enough," he ordered. "Why bring them here? This was a huge mistake."

She melted against him and ran her hands across his body while stealing glances at Tessa. She wasn't shy at what parts her fingers lingered. "I wanted them to see you are now with us. What is the harm in that?"

"The harm is not only will people be looking for you but them as well. You'll never hear them coming, either. If they are found here, it is a death sentence for you and your dim-witted followers."

"Then I guess we should make sure they aren't found alive—or here." She moved away from Chase and grasped Honey's chin and squeezed. "This one we'll give to our men. The tall one can be sold. She is not bad to look at." Taking Tessa by the arm, she threw her into Chase. "Put her in the hole with your men. I want her to suffer for a while before you kill her."

"They are not my men."

He could see them straighten to their full height, but their faces were hidden in shadow. Those expressions he didn't wish to see. These men had followed him to hell and back many times. Not only had he dishonored their service, but now he made them think their relationship was all a scam.

The press of Tessa's body against him threw his body into turmoil. His first instinct was to surround her with his arms and protect her. The desire to turn her away from the evil before her and be the superhero she'd come to expect in every situation washed over him. However, this time, she failed to lean into him with fear as in times past. She pushed free then took a step away. Her steely expression crushed him. How would he ever make this right?

"Take these two women to the grand hall," Soraya ordered the soldiers. As they pushed and shoved the women up the stairs, Soraya stepped in front of Chase and frowned. "I want this Tessa over there." She pointed to the cells without walls, across the wobbly bridge on the other side of the bottomless pit. "Let her try and escape that in the dark." She pushed past him. "Join me in the grand hall while I get this sorted out. This whole thing is beginning to bore me."

"After all your uncle did to rescue you…" Tessa choked. "He loved your mother."

Soraya paused and came back to face her. "My uncle was a lonely seven-year-old when my mother left a brutal family. He remembers nothing about her life and did very little to help us when he was older."

"He was a child."

"Humph. He grew up and became just like my grandfather. My mother hated the royal family."

"You're kidding yourself. He told me he sent your mother money every month to help out after your father died."

"My mother would never ask him for anything."

"He knew that. But he did it on his own, no request or thanks necessary."

"I'm the one who has provided for my family. Not Prince Muhammed."

"Are you sure about that?" Tessa hissed. "Are you sure you threw in with the right guy? Amir betrayed the prince, and if you think the prince won't take revenge, you're mistaken."

She made a lot of sense. You didn't betray the royal family. "She's right, Soraya. We can still escape."

"Amir has a plan, and I want to be a part of the bigger picture. I thought you were with us."

"I am. Just want to make sure you've weighed all your options."

"Do as I said," she demanded, tilting her head at Tessa. "I want the little whore to suffer. Have your way with her if that is what you want because soon, she'll be dead." She left one soldier to stand guard then disappeared up the steps.

A tsunami of guilt washed over him. "Let's go."

Tessa dug in her heels and jerked away at his touch. "Don't do this."

He'd learned a long time ago she feared heights, bugs, and dark, dirty places. Tessa's Hell would be such a place. With a sudden lunge, he captured her upper arm and squeezed. His men yelled words to force him to have a conscience. Where was Darya when you needed him? If he were here, then he could pass her off, kill the guard then go get the other two women.

The bridge bounced gently. A small light well above it made it possible to see for now, but what about when darkness fell or if the storm, radar indicated, moved in. "If you fight this, then you'll send both of us to the bottom and you'll never see your kids again," he told her in a low voice. "So, do what you're told, and I'll come back later."

The team behind bars hushed as the two struggled to cross the bridge. One of the slats cracked and fell through, causing Tessa to scream and reach for Chase who was in the lead.

"Hold on to the ropes," he muttered. "Just a few more steps. Don't look down."

Once on the other side, he pulled her to the landing with one final tug which landed her in his embrace. It was too narrow to stand for long. He pulled her after him to where it was six feet wide and nearly as deep. This would be her cell.

"Don't get close to the edge," he warned. "It can get slick." He turned on a penlight and showed her the edge and what lay beyond.

She caught her breath and stepped backward.

"Stay back here." He showed her the wall with his light, that it was bug free, then the floor. Pulling out his water bottle from inside his jacket, he forced her to drink then set the bottle on the stone floor. The fear in her eyes ripped his heart open.

The guard called across the bottomless pit, and Chase answered then stepped farther back into the darkness with Tessa. He could hear his men yelling for him to remember who he was, who Tessa was, and that they would kill him if he hurt one of their own.

Then she placed her arms around his waist like she used to do when they got in a tight spot.

"Tessa, I'm sorry."

"What did that man say?" she asked.

"He wants to hear you scream and beg."

Tessa tried to step back, but Chase had already pinned her against the wall. "I've never loved anyone but you. Help me do this. Please."

She nodded and let out a scream that would have woken the dead.

When Chase staggered out before the other cells, his men ran to the bars and tried to reach him. The names thrown at him didn't affect him because most of them were true.

"I'm going to kill you," Ken yelled as he shook a fist at his former captain. "How could you hurt her? She would do anything for you."

"You shouldn't have done that," Zoric said with a low pit-bull growl. "It will give me no pleasure to punish you. But I will."

Tessa's sobs carried across the abyss. It served to keep his men stirred up to a murderous rage.

Chase observed them carefully, knowing if they were freed before knowing the truth, he was a dead man. He said nothing in his defense at their false assumptions and strode away. Once he rescued the other two of his team, then, with any luck, Darya would be able to lead them out.

~ ~ ~ ~

If he had been atop a French cathedral, people, if they could have spotted him, would have thought he was a gargoyle wrapped in traditional Middle Eastern garb. Darya blended in next to the tarnished stone, now covered in shadows beneath the barrel ceiling. He stood in the outer corridor parallel to the grand hall. Men gathered around the wells of light. Soraya paced then fumed at the lack of attention, followed by being belligerent to the workers who quickly exited to avoid her outbursts.

Honey and Sam stood still near one of the wells but continued to survey the area. Several times, he noticed their mouths twitched as if they might be speaking. Darya had interacted with Sam on other occasions and was confident she could take care of herself. Honey, he knew by reputation, and with her expertise, she would have an escape plan in the works. He would keep tabs on them nonetheless. Unfortunately, it was a man's world in the Middle East. He'd left instructions for Peshmerga and knew he could count on her.

When he saw Chase arrive at the top of the stairs from the dungeon below without Tessa, he decided to slip away while Soraya focused on him. The captain appeared to hold a kind of power over her bad behavior, but who knew how long that would last.

It was a matter of time before Amir discovered his million dollars had vanished along with his gold coins if he opened the chest where they had been stored. Vernon had given him an earwig of sorts to keep in touch with him and Peshmerga. Thus far, Amir had been kept busy outside. But a storm was blowing in, and he suspected they would soon be on the move. Time was important in matters of death and destruction. Without much effort, he slipped away from his perch and took a secret way into the tunnels he hadn't shared with Chase.

~ ~ ~ ~

When Chase left Tessa behind in the cell, an overwhelming fear engulfed her ability to think straight. How much therapy would this take to get her back to normal? She hoped Dr. Wu, the Enigma psychiatrist, was setting aside plenty of time for her recovery. Did he already know of their circumstances? The man was her rock when it came to healing her brain. But, for now, she couldn't stop the flow of tears and sudden outburst of sobs when her team called out encouragement to her. She could imagine what they must be thinking Chase did to her. But it was all part of the plan.

Her disappointment mixed with rage got the better of her as she punched, kicked, and scratched him. Several times he groaned and she stopped and whispered, "I'm sorry." Then he would twist her arm or pinch her so hard she'd cry out, for the others to imagine a more violent scene. Once, he slammed her several times against the wall when she drew blood. It was a natural response, and he quickly pulled her into his arms and told her again how much he loved her for coming for him.

"I have to leave you here now, Tess. I promise I'll be back and get you out. If not me, then someone else will step up."

"Who? There is no one else. You're the only one I've ever counted on completely. Vernon is missing, and the director is dead. No one knows where we are."

"Trust me one more time," he said, kissing her forehead. "Divine intervention. Isn't that what you always say?"

"Yes. But—"

Before she could finish, he hurried across the bridge without an ounce of fear.

Now she heard the men calling her name. The sound of their voices quieted her, and she prayed for the divine intervention Chase spoke of. Never again would she get herself into this position. What about her children, her parents, her life back home? How sweet and sacred it felt now. She was going to die here in this godforsaken land, and no one would ever find her body. If she dwelled on the facts too long, despair would crowd out any hope of escape.

Then she saw a figure standing past where the men were being held in their cell. It was more of an outline and, at first, she thought it was a statue. He held his palm out as if to tell her to stay away from the edge, so she took a step back, even though the grime came off on her hands when she pressed them against the surface. In the blink of an eye, he disappeared. Divine intervention?

CHAPTER 46

شهيد

The grand hall slowly filled with Amir's men. A few of them Chase recognized and others were the new arrivals. From the black attire they wore, he guessed they were former ISIS. Their gaunt bodies and dirty clothes indicated they may not have fared well as loners. Given their reputation, it surprised him that Amir, an educated man, would invite them to join his rebellion against—whatever it was he was trying to change. Perhaps Prince Muhammed had ignored the man one too many times or reprimanded him in front of important people and devastated his narcissist personality.

The Israel angle was a no-brainer. Everyone in the Middle East resented their success, history, and strength. The world loved an underdog, and they had received their share of support when other countries had been ignored, invaded, or been recipients of embargoes and frozen assets. No wonder this part of the world was such a mess.

His security scan spotted Sam and Honey, hands tied, sitting against two separate columns. The amusement he felt at such a ridiculous thought that tying their hands and separating them would stop an escape was misguided folly on the part of Soraya. They were both staring at him with a measured glare that resembled an impending attack of a pit viper. He decided to take his chances at confronting them.

"Ladies." He stood between the two columns in order to keep a guarded observation of both of them. Underestimating their abilities wasn't a mistake he wanted to make. "You need to play nice with Soraya."

Honey tried to twist her body to see him. "You need to go f—"

"Why are you talking to them?" Soraya said, pulling him a few feet away. "They will poison your mind. Did you hurt the Tessa woman?" Before he could speak, she continued. "How could you want to be with her?"

He'd probably been spotted the night before when he embraced Tessa and carried her inside their quarters.

"Thanks for last night," Sam sounded off.

"According to Chase, he needed us to get the stench of you off him," she moaned, leaning her head back. "The guy has quite an appetite, doesn't he? Whew. Fortunate for us, you weren't woman enough for him."

Soraya's face darkened and took a swing at him when he caught her fist. "I hate you."

"No, you don't," he sighed. "You're having a jealous meltdown. Pay no attention to them." He walked away in hopes to divert her wrath away from his agents. "Can you hold it together for a little while longer?"

She followed like a reprimanded puppy. "Then what?"

"Whatever Amir manages to pull off will determine the next move. If he gets his head shot off, we'll take the money and go back to our uneventful lives. You'll be a bigger star than ever, and I'll be your constant bodyguard."

"I like the sound of that." She tilted her head. "And if he survives?"

"Who knows. Maybe you'll have a shot at being queen of Saudi Arabia."

"And where does that leave you?"

He leaned in and whispered in her ear. "Sneaking around to see you just like now. A win, win for both of us. Speaking of which, where is the million dollars I brought to rescue you?"

"In my travel bag. Packed a few undergarments on top of it so if one of the men takes a peek inside, they'll quickly close it up. They are very offended by seeing such things."

"I'd better take care of it anyway."

After she told him where she'd hid it, Chase made haste to find it. When he returned, Amir was in deep conversation with one of his lieutenants until he saw him carrying Soraya's bag. He eyed it as he joined them. "You got a safe place for this in your vehicle?"

"There's a false door on a compartment in the tan van near the old drawbridge," Amir replied. "There is a chest in there as well. Don't try to open it."

"Don't trust me?" Chase extended his hand holding the bag. "Then, take it yourself."

Amir smirked. "No. No. You have proven yourself over and over. The space is small so it may need adjusting. I apologize, Captain Hunter. I didn't mean to insult you."

"Do you have guards on the vehicle now?"

"And it's locked," he said, tossing him the keys. You'll ride with us. We'll travel to the Jordanian border to watch the weapons being launched into Saudi Arabia. I estimate a thousand men are massing along the border of Iraq and Saudi Arabia even as we speak. I knew Jordan would refuse to cooperate. I'll take care of them much later. But, one thing at a time."

"And Israel?"

"My supporters are the Lebanon-based and Iran-backed terrorist group Hizballah. They remain the most capable people to launch the weapons. Iran jumped at the opportunity to be a part of both threats. There is no love lost between them and the targets." Amir chuckled quietly and put his hands on his hips as he glanced around the room. "This will be a moment in history no one will forget."

"Without a doubt," Chase said as he gave a two-finger salute and hurried to secure Soraya's bag. The longer he waited, the more likely a curious volunteer might discover the money was gone. No way he was leaving a million dollars in cash to a man like Amir.

Thunder rolled across the darkening sky. The first drop of rain fell as he returned to the grand hall where he discovered Sam and Honey had been brought to the largest light well. Since he already knew the wells had heavy duty screens fastened three feet down to protect tourists when the castle had been open for tours, he didn't worry the two were going to be tossed over to their death. His head ached as Amir yelled at Soraya, but she stood unaffected while he ranted. Could he take his final pill to give him some clarity? Or should he suffer through it?

"You are not in charge here, Soraya." Amir stormed up to her and stood nose to nose.

Appearing unaffected by his tirade, she frowned and crossed her arms across her chest. "I want her dead."

"And I want her for myself."

"You can't handle me. How are you going to take her?" she fumed.

In a panic, Chase realized they were talking about Tessa. "Amir, the men are staring. It's a good thing they don't speak English. Soraya,"—Chase took a deep breath and sighed— "I don't know what to say to you." At least both of them stopped arguing.

His two female agents focused straight ahead as if he were invisible. Their extra cover-ups had been removed and with their military fatigues in full view, both appeared to be the lethal soldiers they were in everyday life. There was a kind of beauty in their dangerous appearance, probably why men were drawn to them. Both threatening and tempting, the women showed no fear. Their hands were still tied behind their backs.

A clap of thunder caused most of the soldiers to cower for a split second, but the Enigma agents never budged. A torrential downpour drove a few of the men inside. Amir ran to one of the windows and moaned. Bad weather wasn't good for his timeline. It wasn't good for Chase's, either. By now, bombers were being fueled, or would they use drones? He didn't know and didn't care as long as the job got completed. But he hoped his people were miles away, or at least away from the castle and in a safe place when napalm dropped on those chemical weapons.

Amir rubbed his chin nervously and returned to their side. "What say you, Captain Hunter? You have done many missions."

"Send your weapon trucks to their destination. I checked radar when I went for Soraya's bag. Fast-moving system, and the Lebanon border is already clear. By the time the others reach the Jordanian border, it will have stopped. You have a small window of time before a second front arrives. Even if both convoys drive slowly because of road conditions, chances of meeting any resistance will be smaller."

Amir nodded. "Excellent. I knew you would prove to be an

asset." He ordered his men out to the trucks, except for a small force to be at his side. "Soraya, we'll leave within the hour. Be ready."

Once Amir was out of sight, Soraya peeked over into the light well then at Chase. "I want you to get the Tessa woman, bring her into the light below, and kill her for me. I want to watch."

He stared at her, shocked at her cruelty.

"Do. It. Now." Although she spoke softly, the words came out in a satanic whisper that made his skin crawl.

"I need a gun."

Sam and Honey broke their stare into oblivion to shift their attention to him.

Soraya spoke to one of the soldiers left to watch the prisoners, and he handed over his Glock. Chase checked it then dropped his hand to his side and edged closer to his agents to tell them, "You're next. Be ready."

Their expressions never changed when they lowered their chins in a nod. They blinked a kind of understanding Soraya didn't appear to notice.

Without giving Soraya any more attention, he headed for the open staircase. At the bottom of the stairs, the first thing he missed was the guard from earlier. His team were silent in their cell. Knowing where all the players were was the way to survive. He pulled up his weapon and moved carefully, walking around the circle of light on the floor. Soraya leaned over the rim with her hands firmly planted on the stones.

"The mystery guy who took Vernon killed the guard. The other one Sam picked off earlier," Ken said, grabbing the bars. "Tessa has been quiet for a while. Or do you care?"

Chase didn't respond but walked to the opening of the bridge that crossed the bottomless cavern and stared across. He could feel the shakes and the sweat coming. The ache in his body would soon monopolize his decision-making skills. Could he wait to take the last pill? Never had he second-guessed his strength and power to survive. Now, the love of his life depended on him for one final rescue. Reaching into his pocket he pulled out the pill to manage his self-confidence. His finger caught on the buttonhole, sending the pill into the abyss, along with his power.

CHAPTER 47

شهید

Chase stared down at his feet and willed them to move. He heard movement across the bottomless pit and could barely make out Tessa rising to her feet. The brightness coming from a second light well dimmed as the storm intensified. Water cascaded down the walls. In a few minutes, the surface would become too slick to navigate.

"Go, Chase," called one of his team members.

Stepping out on the rickety bridge, he dug deep to find his faith. *Please let me save her. I'll do whatever you want from here on out.* One step then two. Another. Then another, until he jumped onto the slick surface and skidded into the wall. Reaching through the dark opening, he felt a fragile hand slip into his. He pulled her into the light. He squeezed her hand when she stared up at him with hope shining in her eyes. The woman never gave up on him.

She was wet. The rain seeped into the cell in narrow rivers, growing wider as each second passed. He forced her to take a step back into her cell as he followed. The other agents yelled again for him to hurry, along with threats and unflattering descriptions concerning his manhood.

"Tessa, don't ask me any questions, but I want you to do one more thing for me. Do you trust me?" Although her teeth were chattering as he pulled her camo shirt over her head, leaving her exposed to the elements, there was no resistance.

~ ~ ~ ~

The Enigma agents watched Tessa and Chase emerge back onto the platform in order to cross the bridge.

"What the hell was he doing to her now," Ken said, grasping the bars.

The water coming down on the other side of the abyss had formed a waterfall. The sound of it cascading down into the hole was terrifying, especially since he knew of Tessa's fears of heights. "Don't look down, Tess," he called. "You can do this."

The others shouted encouragement, but the sounds of the water may have masked their words.

Chase stepped out onto the bridge, making it sway slightly. He reached back and held out his hand toward her. When nothing happened, Ken called out to her, "You can do this. Let him help you."

He could barely see Chase now because the light coming through the well above had dimmed. What he could make out was Chase jumping back onto the platform, grabbing her up, and slinging her over his shoulder. Ken didn't know what he said to her, but whatever it was, she had been backing away when he snatched her up.

"Breathe, Tessa. Don't move," Zoric shouted over the rumble of thunder. "Chase will make it if you're limp. Try."

Halfway over, Chase paused. Ken could see him more clearly now. One hand gripped the rope railing and the other was clamped on the back of Tessa's legs. His lips appeared to be moving. They watched in horror as he slowly slid her body off his shoulder and put his free arm around her waist. She stood frozen against him, resting her forehead against his chest then, in slow motion, inch by inch, turned her body to face forward. Chase now gripped both sides of the rope railing as did Tessa. As if in a choreographed ballet, they stepped together and with each inch of progress, Chase leaned down and spoke in her ear. She would nod like a nervous toddler and take one more step. When she jumped off the bridge onto safe ground, followed by Chase, the men behind bars cheered.

To their surprise, Chase bent slowly and picked up his gun then rose to his six-foot-one height. Tessa moved away from him and glanced toward the men behind bars with a forlorn expression.

Ken pushed his arm through the bars and pointed toward the tunnel. "That way, Tessa. Run."

Before she could react, Chase reached out and grabbed her arm then shoved her toward the well of light where he knew Soraya waited to watch her die. He raised his gun at her chest. "I'm sorry, Tessa." Chase used his weapon to wave her away. "Run." Instead, she backed toward the light.

He could hear the others yell their rapid fire of insults and threats. It was all he could do to tune them out as his heart beat faster. When Tessa reached the circle of light, she stopped and turned her attention upward then back to him. There was no alternative. Fear whispered in his ear, his soul, as he aimed the weapon toward her. A tremor touched his hand, making the gun unsteady. He couldn't breathe. His vision blurred as a drop of sweat rolled down the side of his face.

A man came up behind him and placed his hand on Chase's arm to lower it.

Darya. He took the weapon from him and aimed with a steady hand then fired. Tessa's hands flew up as she was knocked to the ground. Darya handed him the gun and ran forward but avoided the well of light and stared momentarily at Tessa. In his ghostly fashion, before he disappeared into the darkness, he held up two fingers and pointed to the grand hall.

Chase continued to be shocked at Tessa's limp body, until the silence of his men was so overpowering, he decided to move forward. He reached the well of light and knelt down next to Tessa before looking up at a smiling Soraya. He'd never hated anyone as much as her. Slipping his gun into his inside vest pocket, he took both of Tessa's hands in his and dragged her body away so the others wouldn't come to admire his handiwork. Once in the darkness, he kneeled down beside her to smooth curls away from her face then cupped her delicate chin in his hand. Gently, he slipped his hands under her back and pulled her up into his arms, burying his face into her neck.

~ ~ ~ ~

Darya watched Soraya lean back from the well of light formation and observe Sam and Honey, who appeared visibly shaken. He'd never seen Sam's olive skin so pale. Honey glared at the singer and chewed on her bottom lip, her face, the color of her red hair. Soraya seemed to enjoy their discomfort as she approached and slapped each of them hard enough to stagger their bodies but didn't bring them down.

"Guess you don't think being slapped is so funny now, do you? I'm sure your agent doesn't, either." She slid her hand down Sam's face then her long messy ponytail and narrowed her eyes. Checking Honey's bonds gave her an opportunity to rub her hand down the woman's backside then whisper into the Irish assassin's ear. Honey turned her head and sneered a reply, receiving a slap to the back of her head.

"Guards, take these two infidels back over there out of my sight. I think I'll finish them off myself before we leave."

With the snap of her fingers, two men jerked and pulled the women to the spot they had been left earlier. They were shoved to the floor in a prone position where they lay motionless until the men moved away.

Darya slipped out of the hidden staircase and edged closer to them in the shadows as the women righted themselves. Gently, he touched Sam's shoulder and felt her jerk away to turn and stare at him. Although nothing showed except his eyes, her expression reflected a kind of recognition that concerned him. He held his finger to his covered mouth and popped open a switchblade. Pointing to the stairs, he tilted his head to indicate their escape route. After slicing through their restraints, the women rubbed their wrists carefully so as to not draw attention to their movements.

Once more, he hunkered down and moved back into the shadows. The women mimicked his movements and followed. For whatever reason, maybe because they had no choice, they showed no fear. He was well aware if they decided to turn on him, he'd have one hell of a time surviving. Sam had plenty of resentment and cause to even the score if she realized who he was. Of course, he was told, Honey enjoyed the smell of blood.

At the bottom of the stairs, they entered the area where Chase had dragged Tessa's body. He held her in his arms with his face buried in her neck. Both tried to rush him, but Darya held them back and mumbled in a gravelly voice, "Wait."

Even from this distance, they could hear Chase speak to Tessa as he pushed her body to arm's length. "Tessa. Tessa, speak to me."

Darya held his breath until he saw her twist her body then laid a hand on her chest where she'd been shot. "Chase?"

Honey and Sam shoved Darya aside and ran to kneel next to their captain.

"That really hurt." She frowned and focused on her two friends. "Some backup you turned out to be," she complained.

Chase stood and, before he could pull Tessa up, his two agents did the job for him then wrapped their arms around her. He cleared his throat. "This is all very touching, but we need to get out of here."

"Who was the guy who cut us loose?" Sam said as he moved past the prisoners and tossed the man named Ken a key. "And where did he go?"

Tessa stared at the figure standing past the cell where Ken was working to get the door open. He stared a hole into her very soul, but there was no reason to believe he wasn't inspecting the mettle of the entire group. He was the one who shot her, not Chase. He must have freed her friends after shooting her. Why? Who was he? Dressed in black, he could barely be made out at this distance.

The group rushed to join the men letting themselves out of their cell. Ken plowed into Chase, knocked him up against the wall then slugged him in the jaw. Zoric and Tom pulled them apart and stood between them.

"Ken, he didn't hurt me," Tessa tried to explain. "We had to pretend he was attacking me earlier." She grabbed his arm and jerked him around to look at her.

"You screamed," he fumed.

Chase shook his head and stuck a finger in his ear. "Yes, and I'll probably need hearing aids from this day forward. I would never hurt her, and I certainly wouldn't force myself on her. It was an act."

"And shooting her?" Zoric asked, pointing at the holes in Tessa's shirt.

"Amir left some of us a bulletproof vest to wear for when and if we got into trouble along the way and had to shoot our way out. I had mine on under my shirt," Chase replied.

"He made me wear it," Tessa said, sending him a grateful thin smile. "It fit poorly, but he tightened it up the best he could. Soraya wanted him to kill me while she watched."

"I wasn't sure it fit snug enough," Chase put in, "and I was getting the shakes second-guessing myself. My meds had worn off."

Ken pointed to the man standing in the tunnel—waiting. "That's why he stepped up and shot her?"

"Yes. I wasn't sure I could make the shot without hurting, even killing her with an off shot."

"Who is he?" Sam asked, following Ken's line of sight.

Tessa took a step in his direction, making him raise his chin in protest. "Khan. His name is Khan." Chase held up his hand for her to stop her approach.

A scream echoed down the well of light. A ruckus at the top of the stairs ensued as Soraya appeared, followed by several soldiers.

CHAPTER 48

شهيد

Soraya hurried down the stairs and stared at them with outrage. Her men were right behind her, leveling their rifles at the Enigma team. She pointed at the two escaped women then Tessa.

"You liar," she snarled at Chase as he stepped in front of the group. "After all I've done for you. Betrayal doesn't become you, Captain Hunter." Unafraid, she stepped off the bottom step and moved closer, her pet monkeys behind her, holding their weapons at waist level to spray bullets indiscriminately. She continued to point an accusing finger at Tessa, and Chase nudged her behind him.

"Come with us, Soraya," Chase coaxed. "This will not end well for you when Amir discovers the money is gone."

"Gone?" she said. "How do you know this? You put it in our vehicle." Her eyes widened. "Oh, I see. You switched it out when you offered to go retrieve it. Clever. And stupid. Amir will kill you for betraying us."

"No, he will kill you for trusting me with his money. You are nothing more than arm candy to use at his leisure," Chase explained.

"Nonsense. He needs me. Wants me."

"Get out while you can. You have a life ahead of you. Go back to performing and calling for recognition of the Kurdish people through your music. It made a difference." Chase understood her influence, once the truth was out, would be finished.

She threw up her hands. "You honestly think I care about all that? It's my angle. Nothing more. Sure, I want the Kurds to be more than the poor relation of the Middle East, but having me as queen of Saudi Arabia would go a long way."

"Amir is Arab, through and through. Do you honestly think he's going to want you, a Kurd, at his side when and if, and that's a big if, he takes the throne? He will throw you away like yesterday's trash."

"That's because she is," Honey chimed in as she eyed the woman from head to toe. "Let her stay. Good enough for her."

Chase shifted his attention between both women. "It's now or never, Soraya."

The team backed toward the tunnel as she continued to approach. Chase turned his head toward Ken. "Go. Khan waits for you with weapons. Hurry. I've got your six, buddy."

Ken put a hand on his shoulder. "I know."

"Sam?" Chase said without looking at her.

"Understood, Captain." She'd do what was best for the team. Time was counting down.

The two soldiers with Soraya raised their rifles, but Chase jumped to Soraya's side and shot them both. It wasn't a clean shot because his aim and clarity remained off. He jerked Soraya behind him, as she covered her ears and cried out. The next time he fired, they went down for good. Turning, he watched his team enter the tunnel. Snatching at Soraya's hand, he jerked her forward then shoved. "Move it."

Without hesitation, she ran to the opening leading to the tunnel. Once inside, he nudged her several times to keep moving. Although torches had been lit to dissipate the darkness, the sections between each torch felt as if he was moving through crude oil. Was his body rebelling?

Chase couldn't gauge time with everything else going on in his body, but if felt like an eternity until he reached the supply room. Darya handed the team weapons, however, it appeared night goggles and bulletproof vests were few. He grabbed the last vest and, in spite of her stomping her foot in rebellion, he forced Soraya to slip it over her head.

"This makes me look fat," she complained.

"Chase, you should be wearing it," Tessa said anxiously as she came to stand before him.

He reached out and laid his palm on her cheek. "I'll be fine. We'll be out of here in no time."

Darya, the man everyone thought was Khan, came to stand beside him. His gaze shifted from Soraya to Tessa and held long enough to make her squirm. He didn't speak, although if he had, he doubted she'd recognize his voice since treatment had changed it during his miracle recovery.

Chase could only imagine that being so close to Tessa would cause Darya pain. Would he decide to reclaim his wife and be the one to give her the life she craved? Now, the man was physically stronger than him and Chase realized in his present state, a standoff meant he had no possibility of winning.

Tessa checked her weapon then slung the strap around her shoulder. Chase noticed she did a double take when she realized how Darya stared at her. She didn't flinch, but her gaze hardened. He'd shot her. Perfectly. If it had been left up to Chase, no telling if he could have hit the protective vest. A chill creeped up his spine at the thought of what would have happened if Darya had not taken the shot.

"Ready?" Sam snapped as she moved in front of Darya, cutting off his line of sight to Tessa.

Chase nodded to Darya to enter the tunnel to where several of his men had taken up positions to watch for trouble. He motioned the rest of the Enigma team to follow while he stayed behind.

"Someone should watch Soraya," Chase said, checking his weapon.

"Oh, let me," Honey cooed as she came up next to the woman. "I wouldn't want anything to happen to her."

Soraya lifted her chin and snorted her disdain.

Honey chuckled. "I'd love to show her what—what did she call me? Oh yes, what Irish trash can accomplish."

"Play nice, Honey," Chase said, although he didn't deny her the job. "Remember she's Prince Muhammed's niece."

"I don't give a rat's—"

"Honey," he snapped.

She sighed then smiled sweetly at Soraya. "After you, your

worship."

If Soraya had known what Honey did for a living, and that she was a sociopath, she might have tempered her, "Humph."

The Irish assassin would do as she pleased, and he had little influence over her.

Darya stepped back inside the room. "We've got company."

~ ~ ~ ~

Tessa appreciated what little light filtered through an occasional abandoned well opening from above, making their progress manageable. Even so, they kept their night-vision goggles on to navigate the heavy darkness that covered them most of the way. Water funneled through the ceiling of the tunnels, sounding at times like it hit metal. The splashes made by heavy boots and unsure steps added a layer of urgency for her. The pungent stench of mildew and decay caused an occasional gag or cough. In spite of the discomfort, the team pressed on, led by the mysterious friend of Captain Hunter, whom he appeared to trust without question.

The strangely quiet man moved like a stalking predator through the tunnels. He'd accepted night-vision goggles and adjusted to them instantly. Fortunately, there had been several more pair for his men. Although the group of rebels had flashlights, Tessa heard this man called Khan to keep them turned off in case they were followed or someone was waiting along the way. This gave the group an edge. Once, he mumbled something to Chase who tilted his head to find Tessa. The goggles they wore prevented her from reading those obsidian eyes of his. For a brief few seconds, Khan turned to stare her way. She wondered if he would address her but moved away to join the other men in the group who took readiness positions.

Did the team wonder what she was thinking or if she was in shock at the events which had happened in the last few hours? Would she pull her weight if push came to shove? She wondered about that herself. At the present, she was both terrified and pissed.

Even though Chase had warned Tessa of his plan, it still surprised her at the force with which he'd attacked her. Something inside him had come unhinged for a few seconds and she'd feared for her life. Now he moved toward her, the others parting to let him pass. "Do you know how to use that weapon?"

The strap hung around her neck and shoulder as she cradled it in her arms. Not once in her whole life had she ever imagined she'd own one of these or even touch one. Then Enigma interrupted a perfectly normal life and forced her to make life choices that affected not only her family but the entire country from time to time.

Chase cocked his head and spoke through gritted teeth, clearly a little on edge. "Tessa, I need to know if you can use that weapon you're holding like a baby."

With a hard swallow, she nodded.

As he turned and marched toward the front of the line, Tessa observed how the mysterious man who led them continued to stare her way. It was difficult to know if he locked onto her or one of the others since the night-vision goggles prevented her seeing too much. When Chase got alongside him, he mumbled something that made him raise his chin then nod at her.

"Up yours," she whispered to both men.

"I heard that," Sam confessed. "Does that guy give you the feeling we've had run-ins with him before? Chase must know him pretty well by the way they keep talking to each other all secret and if that offers any indication."

"I don't know about you two," Honey said, backing into them while keeping watch behind them, along with Ken and Tom, "but that is not the Chase Hunter I know. Even when we went through hell and back, he never acted like he has here. He's dangerous, Tessa. Remember, he tried to kill you."

She moved alongside Sam, who offered her own opinion. "Maybe he's playing both sides against the middle. Ever think about that? He's half out of his mind."

Tessa adjusted her weapon and continued to stare at the two men ahead. "I don't know what to think. To be honest, this is not how I expected our reunion to go. Before he left, he promised it would be different between us, when he returned. That maybe…"

The stranger motioned for them to follow, so the conversation ended.

Tessa followed Ken and Sam, who were in the lead. Zoric had

run ahead to scout out any possible problems. Tom stayed back with Chase, Khan, and his men to level the playing field when the time came. Honey and Soraya were behind her. The constant checking to see if Chase was coming kept her on the edge. Each time she paused to look back, Soraya gave her a sarcastic eye roll and a loud sigh.

Finally, Honey said, "Be a love, Tess, and just say the word."

Soraya glanced at Tessa and gave an eye roll of what appeared to be indifference to what Honey might be suggesting. "Yes, Tessa, do say the word so this piece of trash will shut her mouth."

They were all getting wet now as water pooled in low areas and walking, although careful, splashed up on their pants. The ceiling dripped on their heads and shirts. Tessa felt the cold seep into her bones.

Voices she didn't recognize echoed down the tunnel. Apparently, Soraya recognized them because she screamed Amir's name as Chase and the others joined them. Honey raised the butt of her rifle and smacked the woman in the mouth, sending her toppling back into the rivulets of water cascading down the wall.

She touched her lips, now covered in blood.

"Oops," Honey said coyly as the men arrived. They barely gave Soraya a glance, as Khan's men applied wires to plastic explosives in containers.

The voices down the tunnel silenced, except for one.

"Chase," Amir shouted. "Do you think you can go back to your old life because your friends have come to rescue you? Don't be a fool. You'll be tried as a traitor and spend the rest of your life in prison. I forgive you. Come."

"I'm guessing your big heart has something to do with discovering your gold coins and the million ransom are gone," Chase said sarcastically.

Amir's voice floated down the tunnel. "Maybe a little. There is plenty for both of us, if you live long enough to share. Tell me where it is and I'll let you go once I've killed the others."

The voice was getting closer. Soraya pushed off the wall and came to stand next to Chase, who prevented her from going any farther.

"Amir," she begged, "come get me. They are torturing me." She faked a cry.

"You're the reason the captain has the money," he retorted. "You're the reason he is still alive. So why would I want to do that?"

Soraya let loose enough insults about his physical attributes that Tessa felt embarrassed for the terrorist. "I will have my uncle kill you," the singer shouted. "How dare you treat me this way."

Her rants, along with the rain and thunder rumbling in the outside world, managed to cover the approach of Amir and his men until they appeared at a dead run, bullets flying.

Chase ordered everyone to withdraw, as they returned fire. Amir cowered behind his men until the last second then let loose a spray of bullets that bounced off the wall next to Soraya, who ducked. Chase grabbed her up and stepped in front of her.

"Go," he ordered, pushing her into Honey who jumped into action. Pivoting back to cover Khan so he could finish up the plastic explosives took only a second, but it was too long. Amir emerged and shot indiscriminately, catching Chase three times in the chest.

He teetered then fell into Khan who raised his gun and shot toward Amir. She hoped Chase had only dodged to keep from getting hit. One of the Kurdish fighters and Ken rushed to their side as Khan dragged Chase away from the fray. When all four had gotten clear, Khan nodded to one of his men. "Take cover," he yelled as everyone hunkered down in an area open enough to provide protection. The blast brought the ceiling down, and a wall of dust and debris rumbled in their direction. Finally, Amir's men were cut off.

Tessa, slung her rifle and ran to where Khan had laid Chase down before the blast then covered him with his own body to protect him from flying rock. Khan's body was now covered in Chase's blood.

CHAPTER 49

شهيد

The team rose and took up positions of protection immediately. Sounds of hurried feet came toward them from inside the building attached to the tunnel where they now stood. Khan slowly stood and took Tessa's arm to pull her away from trying to kneel down by the captain.

"He is alive, Tess-sa. I will get him help."

The noise beyond the tunnel increased. There was a chance Amir's men had found their escape route and entered to cut them off. Khan ran toward it then positioned himself between whoever headed their way. They were already lifting their weapons to defend the area when Khan held up his hands.

"Friends. Lower your weapons."

When a flash of lightning lit the room, Tessa could see the bombed-out sanctuary of a large church. Several men dressed in the traditional clothing of Kurdish fighters entered, along with three other people Tessa quickly identified. One man approached her, and she stared in disbelief, until he put his arms around her and pulled her to his chest.

Director Benjamin Clark stared down at the body of the man who had been like a son to him. "Is he..." Tessa understood he couldn't bring himself to speak the horror he felt. She spotted Vernon and felt a wave of relief.

Khan went back to Chase and lifted him into his arms. "We will be safe here." He nodded to Peshmerga to lead the way, and they all followed him, Captain Hunter cradled in his arms. The communion table lay on its side in front of the altar. Several of Khan's men righted it to use as a table for the captain.

"Chase," she pleaded. "I need you to be okay." Tessa touched his cheek with her fingertips, as she watched his chest rise and fall. The shallow breathing terrified her.

Vernon came to stand next to her and dared to place his arm around her shoulders. He was like a little brother to her. Chase used to tease her that she needed to adopt him and be done with it. He had brought him into Enigma and protected him when the big guns at the Pentagon tried to throw him in jail for all his technology shenanigans.

"At least you're okay, Vernon," she said, mind whirling with everything happening too fast and fear for Chase. "And, Director Clark. I want to hear that story, but this isn't the time."

Vernon squeezed her shoulder and moved away as Khan joined her. "We have to peel back his clothes to see what we got. Is anyone here a medic?"

"Chase was the medic," Ken said drily. "I think he's going to need more than a medic now."

"I'm going to try and reach Carter and tell him to get those birds in the air." The director pointed to a prayer room to the east. Tessa figured a computer command center, plus satellite, had been required to pull this mission together.

When Khan cut open the shirt, Tessa covered her mouth at the blood and open wounds. Thunder boomed across the sky and shook the building as wind pounded against the already-shaky building.

Chase opened his eyes enough to search each face bending over him then licked his lips. One of his men handed a bottle of water to Khan. He handed it to Tessa. "He cannot have any water, Tess-sa, but you can wet something to touch his lips. Can you do this?"

"Yes." She nodded as the director grabbed a crumpled napkin from a backpack and handed it to her. Once she unscrewed the bottle and moistened the napkin, she leaned down to touch Chase's lips.

Khan called for Peshmerga to bring some medical supplies she carried and preceded to apply pressure until he could bandage his wounds.

Chase blinked as Tessa fought back tears. "Can you ever stop being the hero?" she tried to sound irritated.

The corner of his mouth twisted up then he turned his head toward Khan and lifted his hand. The masked man took it in his.

Tessa, bewildered at this strong connection between the two men, wondered how they had met. What had formed this friendship between them? For whatever reason, Khan's eyes were mesmerizing and familiar, beautiful and hard, threatening with violence if crossed, all wrapped into a calm demeanor, giving her a sense of safety. If only she could see the rest of his face.

"We're trying to get help, Chase. Just hang on. Can you do that for me?" Tessa picked up his free hand.

"I will try," he said softly. "But if I don't—"

"No. You will. I can't lose you. Promise me."

"I promise you will—never be—alone."

"He needs a doctor," Khan offered in broken English. Tessa jerked her head up to stare at him with a memory of someone else who spoke with that same accent. The voice was coarse and deep, striking a familiar nerve that vibrated throughout her body. "He will die if we don't get help."

"How do you suggest we get one of those?" Ken growled.

Sam peeled Chase's shirt farther back from his chest and frowned. "He's right. Doesn't look good."

Silent tears streamed down Tessa's face. She couldn't believe this was happening to her a second time. Flashbacks of all the lost moments together, when love was unprofessed, crowded in on her until she thought she'd collapse from the weight of the missed opportunities.

"Tessa." Not only was his voice weak, but so was his grip on her hand.

"You hang in there, Chase." She kissed his fingers. "I refuse to lose you, too."

"I know a priest nearby who is a doctor," the mysterious leader said as he locked gazes with Tessa. "At least, if he doesn't make it, a priest can pray him into Heaven." His voice was calm and cold as like the rain dripping through the holes in the roof.

"Then let's get him," Tessa insisted. "Where is he? Here?"

"Nearby. I will get him, but you must come with me. Only you. No one else."

"Not happening, dude," Ken piped in. "She's not going anywhere without us. If you need someone to watch your back, I'll go."

The leader seemed to assess the Enigma team as he took his time staring at each one of them. He then walked around the altar to stand next to Tessa. "I will leave this up to Tess-sa."

She jerked her head around and stared into those familiar slanted eyes. The way he said her name reminded her of Darya. Her mind was playing tricks on her. After all, she'd buried him. At the same time, a kind of peace came over her in spite of knowing he was one more dangerous man in her life. There was no choice but to trust him and find the priest.

"We go now," he announced with a nod to his men.

"I don't think so," Ken snapped, reaching for her.

Khan shot him a dangerous glare as his men lowered their weapons from their shoulders toward the Enigma team, matching the threat.

"Ken," came Chase's weak voice.

"Sir?"

"He can. Be trusted." He dropped Tessa's hand. "Go." He licked his parched lips. "With him, Tessa. No harm—will come to you. I promise."

The leader placed his right hand on the wound and looked upward. "Allahuma rabbi-nas adhhabal ba'sa, ashfi wa entashafi, la shifa' illa shifa'uka shifa' la yughadiru saqama."

Chase nodded. "Thank you, my friend."

The man gently laid his hand on top of the one that held Tessa's. "You understood my words."

"Oh Allah! The Sustainer of Mankind! Remove the illness, cure the disease. You are the One Who cures. There is no cure except Your cure. Grant us a cure that leaves no illness." He appeared to try and smile. "Between you and Tessa, I'll be—fine. Now the rest of you—stand down. That's an order."

Tessa turned to the team. "You heard him. Stand down. I'm going whether you approve or not. If Chase trusts him, so do I."

Khan spoke a command to his men without diverting his

attention from her. Peshmerga didn't appear to be happy being left behind and snarled at Tessa. Jealousy? The man certainly commanded respect. The mysterious aura around him enticed her as well. She couldn't help but wonder about his face behind the mask. The eyes alone were mesmerizing.

A flashback of Darya when they first met in Afghanistan and how he watched her, appraising and evaluating her every move, reminded her of that exact situation. Do I trust him and follow him into the unknown or prepare to fight my way out of an I-should-have-known-better situation?

His penetrating gaze made her fingers twitch at her side, but she returned the steely eyed confrontation. She raised her chin in impatience. "Let's go if we're going."

Creases formed at the corners of his eyes as a slight chuckle escaped through his mask.

Chase coughed and tried to speak again, drawing both Tessa's and the leader's attention back to him. She touched his arm gently and gazed down at his pale face. The stranger laid a hand on the soldier's shoulder.

Chase managed, "If this doesn't. Work out, my friend, you…"

"I will do my best. I promise you, Captain Hunter." He returned his attention to Tessa, still addressing Chase. "No harm will come to your woman."

"That isn't what I—meant."

"What was mine has been given to you for eternity. My gift is not given lightly but with confidence in God's protection for both of you," the man known as Khan replied.

Bewilderment overshadowed what reasoning powers she had left, along with the realization that something remarkable had happened. She continued to feel safe in spite of the others on the team glaring at him as if he had the launch codes for a nuclear device and the willingness to use them.

"We should go," he said firmly to her.

~ ~ ~ ~

Darkness covered their movements as they dodged being in the open for too long. Amid burned-out cars and crumbling buildings that were once-thriving shops and markets, the two navigated their way with caution. Large piles of discarded clothing, furniture, and other goods clogged the streets reminiscent of an apocalyptic movie set. A few small fires smoldered, providing enough light for them to lift their night-vision goggles.

A scrawny rat creeped from under a toppled column and caused Tessa to wonder if the vile creature might possess enough energy to locate a second hiding place. The absence of dogs barking an alarm and people milling around to share tea and swap stories felt louder than the damp wind toying with loose papers that managed to escape the mud puddles in the street.

The day of unexpected brutality weighed like a one-hundred-pound pack on her shoulders. The gurgling noise she heard was her stomach growling for food. When had she eaten last? Her legs hurt from the strenuous attempt at escape but also from being shot and knocked to the ground like a rag doll falling off a shelf. The tortured expression on Chase's face when he hurt her still managed to frighten her. In those few lucid moments, she'd seen his love shine in those dark eyes. Was he afraid for the first time in his life she would find out a secret he feared would cause her to abandon him? What had he done to protect his country and her? The sacrifice must have been more than the weathered soldier could bear. Deep inside her heart, she had no doubt Chase loved her. Having to pretend otherwise had saved her life. There must be a special place in Hell for people like Amir and Soraya. Would the fine man she'd come to cherish be the same after this mess?

Would she see him differently, fear his potential violence, or maybe he would see her differently? That bookish PTA mom had disappeared in pieces over the years. As of today, she had vaporized completely. Although her gardens would now hold greater meaning and beauty, and her children remain a beacon of love, mankind had morphed into an ugly and unpredictable monster. How would she trust the world to do the right thing in the future?

"Someone comes," her escort growled. "Hurry. The doorway is deep, and we won't be spotted."

She could barely see where he'd disappeared to even with the goggles on until he grabbed her hand and led her through the rubble into a doorway. Pushing her to the back, of what must have once been a decorative tile entry, she found herself up against a door, surprisingly still intact. His back pinned her securely against the frame so tightly, she felt him breathe.

"Can you open the door?" he whispered. "Those are Turkish soldiers. They will kill us if they find us."

She reached behind her and felt for the knob but discovered a hole where it had been. Leaning her hip into it had no effect until the man reached around her and shoved it open enough for them to squeeze through. Once inside she saw a wooden beam had partially blocked the ability to swing it wide open.

Tessa adjusted her goggles then followed him to a lopsided door missing a hinge. He squeezed through an opening the size of a child's desk, and she followed clumsily. Once through, he piled available junk and debris near the opening but didn't block it. Then he led her to a second wall he tapped to open and slipped inside. Once more, she hurried to follow him and this time, he replaced the opening with broken furniture and fallen debris to help them remain hidden.

The area was the size of a pantry and surprisingly clean. He led her a few steps toward the back and lifted a black cloth and covered them as they huddled on the floor. She knew it was one more layer of protection. Wearing the goggles was of no use, and he removed his, so she followed suit. Distant voices reached them. Her pulse quickened. By the way the man moved next to her, she knew he'd pulled a handgun and had readied it to fend off if they were discovered.

Voices grew closer, chatting in a nonchalant way. The sound of rubble crunching beneath boots drew closer and louder. Then the men sounded as if they tossed things randomly, perhaps in some kind of an inspection inside the room they had left a few minutes earlier. Voices paused as debris shifted. One male voice let out a shocked gasp followed by a gunshot. Tessa jumped just as Khan covered her mouth with his hand, keeping her from crying out. She grabbed his arm tightly with both of her hands. Her breath was ragged with fear, but she managed to nod, she was okay.

"It was a rat. Nothing more," he whispered against her ear so close, she felt his face against her hair. "They're moving away now. We wait."

"How long?"

"As long as it takes." His voice remained quiet, but there was a lighter tone to it. "They are searching for us, I think. We must have been spotted."

Tessa raised her chin in acceptance as she faced him and realized in spite of him still wearing the mask, they were nose to nose. She wondered if her eyes grew large or if her face glowed with the heat of embarrassment.

"Try to rest," he urged. "This was a difficult day."

Without moving away, Tessa dared quiz him. "Why did you shoot me?"

"Because the captain could not. He was afraid he might kill you. The fog of drugs made him unsure."

"You could have missed."

"I had to take a chance. Soraya and Amir had to believe you were dead to trust the captain."

Tessa rubbed her chest. "I'm going to have a bruise." She took a deep breath. "Can I see your face?"

He remained quiet for a few seconds then slipped his free hand around her back, drawing her closer. At first, she resisted then remembered Darya had touched her in such a way. He meant her no harm.

"This Captain Hunter. Do you love him?"

"Yes. More than I thought possible."

"And what would you do to save him?"

Tessa wondered where this conversation was headed. A nervous admission could change everything. "He has gone through hell for me. I can do nothing less. Are you going to negotiate with me now to get the doctor to save him?"

"No. I will get the doctor for him. He is a lucky man to have such a woman."

She relaxed. "How did you become friends?"

"It is a long story filled with deceit, mistrust, danger, and love. The love being the most important part."

"It always is, I think. I have lost one great love, I don't want to lose another," she admitted.

"Tell me about this great love." His hand moved ever so slowly up her back, urging her closer.

Tessa felt his breath through the mask, warm and sweet. His gaze bored into her and searched her face then rested on her lips. "No. It is none of your business. But"—she watched his expression become hooded—"you remind me of him." She dared touch his cheek. "Is custom or precaution the reason you hide your face from me?"

"The enemy doesn't know my face. I am a ghost to them. One they fear. I want to keep the edge. If you were taken by the Turks or a Russian who helps keep this country divided, you would be able to tell them things, simple things, to help piece together and know who I am, what I look like and then the Syrians would send men to kill me." He took her hand upon his cheek and held it. "I am sorry, Tess-sa."

One more time she was reminded of how Darya had always divided her name when he pronounced it.

"You must sleep a little. In an hour, we can slip out again. They do not stay long. I will keep watch. If they go sooner, then I wake you. We are close to the priest. He knows what Amir is up to." He pushed her back and covered her with the black cloth. "I will wait a few minutes and rest next to you if you do not mind."

Tessa, mesmerized by his voice, closed her eyes so heavy with fatigue. "I will be ready. Thank you for today. I owe you a great debt," she mumbled as sleep overtook her body. Later, she remembered passing into a dreamlike state, when a hand took hers. A thumb rubbed her skin, reminding her of another place and time when love wasn't such a mystery. The man stretched out his legs and moved so their shoulders touched with a familiar warmth. Just a few minutes to catch her breath.

~ ~ ~ ~

Darya waited until Tessa's breathing became deep and slow, before he removed his mask and head covering. The risk was too great to reveal who he was. The woman had toughened up in the year since they'd been together. He let the memories wash over him of how their bodies had entwined during the cold nights of Siberia. Their lovemaking had satisfied them for short periods of time until they reached for one another again. The happiness he felt with her in his arms, watching her walk through the snow and dress like the Snow Maiden of Russia, had filled him with the contentment he had longed for so many years.

Then he died. Somehow, he was resurrected, or maybe he was

just tough enough to live. He'd given Tessa and Chase permission to take care of each other. He'd always known the captain was her first love and, with manipulation and deceit, he'd stolen that same joy he felt from Captain Hunter.

But there was never a moment he doubted the man's devotion and love for her. In many ways, he was a much better man than himself. He had served his country well, took the ethical road with Tessa in hopes she'd save her marriage to the father of her children and, when duty called, he didn't hesitate.

He didn't know when respect trumped the hate he felt for the man. Jealousy and suspicion blinded him because of Tessa. It nearly made him betray the United States. Without the captain, the Russian general would have killed him. Why he'd come back for him remained a mystery, but he felt obligated to return the favor. This time, the captain would take Tessa away from him for good, and he wouldn't have a chance to explain why he abandoned her to a grief carried by her devotion to him.

Leaning back, he let his mind wander back to the moments of intimacy and remembered how her body felt beneath his touch. If only he hadn't seen her again, maybe this wouldn't be so difficult. The dark side of him could easily manipulate the situation and win her back. But Captain Hunter was a man of honor and his equal on so many levels. He respected him and had come to consider him a brother of sorts.

Darya was a hunted man. Tessa wasn't the kind of woman who could endure such a life. Her children certainly could never sustain it. Did he want his own future children to live this way? No. This time, he would surrender to the only man he respected enough to love and create a life for this woman he worshipped with his unreasonable kind of love.

With time, Tessa's memories of him would turn him into a saint instead of what he really was; a ruthless Tribesman who had been a drug dealer, traitor, thief, and manipulator of geopolitics to advance his own future. She had shared the best of him. Maybe that was the reason he loved her.

Tessa twitched, and her breathing was labored. A moan escaped her mouth as she turned her head back and forth. She cried softly and called out, "Darya. Darya. You can't go. Please." She reached her arms out in front of her. "Darya."

He turned on his knees to face her and pulled her trembling body into his arms. "I am here, snow leopard. I have not gone far. Shhh. It is just a dream." He pulled back enough to see her eyes open. Her lips parted as if she might smile.

"Darya," she whispered. With fingers that nervously touched his face then pushed through his shaggy hair, she fell into his arms and wept. "Darya."

He held her, stroked her tangled hair then became a victim of his own longing by capturing her mouth with a passion missing too long in his life. Salty tears mixed with his own silent ones until he withdrew, knowing the darkness hid more than his face. "Sleep now. Soon we will be together again."

"Am I going to die?"

"Sleep now. You are safe."

"You'll not leave?"

"I'm always close, snow leopard." This time he spoke in Pashtu, the language of Afghanistan. "Sthare Mashe." May you not be tired.

Tessa closed her eyes and whispered, also in Pashtu. "Pa Khair Raghla." Thank God you came safe and sound.

It pleased him to hear the words of his people come from her lips. In minutes, her breathing returned to sleep, and he was left to stare at her in the past tense. He touched his face and wiped away the stream of tears that had mingled together in regret and loss.

Slowly he replaced his head covering and mask so not to make such a mistake again. It was a barrier to keep things moving in the right direction. Touching her shook him to the core. It couldn't happen again.

One last time, he reached out and moved a curl from her forehead. "I love you, Tessa Petrov. But you must accept the captain as your forever love now. I will get him home so life can be made new for both of you."

CHAPTER 50

شهید

"Where the hell are they?" Ken asked as he paced then went to the partially caved-in corridor where Darya and Tessa had slipped away.

The darkness was heavy, and the rain continued to beat down with flashes of lightning brightening the sanctuary through what little stained glass remained near the ceiling. Occasionally, a boom of thunder made the rickety building shudder and creak, as if it would rather collapse on them.

Darya's men stood like statues and, from time to time, would sit in the front pew to stare at the door of escape. They didn't complain or wonder aloud where he was but watched as if faithful Labradors waiting for their master.

"You should calm down," Peshmerga said, frowning at the group of Enigma agents. "Khan will be back. There are soldiers in the area. He is careful. It has not been long."

"Why did he take Tessa? That's ludicrous. If it was dangerous, and he needed coverage—" Ken stopped and watched Sam dab cool water on Chase's forehead and lips.

"I do not know," Peshmerga snapped.

Sam glared up at Ken. "She shoots better than you think and, in a pinch, she'd come through. I suspect her Red Cross or State Department credentials might be helpful, too, if they're stopped."

"Then again, maybe he heard about the whole three-way thing we've been planning and thought hmmm." Honey tapped her cheek with her index finger.

"Shut the hell up," Ken growled.

Honey pooched her lips out in a kiss and then pretended to pout by sticking out her bottom lip. Her gaze hardened as it fell on Peshmerga. "Where did you go the other night? Slipped off to avoid being asked a few questions?"

"I was wondering the same thing," Ken growled.

Peshmerga stole a glance at Soraya and snarled, "I wasn't a prisoner, and I was afraid the Turks would find me with you."

"You were protected. That wasn't going to happen." Ken pulled his shoulders back and raised his stubborn chin. "Maybe you didn't want to explain why you went to visit Prince Muhammed or that the two of you—are more than friends."

Director Clark held up his hand for silence. "Care to share now why you chose to visit a prince at such a late hour?"

Soraya laughed as she stood up and moved toward Peshmerga. "You think they were having an affair? And maybe he helped her escape for services rendered?" She rolled her eyes upward in contempt as Peshmerga came to stand in front of her. "She wasn't having an affair. Were you, Peshmerga? Go on. Tell them."

Everyone focused on the now-nervous Peshmerga. "Soraya is my sister."

~ ~ ~ ~

Tessa awoke to find herself alone. She scrambled up and heard voices. Pulling down her night-vision goggles, she spotted Darya standing nearby. He held his finger to his lips as he stepped back and she mimicked his actions. He motioned for her to come to him. Navigating the debris, she joined him as two soldiers managed to push into the room. When they had come within a few feet of them, Khan jumped out and ran his knife into the first one. The second one raised his weapon and had Khan in his sights when Tessa slammed a bucket in his face, causing him to shoot wide. The man, now dazed, staggered back only to have Khan's knife plunge into his chest.

Then, from behind her, came a movement of wood against the

floor. Tessa whirled around and pulled her weapon from a deep vest pocket, but Darya pushed her hand down. "No. It's Father Novak."

The priest went to each man, kneeled then said a few words over them. "May God have mercy on their souls." He stood and shook his head. "These are the two who have been harassing what few Christians are left here. They steal their food and taunt them with threats. The young women are afraid to go out."

"How... How did you find us, Father?" Tessa asked as they picked their way to the door.

"While you slept, I was able to contact the father," Khan admitted. "You must have been watched, Father. I am sorry to put you in such danger. The phone wouldn't work at first." He addressed Tessa again, "I told him where we were hiding. He knew a secret way to join us."

The priest held up his cell phone. "Text," he said proudly. "Yes. Even in hell. Lucky it worked. Most of the time, it doesn't."

"Divine intervention," Tessa said softly.

The priest shrugged. "Could be. Are you a believer?"

"I am."

"Then perhaps it was. Should we go, my friend?" he asked, coming alongside Khan. "I have it on good authority we will be safe." He pointed upward.

Khan pulled down his night-vision goggles and eased out into the outer room then outside. The rain was what they called a toad strangler in Tennessee. Running through puddles and ducking between buildings to keep out of sight felt like a waste of time to Tessa. The streets were empty now because of the storm. Anyone searching for them would be hard-pressed to see them in this downpour. Amazingly, as soon as they slipped into the camouflaged entry to what was left of the church, the storm stopped.

As they shook off the water, Father Novak nodded at her and kissed the crucifix around his neck. "Divine intervention."

She wasn't sure why having him along made her feel better, but it did. The rest of the bunch generally found her beliefs a bit amusing and tolerated her everything-happens-for-a-reason logic. There had been many times when she thought they kept her around as a good-luck charm in case she was right concerning the whole divine intervention scenario. Having another person of faith in the mix made her more confident there was strength in numbers.

"We have to hurry. We've been gone for too long." Tessa was anxious to see Chase.

Khan took the lead. He said he didn't want them walking into trouble in case their position had been compromised. When they joined the others, they found a disagreement going on between Peshmerga and Soraya. The room fell silent, and all heads turned their way as soon as Tessa led the priest to where Chase lay sleeping.

"Let's see what we have here," Father Novak said, setting his medical backpack down. He examined Chase, took his vitals, and appeared to take great pains in assessing his condition the best he could, given less-than-adequate supplies and environment. "Is there another area where we can get out of the draft, where it's warmer and dryer? And how about more light?"

The decision was made to move him to the computer area, a small vestibule off the sanctuary. The men carried the communion table with Chase's sleeping body and placed it carefully away from the door. Since there were no windows, it felt warmer. A number of candles were located and placed in cracked bowls and lanterns that survived bombings, filling the room with light. The priest provided a flashlight for Tessa to hold for him as he continued the examination.

The team stood just inside the room and around the outside of the doorway, cautious not to let Soraya slip from sight, too. Finally, Father Novak turned and frowned. "I don't need an audience. You're cramping my style."

Director Clark motioned for them to return to the sanctuary and left Khan and Tessa to assist when he acknowledged the priest. "Thanks for coming, Father Novak."

"Oh, I'm not really a priest. Well at least not yet. I'm kind of in training. Just call me Mikhail," he said, rolling up his sleeves and letting Khan pour alcohol over his hands into a bucket.

"Nonetheless, we're relieved to have a doctor to take care of Captain Hunter," Tessa admitted.

The would-be priest's forehead wrinkled in surprise. "I'm not a doctor, either." He shifted his attention to Khan. "What have you been telling these people?"

Khan shrugged.

"What?" Tessa gasped.

"I was an army medic in Afghanistan. Saw worse wounds than this." He waved the director away impatiently. "Now, you, man-in-charge, get lost," he said, growing more impatient by the minute. Then he nodded at Tessa. "If you stay, you better not faint, cry, puke, or get in my way. Are we good?"

"Yes."

"Okay, then. Now, let's clean him up and sterilize the area."

Tessa wasn't sure she could keep her word, but Khan did most of the assisting Mikhail required. He explained he believed there to be three bullets, and he'd try and dig them out but could give no promises of success. "I have to stop the bleeding. I'll patch him up as best I can, but this man requires surgery I can't do."

"Help is on the way," Tessa spoke confidently but wasn't sure it would be in time.

Once the bullets were removed, Mikhail explored enough to know if any organs had been hit. There were some questionable areas, but he admitted it was a miracle Chase had survived this much. He shook his head and admitted although Chase's body was muscled and strong, it appeared to have had a great deal of stress to his ribs and other areas, not caused by bullets.

An hour later, after clean bandages were applied, Chase opened his eyes. He blinked at his doctor in bewilderment.

"Aw. Good, you're awake," Mikhail said. "I'm told you're a tough SOB, so I'm expecting you to fight. At least don't be moaning and complaining. I hate that part of being a medic."

Tessa felt a wave of horror at the bedside manner, but Chase grinned. "You. Must. Be a soldier," he said.

At least he was talking, thought Tessa.

"Used to be. I brought some out-of-date antibiotics I'm going to give you."

"How out of date?" Tessa quizzed, concerned.

Mikhail read the pill bottle he held in his hand. "Hmm. Couple years, looks like." He waved her off. "It'll be fine. We'll do four now and see how it goes."

"What?" Tessa snapped.

Chase continued to wear a half grin then nodded. After taking the pills, he stared at something behind Mikhail. "Who is that guy?"

Khan was staring at whoever it was, too, and had unslung his rifle and held it carefully.

Mikhail glanced over his shoulder then at Tessa and focused on Khan. "Oh, that guy?"

"I don't see anyone," Tessa said softly, feeling the hairs stand up on the back of her neck.

"But you see him, don't you, Khan?" Mikhail asked as he checked Chase's pulse.

Khan nodded and took a step back.

"Are you messing with me?" Tessa asked, a bit perturbed.

"No. No," Mikhail said. "Some people say they see an angel looking over my shoulder at times. Let me tell you, it used to scare the bejesus out of me until I saw him, too. Nothing to be concerned about."

"I don't see anything," she repeated.

"That's a good thing." Again, he focused on Khan curiously. "You've seen him before, haven't you?"

"Yes."

"I wouldn't worry about it," Mikhail reassured the others. "He's here to check on the captain. Probably stick around a bit to make sure I don't screw things up." He sighed.

Khan kept staring menacingly at whatever he saw. Putting the fear of God in you just took on a new meaning, considering she was the one who wasn't seeing another person in the room.

Chase reached for her hand, which she grasped like a lifeline. "You okay?"

"Seeing your face does wonders."

"I'm going to give him some pain meds, too," the medic said. "Poking around on him after being shot is going to hurt like…" He glanced over his shoulder as if talking to that other person she couldn't see. "Guess I should watch my language if I plan to be a priest."

Chase winced in pain. "I'm addicted to pain meds."

"Is this new, or has it gone on a long time?" Mikhail's voice was calm now and all business.

"Those guys thought I made a good punching bag," he slurred. "Then they would give me stuff for the pain only to taunt me into another fight." His attention shifted back to Tessa. "Kinda like what you do to me." He closed his eyes.

She took his hand. "Whoever you saw over there in the dark, tell him I'm having none of his threats."

Khan relaxed and lowered his rifle. "Gone now." He sounded relieved as he came to stand next to Tessa.

"Saw an angel on the battlefield myself once. No one saw him but me. Looked like a regular guy, too. That whole angels-among-us thing in the Book of Hebrews—I'm here to tell you it's real." The priest checked over Chase one last time as he spoke nonchalantly.

"Can we talk about something else?" Tessa said, squeezing Chase's hand.

"Did you talk to Tessa?" Chase squinted at Khan now then squeezed his eyes shut for a second as if waiting for an answer. When there was no response, he opened his eyes to stare at him. "I'm thinking no."

"Not the right time. Soon."

"Talk to me about what?" she said, massaging Chase's hand.

"You should rest," Khan said, pulling the linen cloth he'd found in a drawer still wrapped in plastic after being cleaned for the credence table.

In seconds, Chase was sleeping, and Mikhail took his vitals again. "If we can get him real medical help, I think he'll bounce back good as new. The pain meds will enable his body to heal a bit until he can get those repairs. I'm not sure what has been permanently damaged. The guy has been through a lot. Now, I'd like to sit with him awhile and pray. You okay with that?"

Both Tessa and Khan nodded their acceptance.

"Fine. So, get lost." He pulled up a chair next to the table and bowed his head.

CHAPTER 51

شهید

Tessa listened to the storms that came and went all night. Quiet conversation centered around Amir's trucks and whether they'd gotten very far in this weather. Speculation continued on the timing of Israel sending in planes to bomb targets to stop Amir. The sun had broken through in the early morning. Tessa thought it might be a good day to start a war—or stop one. Puddles created a patchwork design on the street and reflected puffy white clouds, giving the day a false sense of serenity. The smell of death and garbage had been washed away.

Vernon announced the planes were in the air and they needed to find a safe place. Bombs would be hitting the target soon. Chase was better, more alert and talking. Ken and Zoric, with the help of Khan's men, found a market cart that once held vegetables. It required repairs, so they'd worked together to fix those during the night. Chase was able to sit up and move to the cart with assistance. Tessa knew he must be exhausted, but he remained awake and refused to take more pain meds until they were completely at a safe distance. He wanted to be alert if his help was needed. Tessa handed him a rifle in case they were attacked.

Tom Cooper, a former Marine, was a big muscled man who reminded Tessa of the Incredible Hulk. He pulled the cart, along with the help of one of Khan's men who was as tall as Tom but slimmer.

Although Tom didn't have a lot to say, he was the guy you knew would complete a job. Methodical and precise, he'd taken courses over the last few years to become a mechanical engineer. The training fit him, but he remained loyal to Enigma and didn't wish to leave to take a job in his line of work. She'd never asked him why. He was no different from the rest of them. The Enigma family came first, and they were all adrenaline junkies. This was one of her problems as well.

Moving down the street at a careful pace, Tessa was glad to see Mikhail had decided to come along to make sure Chase would be okay.

"You're leaving with us, right?" Tessa asked the would-be priest.

"I'm tagging along for now to keep an eye on the captain. But I'm needed here. Got to tie up a few loose ends for my people. Can't abandon them. There's a couple of babies to deliver any day, and I need to make sure everyone has a safe place to go. Then I'll head back to the US. First thing I'm getting when I arrive is a big burger."

"You're a good man," she admitted.

"Not always. But I try." He kept an eye on things around them like a soldier might.

Tessa liked him and hoped their paths would cross again when this was over.

"Besides, Khan will stick around and help me. I'm sick of this place. One step forward and two back, every day. It's a lost cause, I'm afraid." Mikhail fumed. "How a government can turn on its own people is beyond me."

As they moved toward an open landscape, the director told them the real chemical weapons had been moved to an abandoned village on the other side of this small town of al-Husn. Coordinates had been where to find the WMDs and the route the trucks would be taking. Amir was moving to the borders of Lebanon and Iraq. There was enough proof of the intended targets and what the ultimate plans had been to cover Israel's attacks on their northern border. With Saudi Arabia hitting the trucks on the Iraq border, no one would dare call into question the royal family's motivation. Having the two countries work together was a miracle in itself. It might even give the false impression peace was finally coming to the Middle East.

~ ~ ~ ~

Carter waited on the tarmac with two Lockheed Martin Ch-53K helicopters. He was going over his checklist when a Volvo stretch limousine used by the president of Israel pulled up to the nearby hangar. Several well-dressed guys with pistol bumps under their suit jackets jumped out of the car and took positions as the back seat doors swung open. Two more serious-as-a-heart-attack guys eased out then waited for Prime Minister Gilad Levi to exit the limo. He stood like a man with the weight of the world on his shoulders. Carter was sure if he could see beneath the mirror sunglasses he wore, the man's expression would show concern over this mission. Gilad remained at the limousine and turned his head toward Carter who figured that was his cue to join him. Before he reached the car, the prime minister walked inside the hangar, leaving him to follow like an obedient dog.

Once inside, Carter smirked at the two bodyguards and raised his chin. "What's up?" This triggered a rough, all-over pat down then a slight shove. "You boys need to switch to decaf."

"Shut your mouth," the bigger one said. "Be respectful. The prime minister is waiting for you inside the office."

Carter slowly unwrapped a piece of gum and folded it into his mouth, then crumpled the wrapper. He pretended to search for a trash can then handed it to the muscle as he began to chew. "Don't say I never gave you anything."

The man's face resembled stone at the taunt, as his boss appeared in the doorway of the office and motioned for Carter then lifted a phone to his ear and stepped back inside.

Gilad covered the phone with his hand. "I'm waiting to hear an update on Prince Muhammed. We talked last night, and I shared what we now know. He should be here shortly."

Carter choked on his gum and had to swallow it to maintain a little decorum. "Excuse me? I thought I heard you say he was coming here."

"Correct. We sent a USA marked plane there last night to pick him up."

"You don't have a marked US plane."

The prime minister arched an eyebrow as if Carter was an imbecile.

Carter shook his head. "What am I thinking? Of course, you do. I'll be sure to pass this information along when I get home, which poses the next question. How is it he is coming here? Aren't you like the great Satan or something?"

The prime minister pretended to be patient with Carter's lack of knowledge. "Your country is the great Satan. Not Israel. In spite of what you hear on your American news programs, we get along in the Middle East for the most part. There are a few countries resistant to change, but time will tell." Once more, he listened to the phone then clicked off as another limousine pulled up. "Oh, I may have forgotten to mention, Prince Muhammed will be going with you today to pick up the passengers."

"The hell you say," Carter said, cutting off his exit.

One of the bodyguards jerked him back so the prime minister could pass.

"No way. If he gets killed, then you're screwed." Carter pushed off the muscle and caught up with Gilad. "Does your brother know about this?"

Gilad stopped and sighed. "Why spoil a perfectly good plan. Besides, the Saudis publicly said in 2018 that we Israelis have the right to our own land. So, relax."

The crown prince emerged from the second limo wearing a flight suit similar to the one Carter wore. He strode confidently to enter the hangar. He offered an outstretched hand to the prime minister. Gilad grasped his hand, and they exchanged pleasantries like old golfing buddies. Carter was stunned at their friendliness to each other and wondered how long the friendship had gone on.

"Carter has a few reservations on you joining him. Perhaps you can reassure him."

"Of course." He turned to Carter and extended a hand of friendship to him. "You're the one who was in charge of my aerial support in California when an attempt was made on my life. I never got to thank you."

"You're most welcome, Your Royal Highness. I don't think you coming along is a good idea though. So many things can go wrong. It could cause repercussions for both your countries."

"Very true. However, my father, the king, is on board with the plan. At my command, our planes arrived last night in Turkey and will hit the targets in Iraq at about the same time Israel targets the one in South Lebanon. Of course, we know they are fake chemical weapons by now, but hopefully, they have not discovered the switch. And if they weren't switched because of time constraints, then our plan also takes care of that."

"And the actual chemical weapons?" Carter asked.

"Israel will take care of those. They will be incinerated. Great pains have been taken to insure nothing happens to the UNESCO World Heritage site and the small village that cares for it. Your people, along with the rebels, and the Daughters of Kobani, warned them to hunker down and stay inside today."

"Prince Muhammed, why not wait here? I'm hopeful we'll be bringing your niece back with us. The last transmission I received said as much. She is safe. I don't want anything to happen to you to spoil this moment."

The prince and Gilad exchanged glances then the prince offered reassurances. "At the end of the day, however it ends, my father will be holding a press conference as will the prime minister." He nodded toward Gilad. "I'm hoping to return and do it for my father. He does not enjoy being in front of the camera. This is a way to show my people I am looking out for them and want peace."

"For when you become king," Carter added.

"I see you understand. Now, enough talk. Shall we go?"

Carter rubbed his face in frustration. "You don't know anything about helicopters, right?"

The prince tilted his head and acknowledged that to be true with a nod. "I will leave that to you. I fly jets, but Prime Minister Gilad thought that was just too risky. So, you are stuck with me."

"Why? Why would you want to do this? Put your life and reputation in jeopardy?"

"She is my niece, and it is my responsibility to see this through." He twirled his finger in the air and leveled a narrowed gaze. "Knight in shining armor saves the day. Good PR."

"You'll do as I say and not get in the way?"

"Of course. I wanted to fly with the best. You are one of the few men in the world who can fly just about anything, I'm told."

Gilad cleared his throat. "If you keep this up, we'll have to build something to keep his head steady on his neck."

"My people are waiting," Carter said.

"Carter?" Gilad stopped him. "I'll have everything ready when you get back with Captain Hunter. He's a great patriot."

"Get those birds in the air." Carter pivoted and headed out to the helicopter, leaving the prince to follow.

~ ~ ~ ~

The Enigma team continued to move carefully until they exited the village. An hour later, they were at least two miles away. Pulling the cart with Chase and keeping a lookout for trouble slowed them considerably. Tessa could only imagine how he hated this. His whole military career had put him in the driver's seat. Now, they were taking care of him. She watched him force himself to sit up then swing his leg over the edge of the cart which took his breath away.

The director listened to something on his earwig, and Vernon nodded confirmation.

"Everyone take cover now," the director yelled.

Fortunately, there were enough boulders and ditches, along with a cave, for everyone to take cover. They scrambled behind large boulders after helping Chase off the cart. Tom pulled the cart into a ditch where it might stay in one piece a little longer. When the cart stopped, Chase tried to scoot to the edge, but the priest quickly assisted, saying he didn't want his wounds to start bleeding again. The man resembled more of a soldier of fortune than a priest. But what did Chase care? "Chase." Tessa rushed to his side, but Khan had already taken up the job of helping him take cover.

"Tess-sa, you must get down." Even with the gravelly voice, the man reminded her of the Afghan Tribesman she'd married and lost. She stared at him intently and wondered who was the man behind the mask. The way he said her name, the slanted eyes, and the way he walked all reminded her of Darya. Her mind was playing tricks on her. This man and Chase were friends. That had never been the case with the Afghan.

"In one minute," Vernon called.

Tessa put her arm over Chase's back and felt his body rise and fall when Khan put his arm over hers then moved it to lower her head.

"Down, Tess-sa."

She shifted her gaze to him. "Will you come with us, Khan?"

"I cannot. I promised the priest I would help him."

With the roar of the jets overhead, Tessa lowered her body tighter to Chase's. In seconds, there was explosion after explosion. Balls of fire spread out in all directions in the distance.

Tessa thought the heat reached them, but maybe it was the fear that the WMDs weren't destroyed. The jets circled then attacked again until there was no possibility the weapons survived.

In slow motion, everyone slipped out of their safe place and came together. Chase felt a sense of satisfaction being able to claw his way to a standing position. It was all he could do to keep from collapsing. He braced himself against the boulder and faced the others. Everyone stared at the distant smoke rising like a monster eating the world around it.

They returned to the road and, despite Chase's disgust, he agreed to ride on the cart. He was in so much pain and suspected his wounds had opened again when the priest checked his bandages and frowned.

"I want you to be as still as possible." He handed him more antibiotics and a few over-the-counter pain meds."

"These old, too?" he growled.

The priest put his hands on his hips. "Yep."

Chase popped them anyway and grabbed a water bottle he'd set on the edge of the cart.

CHAPTER 52

شهيد

With Chase propped on the cart, he could hold his own weapon. He was concerned about the lack of protection on either side of the road. Other than an occasional grouping of rocks and a burned-out vehicle, the team continued to be sitting ducks. Even if they had decided to abandon the cart and carry Chase, the fact remained they'd be in the open. He wanted to lead but couldn't find the strength or protect his people. All he could do was observe through a kind of fuzzy reality. Would it be enough if danger arrived?

"We're almost to the rendezvous point. My coordinates say it's right around the next bend in the road," Vernon said, pointing to the screen on his tablet. They had stopped and let two other men exchange places with Tom and Khan who had been pulling the cart. Grabbing up their weapons, they nodded to their replacements to get going.

Chase thought he could hear the helicopters enroute, but wishful thinking had become a way of life the last month or so. Maybe he would make it after all. Khan or Darya walked on one side of the cart and Ken Montgomery on the other. The others in the team took various positions, along with Khan's people. Peshmerga hovered next to her sister as if protecting her, but Soraya strolled like it was a walk down Fifth Avenue.

Once around the bend, there were a few trees and boulders on one side of the road and an open field slotted for the helicopters to land on the other. There was a small cinder block building. From around the building, a large vehicle roared into place to create a roadblock. The passenger side door of the transfer truck swung open, and Amir slowly stepped out. Everyone snapped their weapons up and readied themselves. No other men seemed to be present. This couldn't be a good sign.

"Look alive, people," Director Clark said.

"Help me off here," Chase demanded. The priest protested, but Khan waved him off and assisted anyway.

"I see you survived, Captain Hunter," Amir said, straightening up and dropping his hand to his weapon across his chest.

"Thought for sure that blast would have taken care of you," Chase said drily.

"Ah, the will of Allah is a wonderful thing." He appeared to scan the area. "I see you have taken up with the enemy, Soraya."

"I had no choice, Amir. But since I have the money now, and they have destroyed your plans, I think I'll take my chances with them," she snarled, casting a disgruntled glance at her sister. "Although I do find it very distasteful. You are a bumbling idiot, Amir. I should never have believed in your idiotic plans."

Even from where Chase stood, he could see the red of anger rise in his face. "What are you talking about. The plan has—"

"A switch was made on your WMDs," Chase informed him. "Your missile trucks on the borders are probably on fire by now, and you're on the world's most wanted list."

"Liar," he shouted and turned his weapon toward the group as a dozen men popped up out of a ditch and from inside the building. They fired indiscriminately as the team returned fire the best they could while trying to seek protection.

Amir's men were no match for Enigma or Khan's men, and several fell immediately. Soraya's scream got her shoved behind large boulders and told to stay down.

The first wave of panic hit Chase when he realized Tessa was in the open. She stood next to Sam, firing at the enemy, much like any of his men would do. Both women were firing their weapons and backing up, so he fell back against the cart and let it brace him as he also unloaded his weapon.

When Sam paused to reload, she stepped back, and Tessa took

her place, with Honey covering her to the right. In seconds, Sam jumped back in the fray only to take several bullets, one in the leg, which spun her to the ground. In that split second, Tessa turned a look of rage on the others, and yelled, emptying her weapon into Amir's men. Several more fell, but most had taken cover, and the team were running out of ammunition.

Amir stepped out and fired at the slow-moving Chase, catching him in the leg as well, which crumpled him into the dirt, yet he fired back, hitting Amir several times. This caused Amir to fall back into the front seat of the truck then slide out behind the open door to the ground.

Khan was moving fast, taking shots Chase would have thought impossible but showing no fear at fighting the enemy. The Tribesman threw his empty weapon aside and pulled out a long serrated knife and jumped one man after another. Then Chase noticed Tessa standing perfectly still looking up at the sky. The helicopters were landing as the few enemies left alive threw down their weapons and raised their hands in surrender.

Men were running from the helicopters to lend support as everyone took a breath. Chase inventoried his team. Tom had taken a bullet in the arm. Sam's pant leg was soaked in blood, and it appeared her vest hadn't stopped the bullet to her upper chest. She appeared dazed and watched the activity spin around her. Honey and a few of Khan's men were checking the prisoners while Chase's people checked the dead.

"Tessa," he called. She continued to stare at the carnage she helped create and slowly shouldered her weapon. "Tessa."

She turned dull eyes toward him that suddenly widened. Running to him, she kneeled. Removing her belt, she tightened it around his leg. He felt as if life was leaving him. There was too much blood. "I'll always love you, Tessa."

The last thing he heard was, "Hang on, Chase. I can't lose you, too."

The priest kneeled down by Tessa and, while he prayed out loud, he also worked on Chase. "He's just unconscious, Tessa."

A medic from the helicopter joined them and assisted. She spotted Sam and ran to her as a second medic arrived and began working on her. A familiar man jumped out of the nearest helicopter and raced to Sam's side.

"Sam," he said, rubbing her cheek until she opened her eyes. "That's right. It's me. Get the hell up off the ground," Carter said.

"Not this time," she whispered. "I'm glad. To see. You."

"Let's get her back to the chopper and get going," the medic said, standing up. "She's badly hurt."

Carter lifted her into his arms and started back to the helicopter.

Another man emerged from Carter's helicopter, dressed in a clean-and-pressed flight suit. She thought her eyes were playing tricks on her until he got closer. She rose to unsteady feet, her breath caught in her throat.

"Prince Muhammed. Your Highness," she said, stepping in front of him to shield him from the mayhem that had occurred.

He reached out and held both of her arms. "Are you injured?"

"No, Your Highness. I'm not sure it is safe yet for you to be here. Please go back to the helicopter."

"Where is Amir?"

She pointed to the spot where he sat after being pulled out from the vehicle then relieved of his weapons.

"Thank you." He moved like a stalking tiger toward its prey. Amir nervously tried to scoot away. The prince frowned down with intolerance and disgust.

"Your Highness," Amir growled. "I want to—"

Before he could utter another word, the prince pulled out a revolver and shot him in the head. "You have nothing to say that I care to hear." He turned to two of his own men. "Drag his worthless body to the ditch and let the vultures have him if they will."

Director Clark came alongside him. "Your Highness, I would feel better if you returned to the helicopter."

"Where is Soraya?" he asked, stretching his neck.

The director pointed to where she was emerging from behind her hiding place. She came running toward him, carrying the backpack of money she'd taken from Chase earlier in the day.

"Uncle," she called gleefully. "Allah is so good! You came for me. Thank you. Thank you."

He held up his hand to stop her from getting too close. "Is that the ransom money?"

"Yes," she said bewildered.

"Where is your sister? Peshmerga?"

"I am here, Prince Muhammed."

The prince glanced from the groomed Soraya to the shabby clothing of Peshmerga, one of the Daughters of Kobani fighters. He snatched the backpack from Soraya and tossed it to her sister. "Use it as you wish. Keep it or use it for your people in the way you see fit. I do not care."

Soraya morphed into her spoiled persona. "She will waste it on those garbage eaters. It will be gone in a week."

"It is only money, Soraya," he said with disgust. "I trust it will be used to make life a little easier for those who suffer."

She stomped her foot and raised an accusing finger just as the prince once more raised his revolver. He shot her through the heart.

Peshmerga caught her in her arms, a tear squeezed from the corner of her eye.

"It is time to go," he said as he bent to help Khan place Chase onto the stretcher.

Tessa stared on in horror but felt little remorse for the either Amir or Soraya. Maybe it was because the next great leader of Saudi Arabia had executed two people that she was disturbed. He glanced her way and then proceeded to help several of the medics with their equipment as they moved back toward the helicopters.

She boarded with all the others, and they lifted off. After a time, the helicopters floated down to the secret military base in Israel as the afternoon sun played hide-and-seek with the gray clouds forming. With so many people waiting in white coats and masks, the buildings took on a hospital appearance rather than military hangars.

A crew removed everyone who was injured and rushed them away inside, where she heard voices calling out in a what she guessed was Hebrew. Then a group of military personal swooped in to take the prisoners and Soraya's body.

The rest of the team eased out onto the tarmac and waited to be told what to do next. They were exhausted, paralyzed with shock, and in need of nourishment. Tessa was escorted inside by two women soldiers, as was Honey. Since there was only one shower, Tessa sat and waited for Honey to finish as she pondered on those left behind, especially the masked man called Khan.

For reasons unknown, she felt a great loss at him not coming with them. She'd grabbed his hand and tugged at him to follow, but he resisted.

"I cannot go, Tess-sa. You must go take care of the captain."

"Will I see you again before I go home?"

His eyes creased as if he smiled behind the mask. "I will try. But, for now, I must help my friend, Mikhail Novak, one more time. He will make sure the gold coins found in the tunnels get into the hands of the people of the refugee camp Peshmerga told me about. There are organizations that can use the money as well to make life a little easier. She is a good woman, unlike her sister."

"I know it is not acceptable for me to hug you in gratitude," she said, extending her hand in friendship before getting onto the helicopter.

He grasped her hand and pulled her into an embrace. "Perhaps just this once."

Now sitting here, reliving that moment, she thought he'd kissed the side of her ear and whispered something about a snow leopard. But that was crazy. She wanted to sleep.

~ ~ ~ ~

Word came that both Chase and Sam had undergone surgery and were in critical but stable condition. Both were expected to live but had a lot of recovery ahead of them. The plan was to send both of them back to the US once they were able to travel.

Prince Muhammed made an announcement concerning his precious niece Soraya having not survived captivity with the ruthless terrorist group who caused the world to hold its breath for a little while.

"The world has lost a beautiful and talented angel. To honor her, I hope you will play her music often and remember how she wanted the world to be a better place. Therefore, a fund has been set up in her honor. For every download and purchase you make of her work, 100 percent of the money will go to help the Kurdish people she so loved."

Tessa stood with the rest of the Enigma team at the press conference with a touch of satisfaction deep within her, knowing the truth of the way the prince honestly felt. He would get justice for his niece's misplaced attempt at bringing the world to the brink of war every time a coin was put toward the Kurdish coffers. "It is also a message to other terrorist groups who continue to beg for chaos rather than peace in the Middle East. You will be hunted down and dealt with extreme prejudice. That is all."

"Think Soraya is rolling in her grave?" Ken asked, crossing his arms across his chest.

"Muhammed's popularity is soaring here and abroad. His presence in Israel has put the rest of the Middle East on notice."

The prince answered a few questions before the press was ushered out. He was dressed in his traditional Saudi Arabian attire and already moved confidently with the air of a king as he approached the group. Carter extended his hand to him.

"You can fly with me anytime, Your Highness. Let me know when you're ready to take a few lessons on the helicopters."

The prince nodded. "I look forward to it." He then focused on Director Clark. "May I speak to your Agent Scott?"

"Tessa?" the director asked. She nodded, and he pointed for the others to move away.

"I must return home and to my family," the prince told her. "I'm glad to put this all behind us. Thank you again for putting yourself in danger for the sake of not only me but for the peace I pray comes to the world."

"I played a small part, Your Highness. There were a lot of working parts to make this happen."

"One of your strengths as well as charm is your modesty, Agent Scott. I hope you never lose the innocence and selflessness you wear so boldly. If you ever need anything—anything at all, please do not hesitate to contact me. You have my private contact information, so, please…"

"I will. Thank you." She laid her hand on her heart and spoke in Arabic. "Sidiyq lilhaya." Friend for life.

He lifted her hand from her chest and kissed it. "Sidiyq lilhaya." He smiled and turned, met by two of his bodyguards who escorted him away. By morning, he was gone.

~ ~ ~ ~

Sam was awake the next morning and moved out of ICU. The

doctors thought she could go home within a week but relayed that the prime minister thought otherwise until President Austin gave him a call concerning the matter.

"You went behind my back, brother," Gilad said, sharing lunch with Director Clark the next day.

He took a drink of the thick, dark coffee then leaned back in his chair. "I suppose I did. I'm leaving Carter here to personally bring her home. That way I know she'll have a smooth transition without any complications. Do we understand each other?"

"Perfectly."

"Oh, our mother sends her love," the director said as an afterthought. Gilad did not respond. "Wants to know if you'll make it for Thanksgiving this year?"

~ ~ ~ ~

Later that same day, the director told everyone to be ready to return home by evening. Tessa cornered him afterward and voiced her concern.

"Chase can't be left here alone, without one of us. Let me stay until he wakes up. Please."

"No. Your place is at home. It could be a while."

"If he takes a turn for the worse and no one is here—"

"Tessa, I said no. I have made arrangements for his care, and someone is on their way to be with him even as we speak. I will stay to make sure things remain on track until they arrive. Could be a day or so."

"Who?"

"Woman, stop pushing me."

"I'm sorry. But—"

"We're done here. Get your things together and be on that plane at 1900 hours. Got it?"

"Yes, sir," she snapped and left the room.

His phone buzzed, and he answered. "Father Novak. Yes, the team leaves tonight. I appreciate you coming. What about Khan? Good. I look forward to seeing both of you then." He clicked off.

Epilogue

شهيد

And just like that, there he stood. Tall. Rugged. Eyes a bit hooded, and he held a cane at his side. They stared at each other for what felt like eons, but, in truth, it was only a few seconds. Tessa hadn't seen him since she'd left him at death's door in Israel. Every day since then, she'd written to him, sent text messages of support, sent cards and, several times, tried to Skype with him. Not once had he responded.

Her fear was he might die alone, at least surrounded by strangers who didn't love and respect him. Only Sam had remained behind because she, too, was severely injured. Although Carter stayed, he was not able to visit Chase. Apparently, there was some ongoing feud between him and the prime minister that prevented Carter having much access even to Sam. She, too, had pulled through and returned home. Both of them were tough and full of grit.

Chase had undergone several surgeries and, when he recovered enough to be transferred to the States, he ended up in Walter Reed Medical Center in Washington DC. There was never a doubt he would receive the best possible care.

Leaving him had been painful, but Director Clark reminded her that even she needed to take care of her mental health. He also reminded her of her obligation to her family and that they must come first. And, with that, she'd returned home to bubbly children, excited to see her and full of stories of what they'd been doing. Their father, Robert, had expressed concern over her weight loss and the lack of spring in her step.

She'd faked joy for a while but knew she had to have help. Thankfully, Dr. Wu had been available from the time she stepped off the plane. Each day they'd met, worked in his greenhouse full of orchids, and talked about everything from compost to world affairs until she broke down and poured her heart out about Syria, her failed marriage to Robert, the death of Darya, and now a possible loss of a relationship with Chase.

She'd loved Chase almost since the day they met, although she didn't know it then or want such a relationship. He'd survived, but things had changed between them. Had he fallen in love with Soraya and couldn't come to grips with her death? Did he blame her for losing the witch? Why hadn't he responded to her messages?

Dr. Wu suggested Chase needed time to heal both inside and out. Her idea of who and what he was had been crushed, and he might not want to face her high expectations.

Director Clark said he had a lot of physical work ahead of him and no time for her coddling.

The Enigma team said not to worry. Well, except for Honey, who claimed he was having a relationship with his nurse and she should move on. It was always offered with one of her psycho-sweet attempts at humor. For once, she wished Sam was interested enough to bounce her concerns off. At least she'd give it to her straight up, no matter how hard it was to take. Probably the harder it was to take, the more likely she'd tell her the truth.

He stood on her front porch in Grass Valley, wearing military fatigues, solemn and intimidating like always, staring at her with zero emotion. In that moment, she realized for the last few years, every time they'd met up, something magical happened in his eyes, giving her a euphoric sensation. Now, that had disappeared. There had been no notification he'd been released from the hospital or that he was well enough for a visit. His arrival in California must have been kept a secret. She spotted a black SUV parked in her circle drive, and, although she couldn't tell who was behind the wheel, they lifted their hand in greeting, and she returned it.

"Can I come in?" he asked stiffly.

"Certainly." She stepped aside, and he entered the foyer and stood there a moment, scanning the rooms opening off the entrance. There was a moment she thought he'd taken a deep breath and held it before letting it go slowly. Was he remembering the first time he'd entered her home on false pretenses? Maybe he was thinking about the Christmas he stayed with her kids who gave him quite an adventure.

"Would you like a cup of coffee?" Closing the door, she realized the SUV in the driveway was still running.

"No. This won't take long. Okay if I sit down? The leg still gives me a little trouble."

"Of course." She moved to the living room next to the entrance, the room where she placed her biggest Christmas tree. The room he loved to come and visit with the kids. The room where he first saved her life.

Instead of sitting on the couch next to her, he chose a wingback chair across from her next to the fireplace. It felt so far away, it might as well have been in Syria. She folded her hands in her lap and waited. For an instant, as he stared at her, she thought his face softened and the yearning flashed in his eyes, then it was gone.

"You look a lot better than the last time I saw you," she said.

A grin finally touched his mouth. "I imagine so. Thanks for the encouragement, both then and over the last couple of months."

"You never responded to any of my texts or emails." It was hard to keep from bursting into a crying pity party.

He didn't explain, just stared out the many windows flooding the room with sunlight.

"Chase, I understand you may have had feelings for Soraya in spite of everything, but—"

"No! I never had feelings for her," he insisted vehemently.

"Okay. If your feelings have changed for me... If you now see things differently and think you want space, you don't have to worry."

"My feelings have changed for you." She opened her mouth to respond, but he rushed over his next few words. "My love for you has never wavered. If anything, it has intensified. But I do see things differently."

"I don't understand. All I want to do this very minute is wrap my arms around you and begin our lives together."

He stood up and came to sit by her. He took her hand in his and stared at it as he rubbed his fingers over the back of her skin. "I found out something while I was in Syria, Tessa, and I can't marry you."

A choke stuck in her throat. "I love you just the way you are. Nothing can change that. Not what you had to do to stay alive. Not Soraya."

"Yes. There is one thing than can change everything," he interrupted.

"No. I promise you. There is nothing."

He took a deep breath and released it as he softened his gaze. "Darya is alive, and you are still married to him. There is a plane waiting to take us to Montana in a couple of hours. There's a bag packed in the car with everything you need for a few days. He's expecting us."

~ ~ ~ ~

Chase decided it felt good to be able to drive again. Except for the icy silence between them, he almost enjoyed the mountainous landscape before them. The snow was hit and miss, but a storm was predicted for later, around midnight. The plane landed in a small airport in a nondescript town, about an hour's drive from their final destination. A car was waiting for them.

He glanced over at Tessa several times, but she stared stone-faced out the windshield like he wasn't there. He wished he could reach out and hold her hand to help her through this. Reflecting back on the last couple of hours, he replayed her reaction over and over in his mind.

"What?" She stared at him like he'd sprung an extra head. "Chase, are you—"

"I'm not on drugs. I'm clean. Darya is alive. He was—"

"The man you called Khan."

He nodded as she stood and paced. "I should have known. I don't understand. He died. I buried him." Tears squeezed from the corners of her eyes, but she didn't swipe at them. Her voice grew irritated. "Why wasn't I told? Who knew this? Who hid this from me? You?" she accused stubbornly.

"No. I only found out when he showed up at one of the camps. Amir had overdosed me, and he saved my life. He rescued those women and I stayed behind to find the weapons, and, at the time, I thought Soraya was in danger. I suspected she was in on it, but I was there to protect her."

"Darya saved you?" she said incredulously. "The man Khan wasn't Darya. The two of you hate each other. I could tell you and Khan were friends."

"War gives you a new perspective. Director Clark and those scientists we brought back from Russia knew. No one else." He rose to his feet. "Tessa, this is a lot to take in. It's not my story to tell, except the part when I found out he was alive. I refused to keep his secret."

Tessa covered her face with both hands and sobbed. He knew she was grieving yet again for something that wasn't real and for the loss of what they might have had. Daring to step closer to her, he managed to put one arm around her without falling over his cane.

"I'm sorry, Tessa. But we need to go. Your family is being taken care of. The Ervins next door are picking up the kids and treating them to Disneyland this weekend. I know it was Robert's weekend with the kids, so they invited him along."

She stepped out of his touch and glared at him. "Is that why you didn't answer me all these months. Why you didn't tell me you were coming home?"

"I was grieving, too—I'd lost you for a second time."

The road narrowed and turned to gravel as he slowed the car. This he remembered, for he had been at Darya's closed-casket funeral. The land and mountains took your breath away and reminded him of northern Afghanistan where he first had a run-in with the notorious man known only as the Tribesman. No surprise he felt at home here.

Part of Darya's life growing up had been in Afghanistan then the other part had been here. His father, a former Soviet military man, had defected and gone to work for the CIA. He married a woman from the Kyrgyz tribe in Northern Afghanistan. These mountains had made her feel at home away from her people.

Being raised in two cultures had a profound effect on Roman Darya Petrov. One foot in America then, when he'd come home at night, it was a mix of Russia and Afghanistan. He was bright, hardheaded, athletic, and a loner. Somehow, he found his way back to his mother's people and became both an asset to the United States military and a nightmare. Then he met Tessa, and everything changed.

He stopped the car in the middle of the gravel road and let it idle. Tessa sat silently for a good five minutes before she spoke. "Did you ever love me, Chase?"

"With each breath I take."

"Why didn't you tell me he was alive? It wasn't your decision to make for me."

"I'm sure he'll explain everything to you. It's not my story to tell."

"Does he know I'm coming?"

"Yes." Silence. "I'm going to take you to him, Tessa, not because I don't want you. You're married to him. What do you want me to do?"

"You could fight any enemy on any land, in any situation, but you never would fight for me."

He put the car in gear. "The plane leaves tomorrow at one. If you decide you want to go home, then Darya will bring you to the airport."

Tessa sniffed but there were no tears.

He pulled up close to the cabin. There was no drive, just miles and miles of land.

"It's beautiful here."

Chase didn't respond as he kept the car running and put it in park. "I'll get your bag." He started to open the door, but Tessa touched his arm.

"I thought this time we…"

"It's okay, Tess. Do what you want to do. Go on. He's waiting." He limped around the car and grabbed her bag out of the back seat. She took it from him and laid a hand on his chest.

"Stay here." She looked up into his eyes and produced a thin smile. "Deep down, I know you would never hurt me. I don't know why you ignored me these months or why you didn't tell me about Darya. I'm sure you had your reasons."

"Goodbye," he said and kissed her forehead.

He returned to the car and watched her step up on the porch.

The door swung open, and Darya stepped out toward her. Dropping the bag, she covered her face with her hands until the Tribesman stepped forward and pulled her into his arms. He was dressed very much like the first time he'd seen him and still looked wild and untamed. The man turned his head toward Chase and lifted his chin then nodded a thanks. Tessa stared up at him half laughing and half crying as he stepped backward, pulling her back into his life. When the door closed, Chase turned the car around and drove the car back the hour it took to get to the airport.

A snowstorm blew in that night, and his flight home was delayed. Chase did his exercises and used the treadmill in the workout room. The restaurant attached to the hotel fixed him soup and sandwiches and remained open until seven then closed. The workers were given a room since the roads needed to be plowed.

He watched several movies but had no idea what they were since all he could picture was Tessa and Darya in the cabin on such a blustery night. Would she follow him into chaos, or would they go into the witness protection situation? How would this affect the kids? He would never see them again.

He fell asleep around dawn only to be awakened by the desk attendant a few hours later. He received word everything was a go for takeoff at three that afternoon. The runway would be cleared by then and the plane would be gassed and ready for takeoff when the captain arrived.

After a hot shower and breakfast, he mostly pushed around with his fork, he checked his phone to see if Tessa left him a message. Nothing. The familiar pain he used to get when she walked into a room hit him hard. He rubbed the spot and thought it would be advantageous to make a plan. His life was in the crapper, and the one bright spot in his life was in the arms of his former enemy. Best to get the picture out of his head.

Once back at the airport and after turning in the car, he grabbed more coffee and went to his gate. No one was there except for airline personal. Several flights were on hold, but his pilot stopped by to say he had made the final checks and he could board when ready. Chase thanked him and checked the clock. Two thirty. Then he checked his phone. No texts. No missed calls. After all, he'd told Tessa his plane would leave at one, not three. It was over.

He grabbed up his backpack and cane and stared out the plate glass windows overlooking the runways. The mountains in the distance were shrouded in clouds. Tessa would think they were magical. He could almost hear her saying his name in the kind of excitement he admired. It felt so real.

"Chase! Chase!"

He dropped his backpack and turned. There she was, running, all smiles and curls bouncing, like the day he first saw her. Was it a flashback?

"Chase! Chase!"

No. It was real. He dropped the cane and did his best to hurry toward her, but she was there too fast. She fell into his arms, and he lifted her feet off the floor. His arms held her tighter than he ever had before.

"I love you, Chase. I always have and you are the only one I ever want to be with for the rest of my life. It always comes back to you. We have his blessing."

He kissed her long and hard as her fingers ran through his hair. The beat of her heart and the touch of her skin against his was all he ever wanted. Whatever lie in the future could be faced together. Life was finally complete.

COMING SOON

Enigma #9

Enjoy this sample.

The paper on the examining table always sounded louder when it moved in such a small space. It crinkled and stuck to her skin as Tessa tried to slide off the surface until her bare feet touched the ice-cold floor. These yearly exams never got easier and once more she thought of Eve in the Garden of Eden and how she'd screwed it up for women for eternity. She planned to look her up once she got to those pearly gates and give her a piece of her mind. If possible, she planned to shove an apple down her throat.

The appointment had been on the books for a year, as was customary. Only this time, she was miserable and not feeling 100 percent. Going to Syria had beat her up pretty badly, both physically and mentally. There was a chance she'd picked up a bug there and explained why she felt so lethargic and out of sorts. Besides the usual female invasive exam, the doctor had ordered some blood work the day before at her request.

Slipping into her jeans and pullover, she grabbed up her purse and headed out into the hall. One of the nurses smiled her way.

"Hey, Tessa," she called, coming around the high divider that separated the workstation from the patients. "Dr. Pennell is waiting for you. Go right in. Come on. I'll walk you there."

Tessa nodded and followed obediently as the nurse, who she couldn't remember the name, chatted on the short walk. "Thanks," she said, stepping inside.

"Close the door, Tessa," the doctor said without looking up from the stack of papers, she imagined was her medical history.

Dr. Pennell was a young OBGYN doctor with Asian Indian heritage. She was short, cute, and according to rumors, quite the dancer at the local cowboy watering hole in town. Her eyes sparkled, making Tessa grin at the impish expression on her face. However, the woman was serious as a heart attack when it came to her job and her ladies she took care of.

"I don't expect any problems with the exam. Be sure to get your mammogram."

"Mammogram? I thought I had a few years until I had to start that."

The doctor looked back over her chart and nodded. "Oh, you're right. Never mind. Considering your condition, I would have canceled it anyway."

"My condition? What's wrong with me? I feel like crap."

The doctor clicked her tongue. "I'm afraid you have the Egyptian flu." She smiled.

"Egyptian flu," she moaned. "I've never heard of it. Hopefully that isn't the new pandemic."

"No. No. Been around since the beginning of time." She chuckled. "You don't know what I'm talking about, do you?" Tessa frowned. "Egyptian flu?" She shrugged at the doctor. "Tessa, you're going to be a mummy! Get it?"

Tessa could feel herself sway in the chair, when the doctor rushed around to her and called for the nurse. Next thing she knew, someone was putting a cold compress on her forehead and speaking softly to her.

"I'm pregnant?" she whispered.

The doctor handed her a cup of water. "Not very far along. Maybe six weeks. When was your last period?"

Tessa tried to remember. She couldn't. "Pregnant?"

"You had no idea?"

"How—"

"You have three kids. Surely you know how," the doctor said, patting her on the shoulder. "I'm sure Mr. Scott will be excited."

"There is no Mr. Scott," she confessed. "We divorced. Sort of."

"Oh." The doctor sat on the edge of her desk. "So, who is the lucky daddy?"

Tessa got to her feet. "Thank you, Dr. Pennell. I need to go now."

"Sit your butt back in that chair. You're not going anywhere until I know you're okay. Almost lunchtime and I'm buying. It's been too long since we shared a meal. My next appointment isn't until two thirty. You're eating for two now, so no protests. Besides, I want to hear this story."

Tessa sighed and nodded. "Okay. But I'm not sure you're going to believe it."

The doctor shivered with delight. "Come on. Let's blow this joint. I'm starved."

MEET TIERNEY

Tierney James – Adventure, Thriller & Romantic Suspense Author

Tierney decided to become a full-time writer after working in education for over thirty years. Besides serving as a Solar System Ambassador for NASA's Jet Propulsion Lab, and attending Space Camp for Educators, Tierney served as a Geo-teacher for National Geographic. Her love of travel and cultures took her on adventures throughout Africa, Asia and Europe. From the Great Wall of China to floating the Okavango Delta of Botswana, Tierney weaves her unique experiences into the adventures she loves to write. Living on a Native American reservation and in a mining town, fuels the characters in the Enigma and Wind Dancer series. Now with over sixteen books under her belt, Tierney feels there is no stopping her now.

After moving to Oklahoma, the love of teaching continued in her marketing and writing workshops along with the creation of educational materials and children's books. She likes to tell people a little lipstick and danger makes the world go round. http://www.tierneyjames.com. Speaking at conferences, book clubs, school functions, church and community groups are a few of the things Tierney enjoys doing when not writing her next adventure. She also helps beginning writers in their quest to becoming a published author through her workshops and classes. Family, an adopted dog and gardening fill her life with plenty of laughter to share with others.

Tierney has been an Amazon #1 Best Selling author and won numerous awards for her work.

OTHER PUBLICATIONS BY TIERNEY JAMES

The Enigma Series Vol. 1-8
Martyrs Never Die
Invisible Goodbye
The Knight Before Chaos
Black Mamba
Kifaru
Rooftop Angels
The Winds of Deception
An Unlikely Hero

The Dark Side Series
Dark Side of Noon
Dark Side of Morning

Stand Alone Books
The Rescued Heart
Dance of the Devil's Trill
Turnback Creek
Lipstick & Danger – A Collection of Short Stories When Escape is Your Only Option

Other
How to Market a Book Someone Besides Your Mother Will Read
There's a Superhero in the Library
Zombie Meatloaf
Mission K-9 Rescue
African Safari: A Thematic Lesson Book for Teachers